THE GREEK GIRL'S STORY

THE GREEK GIRL'S STORY

Abbé Prévost

FOREWORD BY JEAN SGARD

TRANSLATED AND WITH AN INTRODUCTION BY
ALAN J. SINGERMAN

THE PENNSYLVANIA STATE UNIVERSITY PRESS
UNIVERSITY PARK, PENNSYLVANIA

Prévost, Abbé, 1697–1763, author.
[Histoire d'une Grecque moderne. English]
The Greek girl's story / Abbé Prévost ; translated
and with an introduction by Alan J. Singerman ;
foreword by Jean Sgard.
      p. cm
Summary: "An English translation of the Abbé
Prévost's 1740 novel The Greek Girl's Story.
Includes foreword by Jean Sgard, notes, and
appendices"—Provided by publisher.
Includes bibliographical references and index.
ISBN 978-0-271-06391-1 (cloth : alk. paper)
ISBN 978-0-271-06392-8 (pbk. : alk. paper)
I. Singerman, Alan J., translator. II. Title.

PQ2021.H4E5   2014
843'.5—dc23
2014004357

To

JEAN SGARD, PETER TREMEWAN,

and the memory of

ALLAN HOLLAND

(to all of whom my debt is boundless)

Contents

Foreword

The French language has only one word to designate both a true story and a work of fiction: *histoire*. In the case of the *Histoire d'une Grecque moderne* (*The Greek Girl's Story*), truth and fiction are tightly woven together. As Alan Singerman convincingly demonstrates, it is the well-documented story of a French ambassador who provoked a scandal in Constantinople, locked horns with the grand vizir, was recalled to France, and then publicly indulged such an indecent passion for a young slave that his friends and family feared for his sanity. This chapter of history was no secret for anyone familiar with the rumors circulating in Parisian society when the novel was published. But from the very first words the emphasis falls on the person telling the story, and this narrator informs us that he is incapable of presenting a trustworthy depiction of the Greek girl he has loved. Moreover, he declares that no one will be able to distinguish what is true from what is false in his account. This prologue is highly unusual: what good is a story that can prove nothing? But this uncertainty is precisely the basis of the narrative.

This case is hardly unique in Prévost's literary career; his narratives often seem to rest on a rather fragile justificatory discourse. Cleveland, always full of his rational certainties, alienated his wife, fell in love with his own daughter, and flirted with atheism; that is what he must explain. The dean of Coleraine, with the best of intentions, compounds his errors and loses his moral authority over his whole family: how did that happen, and whose fault is it? Neither the commander of Malta nor Montcal is a very respectable individual. The "memoirs" of these characters, seemingly filled with good conscience, are contaminated little by little by their passions, their hypocrisy, their egoism. Ferriol (let's call him by his historical name) takes bad faith to the limit: sure of himself, of his innate nobility, of his superiority over the defenseless woman he has bought, he is also certain of his own generosity, certain that he is the victim of this ungrateful creature. He constantly attempts to justify himself—and never succeeds.

One day Prévost proposed this problem in casuistry: can anyone say of himself that he has been good? And who will believe him? Accused himself in 1734 of countless serious misdeeds (swindles, apostasy) and subjected to public condemnation, he was forced in his journal *Le Pour et Contre* (The pros and cons) to justify himself and state that despite all appearances he had been honest; for it is permissible, according to him, to claim integrity, but one must do it modestly and indirectly, without making an issue of it; and that is why the whole issue 36 of *Le Pour et Contre* is a kind of extended allegory about Prévost's goodness and the wickedness of his accuser. Voltaire made fun of this enigma whose key is virtue; for his part, he refused to put his own integrity in question and offer it to the public as a subject of dispute. And that is understandable. Prévost's attitude, so unconvincing with respect to morality, is nonetheless very productive when it comes to narrative deceit (*mensonge romanesque*). Moreover, it is rather striking to note that in the same issue of *Le Pour et Contre*, he introduces a plea in favor of des Grieux, this "young man with brilliant qualities," drawn in spite of himself into a "libertine and vagabond existence" and at the same time so likeable, so noble. Although he is somewhat of a rascal, he is justified by his passion, by his misfortune, and by the grace of his narrative, indirectly and unobtrusively.

As regards Ferriol, who has to justify his misdeeds, the scandal he caused by his fits of anger and dubious morality, we see him try to showcase his decency while at the same time, both elegantly and deceitfully, accusing his poor slave. To borrow Voltaire's terms, we may be led to think that the subtle ambassador's pleading is an enigma whose key is virtue: Théophé's virtue. But Prévost scarcely seems concerned with the reality of this virtue: after all, a few lines would have sufficed to tell us that one day she had fled to a convent to finish her days in an edifying way. No, what fascinates the novelist is the web of lies, hypocrisy, and treacherous insinuations in which the narrator entangles himself. That is what drives him to write, to invent the inimitable style of this confession gone astray.

What goal is he pursuing in pushing to its furthest limits this narrative that has no conclusion? I see several, and they are not new to him. The first: to show to what extent every official history is false. Like a true disciple of Pierre Bayle, he will reveal the contrast between the diplomatic version of the history of Ferriol and the internal collapse of this narrator drained by a shameful passion. Bayle did this in so many of his writings: the public history, summarized in such laudatory, authoritative texts, and then the footnotes, which as we know constitute the essential part of Bayle's *Historical Dictionary*. *The Greek Girl's Story* is a long footnote, fundamentally scandalous, on the fringes of official history; perhaps this brilliant ambassador dreamed only of taking his "soul daughter" to bed, and it was this unattainable dream that drove him mad. As he does in all his 1740 novels, Prévost takes pleasure in exposing the imposture of history: the only goal of memoir writers is to honor their own intelligence and character (opening of the *Mémoires pour server à l'histoire de Malte* [Memoirs serving the history of Malte]); it is not always the love of glory that leads them to a military career but more often the desire to make their fortune (opening of *Campagnes philosophique* [Philosophical campaigns]). The history of the great men of the past is scarcely more conclusive: the historian advances in the "labyrinth" of the past with no other guide than the multitude of contradictory testimonies (preface to the *Histoire de Guillaume le Conquérant* [Story of William the Conqueror]) and the spectacle of these testimonies, which "is not greatly to the advantage of history" (preface of *Marguerite d'Anjou*), becomes a sort of shadow play that transforms history into fiction.

A second reason that determines the novelist's choice: since every story is a labyrinth, Prévost will define its path without reaching any conclusions, without intervening, without choosing a way out at the end. On the stage of the novel a trial begins: the characters plead their cause, the readers alone are called to judge; but the readers themselves are multiple and will judge according to their own understanding, their own tastes, and their own passions. What makes for the success of a novel is the multiplicity of possible readings, and Prévost knows this better than most: he experienced it with the success of *Manon Lescaut*, the story of a scoundrel and a prostitute according to Montesquieu, but a tale that moved the public deeply. With *The Greek Girl's Story*, he opens another debate, and to ensure its longevity he multiplies enigmatic characters and equivocal behaviors. Was the ambassador mad or paranoid? Was Théophé a mere slave trained to seduce men or an exceptional woman obsessed with virtue or smitten with liberty? And what about all these decoys strewn throughout the story that turn Synèse, Condoidi, and Maria Rezati into such elusive and disturbing figures? Are they there to enlighten us? I would like to think, on the contrary, that they are there to arouse our interest and our questions, to provoke readings as ingenious and passionate as the one offered by Alan Singerman.

Jean Sgard

Acknowledgments

I wish to express my gratitude to Dr. Gill Holland, professor emeritus of English at Davidson College, for his scrupulous and merciless reading of this complete volume, forcing me to rethink and reformulate a multitude of passages in the quixotic quest for the perfect sentence. I am also deeply indebted to Susan Silver for her meticulous and highly perceptive copyediting of my manuscript, coaxing me gently but tenaciously into making so many improvements in the presentation of the text. Any perceptible shortcomings in this endeavor are entirely my own responsibility. My warm thanks to Kendra Boileau and her editorial staff at Penn State Press for the high professionalism and cordiality they exhibited throughout the preparation of this text. I would be terribly remiss, finally, if I did not express my heartfelt appreciation for the unremitting support of my wife, Véronique, my perennial sounding board, during the several years it took to bring this project to fruition.

INTRODUCTION

The "scandalous" personal life of the abbé Prévost has long been an object of fascination for his readers, which is not necessarily conducive to a proper appreciation of his body of literary works. But, to be perfectly frank, there was certainly enough dirt there to titillate the imagination. It is easy to imagine the first modern biographers of Prévost, from Henry Harrisse to Claire-Eliane Engel, and including Henri Roddier, discovering with astonishment the riveting existence of this ex-Benedictine monk apostate novelist, erudite church scholar, bon vivant, philanderer, occasional crook, apostle of the novel of sensitivity, and spokesman for the passions as well as for moral rectitude.[1]

After schooling by the Jesuits, Antoine-François Prévost devoted eight years of rigorous studies to the Benedictines, then, in 1728, suddenly became famous with the publication of the first volumes of his novel *Mémoires d'un homme de qualité* (*Memoirs of a Man of Quality*, 1728–31). He began to rebel against the strictures of his monastic existence, requested a transfer to a more liberal order, grew impatient, then simply took French leave. Threatened with arrest by his superiors, he "tossed his habit into the nettles," as he says, took refuge in Holland briefly, then crossed the channel into England. Soon dismissed from his job as a tutor in the home of an English gentleman, whom he apparently indisposed by seducing his daughter, Prévost returned to Holland in 1730 and settled down in The Hague. There he composed his famous *Histoire du chevalier des Grieux et de Manon Lescaut* (1731) and continued the writing of his monumental *Le philosophe anglais ou Histoire de M. Cleveland*

(1731–39), begun in England, all the while courting financial ruin through his extravagant spending on his mistress Lenki Eckhart, a lady of ill repute referred to by one of Prévost's contemporaries as a "bloodsucker."

Leaving behind an insurmountable pile of debt, as well as a house full of furniture that the Dutch courts graciously sold for him, he crossed back over the channel in 1733, his beloved Lenki in tow, and took up residence again in England, where he began a weekly journal, *Le Pour et Contre* (The pros and cons), devoted to English culture and current events. Still in desperate financial straits, he was thrown into jail for cashing a counterfeit bill of exchange (i.e., passing a bad check) and just barely avoided an appointment with an Anglo-Saxon hangman before managing, at the beginning of 1734, to negotiate his return to France. Pope Clement XII having granted him an official pardon for all his sins, he was allowed to return to the Benedictines on condition that he do a second novitiate at La Croix-Saint-Leufroy near Evreux. He made peace with the Jesuits and published the first volume of *Le doyen de Killerine* (*The Dean of Coleraine*, 1735–40).

At the beginning of 1736 Prévost was back in Paris. Under the (rather slight) protection of the Prince of Conti, who appointed him his chaplain and gave him lodgings, the abbé quickly became the darling of the Parisian salons, who vied for his presence as much for his notoriety as an unfrocked and somewhat licentious Benedictine as for his fine wit and a vast personal culture acquired during long years of highly varied erudition, historical research for his novels, and popular journalism. He still benefited from the enormous prestige that he had gained with the success of the *Mémoires d'un homme de qualité*, *Manon Lescaut*, and the first volumes of *Cleveland*. His journal *Le Pour et Contre*, henceforth adapted to the French context, was still doing very well. Everything would indicate that Prévost's personal and professional lives were, finally, beginning to look up.

The "Crisis of 1740" and the Genesis of *The Greek Girl's Story*

Unfortunately, this was not the case. Despite the publication of the last volumes of *Cleveland* (1738–39) and the first two volumes of the *Doyen* (1739), Prévost still received no income from the church and was forced to put aside *Le Pour et Contre* for eight months. At the end of 1739 he was flirting with bankruptcy again. Thanks to Harrisse (*Abbé Prévost*, 299–302), the facts have become well known: because he was unable to pay fifty louis of debts, Prévost was threatened with arrest by a group of creditors led by his tailors and upholsterers. On January 15, 1740, he wrote a desperate letter to Voltaire in which he offered to write a "Defense of M. de Voltaire and of His Works" in exchange for the fifty louis he needed so badly; the illustrious philosopher politely declined the proposal. The debts continued to pile up, reaching "four or five thousand francs" at the end of the year. Prévost, his back to the wall, compromised himself in a shameful venture into scurrilous journalism and was forced once again to go into exile in January 1741, first to Brussels, then to Frankfort, before he was finally able to show his face again in Paris in September 1742 (Weil, "Abbé Prévost").

Squarely in the throes of the 1740 crisis, in the second half of September, Prévost's second literary masterpiece came out: *Histoire d'une Grecque moderne* (*The Greek Girl's Story*). But this novel was buried, so to speak, in an intense literary production that also included, the same year, the publication of the last three volumes of *Le doyen de Killerine*, the two volumes of the *Histoire de Marguerite d'Anjou*, and volumes 19 and 20 of *Le Pour et Contre*, as well as the writing of the *Campagnes philosophiques* (1741), the *Histoire de la jeunesse du commandeur de . . .* (1741), and the *Histoire de Guillaume le Conquérant* (1742). That is a remarkable amount of writing, and it is difficult to avoid seeing a link between this frantic literary activity and Prévost's financial dilemma—which led André Billy, a trifle cavalierly, to characterize all of the production of this period as "alimentary literature" (*Un singulier bénédictin*, 233)!

There has been no lack of reflection over the causes of the ruinous expenditures of Prévost, who seems to have squandered a fortune to put himself in such a fix. According to a suggestion from Roddier (*Abbé Prévost*, 43–44), based on comments by the chevalier de Ravanne (J. Gautier de Faget de Malines), the abbé's former secretary in The Hague, Prévost picked up again in Paris with Lenki; it was for her, under the name of Mme de Chester, that Prévost courted financial ruin a second time, before she finally disappeared from his life upon marrying a certain M. Dumas in 1741. If we are interested in Prévost's personal woes during this period, it is because one is tempted to see a connection, as do Jean Sgard and Robert Mauzi, between the sentimental tribulations of the abbé with Lenki–Mme de Chester and those of the narrator-hero of *The Greek Girl's Story*. Prévost and his hero, in this perspective, were both "exhausted and aged" by the "miserable end of a long affair" and "in the portrait of the solitary old man, impotent, fallen, one can read a strange and ironic judgment by Prévost on himself" (Sgard, *Prévost romancier*, 406, 483). *The Greek Girl's Story* would thus be, in Mauzi's view, the transposition of the "suffering from passion" that Prévost experienced personally (Prévost, *Histoire d'une Grecque moderne*, ix). These are, of course, only hypotheses, however seductive they may be.

"Neither a Key to the Names nor Any Clarification of the Facts"

If the autobiographical conjectures must be treated with caution in any consideration of the genesis of *The Greek Girl's Story*, this is hardly the case with the historical models for the two main characters, for there is no doubt that this is a roman à clef. To make the readers aware of this (and to arouse their curiosity, of course), Prévost declares that his preface "will serve only to notify the reader that we promise him, for the work we are introducing to him, neither a key to the names nor any clarification of the facts nor the slightest information that will help him understand or guess what he cannot comprehend through his own discernment." What better way, as many commentators of this novel have already noted, to suggest that there is, in fact, a "key to the names"?[2] In any case the author's contemporaries were in no way fooled, as several texts from the period clearly attest. In a letter from September 29, 1740, scarcely a week after the publication of the novel, the journalist Gastellier offers a commentary in which he names the main actors in the drama that served as Prévost's inspiration: "The beautiful Aïssé, whose story, I was informed, was told by the abbé Prévost, was a young Greek girl that M. de Ferriol had also brought with him from Constantinople to Paris." Then, in a letter from October 17, 1740, we read, "The abbé Prévost d'Exiles continues to produce the type of novel he specializes in. He has just brought out *The Greek Girl's Story*; it is, people say, essentially the adventure of M. de Ferriol when he was our ambassador at the Sublime Porte." And again, a few months later, Mme de Staal-Delaunay writes to a friend, "I began *The Greek Girl's Story* because of what you told me about it: it is believed indeed that Mademoiselle Aïssé inspired it, but there have been a lot of embellishments, because she was only three or four when she was brought to France."

The two individuals concerned here are Charles-Louis-Augustin, marquis d'Argental, comte de Ferriol, the French ambassador in Constantinople
from 1699 to 1711, and a young Circassian (Russian) girl, Charlotte-Elisabeth
Aïssé (whose real name is "Haïdée") whom Ferriol had bought at a slave
market in Constantinople before his ambassadorship began and brought
with him to France in 1698 when she was four years old. The diplomat put
his "goddaughter" in the care of his sister-in-law Mme de Ferriol, the older
sister of the celebrated Mme de Tencin, who reigned over one of the most
famous salons in Paris in the eighteenth century, frequented by Prévost
among other literary luminaries. Mme de Ferriol raised the young girl along
with her two sons, the comte d'Argental and the comte de Pont-de-Veyle.

In 1711, when Ferriol showed signs of madness and was recalled to France,
it was rumored that despite his sixty years he nonetheless insisted on his
"rights" over his protégée, who had become at age eighteen a strikingly beautiful woman, courted by a number of eminent contemporaries, including the
regent himself, the duc d'Orléans. This "rumor" is confirmed, moreover,
quite explicitly in a letter from Ferriol to Aïssé published in the *Bulletin of
the Society of French Bibliophiles* in 1828, where we read, in particular, "When
I delivered you from the hands of the infidels and purchased you . . . it was
my intention to benefit from destiny's influence on men's fate to dispose of
you as I wished, and to make you one day either my daughter or my mistress. The same destiny has decided that you have become both of them,
since I have found it impossible to separate love from friendship and intense
desire from a father's affection" (Sainte-Beuve, *Portraits littéraires*, 137). The
scandalous character of the relations between Ferriol and Aïssé—an open
secret in Parisian salons between 1735 and 1740—was certainly germane to
Prévost's motivation when he undertook the writing of *The Greek Girl's
Story*. He was desperately in need of a quick success, even if it were a *succès
de scandale*, to extricate himself from his financial morass.

The Aïssé personage lent itself particularly well to this purpose, and not
only because of her relations with Ferriol. Around 1720 she had become the
mistress of a young Knight of Malta, Blaise-Marie d'Aydie, who is said to
have abandoned, out of love for her, his existence as a "rake of the Regency"
and become "the most faithful and tender lover" (Asse, "Baron de Ferriol,"
169). In 1721 their liaison produced, in the utmost secrecy, a baby girl known
as Célinie Le Blond. After Ferriol's death in 1722, Aïssé refused a marriage

Fig. 1   Mademoiselle Aïssé. From Courteault, *Mademoiselle Aïssé, le chevalier d'Aydie et leur fille*, 1908. Bibliothèque nationale de France.

proposal by the knight—because of her socially inferior position, according to Maurice Andrieux (*Mademoiselle Aïssé*, 136)—then, ill with tuberculosis around 1730, was overcome with remorse and embraced repentance and religion until her death in 1733. The couple was surrounded by a veritable legend of mutual love, devotion, and fidelity that will be magnified by posterity, thanks to the publication, a half century after Aïssé's death, of her letters, in which one can perceive an extraordinary sincerity in the expression of her love for the knight, as well as in the repentance that marks her last years. In her correspondence "she invites us to witness day by day," as Asse remarks, "the struggle between the Christian who is repenting for her failings and does not wish to recidivate and the lover who cannot extinguish her love but only conserves its immaterial and ethereal qualities" (*Lettres de Mlle Aïssé*, 169)—a struggle therefore, from the thematic perspective, between virtue and desire that the novelist exploits fully in *The Greek Girl's Story*.

Having frequented the social circle of the relatives or friends of Ferriol since his return to Paris in 1736, Prévost could not have been unaware of the rumors about Aïssé's fate. On the one hand, the facts concerning the ambassadorship of Ferriol to the Sublime Porte had been related not only by the count himself in the *Explication des cent estampes* (*Explanation of the One Hundred Engravings*, 1715) but also in several travel narratives that were very widely known at that time, including those by Joseph Pitton de Tournefort (1717) and, especially, Antoine de La Motraye (1727). His tenure there was also related in *The History of the Growth and Decay of the Othman Empire* by Demetrius Cantemir, a book Prévost had known very well in its 1734–35 English version before applying himself to its translation into French at the very moment of the publication of *The Greek Girl's Story*.[3]

It is not difficult to find in the stories of Ferriol, Aïssé, and the chevalier d'Aydie the elements that the novelist seems to have transposed. Prévost was especially struck, for example, by the multiple incidents recounted by Cantemir and La Motraye that marred the relations between Ferriol and his Ottoman hosts, including the episode in which the diplomat's "madness" manifests itself (see app. 1). The *fête du roi*, or king's party, in his novel is thus a quasi-literal transposition of a celebration organized by Ferriol in 1704 in honor of the birth of the grandson of the king, the Duke of Brittany, that nearly provoked a highly serious diplomatic incident. The aberrant behavior of Prévost's narrator, who, like his historical model, threatens to blow up his house with all his guests, is a transparent evocation of Ferriol's lapse into madness that will significantly contribute to his recall, although it was in fact a completely different incident that led to his disgrace. Accordingly to La Motraye, Ferriol became severely indisposed following an argument with a French nobleman during an outing on horseback. Extremely upset, Ferriol is said to have become so furious that he began to shout deliriously, which forced his entourage to lock him up in a room. Informed of the "madness" of his ambassador, who was in fact suffering from a kind of nervous illness, the king relieved him of his charge and recalled him to France. The suggestion of "madness," which we find again in Prévost's novel, is clearly a reference to Ferriol; just like him, the narrator is relieved of his diplomatic functions and ordered back to France.

The incident that we have just mentioned will give rise, moreover, to another circumstance that is of the utmost interest as regards the genesis of *The Greek Girl's Story*. Again according to La Motraye, "But what upset M. de Ferriol even more was that they took away from him an Armenian girl whom he called his *figlia d'anima*, or his 'soul daughter' [*fille d'âme*, as adopted girls are called], and whom the malicious gossips called his 'body daughter' [*fille de corps*]. This girl accompanied him, holding his hand, even out in the streets" (*Voyages*, 1:410).[4] The "figlia d'anima" is Lucie-Charlotte de Fontana, whom Ferriol will bring to France with him when he returns in 1711, and with whom he will continue to live for around ten years more before marrying her off. Prévost's heroine Théophé thus evokes both Aïssé and Fontana, while nonetheless being different from them and possessing her own individuality. In creating Théophé, Prévost was clearly inspired by the relations Ferriol entertained with Fontana in both Constantinople and Paris as well as by those that united the ex-ambassador to Aïssé in Paris, the two women sharing the equivocal and scandalous status of both "daughter" and "mistress."

It is easy to recognize the historical reference point of the narrator-hero's project in which he strives more and more desperately to transform his status as "father" to that of "lover." The Aïssé figure furnishes, in addition, as we have suggested earlier, the theme of moral conversion, of devotion to virtue, indeed, of the desire to expiate her sins that Théophé will erect as an obstacle to the diplomat's amorous desire. Greedy for scandals, the Parisian public wasted no time identifying the "key to the names" that Prévost so coyly denies them in his preface, all the while inviting them to see the obvious. The commotion caused by the title of the novel alone, before its publication, was enough to mobilize the friends of Aïssé, who was known as "the young Greek lady" (whereas Ferriol was widely referred to as the "pasha" or the "aga"). It is only after the intervention of the comte d'Argental and of the chevalier d'Aydie himself, concerned about Aïssé's reputation, that Prévost agreed to change the name of the last suitor of Théophé in the novel: the comte de . . . was originally named "le chevalier D." Well, when we know that the knight's name "d'Aydie" was often written "Daydie" at the time, we can understand the alarm of the defenders of the beautiful Circassian (Breuil, "Une lettre inédite").

Along with Ferriol, whose character does not always correspond to that of Prévost's narrator-hero, we need to take into account a second important source of inspiration: the comte Charles-Augustin de Bonneval. This rather colorful character was a former general during the reign of Louis XIV who defected to the Germans before taking refuge in Constantinople around 1729 to escape his numerous enemies. He converted to Islam and was completely assimilated into Ottoman society. Speaking Turkish fluently like Prévost's diplomat and, like him, enjoying high favor among his hosts (very unlike Ferriol), he was elevated to the rank of pasha of three tails (provincial governor). His defection, both religious and political, was a broad public scandal provoking heated polemics between 1737 and 1740 in which Prévost himself took part, coming to the defense of the renegade in a text published in 1739. Bonneval's stay in Turkey is related in 1737 in apocryphal "new" memoirs fabricated by his detractors, the *Nouveaux mémoires du comte de Bonneval* that Prévost had read and that enjoyed a resounding success in that period. It is highly likely that Prévost wanted to take advantage of this craze in offering the public some more apocryphal oriental memoirs, those of the comte de Ferriol.

Certain passages of the *Nouveaux mémoires*, moreover, may have played a specific role in the genesis of *The Greek Girl's Story*. In the excerpts in appendix I, the reader will note, in addition to the locale and the atmosphere, a number of striking similarities regarding situations and themes: the unhappy slave (like Théophé) who tells her story to a Frenchman and who appeals to his sense of honor and generosity to free her from her unbearable concubine's existence; the attack of the Turkish pirates in which the young European woman (like Maria Rezati) is taken prisoner and finds herself in a harem; the old slave who attempts (like Bema) to persuade the girl to accede to her master's desires; the thousand crowns spent to purchase the mother's freedom (same sum to liberate Théophé); the questioning of the *motives* of the beautiful Persian girl, who is of noble birth (like Théophé may be) and who, in addition, exhibits a fine mind. . . . These similarities may be coincidences, of course, but they are numerous enough to lead us to suspect otherwise.[5]

If questions of genesis may elucidate the novelist's inspiration and motivation, they can hardly explain the value of a literary work, which is, of course, a matter of intrinsic qualities. Moreover, an excessive concern with sources may even obscure the work itself. The reputation of *The Greek Girl's Story*, considered by many today to be a masterpiece, has long suffered, since its first appearance, from its status as a *roman à clef* and as a *roman à scandale*; readers were more interested in the key, in the private lives of the historical models, than in the work of art. Prévost took great pains, in fact, to foster this interest. If there is something "miraculous" about *The Greek Girl's Story*, as Allan Holland once suggested ("Miracle"), it is that Prévost succeeded, despite the material problems of the writing and the scabrous rumors that inspired him, in producing a literary work of the first rank.

A "Perpetual Enigma"

Falling in love with a former concubine is already hardly a banal event. When it is the French ambassador to the Sublime Porte, a worldly libertine, who has purchased the freedom of the young lady, and when said damsel proceeds to reject even the most "honorable" of her benefactor's advances, condemning him to unbearable frustration, driving him to spasms of jealousy, it becomes a most singular case. Moreover, it is the diplomat himself who, after the death of his protégée, relates this story and who, tormented by doubts, asks the reader to render a judgment on her. This young lady, an experienced odalisque who aspires, upon leaving the harem, to devote her life to the cultivation of the most severe virtue, can she be sincere? Is it conceivable that a harem girl, raised expressly to satisfy carnal desires, acquires instantly a moral conscience and suddenly converts—upon her first encounter with the idea of virtue—to a life of chastity and striving toward moral perfection? Hasn't the narrator been duped by the "fine principles" of the young Greek woman, who attempts to flee with Synèse (this "brother" whose highly suspicious caresses she later countenances), who proves to be receptive to the advances of the "first fellow who came along" as soon as she arrives in the West, who participates in licentious parties in Paris, and who will be accused of receiving lovers in her room at night? What a litany of serious charges!

Nonetheless, Théophé's defense is always convincing. If she had tried to flee, it was solely to escape the diplomat's gaze (as in Sartre's imprisoning *regard*), which reminded her constantly of her shameful past. If she accepted Synèse's caresses, it was because he had convinced her—and she had no reason to suspect his sincerity—that it was an accepted practice for brothers and sisters to give each other marks of their mutual affection. If she didn't resist her attraction to the comte de M. Q. in Livorno, it was because, she explains, "I didn't believe that he had any knowledge of my wretched past, so I flattered myself that I could enjoy with him the ordinary rights of a woman who has pledged herself to honor and virtue." And so on.[6] What or whom are we to believe? The narrator-hero's doubts, his suspicions, and his accusations, or the apparently sincere and coherent explanations of Théophé? The narrator himself, clearly unable to sort things out, asks the "reader" to decide for him. This intratextual narratee, condemned to silence, passes the burden on to the implied (real) reader, that is, to us.

Faced with this exegetical dilemma, the prudent reader would be tempted not to decide at all. It is thus hardly surprising that a persistent critical tradition has developed that holds that the enigma itself, and the ambiguity this implies, is in a certain sense the very message of the novel—the "enigma" of Théophé's character and the "ambiguity" of her motivation and behavior. From this perspective, Théophé is just another example of the *éternel féminin* embodied by Manon Lescaut in Prévost's earlier novel. We will never know if the heroine is really sincere, if she is virtuous and chaste, if her conversion is authentic; she *could* be, as various talented critics have maintained, a "talented liar," a "hypocrite," an "amoral" creature, an "ambiguous and fickle girl" who abuses both the generosity and the gullibility of the diplomat to guarantee her material security while retaining all of the advantages of personal liberty.[7] Prévost, according to this hypothesis, has deprived the reader of any enlightenment on these questions, preferring, as Mauzi maintains, "that she remain forever an enigma" (*Histoire d'une Grecque moderne*, xxxii). In this case, doubt itself dominates the semantic field of the novel, "a doubt concerning the very nature of love and virtue," according to Sgard, who lumps *The Greek Girl's Story* together with the two other novels in the "1740 trilogy," the *Mémoires pour server à l'histoire de Malte* and the *Campagnes philosophiques*, works whose deep cynicism is well known to Prévost's readers (*Prévost romancier*, 418–19).

In the same vein we may choose to agree with Jean Rousset, who emphasizes the hermeneutical problem and states that the principal interest of the novel is "the uncertainty of reality and the plurality of interpretations that it accommodates" (*Narcisse romancier*, 153–54).[8] There is no doubt that the novel demonstrates the impossibility for the narrator-hero, a prisoner of his natural egocentrism as well as of his jealous character, to establish any kind of "truth" as regards the history of his relations with the heroine. But are we forced to conclude that the real reader—who does not have to identify with the fictional (and passive) "reader" to whom the narrator addresses his narrative and his plea—is reduced to the same impotence? It would seem legitimate to ask ourselves, as Francis Pruner does, if we are faced here with the impenetrability of the female heart or, simply, with the blindness of the narrator ("Psychologie," 140).

An Insidious Narrative

The "enigma" label that has been attached so tenaciously to *The Greek Girl's Story*, and that is sometimes accompanied by a thinly veiled skepticism regarding the heroine's sincerity, is hardly gratuitous. It is the narrator himself who strives, and quite successfully, to impose this image of Théophé, sharing over and over again his incomprehension, his perplexity, indeed, his consternation before the behavior of the young woman. Ultimately he will admit that "everything about her, from the first moment I had laid eyes on her, had been a perpetual enigma for me."[9] But we are faced with a text that puts explicitly into doubt its own credibility. Théophé's actions, like the hero's motives, are presented to us by a narrator whose vision is circumscribed and deformed by the exacerbated subjectivity wrought by his passion, which renders his testimony exceedingly problematical. He gives us fair warning from the outset of his memoirs: "Who will believe in the sincerity of this account of my pleasures or of my suffering? Who will not be skeptical about my descriptions and my praise? Will my violent passion not distort everything that passes through my eyes or hands?" There is, indeed, good reason to be suspicious, and Prévost gives birth to the "unreliable narrator" long before it will become one of the hallmarks of the twentieth-century novel.[10]

His memoirs, moreover, take on the form of a "trial" in which the pleading and the prosecution—the defense of the diplomat himself and the indictment of Théophé—are subtly intertwined. It is tempting to see in the narrator a kind of prosecuting attorney who connives with the hero, acting as an investigating magistrate (*juge d'instruction*), to lead an insidious campaign to convict the heroine, all the while insisting on the honesty of his own motives, on his sincerity, and on his sense of justice.[11] Throughout his tale the diplomat seems to strive to create doubts in the readers' (the "jurors'") minds by inviting them to share either his uncertainties and suspicions or his spite, even his scorn, toward Théophé. The entire text—you, the reader, will decide for yourself—may appear to be a mass of innuendo whose only real purpose is to discredit the young Greek woman, to create an impression of ambiguity that prevents us from believing unreservedly in the sincerity of the former concubine.[12]

However, there remains a critical question: Is the narrator doing it on purpose? Is he consciously attempting to discredit his protégée, or does he sincerely believe that he is being objective and just, that, indeed, he is giving her the benefit of all the doubt he has created? Is he really appealing to the readers' judgment, or is he only asking them to share his suspicions? As regards narrative ambiguity, that is perhaps the essential question.[13] Whichever the case, Théophé's explanations, as well as her repeated refusals of the diplomat's advances, are not without credibility. Mauzi, who proposes a "solution" to the "enigma," is the first to recognize it: "Obsessed with expiation and purity, Théophé dreams of forgetting a past of which she is ashamed. She is therefore unable to love the narrator, whose most generous actions just remind her of the past, and whose demands sometimes plunge her back into it" (Prévost, *Histoire d'une Grecque moderne*, xxxv–xxxvi). This is what the young woman attempts, in vain, to get her benefactor to understand: "Your friendship and your generous protection," she said, "repaired instantly all of my misfortunes; but the regrets, the determination, the efforts I will need to make for the rest of my life will never repair the immorality of my past. I am indifferent to anything that will not help to make me more virtuous, because virtue is henceforth the only treasure I desire, and every day I discover more and more that it is the only one I lack." While agreeing that "this is perfectly coherent," Mauzi remains nonetheless skeptical: "But then there is no enigma, and doesn't that put into question the whole meaning of the work? One may draw that conclusion. But it must be said that neither the author nor the narrator find this explanation satisfactory" (xxxvi).

The cult of enigma is tenacious, and Mauzi, like many others, remains convinced that the heroine "disappears with all of her mystery" because the reader, he maintains, is reduced to the narrator's testimony alone. To elucidate the case, "he [the reader] would have to be able, like a true judge, to undertake his own investigation and complete the file" (Prévost, *Histoire d'une Grecque moderne*, xxxiii), which Mauzi feels is impossible, as does Rousset, who follows the same line of reasoning: "Prévost's reader . . . would be able to establish the truth if the file he is given contained the complementary testimony which is needed; this testimony is missing" (*Narcisse romancier*, 154). Nonetheless, as may be demonstrated, it is not clear that this "complementary testimony" is completely missing nor, by the same token, that Prévost wanted Théophé to "remain forever an enigma." The author's "strategic location" in the text (to borrow Edward Said's terminology), as conveyed through a number of rhetorical devices, gives considerable pause for reflection in this regard.

Complementary Testimony: The "Doubles"

The reader may, in fact, achieve a perspective that transcends the narrator's biased and somewhat tendentious vision through a whole series of secondary characters in Prévost's novel whose function seems to be, in addition to their role as actors in the story, to provide information on the hero's and heroine's behavior. This concerns, above all, characters who appear to serve as "doubles" for the diplomat by suggesting his true sentiments, his motives (whether intentionally dissimulated or buried in his unconscious mind), and even his psychological conflicts. This technique of "psychological decomposition," which the abbé had already put into practice in *Cleveland*, where the behavior of both the duc de Monmouth and don Thadéo, for instance, serves to elucidate the hero's ambiguous and semi-incestuous feelings toward his daughter, Cécile, seems to become in *The Greek Girl's Story* a systematic practice.[14] Thus the selictar, the closest Turkish friend of the diplomat's, may be seen to reflect, by his comments and comportment, the complete evolution of the hero's love for Théophé, from the immediate conception of a desire that he refuses to recognize as such until his marriage proposal, a function that exposes in an ironic mode all the blindness and bad faith of the diplomat as regards his own motives. Elsewhere the highly ambiguous and suspicious relations that Synèse establishes with Théophé as both her brother and lover, relations that he would like to push yet further by denying their familial bond, clearly suggest the no less incestuous character of the project elaborated by the diplomat, who attempts to rid himself of his "paternal" status (as the person who has "fathered" Théophé's moral rebirth) to make her his mistress. And so on to the end: Théophé's Parisian governess herself may be perceived as a final image of the pathological jealousy of the narrator-hero, of his own "ridiculous fantasies," his probably gratuitous suspicions and accusations, his persecution of the Greek girl, his unavowed desire to avenge himself.[15]

As for the "enigma" of Théophé—Is her conversion to virtue authentic? Is her behavior irreproachable? Is her devotion to her benefactor sincere?— here also the text may provide some "complementary testimony" that permits us to establish a certain level of "probability" in this matter, without, of course, claiming to establish indisputable truth, which is obviously impossible and would be intolerably reductive to even attempt. Théophé too has a parallel character in the novel who may be able to help us pierce this "veil" that certain critics find impenetrable: Maria Rezati. Sgard saw clearly the symbolic overtones of the story of the young Sicilian girl, so "similar," in his opinion, to Théophé's own story that he perceived it to be "one of these parallel destinies that illuminate the contours of the main character" (*Prévost romancier*, 462). For him, Maria is a "troubling double" whose dissolute conduct constitutes a bad omen for Théophé's behavior: how can we believe in the moral rehabilitation of a former concubine if Maria, despite the most rigorously virtuous upbringing, falls into debauchery and tries to coax Théophé into following her example? That sounds logical, but what if Maria Rezati is not a double for Théophé but rather a foil who, on the contrary, serves to validate the authenticity of her conversion?

If we return to the respective upbringings of the two characters, we note that the personal itineraries of the two girls are in fact diametrically opposed. Sequestered in the country by her father, under the strict surveillance of "two old and virtuous women," Maria is raised until the age of seventeen "in the constant practice of all the virtues," in complete ignorance of her beauty as well as of its effect on men. This does not prevent her, upon seeing herself for the first time in a mirror, from realizing immediately the power of her physical charms, fleeing with the first young man who comes along, and plunging into a licentious existence. Théophé, on the other hand, after a long upbringing whose sole purpose was to turn her into purely carnal creature, undergoes at exactly the same age, seventeen, an instantaneous transformation "at the first mention of the name and concept of virtue" when she meets the diplomat in the harem. In both cases it is the "natural traces" that win out over the "acquired traces," to borrow the vocabulary of the moral philosopher Nicolas Malebranche, whose themes so profoundly affected Prévost's thought (see Deprun, "Thèmes malebranchistes," 162–67). Théophé and Maria both return to their natural character, which their education had only repressed.

How can we ignore this reverse symmetry, this striking antithesis that seems to be a confirmation of the sincerity of Théophé's conversion? Théophé and Manon are often compared as two objects of an "unworthy love," whereas there is a clearer parallel between Théophé and the chevalier des Grieux, both experiencing a *coup de foudre* (love at first sight), one sentimental, the other moral. Like des Grieux, a model of virtue who had been oblivious to female charms and is "suddenly overwhelmed with passion" the first time he sets eyes on Manon (Prévost, *Manon Lescaut*, 19), for Théophé, a purely carnal being, the meaning of the ideas of virtue, honor, and proper conduct "was clear in a flash, as if [she] had always known them." This experience of the coup de foudre is described, moreover, in virtually identical terms in the two cases, the chevalier feeling that he has been "transporté dans un nouvel ordre de choses" (swept into a new order of things, 45), and Théophé finding herself "transportée dans un nouveau jour" (swept into a different world).

But how can we believe in a "moral coup de foudre"? The diplomat cannot bring himself to do so, any more than many readers of the novel, despite the fact that the coup de foudre and religious conversion, as Denis de Rougemont reminds us, have been linked in the Western world since the Middle Ages: "The first gaze exchanged by lovers, which is going to change their whole life, corresponds to the first touch of divine love, to the Christian's conversion" (*L'Amour et l'Occident*, 315). We note, in this respect, the name that Prévost gives to his heroine when she leaves the harem: Zara becomes "Théophé." Can it be a simple matter of chance that this name seems to be derived from the Greek noun *Théophèmi* (Θεοφημη) that means "she who loves the gods," "she who is dear to the gods," or "she who announces God's will"?[16] Doesn't this suggestion of divine action tend to reinforce the idea of "conversion"? It seems to us that "rectifying interventions," for anyone who is listening carefully, are scarcely absent from *The Greek Girl's Story*. If it would be imprudent to speak of incontrovertible evidence of the heroine's sincerity, we may at least agree that the novel provides us with perspectives that clearly transcend the limited vision of the diplomat. The rhetorical devices deployed in the text are addressed directly to the reader, through but beyond the narrator's knowledge, and create the conditions for the layer of irony that underlies the entire narrative and that fosters a complicity between author and reader at the expense of the narrator-hero.[17]

The "Meaning" of the Novel

Assuming the hypothesis according to which Théophé's character is an enigma only for the hero himself—a "false enigma," states Henri Coulet, "born of his male egoism" ("Sur les trois romans," 13)—what then might be the "meaning" of this novel? Again, without wishing to take a reductive stance toward a work whose "open," that is, modern, character is undeniable, we might situate one of the principal thematic axes in the dilemma of the hero, who is blinded both by an unworthy passion, as des Grieux was, and by his "male egoism" that prevents him from understanding Théophé's aspirations.

Prévost presents us with the step-by-step spectacle—this is the clear goal of his demonstration—of a growing passion constantly repulsed (growing *because* it is constantly repulsed, as is typical of the Don Juan character) and with the debilitating drama of an inextinguishable and perpetually unrequited desire. Faced with Théophé's unwavering resistance, the diplomat is condemned to a state of increasingly intense and ultimately intolerable frustration that will bring him to the edge of madness before plunging him into the aberrations of the pathological jealousy that characterizes his behavior during the whole latter, occidental, section of the novel.

The very intransigence of the heroine, moreover, is the intersection with a second thematic axis that is just as fundamental to Prévost's work. In this battle between the sexes, because that is indeed what is involved here,

Théophé seems to have spontaneously understood the rule of the game: if she yields to the diplomat's desires, even as his wife, she will reassume her former status as a sex object, and scorn will replace the respect and esteem that her virtuous resistance has earned her. While virtually pleading with her to grant him "voluntarily" what he desires, the hero has nonetheless made it clear to her that it is precisely "misdeeds that are committed intentionally [that] are worthy of contempt." She understands what is at stake here. Radicalized by the feeling of shame that is associated with the memory of her existence as a concubine, considering physical love itself to be a form of debasement, Théophé is profoundly convinced that her personal value now depends entirely on her status as a moral being. She will not forget the premises of the new existence that the diplomat had painted in such glowing colors with his references, in the harem, to the relationship between "happiness" and "virtue." Ignorant of gallant circumlocution and taking her interlocutor at his word, the young slave will retain only what resonates with her newly discovered inclinations: "There are men who value in a woman something other than physical charms! Women can distinguish themselves by other qualities and can hope for other kinds of pleasure!" And she will not give up an iota of that dream.

Prévost, as we know well, is drawn to "experiments." In *Manon Lescaut* he delivers up to the ravages of passionate love a young male virgin, a Knight of Malta who is a paragon of virtue and innocence and destined for a brilliant career in the church. In *Cleveland* he puts philosophy and rationalism to the test of life, that is, the test of misfortune, suffering, and all the worldly passions. He returns to the well again in *Le doyen de Killerine*, putting Christian morality itself to the test of the principal passions, love and ambition. Like a proto-Zola "experimental" novelist, he sets all the social, psychological, and moral conditions of the experiment, lets it play out, and notes the results—or rather the havoc that is wrought. His approach is hardly different in *The Greek Girl's Story*, in which he imagines the admittedly more original hypothesis of a moral coup de foudre that opposes a libertine in the full flower of manhood and a gorgeous young woman—a sex object par excellence—who owes him everything, beginning with her conversion to virtue, to "see" what will happen. Manon's sexual liberty is replaced by Théophé's moral liberty, which will prove, mutatis mutandis, to be just as devastating for the hero. There results in this novel a monumental conflict, rising from a fundamental and mutual *malentendu* that condemns to failure from the outset any attempt by the two characters to achieve a harmonious relationship.[18] Théophé immediately imposes on the diplomat the role of moral mentor, while he, on his part, can imagine them only as lovers. This is a novel about the irreconcilable. In the final analysis the protagonists both imagine themselves in the wrong "novel," Théophé taking her benefactor-mentor for the doyen de Killerine, the diplomat taking *her* for Manon Lescaut. Hell is others.

A Metaphorical Orient

But what are we to make of all these harems, concubines, and pashas? We may, of course, consider the depiction of the Orient to be its own justification. At the time of the writing of Prévost's novel, the Orient had held an increasing fascination for Europeans since the preceding century, as witnessed by Racine's *Bajazet*, Molière's *The Bourgeois Gentleman*, *The Turkish Spy* by Giovanni Paolo Marana, and the history of the Ottoman Empire by Paul Rycaut, as well as the more recent travel narratives of Jean-Baptiste Tavernier, Jean Chardin, Jean de Thévenot, Antoine de La Motraye, and others; the innumerable editions of Antoine Galland's 1704 translation of the *Arabian Nights*; and the wide success of Montesquieu's *Persian Letters* (1721). The contemporary public yearned for exoticism; reveled in harem intrigues, slave markets, and palace revolutions; and was intoxicated by the whiff of blood and sensuality that seeped from Turkish tales. It is easy to understand that Prévost, in desperate need of money, would be eager to take advantage of this infatuation, which reached its height precisely around 1740.[19] This, however, sheds no light on the signification of the oriental elements in his novel, the possible meanings that the work lends to the extremely conventional image of the Levant that he offers his readers.

It is virtually impossible today, since the appearance of Edward Said's luminous study *Orientalism* in 1979, to discuss a literary work involving the Orient without reflecting on its possible relationship to colonialism. Does Prévost's oriental novel contain images or themes that are informed by colonialist attitudes during the Ancien Régime and, more precisely, under the reign of Louis XV in Prévost's time? Is the French ambassador's behavior "imperialist"? Is his treatment of Théophé a metaphor for the exploitation of the Orient by the Occident? To the extent that, as Said states, "the essence of Orientalism is the eradicable distinction between Western superiority and Oriental inferiority" (*Orientalism*, 42), there is an undeniable colonialist cast to the French ambassador's smug, condescending attitude toward his Turkish hosts, most likely shared by Prévost himself, since oriental backwardness, along with despotism, was a prominent *idée reçue* of the Ancien Régime.[20]

But orientalism refers more broadly to "a Western style for dominating, restructuring, and having authority over the Orient" (*Orientalism*, 3), and from this primarily political perspective, it is difficult to apply this concept to writings of much of the French eighteenth century. While it is true that by the early years of the century, the French had established a significant trade advantage in Turkey, the Ottoman rulers remained fiercely independent and were hardly a colonized people, despite their recent military defeats by Austria, Russia, and Venice and the humiliation of the treaties of Carlowitz (1699) and Passarowitz (1718). They pursued an active politics of détente with the West, and with France in particular, in the dozen years following the Belgrade defeat, the so-called Tulip period (1718–30), during which they condescended to dispatch their first real ambassador to Paris (1720).[21]

Orientalism, as defined by Said, is largely a post-Enlightenment phenomenon. It is reflected primarily in texts from the nineteenth and twentieth centuries, beginning with the *Description of Egypt* (1809–28) mandated by Napoleon during and after his failed occupation of that country (1798–99) and continued with the subsequent broad expansion of Western colonization of the East. The French ambassador in the early eighteenth century, while enjoying considerable prestige as the official representative of France, and despite a pervasive assumption of cultural superiority, could not be domineering in his relations with the Ottoman Porte, as such attempts by failed diplomats like Ferriol demonstrate. The ambassador did not exercise political power over his Turkish hosts. Prévost's diplomat is respected by the Ottoman officials but is no less respectful of them and their authority, other than in the episode of the king's party, in which his behavior is clearly deranged. Despite the clear existence of French imperialist fantasies regarding the Orient during the Ancien Régime, it would seem hazardous to interpret, as some have done, the diplomat's rather despotic treatment of Théophé as a metaphor for French colonization of Turkey, no matter how attractive this idea may be today.[22]

So what might Prévost's aim be here? Did he, as Mauzi claims, simply want to create an opposition between two worlds in which the Orient, "entirely devalued," serves only as a foil for Western society and Christian values, which are proposed as "absolute models" (Prévost, *Histoire d'une Grecque moderne*, xxxvi–xxxxvii)? Insofar as it is the Frenchman and not the Turk who is disgraced in this novel, there is room for doubt. If it is true, as noted earlier, that the diplomat manifests a certain scorn for his hosts, declaring haughtily at one point that "a Frenchman was not guided by Turkish customs" or alluding to "what we would find disgusting in a Turk," the reader shouldn't be misled by the prejudices displayed by the narrator, who is himself forced to recognize that "there are few nations where the sense of equity is more pronounced" than in Turkey.[23] The complete honesty and sincerity of the selictar, the principal Turkish character, serve to highlight moreover the hypocrisy of the Frenchman as well as the ambiguity of the Western mores that he had boasted of so proudly to his Turkish friend, beginning with the character of amorous relations between men and women. Pruner is certainly right to wonder aloud if "the Western libertinage that he intends to practice with a kept woman is any better than oriental polygamy" ("Psychologie," 141); indeed, the diplomat is forced to confess to Théophé, "Although they may have very sound ideas of virtue in Europe, they scarcely practice it any better than in Turkey." As Julia Douthwaite sums it up, Prévost's novel "demystifies the moral superiority of his Christian nation" (*Exotic Women*, 65).[24]

It is precisely in this ironic allusion to the mores and values of Western peoples that we may find the principal significance of the image of Ottoman society in this novel. The oriental world offers us a rich series of potential metaphors in which the harem, for instance, may be seen to represent the reign of the flesh, "the love of the world" and of its pleasures, the universe of perishable goods devoid of spirituality; in which the Turkish pasha brings to mind Western man in his relations to women, the tyrannical character of carnal desire that aspires to the absolute possession of its "object"; in which the concubine, finally, may be seen as an image of women as pure sex objects, relegated to this status by a male-dominated ideology no less occidental than oriental and which ultimately circumvents any moral values.[25] From this perspective the Orient proposes a feminine "ideal" that evokes and denounces the erotic fantasies of Western men, the myth of the female sex slave submissive to masculine desire, which collides violently with this other Western myth, the pure, chaste, and inaccessible woman that is conveyed by both Christian morality and the courtly tradition.[26]

The oriental metaphor thus certainly offers a commentary on the status of women in both the East and the West, but it is also a reference to the particular dilemma of the narrator-hero, this Turkified Frenchman who is caught between two cultures, between two sociocultural codes, entangled in contradictory aspirations and reduced to the artifices of his desire and of his pride (*amour-propre*) before this young woman that he "possesses" but who escapes his grasp up to the end. The diplomat constantly oscillates between his desire to possess the sex object he has purchased and his Pygmalion-like admiration for the moral being he has created. But are we not speaking here of the attitude of Western man in general confronted with the very Cartesian duality of women, both mind and body, a duality that the desiring subject has difficulty accepting but that he cultivates hypocritically in the hope of a more complete possession, both moral and physical? What, then, becomes of the male when the female refuses to be reduced to the compass of his desire alone? Might this not be, in the final analysis, the essential question of this experiment in applied psychology that the abbé Prévost offers us in *The Greek Girl's Story*?

A Word on the Translation

The abbé Prévost published the *Histoire d'une Grecque moderne* in 1740, followed quickly by a corrected version the following year. The rapid success of the novel is indicated by the appearance in 1741 of the first English translation (anonymous), *The History of a Fair Greek, Who Was Taken Out of a Seraglio at Constantinople, and Brought to Paris by a Late Embassador at the Ottoman Port*, published by J. Roberts in London. The Roberts translation is based on Catuffe's second edition of the novel in 1741, clearly indicated by its inclusion of an additional paragraph in Prévost's foreword referring to Mlle Aïssé, the "Fair Circassian," which is not in the original edition. The Catuffe edition of the *Grecque moderne* is the last one published during Prévost's lifetime, and the best version we have. It contains several dozen corrections, some of them important for the sense of the novel. The first edition was brought out in Paris by Prévost's regular publisher, François Didot, under a false name and address, "chez François Desbordes à Amsterdam." Censorship of novels in France was so stringent in the period from 1730 to 1750 that publication in Paris with a false foreign address was widespread. The Roberts translation is generally accurate and well written but, of course, in an antiquated eighteenth-century English style.

The first modern English translation we have of Prévost's novel, *The Story of a Fair Greek of Yesteryear*, appeared under the name of James F. Jones Jr. in 1984. Jones bases his work on the Robert Mauzi edition of the *Grecque moderne*, which is itself based on an error-ridden, pirated edition of the original publication that appeared a year later, in 1741. Jones's translation is, unfortunately, unusable by any serious scholar or student, which is one of the principle reasons why we undertook this new translation of Prévost's novel. In addition to dozens of blatant mistranslations of basic French, distorting the meaning of the text, a whole eight-page section near the denouement, one of the most intense episodes (260–69 in the Mauzi edition), was incomprehensibly left out of Jones's book.

A second, far more accurate, translation of *Histoire d'une Grecque moderne*, "The Story of a Modern Greek Woman," done by Lydia Davis, was published as a part of a 1300-page volume, *The Libertine Reader: Eroticism and Enlightenment in Eighteenth-Century France*, with a short introduction by Joan DeJean but no footnotes. An excellent unpublished English translation, finally, was produced in 1995 (then revised in 1999) by Peter Tremewan for classroom use at the University of Canterbury in Christchurch, New Zealand. It includes, however, neither introduction nor notes. I wish to recognize here my debt to Professor Tremewan, whose text often served as a guide when I was wrestling with difficult passages.

The translation I am offering here is based on my own edition of Prévost's novel, published in the GF-Flammarion collection in 1990. The text of reference in that volume is the 1741 corrected Catuffe edition, to which I restored most of the punctuation from the original publication. An overzealous proofreader or typographer in Holland had completely changed the punctuation, adding commas everywhere and radically modifying the characteristic rhythm of Prévost's somewhat convoluted sentences, with their concatenation of subordinate and participial clauses. The introduction is an updated version of my introduction to the GF-Flammarion edition, and the extensive footnotes to the novel have been revised or, if deemed inessential in retrospect, simply eliminated. My goal here is to provide readers with a reliable single-volume translation of this classical literary masterpiece, written in natural and contemporary English, with a critical apparatus that provides sufficient context and information to help the reader reflect in some depth on the novel's genesis, characters, action, techniques, and possible meanings.

THE GREEK GIRL'S STORY

Abbé Prévost

HISTOIRE

D'UNE

GRECQUE MODERNE.

PREMIERE PARTIE.

A AMSTERDAM,

Chez FRANÇOIS DESBORDES,
près la Bourse.

M. CC. XL.

Fig. 2   Title page from the original French edition. From Prévost,
Histoire d'une Grecque moderne, 1740. Bibliothèque nationale de France.

Preface

This story has no need of a preface, but custom requires one at the beginning of a book. The present one will serve only to notify the reader that we promise him, for the work we are introducing to him, neither a key to the names nor any clarification of the facts nor the slightest information that will help him understand or guess what he cannot comprehend through his own discernment. The manuscript was found among the papers of a man who was well known in society. We have attempted to give it a tolerable style without changing in any way the simplicity of the narration or the intensity of the feelings. Along with love, the story is suffused with honor and virtue. Let it go forth under such favorable auspices, and may it owe its success to itself alone.

We will not try to hide the fact, nonetheless, that its interest may be magnified for those who have had some knowledge of the main characters. But let great care be taken not to confuse the heroine with a lovely Circassian lady who was known and respected by a multitude of fine people, and whose story bore no resemblance to this one.

We have omitted a display of Turkish erudition that would have hampered the narration and replaced all foreign words with French ones when at all possible. Thus, we have used the word *seraglio* [*sérail*] instead of *harem* even though it is well known that *harem* is the name given to private *seraglios*, *market* instead of *bazaar*, and so on. This is for the benefit of those who are not familiar with writings on the Levant, for there are scarcely any of these works that do not contain an explanation of all these terms.

BOOK ONE

Will I not arouse suspicion by the very confession that serves as my introduction? I was in love with the beautiful Greek girl whose story I begin here. Who will believe in the sincerity of this account of my pleasures or of my suffering? Who will not be skeptical about my descriptions and my praise? Will my violent passion not distort everything that passes through my eyes or hands? In short, how much objectivity can one expect from a pen guided by love? Those are the reasons that should keep a reader on his guard. But if he is perceptive, he will quickly understand that I would not have stated them so frankly were I not sure that another admission would soon erase the impression they have made. I was in love for a very long time, I don't mind admitting it, and perhaps I'm not so free of this fatal poison as I've managed to convince myself. But love has given me only heartbreak. I've known none of its pleasures or even its illusions, although the latter, in my state of blindness, would certainly have sufficed for lack of the real thing. I am a suitor who has been rebuffed, indeed betrayed, if I am to believe the appearances that I will leave the readers to judge. I was held in esteem nonetheless by the woman I loved, listened to like a father, respected like a mentor, consulted like a friend; but what meager consolation for sentiments like mine! And in the bitterness that still engulfs me, can you expect me to offer flattering praise or sentimental flights regarding an ingrate who has filled my life with constant torment?

I was the king's emissary in a court whose customs and intrigues held no mystery for me. My advantage in speaking perfectly the Turkish language upon arrival in Constantinople helped me gain almost immediately a measure of acceptance and confidence that most officials achieve only after a long period of probation; and the very rarity of a Frenchman who appeared just as Turkish, if I may use this expression, as the native inhabitants of the country, brought me from the outset of my stay an unending stream of compliments and honors. Indeed, my show of preference for the customs and mores of their nation served to increase even more their affection for me. They went so far as to imagine that I could not have so much in common with Turks without being drawn to their religion as well; and with this idea fueling their esteem for me, I found myself as free and as comfortable in a city where I had scarcely lived two months as in my hometown.[1]

My official duties left me so much free time that I decided to benefit from my situation as much as possible to satisfy my general desire to learn. I was moreover at an age where a penchant for pleasure was not incompatible with an interest in serious business, and my plan, in going to Asia, had been to divide my time between these two dispositions. The diversions of the Turks did not seem so foreign to me that I could not hope to soon begin enjoying them as much as they. My only fear was to find it somewhat more difficult to satisfy my penchant for women. Their lack of freedom and the great difficulty there is in managing to see them had already led me to the decision to repress this particular predilection and choose a tranquil existence over such troublesome pleasures.

However, I had developed friendships with prominent Turks who were reputed to be the most discriminating in their choice of women and to have the most magnificent harems. In their palaces they had often flattered me with their ingratiating behavior and marks of esteem for my person. I was struck by the fact that they never evoked the objects of their affection in the course of our conversations, and that their most playful remarks revolved only around fine dining, hunting, and the trivial events of the court and the city that lent themselves to mockery. I maintained the same reserve, and I pitied them for denying themselves, out of excessive jealousy or a lack of refinement, the most agreeable subject that could enliven a conversation. But I misunderstood their intentions. They were only testing my sense of discretion; or rather, knowing the appreciation of the French for fine women, they had all resolved, as if in concert, to allow me to reveal my desires in my own time. At least this was the conclusion that they soon led me to draw.

A former pasha, who was living tranquilly on the wealth he had accumulated through long years of service, had shown me great consideration, and I made every effort to respond in kind by assuring him often of my gratitude and friendship. His house had become as familiar to me as my own. I had visited all the apartments, except for the quarters reserved for his women, which I made a point of ignoring completely. He had noticed this affectation, and having no doubt that I knew at least the location of his harem, he had invited me several times to go for a walk with him in his garden, which was next to the building. Finally, conquered by my stubborn silence, he said to me, smiling, that he admired my discretion. "You are not unaware," he added, "that I have beautiful women, and it is unlikely that either your age or your temperament would make you indifferent toward the fair sex. I am amazed that you seem to have no curiosity to see them." "I am aware of your customs," I responded coolly, "and I will never ask you to violate them in my favor. A little experience of the world," I continued, my expression unchanged, "helped me to understand, upon arriving in this country, that since such care is taken to guard women, the most intolerable vices must be curiosity and indiscretion. Why would I take the risk of insulting my friends with questions that might displease them?" He praised my response warmly, and confiding in me that several examples of the effrontery of the French had made the Turks leery of my countrymen, he was all the more pleased at my sensible attitude. He immediately offered to let me see his women, a favor I accepted quite calmly. We entered a place whose description is of no interest here, but I was too struck by its organization not to remember it in detail.

The pasha's women, twenty-two in number, were gathered in the apartment reserved for their activities. Each of them was free to pursue her own interest, some painting flowers, others sewing or embroidering, according to their talents or inclinations. The fabric of their dresses appeared to be the same; the color was uniform, in any case. But their coiffure was varied, and I realized that it was arranged in harmony with each woman's face. A large number of servants of both sexes, the males being eunuchs, stood ready in the corners of the apartment to carry out their slightest wishes. The crowd of slaves withdrew as soon as we entered, and the twenty-two ladies, rising without leaving their places, appeared to be awaiting the orders of their lord and master, or the explanation of a visit that they apparently found quite surprising. I examined each one in her turn, noting the differences in age;

but while none seemed to be over thirty, I didn't see any as young as I had imagined, the youngest being at least sixteen or seventeen.

Cheriber, as the pasha was named, asked them politely to come closer. After briefly explaining who I was, he suggested that they provide me some entertainment. They had various instruments brought, and some of them began to play while the others danced quite gracefully. After an hour or so the pasha had refreshments served to each of the women, who had regained their original places. I hadn't yet had the opportunity to say a word. He asked me, finally, what I thought of this charming group, and upon hearing my praise of such attractive creatures, he offered several judicious reflections on the force of education and habit, which render the most beautiful women obedient and tranquil in Turkey, whereas, he told me, he had heard all the other countries complain of the turmoil and disturbance that their beauty causes there. I responded with some flattering comments about Turkish ladies. "No," he continued, "it is not something that is more characteristic of our women than of those of any other country. Of the twenty-two women you see here, there are not even four who were born Turkish. Most of them are slaves I bought at random." And pointing out one of the youngest and most attractive: "She is a Greek girl," he said, "whom I have only had for six months. I have no idea who owned her before me. I took her on a whim, for her appealing looks and engaging turn of mind, and you can see that she is as content with her lot as the rest of her companions.[2] However, given the perspicacity and quick-mindedness she has shown me, I am sometimes amazed that she could adjust so quickly to our customs, and I can find no other reason for it than the power of example and habit. You may chat with her for a moment," he told me, "and if I'm not mistaken you will find in her all of the fine qualities that elevate women to the highest stations in your country and allow them to be party to the loftiest enterprises."

I approached her. She seemed to enjoy painting, and having little apparent interest in what was happening in the rest of the room, she had taken up her brush again as soon as the dancing was over. After excusing myself for taking the liberty of interrupting her work, I could find nothing better to talk about than what I had just learned from Cheriber. I congratulated her on the personal qualities that had endeared her to her master, and making it clear that I knew how long she had been in his harem, I expressed surprise that she had been able to conform so perfectly, in so short a time, to the habits and activities of the Turkish ladies. Her answer was simple. Since a woman

Fig. 3   Turkish dancer. From Ferriol, *Recueil de cent estampes*, 1714. Art and Architecture Collection, Miriam and Ira D. Wallach Division of Art, Prints and Photographs, The New York Public Library, Astor, Lenox and Tilden Foundations.

can hope for no other happiness, she said to me, than that of pleasing her master, she considered herself quite fortunate if Cheriber indeed thought so well of her, and I shouldn't be surprised that, with this goal in mind, she had adapted so easily to the laws that he had established for his slaves. This fervor to cater to the desires of an old man, in a charming girl who was indeed no older than sixteen, struck me as more remarkable than anything I had heard from the pasha. Both the manner and the words of the young slave convinced me that she was completely sincere in what she was saying. The comparison that occurred to me between the principles of our Western women and those that she professed prompted me to remark, offhandedly, how sad it was that she should be born for a fate other than the one she deserved so richly for her great devotion and kindness. I deplored the misfortune of Christian countries, where men, who spare nothing to make women happy, treating them like queens rather than slaves, devoting themselves to their lady and asking in return only sweetness, love, and virtue, almost always discover that they have made a bad choice of spouse, the woman with whom they share their name, their station, and their property. Noting that my complaints were receiving rapt attention, I continued to speak enviously of the felicity of a French husband were he to find in his life's companion those virtues that were wasted by Turkish ladies, since they have the misfortune of never receiving from their men a response worthy of their sentiments.

This conversation, during which, I confess, I was so carried away by my feelings of pity that I didn't give the young Greek girl a chance to respond, was interrupted by Cheriber. He may have noticed the enthusiasm with which I was addressing his slave, but since the innocence of my sentiments assured me that I was not abusing his confidence, I rejoined him with a clear conscience. His questions, in any case, showed no sign of jealousy. On the contrary, he promised to invite me to share this entertainment again if it was to my liking.

Several days passed during which I intentionally avoided seeing him, for the sole purpose of forestalling all his suspicions by feigning indifference for women. But during a visit he paid me to reproach me for neglecting him, a slave in his retinue gave a note to one of my servants. It happened to be my valet, who brought it to me as mysteriously as he had received it. When I opened it, I discovered that it was written in Greek, which I had not yet mastered, although I had been studying it for a while. I immediately sent for my Greek tutor, who was known to be a very respectable Christian, and asked him to explain the contents of the letter as if it had come into my possession by pure chance. When he had written out the translation, I recognized at once that it came from the young Greek girl to whom I had spoken in the pasha's harem. But I was quite unprepared for its contents. After a few remarks on her unfortunate station in life, she begged me, in the name of the high regard I had expressed for women who were devoted to virtue, to use my influence to free her from the pasha's service.

I had not developed any particular feelings for her other than a rather normal appreciation of her feminine charms; and in light of the rules of behavior I had adopted, nothing was further from my intentions than to get involved in an intrigue that no doubt promised more trouble than pleasure. It was clear to me that the young slave, enchanted by the image I had briefly evoked of the good fortune of our women, had begun to find harem life distasteful and, hoping I was typical of the gallant men of my country, wanted to engage me in a love affair. Upon reflecting on the danger of such an enterprise, I became all the more firmly convinced that my first reaction was the best. Nonetheless, the natural desire to do a favor for an attractive woman, whose existence was probably going to become torture for her, led me to wonder if there wasn't some decent and proper way to come to her aid. It occurred to me that I could try an approach that would only engage my generosity, by offering to buy her freedom. The fear of shocking the pasha by my proposal was enough to keep me from acting, but I came up with a plan that satisfied my sense of propriety. I was close friends with the selictar, one of the most important officials of the empire.[3] I decided to confide in him my desire to buy a slave who belonged to Cheriber and to get him to negotiate the deal as if he were doing it for himself. The selictar agreed, without making much ado over such a minor favor. I gave him carte blanche as to the price. Cheriber's respect for his rank made it much easier than I had dared hope. That very day I had the selictar's word that the deal was done and learned that it would cost me one thousand crowns.

I was delighted to put this sum to such good use, but just as I was on the point of concluding the arrangement, it occurred to me that there was a problem I had overlooked in my enthusiasm. What was to become of the young slave, and what were her intentions in leaving the harem? Did she plan to take up residence in my house? I found her sufficiently appealing to deserve my help, but in addition to the decorum that I had to maintain before my servants, how could I prevent the pasha from learning sooner or later where she had gone, and wasn't I going to run the same risk I thought I had avoided? This thought made me so reluctant to proceed with my plan that when I saw the selictar the following day I expressed some regret at having involved him in an affair that, I feared, might indispose the pasha. And with no mention of the thousand crowns I was supposed to give him, I took leave of him to pay my visit to Cheriber. Torn between the desire to come to the aid of the slave, the troublesome consequences that I apprehended for myself, and the fear of displeasing my friend, I would have liked to find some pretext to extricate myself from this affair. I wondered if it wouldn't just be best to confide in the pasha himself, to learn at least if the sacrifice I had imposed on him was not too great. It seemed to me that with an excuse so legitimate as the respect due a friend, I could certainly decline to satisfy a woman's whims without appearing insensitive. Cheriber was so pleased by my visit that his joy prevented me from broaching the subject I had on my mind. At the same time he informed me that one of the women in his harem was leaving; the young Greek girl with whom he had let me chat had been sold to the selictar. His remarks appeared so nonchalant that I concluded that he was hardly affected at all by his loss. I also came to understand that he had no passionate attachment to his women. At his age he did not suffer from the urges of the flesh, and the expenditures he allotted to his harem were motivated less by sentiment than by vanity. This realization having soothed all my scruples, I abandoned my plan to share my concerns with him and thought it best just to leave him the satisfaction of thinking he had earned a large debt of gratitude from the selictar.

However, having suggested we go spend a few moments in his harem, he seemed troubled by how he was going to break the news to his slave. "She doesn't know," he told me, "that she is going to have a new master. After all the proof she has had of my affection, her pride will be hurt at the idea that I found it so easy to give her to someone else. You will be witness," he added, "to her reaction to my farewell, for I am going to see her for the last time. I've told the selictar that he is free to have her brought to him whenever he deems it appropriate." I foresaw that this scene would indeed be entertaining for me, but not for the reasons that it might be embarrassing for the pasha. Since I hadn't dared risk sending an answer to the missive from the young Greek girl, I expected that she would be quite chagrined to learn that her servitude would just be continued in the selictar's harem. How would she react if she learned it in my presence and didn't dare show her resentment by complaining? Cheriber's slave had come twice to ask for my response, but I had seen fit to tell him only that I would do my very best to be worthy of the good opinion she had of me.

Instead of taking me to the women's apartment, the pasha had his slave instructed to join us in a private room, where he gave orders that only she was to be admitted with us. As she approached us, her constrained manner betrayed her excitement. She could hardly see me with her master without jumping to the conclusion that I had agreed to her request, and that I was bringing her the happy news of her liberation. The pasha's first comments certainly confirmed this impression. He informed her, politely and gently, that in spite of the great fondness he felt for her, he hadn't been able to avoid ceding to a powerful friend the rights he had to her affections; but he was consoled, he added, that although he was losing her, he could assure her that she couldn't fall into the hands of a finer gentleman—in addition to the fact that he was one of the highest-ranking lords of the empire and the most capable, given his wealth and his sentimental inclinations, to make a happy life for the women who succeeded in putting him under the spell of their charms. Then he uttered the selictar's name. The frightened look she gave me, as well as the sadness that suddenly spread over her features, seemed a tacit reproach for misunderstanding her intentions. She imagined that it was indeed I who was freeing her from Cheriber's harem, but only to change the nature of her bondage, and that I thus had not understood or had ignored the motives that had prompted her to ask for my help. There was no doubt in Cheriber's mind that her emotion was caused by her regret at the thought of leaving him. She compounded his error by protesting that if she were to continue the existence that was her lot in life, she desired no other master than him; and in her sorrow she added to her protest such tender and urgent entreaties that I could see that the pasha was on the point of forgetting all his promises. But considering his uncertainty to be a passing impulse, which moved me far less than the tears of the beautiful Greek girl, I hastened to help both of them recover by remarking to her, "You should be consoled by the grief that the pasha feels at losing you; and if you have any doubt concerning the happy state that awaits you, I am on good enough terms with the selictar to guarantee that he will let you determine your own fate." She looked into my eyes, where she clearly read my meaning. Cheriber, for his part, saw in my words only a confirmation of his arrangement with the selictar. The rest of our conversation was more pleasant. He showered her with presents, which he asked me to help choose. Then, having begged me to excuse him while he tended to some private business with his slave, he accompanied her into another room, where they stayed together for over a quarter hour; it was clear to me that he was indulging, a final time, his affection for her. It is also clear that I had no particular feelings for the girl, since the thought of what was transpiring left me indifferent.

In any case, having gone too far to back out, I hurried home to get a thousand crowns, which I immediately brought to the selictar. He asked me, smiling, if I was going to keep my intrigue a secret from him, and he bid me, in return for the favor he was going to do for me, at least to explain to him by what circumstance I had become acquainted with one of Cheriber's concubines. Having no reason to hide anything, I shared with him the origin and the nature of the affair. And when he expressed some skepticism at the idea that it was my generosity alone that had moved me to come to the aid of a young lady as comely as I had described her, I insisted so sincerely that I had no amorous designs on her and was only helping her to obtain her freedom, and that I was even somewhat at a loss about what she was to do upon leaving her present bondage, that all of his suspicions about my motives disappeared. He indicated the time at which I could come for her at his home. I felt no impatience as I waited. We had agreed to act at night to keep the matter out of the public eye. I sent my valet in an ordinary conveyance, around nine in the evening, with orders to alert the selictar alone that he had come on my behalf. He was informed that the selictar would see me the next day, and that he would apprise me at that time of what he had done for me.

This delay caused me no concern. Whatever the reason might be, I had been guided solely by my sense of honor and generosity, and any pleasure I felt at the success of my endeavor was derived entirely from those two motives. I had reflected seriously during this interval about my future demeanor with the young slave. There were innumerable reasons not to take her to my home; and even considering the most flattering aspect of her appeal to me, which was perhaps the hope that she would reward me with her favors, I had no intention of making her my official mistress. I had enlisted the help of my Greek tutor, whom I had finally taken into my confidence. He was married. His wife was to receive the girl from my valet, and I planned to learn from her own lips, the next day, how else I could be of service to her.

But the reasons that had governed the selictar's behavior were more compelling than I could have imagined. Since I had arrived at his residence at the very moment he intended to pay me a visit himself, he was quite disconcerted by both my arrival and my initial questions. He was silent a moment before answering. Then, embracing me more affectionately than I had come to expect from him, he entreated me to reiterate what I had told him the day before in such unequivocal terms that he had been absolutely convinced of my sincerity. After I had reassured him, he heaved a sigh of relief and, embracing me again, proclaimed himself the happiest man on earth, since he was passionately in love with Cheriber's former slave, and he saw now that he need fear neither competition nor opposition from his friend. He kept nothing from me. "I saw her yesterday," he said. "I spent only an hour with her; I didn't utter a word of love. But I am so completely taken with her charms that I simply cannot live without her. Since you do not have the same feelings for her," he continued, "I assumed that you would have no objection to yielding to a friend someone of so little importance to you. Ask any price you deem appropriate, and don't be like Cheriber, who obviously did not recognize her worth."

While I hadn't expected this proposition, after the favor he had done me, I had no sentimental involvement that might have caused me to resent it; I therefore voiced no complaint as regards honor and friendship. But the same motives that had prompted me to help the slave made me loath to impose a new master on her against her will. That was the only objection I made to the selictar. "If you were to inform me," I said, "that she shares your sentiments, or that she is at least willing to have you as her master, I would forget all my plans, and heaven is my witness that you would not have to ask me twice for a favor I would be only too happy to grant you. But I know, on the contrary, that she would consider it the greatest of misfortunes to find herself back in a harem, and that is the only reason why I became interested in her fate." He couldn't resist reverting to his country's customs: "Must we take into consideration," he said, "the desires of a slave?" I hastened to oppose this line of reasoning. "Do not call her a slave anymore," I answered. "I only bought her to set her free, and she has been free since the moment she left Cheriber's home."

He appeared extremely dismayed by this declaration. However, as I wished to keep his friendship, I added that it was quite possible that the love and offers of a man of his position might touch the heart of a girl so young, and I gave my word that I would consent to anything she agreed to. I told him that I saw no reason to put off his overtures. He seemed to gain heart. The young Greek girl was summoned. I served personally as the interpreter of the selictar's sentiments, but I wanted her to be aware of all her rights so that she could make her decision in complete liberty. "You belong to me," I said; "I bought you from Cheriber with the help of the selictar. My plan is to help you achieve a happy existence, and you already have, here and now, an excellent opportunity. You can find in the affection of a man who loves you and in the luxury he can offer you a happiness that you would seek in vain in the rest of the world." The selictar, who found my words and my behavior sincere, hastened to shower her with flattering promises. He swore by his Prophet that she would enjoy the highest position in his harem. He described in detail all the pleasures that awaited her and all the slaves she would have at her beck and call. She listened to his proposal, but she had grasped quite clearly the sense of my own. "If you want to make me happy," she said to me, "you'll have to put me in a position to take advantage of your kindness." Given the unequivocal nature of this response, my only thought was to provide her with whatever means of defense she needed against violence, and even though I feared none from a man such as the selictar, there were a multitude of reasons to take this precaution. While Turks may act despotically toward their slaves, they treat free women with great respect. I wanted her to be protected from all the dangers of her current social station. "Do as you please," I told her, "and have no fear, either of me or of anyone else; you're no longer a slave. I renounce all rights I have to you and grant you your freedom."

She knew, having heard about it a thousand times since she had been in Turkey, how differently the Turks treat free women. However overcome she was with joy at my declaration, her first reaction was to assume the attitude and the expression that she thought appropriate to her new status. I couldn't help admiring the air of modesty and respectability that suddenly swept over her. She was concerned less with expressing her gratitude to me than with making it clear to the selictar what her sense of duty dictated in the light of the favor I had just granted her. He was himself forced to recognize her new rights, and his displeasure being evidenced only by his silence, he appeared prepared to give her the liberty to leave. I had no idea where she intended to be taken, but she was herself surprised that I had not made my own intentions clear to her on this subject and approached me to inquire. I did not think it appropriate to enter into a long discussion in front of the selictar, so while assuring her that I would continue to help her in any way necessary, I led her to the door, where I entrusted her to one of my servants, whom I ordered to drive her secretly to the home of my Greek tutor. There are vehicles suitable for women in Constantinople.

I was astonished by the fact that the selictar, far from objecting to her wish to leave, gave the order himself for the door to be opened for her and greeted me quite calmly when I came back in. He asked me, just as calmly, to listen to his thoughts. "I must praise your generosity," he said, "in taking an interest in the happiness of this young Greek girl, and I find it so unselfish that I can only express my admiration. But since you find her worthy of your action, your opinion of her only serves to confirm my love for her. She is a free woman now," he continued, "and I will not accuse you of preferring her interests to mine. But I ask you a favor that I promise not to abuse. Please don't let her leave Constantinople without my knowledge. And you will not be bound long by your promise," he added, "because I give you mine that you will know my intentions within four days." I readily granted him such a simple request. Since I had feared that he might still feel some resentment at my behavior, I was delighted to keep his esteem and friendship at so little cost.

Some business that I needed to finish the same day forced me to put off until evening the visit that I owed my Greek girl. I chanced to meet Cheriber. He told me that he had seen the selictar, and that he had found him extremely happy with his slave. This could only have been after I had left him. His discretion in so carefully concealing our affair gave me an even better opinion of his integrity. Cheriber's praise of me had also elevated his opinion of my character; judging by the manner in which the selictar had spoken about me, he assured me that I had no more devoted friends than the selictar and himself. I received his compliment with the appropriate gratitude. Having no particular reason to wonder where this great show of friendship and the promise that the selictar had extracted from me would lead, both my imagination and my heart were at peace, and that was the state of my feelings when I arrived that evening at the home of my language tutor.

I was informed that the young Greek, who had already changed her name from Zara, as she was known when a slave, to Théophé, was awaiting my arrival most impatiently.[4] I went to see her. She instantly threw herself to the floor and wrapped her arms around my knees, sobbing. I tried in vain to lift her back up to her feet. At first she could only manage a series of sighs, but as her violent emotions subsided, she called me over and over her liberator, her father, and her God. There was nothing I could do to restrain this initial outburst, during which she seemed to pour out her entire soul. And moved to tears myself by such an intense expression of gratitude, I was powerless to defend myself against her tender caresses and thus left her free to satisfy her need. Finally, when it appeared that she had calmed down a little, I lifted her in my arms, seated her in a more comfortable place, and sat down beside her.[5]

When she had caught her breath, she repeated more coherently what she had tried to say twenty times but couldn't get out. She gave warm thanks for the favor I had done her, marveled at my kindness, and prayed fervently to heaven to shower me with its favors for what she could never repay me with all her strength and all her blood. She had had to make a violent effort to contain her joy in front of the selictar. She had suffered no less from having to wait for my visit, and if I wasn't convinced that her every living breath would be devoted henceforth to making herself worthy of my kindness, I would make her more unhappy than she had been in slavery. I interrupted her to assure her that such deeply sincere sentiments were already ample reward for my services. And in an effort to head off a new wave of effusion in the making, I asked her to be so good as to explain how long and by what misfortune she had lost her freedom.

I swear to my reader that in spite of her beautiful features and her touching dishevelment at my feet and in my arms, I had felt no other sentiment toward her than compassion. My scruples had naturally prevented me from feeling anything more for a young woman who had just left a Turk's arms, and in whom I did not expect to find anything but the physical attractiveness that is so common in the harems of the Levant. Thus, not only did I still feel that I was acting purely out of generosity, but it had occurred to me more than once that if it were to come to the ears of the local Christians, I would have had to endure the censure of the stricter among them, who would have considered it a crime not to have used such a sum—that they would have accused me of lavishing on my pleasures—to benefit our religion or to liberate a few unfortunate captives. You will have to judge for yourself whether the rest of this story serves to vindicate me, but if I deserve any criticism in its beginnings, I'm afraid that what follows will hardly help to justify my conduct.

My slightest wishes appearing to be a command for Théophé, she promised to tell me candidly what she knew of her birth and the life she had led up until then. "My earliest memories begin," she said, "in a town in Morea, where my father was considered to be a foreigner, and he was the one who gave me to understand that I am Greek, although he never revealed where my birthplace was located.[6] He had little money and, not having any means to improve his situation, raised me in poverty. However, I was not aware of our destitute condition and have no memory of anything about it. I was scarcely six when we moved to Patras; I remember this name because it is the earliest clear recollection I have of my childhood. The relative comfort we knew there, after the hard life we had led before, also left an indelible impression on me. I lived with my father, but it was only after having spent several years in this city that I clearly understood my situation upon learning the fate that was reserved for me. Without being a slave himself and without having sold me, my father had insinuated himself into the governor's circle.[7] A certain comeliness in my features had attracted the interest of the governor, who had promised to provide for him for the rest of his life and to have me brought up properly, on the condition that he would turn me over to him when I had become old enough to gratify his desires. Along with room and board, my father was given a little job. I was brought up in his presence, but by one of the governor's slaves, who scarcely waited until I was ten to speak to me of my good fortune in having aroused the interest of her master, and of his reasons for tending to my upbringing. What was presented to me as the height of good fortune was thereafter how I always imagined it. The splendor of the several women who composed his harem, and whose happy existence was described to me, made me impatient to join them. However, the governor was so old that my father, fearful that he would not be able to enjoy forever the advantages that had brought him to Patras, began to regret an agreement whose benefits would be so short-lived. He did not yet share these reflections with me, but having no obstacle to fear from the principles I was being taught, he made a secret deal with the governor's son, who was already showing an intense interest in women, arranging with him to enjoy his father's rights under the same conditions. The young man, who was allowed to see me, was passionately attracted to me. Less patient than his father, he demanded of my father that the time specified in their agreement be shortened. I was put in his bed at an age when I still hardly knew the difference between the sexes.

"You can see that my misfortune was not the result of a penchant for pleasure, and that I did not fall into debauchery; I was born into it. Consequently, I never knew either shame or remorse, and growing older hardly enlightened me in any way that could serve to change my principles. Nor did I experience during this period the desires normally associated with love. It was just a question of habit. This situation lasted until the time that the governor had set to bring me to him. His son, my father, and the slave who had been in charge of my upbringing all found themselves in the same frightful dilemma, but far from sharing their consternation, I was still convinced that I was meant to belong to the governor. He was proud and cruel. My father, who had mistakenly counted on his death, found himself in such a terrible predicament that, losing his head, he decided to flee with me, without sharing his intentions with either the slave or the young Turk. But his plan was so ill conceived that we were arrested before even making it to the port. Since he was not a slave, his attempted escape was not a crime punishable by flogging. Nonetheless, he had to bear the full anger of the governor, who treated not only his flight as treason, but all the benefits he had received as a theft. I was shut up that very day in his harem. I was told the following night that I would have the honor of becoming one of my master's women. I took this announcement as a sign of favor, and since I hadn't understood why my father had felt forced to flee, I was astonished that he would suddenly want to give up his good fortune and mine.

"Night falls. The servants prepare me for the honor I am to receive, and I am taken to the governor's quarters; he greets me very kindly and affectionately. A moment later, he is informed that his son absolutely insists on speaking to him, and that the matter that brings him is so urgent that it cannot wait until the next day. He receives him and gives orders to be left alone to listen to what he has to say. I am still with them, but the father and his son step into an inner chamber for a moment. I heard angry voices that made it clear there was trouble. Their words were followed by some loud noise, which was really beginning to worry me when the son comes out of the room and, obviously distraught, grabs me by the hand and urges me to flee with him. Then, realizing, I imagine, that he had to be wary of the servants, he goes out alone, dupes them with fake orders from his father, and leaves me as I was, that is, trembling from his panic and not even daring to go into the room to see what had happened there. However, the young Turk had told the slaves that his father wanted to be alone for fifteen minutes, and when they returned after this time had lapsed, finding me in the state I have described, they become suspicious about my distress. They question me. I just point at the room, unable to utter a sound. They discover their master on the floor, covered with blood and dead from two dagger wounds. Their cries immediately attract all the women in the harem, who ask me to explain this tragic event. I relate less what I had seen than what I imagined I'd heard, and as I had no greater understanding of what had happened than the others, my bewilderment and fear turn into a torrent of tears.

"There could be little doubt that the governor had been slain by his son. This certitude, which was confirmed by the flight of the young Turk, produced a bizarre effect. The women and slaves in the harem, believing they no longer had a master, grabbed everything of value in sight and, fleeing their prison, disappeared into the night. All the doors being open, I decided to leave too, having become aware that no one was concerned with my anguish or with my presence. It was my intention to return to my father's lodgings, which were near the harem, and I felt sure that I could easily find my way. But hardly had I taken a dozen steps in the dark when I thought I saw the governor's son. I didn't recognize him for sure, however, until I asked him to identify himself. Terrified by the deplorable act he had just committed, he said, he was trying to learn if his father was dead, in which case he would have no choice but to flee. I shared with him everything I had seen. His grief seemed sincere. He explained to me briefly that he had gone to see his father more out of fear than anger, wanting to explain the relationship he had had with me, but that his father, furious at his admission, had attempted to kill him with his dagger, and that he had only been able to avoid death by defending himself with his own weapon. He invited me to flee with him, but at the very moment he was pressing me most urgently, we were surrounded by several people who had recognized him and, having heard the news of his crime, proceeded to arrest him. I was not detained. I found my way discreetly back home and to my father, who was delighted to see me.

"Having no part in these tragic events, he immediately decided to gather up all the money he had saved during his stay in Patras and leave the city with me. He offered me no explanation of his plans, and I was too naïve to have any fears. Our departure was unhindered, but our ship had scarcely put out to sea when he shared thoughts that caused me great distress. 'You are young,' he said, 'and nature has bestowed upon you all the charms necessary to guarantee a woman the brightest fortune. I am taking you to a place where you can best profit from these advantages, but I want you to swear to me to follow my advice.' He urged me to make this promise in such a way as to make it virtually impossible to violate. I felt an extreme repugnance at being subjected to his will in this fashion. Considering the relationships he had arranged for me with men up to then, it occurred to me that I might find it more enjoyable if I chose them myself. The son of the governor of Patras, whose bed I had been forced to share, had never touched my heart, whereas I had seen a thousand young men with whom I would have willingly shared the same intimacy. However, since I hadn't the strength to resist my father's authority, I submitted to his demands. We arrived in Constantinople. During the first months I was taught the manners and sophistication that make a woman alluring in this metropolis.[8] I was no more than fifteen. Without revealing his plans for me, my father constantly tantalized me with the prospect of a life beyond my fondest dreams. One day, as he was returning home, he didn't notice that he had been followed by two individuals who observed carefully the house that he had entered and then followed him in, accompanied by several neighbors. We occupied only a small part of the house. They knocked so sharply at our door that, frightened at the noise, he sent me into the next room. Having opened the door, he was immediately confronted by a man whom he must have recognized, since he was struck dumb and was unable for a time to answer several contemptuous rebukes that I heard quite clearly. He was called a traitor and a coward who was going to get what was coming to him, and who would be forced to admit his treachery and his thefts. He made no attempt to claim his innocence, and seeing no possibility of defending himself, he went meekly before the *cadi*.[9] As soon as I had recovered from my shock, I covered my head with a veil and hurried off in the direction he had been taken. Since court hearings are public, I arrived early enough to witness the accusations against him and the sentence that immediately followed his confession. He was charged with having seduced the wife of a Greek nobleman who employed him as his steward, with having kidnapped her along with the Greek couple's two-year-old daughter, and with having stolen, in addition, all the valuables he had found in his master's home. Unable to deny these allegations, he attempted to defend himself by swearing to God that it was all the woman's idea, and that he had let himself be pressured into it; she alone had committed the theft, and he had not derived the slightest benefit from it, since he had himself been cruelly stripped of everything by thieves and reduced to the most extreme poverty. When questioned about the fate of the woman and her daughter that he had kidnapped, he maintained that both of them had died. On the basis of his admissions alone, the judge sentenced him to death. I heard him give his verdict. Despite all the shame I felt at being the child of such a villainous father, I was overcome with grief and couldn't stifle my cries and tears. But having begged to be heard a moment in private, what he said appeared to appease the judge and served at least to postpone his punishment. He was taken to prison. Such an unusual delay was a hopeful sign. As for me, I had no other choice, in my sad situation, than to go back home and await the outcome of this awful event. But as I approached the house, I saw an unruly mob of people out front; I asked the cause of all the commotion, afraid to go any farther. In addition to what I already knew only too well, I was informed that since the usage in Constantinople was to seize the property of a criminal as soon as his sentence was pronounced, this pitiless custom was already being executed with regard to my father's belongings.[10] I was so terrified that I began trembling and, not having the strength to disguise my identity, beseeched a Turkish woman in the street to take pity on the unfortunate daughter of the Greek who had just been sentenced to death. She lifted my veil to study my face and, appearing to be moved by my grief, took me into her house with the consent of her husband. They both made it clear to me that they were doing me a big favor. The state of fright I was in led me to exaggerate it even more. I put my fate in their hands and felt I owed them my life when they promised to take care of me. I still had, nonetheless, the shred of hope that everyone had drawn from the judge's delay of the execution. But after a few days I learned from my hosts that my father's death sentence had been carried out.

"In a city where I knew no one and was only around fifteen years old, with so little worldly experience and tormented by such a humiliating disgrace, I thought at first that I was condemned for the rest of my life to misery and misfortune. However, my extreme situation prompted me to reflect on my early years to seek some rule to guide my behavior. Among all my memories I could find only two principles that had served as the basis of my upbringing: one of them was that I should look upon men as the unique source of the good fortune and happiness of women; the other had taught me that by our willingness to please, our submissiveness, and our caresses, we could gain a certain ascendancy over men that made them submissive to *us* and helped us obtain from them everything we needed to be happy. Despite the secrecy of my father's designs, I remembered that all of his plans for the future revolved around wealth and luxury. While taking great pains to cultivate my physical charms since our arrival in Constantinople, he had constantly emphasized that I could aspire to a fortune infinitely superior to that of ordinary women. He was thus expecting the prosperity to come from me, rather than having the power to obtain it himself; or if his ingenuity was to play any role at all, it was simply by exploiting my own capacities, intending to take his share of the riches with which he filled my dreams. Had his death stripped me of those qualities that, as he had repeated incessantly, were a gift of nature? This line of reasoning, which became ever stronger in my thoughts during a few days of solitude, produced an idea that I thought would permit me to repay the debt of gratitude I owed to my hosts. My idea was to explain to them what my father had in store for me and to offer them to share the fruits in his place. I had no doubt that, knowing their own country, they would understand instantly what I could do for them and for myself. I was so pleased with this idea that I decided to share it with them that very day.

"But these people were far more cunning than I, and the plan I had conceived in my naïveté had already occurred to them. The Turkish woman had taken an interest in my dilemma only because she had noticed the attractiveness of a foreigner who was alone in Constantinople with no refuge. She had concocted a plan she hoped to persuade me to accept, and she had chosen the very day I intended to share mine with her to propose hers to me. She asked me several questions about my family and my birthplace; my answers appeared to encourage her to pursue her scheme. Finally, after flattering me on my good looks, she offered to make me happy beyond my wildest dreams if I would take her advice and put my trust in her. She knew a rich merchant, she told me, who adored women and who spared nothing to make them happy. He had ten of them, the prettiest being far inferior to me, and I could be certain that he would shower me with affection and do more to make me happy than for all the others put together. She dwelled at length on the luxury in which he lived. I should take their word for it, because she and her husband had been in his employ for a very long time, and they were amazed every day at the abundance of blessings this gracious man had received from the Prophet.

"Her description was clever enough to convince me, and all the more easily since I was on the point of making the same proposition to her. I was delighted that she had spared me the trouble by suggesting it herself. But the suitor she was proposing to me met only half my expectations. My father's plans for me had always included both wealth and an elevated station. The idea of belonging to a simple merchant wounded my pride. I made this objection to my hosts, but far from respecting it they emphasized even more insistently the advantages they were offering me and eventually became offended at my resistance. I understood that what they had pretended to leave up to me had already been decided by them, and perhaps in concert with the merchant in whose name they were acting. Although I felt all the more reluctant to yield to their urgings, I hid my chagrin and asked them to give me until the next day to make up my mind. My repugnance increasing as I reflected during the rest of the day, I made a decision that night that you would certainly attribute to despair if I didn't assure you that I made it in a state of complete calm. My father's lofty aspirations, which never left my mind, gave me the strength I needed. As soon as I thought my hosts were asleep, I left their house as I had come and ventured alone out into the streets of Constantinople, with the vague intention of appealing to some person of high station to take my fate into his hands. Such an ill-conceived plan had little chance of success. I didn't become fully aware of it until the next day— after having spent the rest of the night in a state of terrible anxiety—when I still had no idea how to solve my dilemma. In the street I met only common people, who could be no more helpful to me than the couple I had fled. Although it was easy for me to identify the residences of the rich, I saw no possibility of gaining admission, and my fear getting the best of me, despite my efforts to keep up my courage, I felt even more miserable than I had following the death of my father. I would have returned to the house I had left if I had had any hope of finding it again, but realizing now the full extent of my rashness, I was so frightened that I thought I was surely doomed.

"I had no clearer idea of the misfortunes that threatened me, however, than of the riches I had desired. My fears had no particular object, and my growing hunger was my most immediate concern. Happening, by pure chance, to walk by the market where slaves were being sold, I asked who were the group of women that I saw lined up under a canopy. As soon as I learned why they were there, I realized this was an opportunity for me too. I walked up to the women and took my place at the end of the line. I calculated that if I were as attractive as I had been led to believe so many times, I wouldn't have to wait long to be noticed. Since all of the other women had their faces hidden, I resisted the urge, for the moment, to reveal mine. However, the time having come for the slave market to open, I couldn't bear watching various people examine women who were clearly inferior to me without feeling impatient to remove my veil. No one had noticed that I did not belong to the group, or, rather, no one could figure out why I was there. But scarcely had they caught sight of my face when all the spectators, surprised at my youth and beauty, gathered around me. I heard them asking on all sides to whom I belonged, and the slave dealers, astonished, were asking the same question. Since no one had an answer, they decided to ask me. I announced that I was for sale and immediately asked who among them would like to buy me. The crowd around me continued to grow as news of this extraordinary event spread. The dealers, as covetous as the spectators, made me offers that I spurned. There were several people who responded by identifying themselves and their social station, but since I heard nothing impressive enough to satisfy my ambitions, I continued to reject their offers. The astonishment of my admirers grew yet greater when, my hunger becoming unbearable, I walked rapidly over to a woman who was carrying some food. I begged her not to refuse me the sustenance I so urgently needed. She gave me something to eat. I consumed it so voraciously that everyone just stared, mystified. I could see compassion for me in the eyes of some, curiosity in the eyes of others, and in almost all the men's faces signs of lust. These latter impressions vindicated the opinion I had of my charms and persuaded me that this scene would turn to my advantage.

"After I had been subjected to a flurry of questions that I refused to answer, the crowd finally opened to make way for a man who had inquired in passing about what had drawn the great crowd he saw at the market. He had been told the source of everyone's astonishment and had come closer to satisfy his own curiosity. Although the respect he commanded prompted me to show him more courtesy, I agreed to answer his questions only after I had learned from him personally that he was the head steward of the pasha Cheriber. I also demanded to know a few facts about his master. He informed me that he had been the pasha of Egypt, and that he possessed immense wealth. Whispering into his ear, I told him that if he thought I would be to the pasha's liking, I would be very grateful if he would present me to him. Without waiting for me to repeat my request, he took me by the hand and led me to his conveyance, which he had left to come see me. I heard both the regrets of the other men, who saw me leaving, and their conjectures about an event that they found more and more incomprehensible.

"In the carriage the pasha's steward inquired about my plans and asked by what trick of fate a young Greek girl, as he presumed me to be from my attire, happened to be alone and free to dispose of herself as I was. I invented a fairly plausible story, but my naïveté must have been so apparent that he concluded that there was some personal gain to be made from the business he was going to conduct for his master. Any concerns I might have had about my own interests were eclipsed by the joy I felt at falling into such good hands, and I was intent only on demonstrating my gratitude to my new hosts. I made no objection to the steward's request that I confirm that he had bought me from a slave dealer. He promised me that in return he would speak so favorably of me to the pasha that I would soon be his favorite concubine, and he gave me a few tips about how best to gain his master's favor. Having informed the pasha of my arrival, he did in fact arrange for me such a lavish welcome that I thought all my dreams had already come true. I was given the magnificent quarters you have seen for yourself. A large number of slaves were assigned to serve me. I spent some time alone, receiving the training appropriate to my new state, and in those first days when I enjoyed so thoroughly being waited on hand and foot, receiving everything I could wish for and having even my slightest whims satisfied, I couldn't imagine a greater happiness. My contentment increased yet further when, after two weeks of training, the pasha told me I was the most adorable woman in his harem, and in addition to the proofs of his generosity I had already received, he gave orders that I was to receive a thousand new presents, whose very abundance I sometimes found excessive. Although because of his age his own desires were quite modest, he regularly saw me several times a day. He seemed to delight in my vivaciousness and gaiety in everything I did. This situation, which lasted two months, was no doubt the happiest time of my life. But I gradually grew accustomed to the things that I had at first found so exciting. The idea of my happiness no longer had any effect on me, because there was nothing that brought me pleasure any more. Not only was I no longer flattered by the promptness with which I was served, but I had no more orders to give. The luxuriousness of my quarters, the profusion and beauty of my jewels, the sumptuousness of my wardrobe, nothing had the effect on me that it had had at the beginning. Again and again, when I was feeling depressed, I beseeched everything around me: 'Make me happy,' I said to the gold and the diamonds. There was no answer, only wooden silence. I thought I was the victim of some unknown illness. I spoke of it to the pasha, who had already observed the change in my mood. Since I spent part of each day alone, he thought that my melancholy might be caused by my solitude, even though he had given me a painting teacher when he saw that I was attracted to that particular art. He suggested that I move into the common quarters occupied by his other women, from whom he had kept me separate until then as a sign of distinction. The novelty of the surroundings served to perk me up a bit. I enjoyed participating in their parties and their dances, and I assumed that by sharing their existence I would discover that we had much in common. But while they were very eager to get to know me, I almost immediately found their company distasteful. They seemed to have only petty interests, which were completely alien to my personal preoccupations, as they were to a thousand things that I desired without knowing what they were. I lived for around four months in their company without sharing their life, performing my duties diligently, not offending anyone, and more popular with my companions than I would have liked. Although he never neglected his harem, the pasha seemed to lose his particular affection for me. I would have been deeply wounded at the beginning, but it was as if my whole attitude had changed with my frame of mind; I was simply indifferent to his loss of interest. I caught myself daydreaming now and then but could remember nothing when I came out of it. I had feelings that I could not comprehend, and it seemed to me that my soul thirsted after some kind of good that I knew nothing about.[11] I asked myself again, as I had done in my solitude, why I wasn't happy when I possessed everything I could imagine wanting. I sometimes wondered if, amid all these pleasures and luxuries, there might be some gratification that I hadn't yet tasted, some change in my existence that might dispel my constant state of uneasiness. You saw me painting; that's the only pleasure I had left, after having such high hopes. And I couldn't even keep my mind on that, I was subject to such mystifying lapses of attention.[12]

"That was my situation when the pasha invited you to visit his harem. This unprecedented favor piqued my curiosity, and I wondered what would come of it. He ordered us to dance. I did so, but in an extraordinarily dreamlike, absent state. Afterward, filled with anxiety, I quickly went back to my place. I have no idea what I was thinking about when you came over to me. If you asked me any questions, my answers must have appeared troubled. But my attention was quickly caught by the striking thoughts I heard you express. A charming instrument I was hearing for the first time could hardly have made a greater impression on me. I could recall nothing that was in such instant harmony with my feelings and thoughts. This impression grew yet stronger when, evoking the happiness of women in your country, you explained its source and how men contributed to it. The meaning of the words 'virtue,' 'honor,' and 'morality' was clear in a flash, as if I had always known them.[13] I strained eagerly to hear every word you added. I didn't interrupt you with questions, because everything you said struck a chord in my innermost being. Cheriber put an end to this wonderful conversation, but I had not lost a single word, and no sooner had you left than I began to mull over every detail. I found it all marvelous. It became immediately my sole preoccupation, filling my thoughts day and night. So there is a country, I said to myself, where one can find another kind of happiness than material success and wealth! There are men who value in a woman something other than physical charms! Women can distinguish themselves by other qualities and can hope for other kinds of pleasure! But how is it that I have never heard of this idea that I find so alluring and that is in such perfect harmony with my own inclinations? Although I would have liked answers to so many questions I wanted to ask you, the very fact that I was consumed by such desires was enough to help me grasp the importance of my emotional turmoil. I would not have hesitated to leave the harem had it been possible. I would have sought you out anywhere in the city if only to learn about a thousand things I still needed to know, to have you repeat what I had heard, to hear your voice again and satisfy my desire for a pleasure I had barely tasted. I recalled, in any case, a hope that I had always retained, and without which I would have taken more precautions in my dealings with the pasha's steward. Not being born a slave, and having no obligation to become one, I was convinced that, were I to grow weary of my situation, no one could force me to stay in the harem. I imagined that all I had to do was explain things to the pasha. But since I occasionally saw the steward, who was in charge of maintenance in the harem, I wanted to confide in him first. He had kept his word to me. I was satisfied with his services up until then, and I had no reason to doubt that he would be willing to help me in this matter too. However, as soon as he had understood what I wanted he became cold and somber and pretended not to understand the legitimacy of my claims. And when I tried to remind him how I had come to the harem, he expressed surprise that I could have forgotten that he had bought me from a slave dealer. I saw clearly that I was a victim of treachery. Despite my violent chagrin I understood that it was useless to rail against him and complain. I begged him, with tears in my eyes, to treat me fairly. He became harsh with me as never before, and declaring pitilessly that I was to be a slave for the rest of my life, he advised me never to bring up the subject again, or he would report it to his master.

"The illusion that had concealed my fate from me for such a long time finally dissolved. I don't know how, but my whole manner of thinking had changed more since my short conversation with you than during my whole life until then. I saw nothing but shame in my past existence and could not even stand to think of it. Guided solely by the principles that you had planted in my heart, I felt as if I had been swept into a different world by a multitude of thoughts that cast everything in a new light. I even felt a surge of courage, which surprised me, given my dreadful predicament, and more determined than ever to open the gates of my prison, I concluded that before resorting to desperate means there were an infinite number of less reckless solutions I might discover through my own ingenuity. The idea of confiding in the pasha seemed the most dangerous. In addition to risking his indignation, it would inevitably earn me the hostility of his steward, which would make all other avenues more difficult. It was then that it occurred to me to ask you for help. My transformation not only was your doing but could be consummated only by you. I hoped that the favorable attitude you had shown toward me was an indication that you would not refuse your help.

"The only difficulty was to communicate my request to you. I took the risk of sounding out a slave who had been devoted to me since my arrival in the harem. She was quite willing to help me, but she was as much a prisoner as I. Since leaving the harem would be considered a criminal act on her part, her only recourse was to offer me the help of her brother, who was also in the pasha's employ. I decided to take the risk. I entrusted to my slave the letter you apparently received, since you could have had no other reason to help me achieve my freedom, but which, for a few days, created a new source of anxiety. One of my companions, who tended to keep an eye on me, noticed I was troubled and concluded that I was planning some unusual enterprise. She observed me while I was writing my letter and was clever enough to discover that I had given it to the slave. She thought that she had caught me in an affair with a man. That very day she found the opportunity to speak to me in private, and revealing the power she had over me, she confessed that she too had been involved in a very dangerous liaison for several weeks. She was entertaining a young Turk who was fearlessly risking his life to see her. He would creep from roof to roof until he was just above her window; then he would let down a rope ladder and climb down to her room. Despite the fact that I now had a room in the same area as the pasha's other women, I had kept my former quarters, and my shrewd companion found them most convenient. The favor she expected of me was to hide her lover there for a few days, since her own room didn't afford her the liberty to see him as much as she liked.

"I found this request quite alarming but was bound by the fear that she might betray me. My own knowledge of her intrigue gave me no power over her, since I had no proof of her admission, and were I to refuse to help her, she could simply erase any trace of her affair by putting a stop to her lover's visits, whereas my letter and the two slaves I had taken into my confidence could be used as evidence against me at any time. I submitted to all her demands. Her lover was brought in the following night. In order not to be seen by my slaves, I had to leave my room while they were asleep and lead the Turk to a small room to which I alone had a key. This was where my companion planned to see him during the day. It took some ingenuity to escape the attention of a large number of women and male slaves, but in a closely guarded harem no one was concerned if we disappeared now and then, and the numerous rooms rather facilitated these short absences.

"The Turk, however, who had gotten only a brief glimpse of me in the candle light, fancied me more than my companion. From her very first visit to him, having let herself in with my key, she noticed a lack of enthusiasm she couldn't long attribute to his fear. He made up reasons to invite me to join them in the room. They were so frivolous that, suspecting him of betraying her affections, she resolved to find out the truth by playing along with him. I agreed to her request to accompany her. Her lover was so indiscreet that, shocked at how little attention he paid her, I couldn't help sympathizing with her spite and her decision to dismiss him that very night. He further provoked her jealousy by his show of disappointment, and the looks he gave me told me only too clearly that I was the cause of his regret. But the punishment was far more severe than his offense. While helping him out of her window to climb back up to the roof, she pushed him so violently that he fell to his death. She informed me herself, the next day, of her brutal revenge.

"It had not occurred to her, however, that his rope ladder had been dragged down with him, and that this piece of evidence, added to his sad fate, would inevitably betray the nature of his business there. In fact, it wasn't clear which window he had fallen from, since there were several that looked out upon the same courtyard. Cheriber's household was, nonetheless, deeply alarmed, and the effects were immediately felt in the harem. Cheriber himself questioned all his women. He had his staff examine every spot that provoked the slightest suspicion. They discovered nothing, and I was amazed at the composure of my companion while all this activity swirled around her. The steward's suspicions finally fell on me, although he didn't share them with his master. He told me that, given the ideas I was entertaining, there could be no doubt that I was the source of the trouble in the harem and had perhaps resorted to criminal means to achieve my freedom. While I was not at all intimidated by the threats he employed to obtain my confession, I thought my fate was sealed when he spoke of arresting my most devoted servants. Struck by my fright, he began to give orders, forcing me to tell him what I couldn't let him discover by himself without exposing my unfortunate slaves to a terrible death by torture. Thus, the investigation of someone else's misconduct led me to betray my own secret. I confessed to the steward that I was seeking my release from the harem by means which even the pasha couldn't disapprove, and no longer insisting on my rights, I assured him that I was attempting to have myself bought as a slave and at whatever price was asked. He wanted to know whose help I had enlisted. I could not hide that it was you I had contacted. My sincerity helped my companion, whose intrigue remained secret, and the steward, apparently pleased by what he had learned, assured me that he would be glad to help me achieve my aims in the manner indicated.

"I was as surprised by his indulgence as I had been terrified at his severity. I still do not know what motives he had. Only too happy, however, to have overcome such a redoubtable obstacle, I inquired several times if you had been touched by my request. Your answer wasn't clear. Nevertheless, the recent events have happily proven that you were sensitive to the fate of an unfortunate slave, and that I owe my liberty to the most generous man in the world."[14]

If you have shared but a part of the reflections this story provoked in me, you should expect those that will follow. Putting aside the obstacle of language, I found the young Greek girl just as intelligent as Cheriber had boasted.

I even found it admirable that, with only nature as a guide, she had presented the vicissitudes of her existence with such clarity, and that in explaining her musings and meditations she had given such a philosophic turn to most of her ideas. Their development was impressive, and I couldn't suspect her of borrowing them from someone else in a country where it is uncommon for people to indulge in this sort of exercise. I was therefore convinced that she was endowed with unusual intellectual qualities, which, combined with her extremely attractive features, made her most surely an extraordinary woman. Her adventures were in no way repugnant to me, since in the several months I had been in Constantinople I had learned every day about the most bizarre events concerning slaves of her sex. The rest of this narrative will offer many other examples. Nor was I surprised at her description of her upbringing. All the provinces of Turkey are filled with these vile fathers who raise their daughters for sexual exploitation, and who have no other livelihood or means of improving their lot in life.

But in reflecting upon the powerful impact she claimed to have felt from a brief conversation, and the reasons she gave for appealing to me in particular to gain her freedom, I wasn't so gullible as to let myself be taken in by the ingenuous and innocent manner she had assumed. The more astute I found her, the more I suspected her of guile, and the care she had taken to emphasize several times her naïveté was precisely what made me suspicious of her. Today as in ancient times, "as sincere as a Greek" is an ironic saying.[15] In the best of scenarios I could imagine that she was weary of the seraglio and had decided to leave Cheriber in the hope of gaining more freedom. Bent on gaining my affections, she had deduced from my remarks the best way to approach me. If I were to lend any credence to the description she had given me of her distressed emotional and mental state, it was easy to attribute it to the situation of a young woman who must not have known much pleasure in the company of an old man. She had in fact alluded to the pasha's modest demands. And to be perfectly frank, I was in my prime; while I may not be particularly handsome, my looks could have made an impression on a young harem girl whose keen intelligence was probably matched by her sensuality. I would add that in her cries of joy I had observed an extreme excitement that was out of proportion with the attitude she had always had toward the events of her life. These fits of ecstasy were too sudden and had no discernable cause. After all, unless the power of God was responsible for her newfound principles, what reason did she have to be affected so extravagantly by the favor I had done her, and how could she suddenly look with such horror upon a place where she could complain only about being satiated by luxury? I concluded from all these musings, some of which had come to me while she spoke, that I had done a pretty woman a favor I had no reason to regret, but that all the beautiful slaves would have been entitled to the same consideration. Although I was flattered, given her beautiful looks, by what I assumed to be her desire to attract me, the very thought that she had just come from Cheriber's arms after having been in those of another Turk, and perhaps in those of a host of other lovers that she had concealed, was enough to fortify me against any temptation to which my natural desires might have exposed me. I was curious, however, to learn precisely what she planned to do with herself. She must have understood that I had no right to demand anything of her, having freed her, and that, on the contrary, I was waiting for her to explain her intentions. I asked her no questions, and she was in no hurry to enlighten me. Returning to the subject of our women in Europe, and to the principles I had told her they were taught when young, she asked me to explain a hundred details that I was pleased to elucidate. We were far into the night when I realized it was time for me to take my leave. Since she had expressed no wish, dwelling rather on her happiness, on her gratitude, and on the pleasure of listening to me, I renewed, upon leaving, my offer of help and assured her that as long as she was content with her host's home and his services she would want for nothing. She took leave of me in a most passionate manner, calling me her master, her king, her father, and all the affectionate names that are in common use among women in the Orient.

After tending to some important matters, I couldn't go to bed without reflecting on everything that had transpired during my visit. It even filled my dreams. I could still think of nothing else when I awoke, and my first gesture was to send someone to inquire of the tutor if Théophé had slept well. I didn't feel attracted to her in a way that might have given me cause for worry, but my imagination being filled with her charms, and having no doubt that they were at my disposal, I confess that I had second thoughts about the initial repugnance I had felt at the idea of having intimate relations with her. I asked myself just how much I could indulge this whim without going too far. Had the caresses of her two lovers left some indelible stain, and was I supposed to be disgusted by something I would not even have noticed had I not been informed of it? Couldn't a blemish of this sort be erased by rest and several days of care, especially at an age when nature, through its own vitality, is continually renewing itself? Moreover, the part of her story that I had found the most believable was her complete ignorance of the sentiment of love. She was barely sixteen. Cheriber certainly hadn't touched her heart, and her extreme youth in Patras, in addition to the distaste she had described to me, must have prevented her from forming any sentimental attachment to the governor's son. I imagined that there would be some pleasure in introducing her to love, and I hoped, as I thought about it more and more, to have been fortunate enough to have already aroused some desire. This thought was more effective than my previous rationalizing in overcoming my scruples. I got up completely changed in comparison to the day before, and while I had no intention of rushing into an involvement, I was resolved to lay at least the groundwork before the end of the day.

I was invited to dine with the selictar. He questioned me extensively about my slave's situation. I reminded him that he could no longer refer to her as a slave, and assuring him that it was my intention to permit her to exercise fully the rights I had given her, I confirmed unequivocally his understanding that I had no particular attachment to the girl. He felt all the more justified in asking me where she was staying. This question made me uneasy. I managed to dodge it by joking that she needed rest after leaving Cheriber's harem, and that I would be doing her a disservice by revealing her refuge. But the selictar swore so earnestly that she had nothing to fear from his attentions, and that he intended neither to disturb her nor force her into anything, that I couldn't decently question his word of honor after he had shown such confidence in mine. I informed him of the location of the Greek tutor's residence. He gave his word once again, so sincerely that I felt reassured. We continued our conversation about Théophé's extraordinary qualities. It had cost him dearly to control his desires. He confessed that he had never been touched so deeply by a woman's beauty. "I hastened to turn her over to you," he said, "out of fear that I might grow even more attached to her as I got to know her better, and that my love might overwhelm my sense of justice." The selictar's remarks were clearly those of a man of honor, and I owe it to the Turks to testify that there are few nations where the sense of equity is more pronounced.

While he was expressing these noble sentiments, he was informed of the arrival of the pasha Cheriber, who appeared almost immediately in such an agitated state that we asked him what was wrong. He was on as close terms with the selictar as with me, and it was on his recommendation that I had

Femme Turque
qui repose sur le Sopha sortant du bain.

Fig. 4 Turkish woman resting on a couch after her bath. From Ferriol, *Recueil de cent estampes*, 1714. Art and Architecture Collection, Miriam and Ira D. Wallach Division of Art, Prints and Photographs, The New York Public Library, Astor, Lenox and Tilden Foundations.

become friends with the latter. He responded to our queries by throwing at our feet a bag of sequins containing my thousand crowns. "What a pity it is," he exclaimed, "to be duped by one's own slaves! Here is a bag of gold that my steward stole from you," he added, speaking to the selictar. "And this is not his only theft. I've just obtained from him, under torture, a horrible confession. If he's still alive, it's only so that he may repeat it in your presence. I would die of shame if this wretched slave did not do me justice." He requested the selictar's permission to have him brought in, but we both begged him to prepare us first with some sort of explanation.

He informed us that one of his other servants, who was jealous, in fact, of the power the steward had usurped in his house and thus motivated to keep an eye on him, had noticed that the selictar's eunuch, who had come for the young concubine, had given to the steward a large quantity of gold coins before she was handed over to him. Having no reason to be suspicious, he mentioned to him what he had seen, out of curiosity about the size of the payment. But the steward, disconcerted at having been overseen, had entreated him urgently to keep silent about it and had given him a substantial gift to that effect. He had only succeeded instead in heightening the servant's desire to bring about his downfall. Convinced that the steward was guilty of some act of treachery and feared punishment, he had immediately shared his suspicions with the pasha, who had no trouble getting to the bottom of the matter. The steward had confessed, under the pressure of his master's threats, that when the selictar had come to negotiate the purchase of the young Greek girl, he had heard these two lords argue politely over the price, and had also heard his master protest that, being only too happy to oblige his exalted friend, he was determined to let him have his slave for nothing. Having observed that they had taken their leave without resolving this courtesy contest, he had followed the selictar and told him, as if he were acting under orders from the pasha, that since he continued to refuse to accept the slave as a gift, he would set her value at one thousand crowns. He had added that he was authorized to receive the money and to turn the slave over to whoever was sent for that purpose by the selictar. Cheriber, who had instructed the steward, on the contrary, to take her to his friend's home, had had absolutely no reason to distrust his account of the transaction. When he learned, however, that both he and the selictar had been duped, he was furious. Moreover, he had suspected that this example of deception was not the first, coming from a man to whom he had blindly confided the management of his affairs. To obtain from him a confession of his other crimes, as well as to punish him for the most recent one, he had had him tortured so cruelly, in his very presence, that he had forced him to reveal just how badly he had been abusing his trust. The episode concerning Théophé had struck Cheriber as one of his blackest deeds. He couldn't forgive him the injustice he had perpetrated against a free person.[16] "Far from treating her like a slave," he insisted, "I would have welcomed her into my home as a daughter, I would have taken pity on her misfortune, I would have seen to all her needs. My only surprise is that she never once complained and revealed the truth to me."

This tale held far less surprise for me than for the selictar. Nevertheless, I continued to hide what they had no need to know, and the selictar understood from my remarks to Cheriber that I still wished to conceal my involvement in this matter. The steward having been brought in, his master forced him to tell us the circumstances of his first meeting with Théophé and his treachery in taking advantage of her naïveté to reduce her to slavery. We had little interest in the fate of this wretch, who was immediately sent to his execution, as he deserved.

After this explanation the selictar readily agreed to take back my sequins, which he sent back to me the following day. But scarcely had Cheriber taken his leave when, returning excitedly to the subject of Théophé, he asked me what I thought of such a bizarre story. "If she wasn't born into slavery," he reflected, "she must be of much higher birth than we thought." His reasoning was based on the fact that outside of lowly social stations where certain talents are developed in young people for commercial reasons, good upbringing, in Turkey as elsewhere, is a sign of high birth—rather like the case of a dancing master whose graceful and polite manner are no surprise to us, whereas were it a stranger, we would take the same appearances as an indication of noble origins. I left the selictar to his conjectures. I didn't even give him any information that might have shed some light on them, but I was no less struck by his observation, and recalling the part of Théophé's story about her father's death, I was amazed that I had paid so little attention to the kidnapping of a Greek lady and her daughter of which he had been accused. It did not seem impossible that Théophé could be the two-year-old child who had disappeared with her mother. But how on earth could I verify that? And wouldn't she have suspected it herself if she had made the slightest connection between that story and her own? Nonetheless, I decided to ask her a few more questions to satisfy my curiosity and to do so at my very next visit.

My valet was the only one of my servants who was aware of my relationship with Théophé. I was determined to keep this intrigue secret and to go to the Greek tutor's home only in the evening. I went there as soon as night fell. He informed me that an hour earlier a very handsome Turkish gentleman had come and requested insistently to speak to the young Greek girl, calling her Zara, her former name in the harem. She had refused to see him. Greatly disappointed, the Turk had entrusted to the tutor an elegant box for Théophé, along with a missive in the Turkish style that he insisted she was to read. The girl had refused them both, and the tutor turned them over to me. I took them with me into Théophé's room and, more curious than she to get to the bottom of the matter, encouraged her to open the letter in my presence. It was easier for me than for her to recognize it as a romantic overture from the selictar. The terms were moderate, but they appeared to come from a heart deeply smitten by her charms. He begged her to have no fear for the future as long as she would deign to accept help from a man whose entire fortune was at her disposal. In sending her a large sum of money, with other gifts of considerable value, he referred to his generous offering as a trifle that he would be ready to renew at any time. I explained forthrightly to Théophé who I thought had written this letter and added, to encourage her to reveal her feelings, that the selictar's love for her was no greater than his respect, now that he no longer regarded her as a slave. But she appeared so indifferent to what he thought of her that, presuming she was serious, I gave the box back to the tutor to return to the selictar's messenger when he returned. She felt some regret at having opened his letter and, consequently, not being able to pretend she didn't know what it contained. But then she had a new idea, which was to send him an answer. I was curious to see the terms she would use, since she made no effort to hide her plans from me. A Parisian lady, with worldly experience to complement her intelligence and virtue, could not have found a better tone to quell a suitor's love and shatter his hopes. She gave this answer calmly to the tutor, asking him to spare her in the future anything else to do with this matter.

I will not hide that my vanity took this sacrifice as a favorable sign for me, and not having forgotten the plans that had preoccupied me that morning, I set aside everything concerning the selictar in order to begin, gradually, tending to my own interests. I was interrupted, however, by a flood of spontaneous observations from Théophé that were clearly related to a few casual remarks I had made the previous evening. Her mind had a reflective bent and seized on each idea, considering it from every angle. I could see that this had been her sole occupation since I had last seen her. She peppered me with new questions, as if all she could think of was preparing her meditations for the night to come. Were she struck by one of my country's customs or by some principle she was hearing for the first time, I would see her turn inward for a moment to engrave it into her memory. Sometimes she would ask me to repeat it, fearing that she hadn't grasped its entire meaning, or that she might forget it.[17] Despite the serious nature of this conversation, she still managed to include various expressions of gratitude to me. She had diverted me so far from my original project, however, by the reflections that preceded her affectionate gestures, that I found it impossible to get back to my own amorous designs, which I had hoped to further. In any case, there was little opportunity; by a stream of questions, each leading me immediately into a new subject, she constantly forced me to appear more serious and solemn than I would have preferred.

In the enthusiasm that drew her incessantly to this sort of philosophical rumination, she scarcely left me time to tell her of the conjectures the selictar had made concerning her birth. However, since I needed no preparation to speak to her of her father, I begged her to interrupt a moment her queries and reflections. "I have had some suspicions," I said to her, "and you will understand immediately that they stem from my admiration for you. But before I explain them to you, I need to know if you ever knew your mother." She responded that she didn't have the slightest memory of her. I continued, "What? You don't know how old you were when you lost her? You don't know, for example, if it were before or after the kidnapping of which your father was found guilty? And you don't even know if she was a different woman from the Greek lady he had lured away from her husband, and who was accompanied, if I remember your story correctly, by a two-year-old girl?"

She blushed at my words, although I couldn't yet divine the source of her embarrassment. She stared at me fixedly: "Has the same thought simply occurred to you," she asked, "or have you happened upon something that might elucidate a suspicion I haven't dared share with anyone?" "I'm not sure I understand what you mean," I continued, "but I can't help admiring innumerable natural qualities that set you above ordinary women and just cannot convince myself that you are the daughter of such a foul individual as you've described your father. And the more ignorant I find you about the earliest period of your life, the more I'm inclined to believe you may be the daughter of this same Greek nobleman whose wife was ravished by the wretch who claimed you falsely as his own offspring." This declaration produced a surprising effect on her. She leapt to her feet excitedly. "Ah! That's exactly what I've thought for a long time now," she said, "without being so bold as to be absolutely sure of it. Do you really think it might be true?" Her eyes filled with tears as she asked this question. "Alas!" she added immediately, "why tempt me with an idea that can only serve to increase my shame and misfortune?"

Without grasping what she meant by "misfortune" and "shame," I brushed away these gloomy thoughts by suggesting to her that she could in fact hope for no better fortune than being the daughter of some other father than the scoundrel who had usurped that title. And the very suspicion she felt being enough to vindicate my own, I urged her not only to recall everything that might shed some light on her childhood, but to tell me if she hadn't learned at the hearing in court the name of the Greek lady who I thought was her mother, or at least that of the plaintiffs who had dragged to his death sentence the miserable author of all her misfortunes. She could remember nothing, but in speaking of the cadi, it occurred to me that this magistrate might be able to elucidate the matter. I promised Théophé to look into it the next day. Thus, this evening, which I had intended to devote to my amorous desires, was spent discussing her personal interests.

Upon leaving I chided myself for showing such restraint with a woman who had just left the harem, especially after she had revealed to me the life she had led before. I asked myself, assuming she was as well disposed toward me as I still thought, if I were prepared to form with her the type of liaison that is referred to in France as keeping a mistress. Feeling less repugnance than I had at first about getting involved with her in this manner, it seemed to me that all I had to do was propose it to her outright, without taking the normal roundabout approach. If she reacted as favorably as I felt sure she would, the selictar's passion would be no cause for concern, since he had himself declared that he had no intention of using force to achieve his ends. And in the event that the information I sought proved her high birth— which would enhance her status a little in my eyes without changing the fact that she had suffered the dishonorable experiences that she had recounted— I could only expect that any discoveries I might make would increase my desire for her without making her any less proper for the relationship I intended to propose. My designs went absolutely no further than this. It's easy to see how far I still was from anything resembling love.

The next day, having sought out the cadi, I reminded him of the case of the Greek man he had condemned to death. Not only had he not forgotten it, he related the case in detail and, to my great pleasure, repeated several times the names I was seeking. The Greek nobleman whose wife had been abducted was named Paniota Condoidi. It was he who had recognized the kidnapper in the street and had had him arrested. But, the judge added, the only satisfaction he obtained was his vengeance; neither his wife nor his daughter nor his jewels were ever found. I was surprised by this observation, since it seemed to me that he had, in effect, neglected all the means at his disposal to locate them. I even shared my surprise with him. "What more could I do?" he asked. "The perpetrator maintained that the lady and her daughter were deceased. This statement must have been truthful, since the only way he could have saved his life would have been to produce them before the court, had they been alive. And wouldn't you know it, no sooner had he heard his sentence pronounced than he tried to trick me with silly stories; but it didn't take me long to realize that he was only trying to escape justice."

As I indeed remembered that his execution had been postponed, I asked the cadi to explain this incident to me. He told me that the criminal, having asked to speak to him in private, had offered, in return for his life, not only to produce Condoidi's daughter, but also to have her brought secretly to the judge's harem. The details he had revealed concerning several circumstances had been sufficient to make his promise seem plausible. All the efforts they had made to find her, however, were fruitless, and concluding that the miserable wretch was just lying to delay the execution of his sentence, the judge, indignant at his audacity and ignoble behavior, dispatched him all the more quickly to his death.

I couldn't resist sharing with this elevated Turkish magistrate a few reflections on his handling of the case. "What prevented you," I said, "from keeping your prisoner a few more days and taking the time to seek information in the places where he had lived after committing his crime? Couldn't you force him to reveal where the Greek lady had died, and in what manner he lost her? And finally, wasn't it a simple matter to retrace his movements and study them in minute detail? That is our method in Europe," I added, "and if we are no more devoted than you to justice, we are more adept at investigating crimes." He found my advice so sound that he offered his thanks, and a few remarks that he added about how he exercised his office convinced me that the Turks are more solemn than enlightened in their judicial proceedings.[18]

Along with the Greek lord's name, I managed to obtain from the cadi his place of residence; it was a little town in Morea that the Turks call Acade. It didn't appear to be an easy matter to get in touch with someone there, and I thought at first that I might do well to contact the pasha of that province.[19] I heard, however, that there were in Constantinople numerous slave dealers from the same area. I began to contact them and was so lucky that the first one I spoke to assured me that Lord Condoidi had been in Constantinople for more than a year, and that all of his countrymen in the city knew him well. The only problem was locating his place of residence. The slave dealer immediately came to my aid. I wasted no time making my way to his home, and my excitement growing at this initial success, I was sure I was on the verge of discovering what I sought to know. The Greek's house and personal appearance left the impression that he was of modest means. He belonged to one of those old families whose pride in their noble origins far surpassed their present fortune, and who, given their humiliating domination by the Turks, would not even dare to exhibit their wealth, assuming they had enough to live more opulently. Condoidi, who resembled in short a modest country gentleman, greeted me politely without knowing who I was, since I had dismissed my carriage and footmen upon leaving the cadi. Appearing to have little interest in what I was going to say, he gave me ample time to present things as I had planned. After demonstrating that I was quite aware of his past misfortunes, I begged him, alleging several important reasons, to excuse my curiosity on a point he could clarify easily. I wished to learn from him personally how long ago he had lost his wife and daughter. He replied that it had been fourteen or fifteen years. This period corresponded so perfectly to Théophé's age, taking into consideration, of course, that she was two at the time, that I had practically no more doubts. "Do you suppose," I continued, "that despite the kidnapper's statement it may be possible that one of them is still alive? And if it would seem preferable for you that it be your daughter, wouldn't you be grateful to those who could provide some hope of getting her back?" I expected this question to generate some excitement, but he replied indifferently that time, which had healed the wound caused by his loss, prevented him from wishing for miracles to remediate it; that he had several sons whose inheritance would be barely sufficient to sustain their honorable birth; and that even assuming that his daughter were still alive, it was so unlikely that she had preserved her virtue in the clutches of a scoundrel and in a country like Turkey that he could never be convinced that she was worthy of becoming a part of his family again.

I found this final objection the most formidable. However, considering that the first reaction is critical where natural affection is concerned, I resolved to use every means possible to rekindle his paternal sentiments. "I will not dwell on the substance of your scruples or reasons," I replied sharply, "because they cannot change this simple fact: your daughter is alive. Let's put aside the question of her virtue, which I cannot guarantee. I can assure you, however, that you will find nothing wanting in her intelligence and her beauty. You may, if you so wish, see her immediately, and I'm going to leave you her address." Requesting a pen, I wrote down the name of my Greek tutor and quickly took my leave.

I was convinced that if he were not completely insensitive his natural impulses would take over, and I left so full of hope that, to be able to witness the joyous scene, I went directly to the tutor's house where I imagined he might arrive at the same time as I. To have the pleasure of witnessing Théophé's surprise, I waited outside. But after several hours of waiting in vain for his arrival and beginning to fear that I had been too optimistic, I proceeded to reveal to the person whom it was now impossible not to regard as his daughter what I had done to keep my promise. The testimony of the wretch who had abused her youth had a greater effect on her than all the rest. "I would not be unhappy," she said, "to remain unsure of my birth; and even if I were convinced that I owe it to your Greek lord, I would not complain if he were unwilling to recognize me as his daughter. But I thank heaven for giving me the right, henceforth, to refuse to consider as my father the man whom I should hate and despise more than anyone in the world." She seemed so moved by this thought that, her eyes filled with tears, she repeated over and over that she owed her birth to me, since I had given her a second one in delivering her from the disgrace of the first.

Nonetheless, I didn't feel that my work was done, and in my continuing enthusiasm I suggested that she accompany me to Condoidi's residence. Nature has rights against which neither vulgarity nor interest can harden one's heart sufficiently. It seemed impossible to me that upon seeing his daughter, upon hearing her voice, and under the effect of her embraces and the look in her eyes, his natural affection for her would not be revived.[20] He had made no objection to the possibility of finding her. I hoped that nature would vanquish all the others. Théophé expressed some apprehension: "Wouldn't it be better for me," she ventured, "to remain unknown and even hidden from everyone's view?" I didn't probe the cause of her reservations and practically forced her to accompany me.

It was rather late. I had spent part of the day alone at the teacher's house, and as I was already becoming accustomed to this aura of secrecy, I had had my dinner brought to me by my valet. By the time I had persuaded the Greek girl to go with me, night had begun to fall, and it was completely dark when we arrived at Condoidi's domicile. He hadn't returned from the city, where he had gone on business in the afternoon, but one of his servants, who had seen me that morning, told me that I could speak to his three sons while awaiting his return. Far from rejecting this proposition, it appeared to me that I couldn't have hoped for anything better. I entered with Théophé, whose head was covered by a veil. Scarcely had I informed the three young men that I had paid a visit earlier that day to their father, and that I had returned for the same reason, than they seemed informed of the subject of my visit. The one whom I took, by his attitude, to be the eldest replied coldly that it was very unlikely that his father would be convinced by such a vague and implausible story. I responded by presenting and defending all the reasons that supported my position, after which I asked Théophé to lift her veil to give her brothers an opportunity to detect any family resemblance in her features. The two elder sons were unmoved, but the youngest, who didn't appear to be older than eighteen, and whose resemblance to his sister had already struck me, had no sooner seen her face than, opening his arms, he approached her and embraced her passionately. Théophé, not daring to respond to his caresses, attempted chastely to ward them off. The other two brothers came to her rescue. They rushed forward and snatched her from their brother's arms, threatening him with the indignation of their father, who would be deeply offended by his disobedience. I was myself indignant at their severity and rebuked them sharply, although this did not prevent me from inviting Théophé to sit down and await the arrival of Condoidi. In addition to my valet, I had brought with me the Greek tutor, and two men sufficed to shield me from any insulting behavior.

Their father arrived finally, but—this I had not foreseen—no sooner had he learned that I was awaiting him, and that I was accompanied by a young lady, than he left as precipitously as if he had been threatened by some peril, charging the servant who had admitted me to inform me that after our earlier discussion he was surprised at my attempt to force upon him a girl whom he did not recognize as his daughter. Shocked by this coarseness, I took Théophé by the hand and told her that since her birth did not at all depend on her father's whims, it didn't really matter if she was recognized by Condoidi or not, when it was quite obvious that she was his daughter. "The testimony of the judge and my own," I added, "will carry as much weight as your family's acceptance, and their refusal to grant you their affection is no great loss." When we took our leave, they didn't even show us the elementary courtesy of accompanying us to the door. Having no reason to expect any deference from three young men who had no idea who I was, I excused more readily their rudeness toward me than the harshness they had shown toward their sister.

This unfortunate girl appeared more distressed by this humiliating experience than I would have thought possible after her reluctance to accompany me to Condoidi's home. I postponed the declaration of my intentions toward her until we were back at the Greek tutor's home, and what had just transpired favored my plans. But the shroud of sadness that had fallen over her throughout the evening led me to conclude that this was not the right moment. I simply repeated several times that she should be happy, knowing that she would want for nothing with me. She replied that what she found the most touching in my offers was the assurance that my sentiments toward her hadn't changed. Although this remark appeared affectionate, it was delivered with such heaviness of heart that I thought it best to give her the night to get over her mortification.

I spent mine more tranquilly, for having finally made up my mind, the certainty of Théophé's elevated birth had by now chased away the nagging thoughts that had regularly assaulted my sense of honor. She had undergone some revolting ordeals, but with so many fine qualities and her noble origins, would I truly have wanted to make her my mistress if her honor were unstained? This combination of attractiveness and blemishes seemed to make her perfect for the relationship I planned for her. I fell asleep with this thought, which must have been far more appealing to me than I had previously imagined, since I was so troubled by the news that greeted me upon awaking the next morning. It came from the tutor, who insisted upon speaking to me at nine o'clock. "Théophé," he said, "has just departed in a carriage brought by a stranger. She left with him willingly. I would have stopped her," he added, "if you hadn't given me strict orders to leave her free to do as she pleased." Without thinking, I interrupted his agonizing account, shouting, "Oh! Why the devil didn't you stop her? How could you have misunderstood my orders so badly?" He hastened to add that he had stressed to Théophé when she left that I would be surprised by such an abrupt decision, and that she owed me at least an explanation of her behavior. She had replied that she herself had no idea what lay ahead for her, and that whatever misfortune might befall her, she would be sure to inform me of her fate.

You may draw whatever conclusions you like as regards the true reasons for my violent reaction. Even I do not understand them. But I arose from my bed with emotions I had never felt before, and bitterly repeating my complaints to the tutor, I declared with the same vehemence that my good will or my indignation would depend on the success of his efforts to discover where Théophé had gone. Being aware of everything that had happened since she had arrived in his home, he told me that if nothing about the Greek girl's story was being hidden from him, the stranger who had come for her could only be someone sent either by Condoidi or by the selictar. That it was one or the other seemed just as clear to me. But either alternative was no less troubling for me, and without seeking to understand why this was so, I ordered the tutor to go to both the selictar's and Condoidi's homes. I gave him no instructions regarding the first other than to find out from the doorman who had been there since nine that morning. As regards the other, I ordered him specifically to inquire of Condoidi himself if it was he who had sent for his daughter.

I awaited his return in an unspeakable state of impatience. His trip was so fruitless that in the fury I felt at being left even more in the dark my suspicions fell on him. "If I dared to take seriously the suspicions that I am entertaining," I said, staring at him fiercely, "I would have you subjected immediately to such cruel treatment that I would drag the truth out of you." He was terrified by my threats and, throwing himself at my feet, promised to confess what he had agreed to do, he said, only with the greatest repugnance and for no other motive than compassion. I was burning with impatience to hear what he had to say. He informed me that the day before, shortly after I had left Théophé, she had called him to her room and, after a very touching explanation of her situation, had asked him to help her with a plan she was absolutely resolved to carry out. Finding it intolerable, she had told him, to be in the presence of people who were familiar with her shame and misfortune, she had decided to leave Constantinople secretly and to go to some city in Europe where she could find refuge in the generosity of some Christian family. She confessed that after all the favors she had received from me it was ungrateful of her to steal away without informing me and to show so little confidence in her benefactor. But precisely because I was the person to whom she owed the most, I was also the one whom she revered the most and, consequently, the one whose presence, words, and friendship reminded her the most vividly of the shame of her previous life. In the end, her entreaties rather than her motives had convinced the tutor to take her at daybreak to the port, where she had found a Messinian ship that she was determined to board to go to Sicily.

"Where is she?" I interrupted with mounting impatience. "That's all I want to know from you and what you should have told me immediately." "I have no doubt," he said, "that she is either on the Messinian ship, which won't set sail for two days, or in a Greek inn where I left her at the port." "Get back there," I ordered harshly, "and convince her to return to your home immediately. Don't you dare show yourself in my presence again without her," I added threateningly. "I don't need to tell you what you have to fear from my wrath if I don't see her back here before noon." He was going to leave without comment. But in the grip of my emotions, troubled by a multitude of fears that I didn't stop to sort out, it occurred to me that whatever I didn't do myself would be too slow or too unsure. I called him back. With my knowledge of the language, it seemed to me that it would be easy to go to the port and to mingle in the crowd without being recognized. "I want to go with you," I said. "After your vile betrayal, I can no longer trust you."

My plan was to go on foot, dressed plainly and accompanied only by my valet. While I was dressing, the Greek tutor attempted to get back into my good graces by his submissiveness and all sort of excuses. I hadn't the slightest doubt that he had acted out of self-interest. But paying little attention to what he was saying, I could think only of what I was going to do. Despite my passionate desire to keep Théophé in Constantinople, it seemed to me that if I could confirm her intentions and convince myself that she really wanted to devote herself to a sensible and sheltered existence, I would have been less inclined to oppose her plans than to support them. If I were to suppose her sincere, however, how likely was it that at her age she would be able to resist all the temptations she was going to meet to get into new involvements? The Messinian captain, the first passenger she would run into on the ship, I was suspicious of everyone. And if she didn't appear destined to a more virtuous existence than her previous one, why would I let someone else enjoy the favors I had reserved for myself? I thought at this time that my feelings for her went no further than this. I arrived at the inn where the tutor had left her. She hadn't left her room, but we were informed that she was there with a young man whom she had caught sight of at the port and had sent for. I was curious to know the circumstances of this visit. I was told that Théophé, whom the young man had recognized immediately, and whom he had embraced with great affection, appeared to receive his caresses willingly. They had gone to her room together, and no one had interrupted them for over an hour.

I thought that all my fears had already come true, and overcome by spite I very nearly renounced any further involvement with Théophé and returned home without seeing her. However, still blind to my true motives, I tried to attribute to simple curiosity my continuing interest in the matter. I sent the tutor up to inform her that I wished to speak to her. Her dismay at hearing my name left her speechless for a long while. Finally, the tutor returned and told me that the young man he had found with her was the youngest of the three Condoidi sons. I went up to her room immediately. She tried to throw herself at my feet, but I wouldn't let her; and much calmer in recognizing her brother than I should have been after so much emotional turmoil, if my feelings hadn't been quite different from what I still believed, I was much less inclined to chide her than to express the joy I felt at getting her back.

Indeed, as if my vision had undergone some change since the day before, I found myself staring at her with an inclination, or rather a burning desire, that I had never felt before. I found her whole countenance, which I had only moderately admired until then, so enchanting that I pulled my chair up next to her in a burst of passion. The fear I had felt at the idea of losing her seemed to grow now that I had found her again. I would have liked her to be back at my tutor's house already, and the sight of several ships, one of which I presumed belonged to the Messinian, made my blood boil with anxiety. "So you were leaving me, Théophé," I said dolefully, "and when you decided to abandon a man who is devoted to you, you cared nothing about the pain that your departure was going to cause me! But why leave me without letting me know of your plans? Have you ever found your confidence in me misplaced?" She kept her eyes lowered, and I saw some tears slide down her face. However, lifting her gaze up to me, with some embarrassment, she assured me that she could not be accused of lacking gratitude. If the tutor, she said, had reported the feelings she had conserved for me upon leaving, I couldn't suspect her of being ungrateful. She continued justifying her conduct by the same reasons he had given, and coming to the Condoidi boy, whose presence in her room I could find surprising, she admitted that having seen him walk by, the memory of his affectionate behavior the day before had prompted her to hail him. What she had just learned from him gave her even more reason to leave quickly. Condoidi had declared to his three sons that he no longer had the slightest doubt that she was their sister, but not being any more inclined to admit her into his family, he had forbidden his sons to entertain any relationship with her, and without revealing his thoughts, he seemed to be concocting secretly some sinister plan. The young man, delighted to see his sister, for whom his affection continued to grow, had himself urged her to beware of his father's disposition, and finding her determined to leave Constantinople, he had proposed to accompany her on her trip. "What advice would you give to a wretched girl like me," Théophé added, "and what choice do I have but to flee?"

I could have replied that the most important reason she had to flee being the fear she had been led to have of her father, the basis for my complaints was still valid, since she had learned of this new misfortune only after her decision to leave. But thinking only of my desire to keep her, and not even trusting her brother, I pointed out that if her departure was wise and necessary, it should have been undertaken with enough precautions to guarantee her safety. And accusing her again of lacking confidence in my devotion to her interests, I urged her to postpone her plans in order to give me time to seek out an alternative that would be less dangerous than a captain of whom she knew nothing. As for young Condoidi, whose good character I applauded, I offered to take him into my home, where she could easily see that as far as material comforts and his education were concerned, he would be far better off than at his father's. I don't know if it was her timidity alone that led her to submit to my proposals quietly, but assuming by her silence that she agreed to come with me, I sent for a carriage to take her back to the home of my tutor, who whispered something to her that I couldn't hear. Condoidi, who had learned from her who I was, appeared so overjoyed by my offer that

I thought even worse of a father whose son was so happy to escape from, and one of my motives was my desire to learn everything I could about this family.

Returning to the tutor's house, I intended to put off no longer the proposition I had in mind for Théophé. But finding no proper way to dismiss the Condoidi boy, who seemed to be afraid that I might forget my promise once he was out of my sight, I was obliged to resort to vague comments whose meaning she could not have been expected to grasp. My manner of speaking to her was nonetheless so different from what she was accustomed to from me that she was too intelligent not to notice that something had changed. The only change that I instituted at the tutor's home was to leave my valet there, with the excuse that Théophé had no servants at her disposal, but in fact to keep an eye on her until I had found a slave for her that I could count on. I planned to acquire two of them, one of each sex, and to bring them to her that very evening. Condoidi followed me back to my residence. I had him immediately take off his Greek clothes and had him dressed more properly in the French style. This change of garments became him so well that I had seen few young men so handsome. He had the same features and eyes as Théophé, with a fine physique whose attractiveness had been hidden by his former clothes. His education was so deficient, however, in so many ways that my poor opinion of the practices and mentality of Greek nobility was reinforced. But the fact that he was so closely related to Théophé was enough to motivate me to do everything I could to perfect his natural qualities. I gave orders for him to be treated by the servants with the same diligence they showed me, and I hired the same day various tutors to tend to his general education and refinement. I also proceeded to question him about his family. I knew that their nobility went far back, but the precise information I was seeking was only what I thought could be useful to Théophé.

Repeating what I already knew of his father's ancient lineage, he told me that he claimed to be the descendant of a Condoidi who was a general for the last Greek emperor, and who had given Mohammed II a serious fright shortly before the fall of Constantinople.[21] He was in the field with a large body of troops, but the position of the Turkish army preventing him from approaching, he made the decision, based on a report of the desperate state of the city, to sacrifice his life to save the Eastern Empire. Choosing one hundred of his bravest officers, he asked them to follow him down out-of-the-way paths too small for an army to go through, and riding at their head in the darkest hour of the night, he arrived at Mohammed's camp with the intention of killing the Sultan in his tent. The Turks thought there was so little danger of an attack from that side that the forces there were negligent and off their guard. While he didn't make it to Mohammed's tent, he did manage to get to those of his staff surrounding it. Not stopping to attack enemies he found fast asleep, his only thought was to reach the Sultan's tent, and he almost made it. But a Turkish woman who was apparently stealing from one tent to another was frightened by the muffled sound of steps. She turned back, and in her terror aroused everyone around her. Condoidi, who was no less sensible than brave, knew immediately that his mission was doomed, and believing it necessary to save his life for his master if he could not succeed in ridding him of his enemy, he turned his courage and prudence to the task of opening a breach to save himself and his companions. In the general confusion he managed to escape losing only two men, but he had saved his life only to lose it more gloriously yet in the horrible revolution that came two days later. His children, who were still very little, lived under Turkish domination, and one of them settled in Morea, where his descendants were involved in a multitude of adventures. Finally their family was reduced to those who were now living in Constantinople and a Greek bishop of the same name whose seat was in some town in Armenia. Their whole fortune consisted in two villages, which brought them around a thousand crowns a year, and whose property was passed on to the eldest sons by a privilege that was rather unusual in the estates of the Turkish emperor, and that was the only distinction their family could claim.

But other hopes had brought the father and his children to Constantinople, and these were apparently the cause of their harshness toward Théophé. A rich Greek, a close relative, had bequeathed his entire fortune to them with the sole condition that the church had nothing to reproach them as regards religion and freedom, two areas of distinction that the entire Greek nation values most highly. The church, that is, the patriarch and his suffragan bishops, who had been appointed arbitrators in this matter, were all the more motivated to be severe in that they would themselves become the heirs in the event that the Condoidi family violated the conditions of the will.[22] The abduction of Condoidi's wife had occurred in this context, and the Greek prelates had pounced upon the uncertainty of her fate and that of her daughter to contest the execution of the will. That was why Condoidi, when he had recognized his former steward, had made no effort to learn about what had happened to his wife and daughter, seeking only to punish their kidnapper as soon as he had confessed to his crime and declared them both dead. He had hoped that whatever had befallen them, any knowledge of it would be buried with the steward. While he was even aware of the information that this wretch had given the cadi in private, he had been the shrillest of all in denouncing it as a lie and had not rested until he had seen the sentence carried out. In fact, the patriarch showed no greater inclination to grant him his inheritance; not satisfied with the steward's report of their death, he demanded proof that Condoidi thought unnecessary. His daughter, presented to him as if she had fallen from heaven, threw a terrible scare into him. Not only was he disinclined to examine the validity of her pretensions and to learn how she came to be in Constantinople, he was in mortal fear of any information that might put his inheritance in danger. In the end, being convinced that after the death of the steward she would find it very difficult to prove her birth, he had resolved not only to refuse to recognize her as his daughter but to accuse her of imposture and to seek to have her punished if she attempted to make public the rights she claimed.

"And unless I am mistaken," the young man added, "he has much worse things planned. Since your visit we have seen him in a cold fury that in the past has always resulted in some extraordinary action, and I don't dare tell you what his hate and anger have made him capable of doing."

This account convinced me that Théophé would have great difficulty establishing her rights; but I was unconcerned by her father's intentions, and whatever attempt he might make to harm her, I was sure that I could defend her from him. This thought even prompted me to change my plan to keep my identity from him, or at least to hide from him my interest in his daughter. Instead, I encouraged his son to see him that very day to inform him not only that I was taking Théophé under my protection but also of the friendship I was extending to this young man in welcoming him into my home. I immediately sent for two slaves whom I considered necessary for the new arrangements I was contemplating, and intending to implement them that very evening, I went to the tutor's home at nightfall.

My valet was waiting impatiently for me. He had been sorely tempted during the day to leave his post to come inform me of a number of observations that he thought important. The selictar's messenger had come with expensive presents, and the tutor had spoken with him at length in a very mysterious manner. My valet, who didn't understand Turkish, had pretended all the more easily to notice nothing, and having no hope of understanding their exchange, he had been content to observe them at a distance. What appeared most strange to him was to see the tutor accept the selictar's gifts graciously. There were precious fabrics and a large number of jewels intended for women. He had made an effort to see how Théophé would receive them, but he assured me that although he had kept the door to her apartment under constant surveillance, as well as Théophé herself as much as he could, he hadn't seen anyone bring the amorous offerings into her room.

I owed the tutor so little consideration that, wanting to hear his explanation from his own lips, I had him brought to me immediately. He understood instantly that he was in deep trouble. Realizing he wasn't going to be able to bluff his way out of it, he decided simply to admit that, with Théophé's complicity, after he had shared with her his financial woes, he had kept the selictar's gifts for himself, both the money and the expensive cloth. "I am poor," he said. "I explained to Théophé that the gifts belonged to her, and that they had been given with no strings attached, but her gratitude for a number of small favors I had done for her prompted her to let me keep them for myself." I had no trouble, after this admission, figuring out why he had been so eager to help Théophé run away. I immediately lost all confidence in a person capable of such vile behavior, and although I couldn't really accuse him of lacking integrity, I told him that he could no longer count on my friendship. This angry reaction would prove to be unwise. I didn't realize it at the time because of the power I had over a man of this lowly station whose services I no longer needed, since I intended to move Théophé out of his home.

The two new slaves I engaged had been recommended to me by someone in whom I had such complete confidence that I knew I could count on them absolutely. I had explained my intentions to them and had promised to grant them their freedom as a reward for their loyalty and dedication. The woman had served in several harems. Like Théophé, she was Greek. The man was Egyptian, and although I hadn't paid much attention to their looks, they both seemed to be more highly born than their current station in life. I introduced them to Théophé. She had no objection to them, but she asked me why she needed them given the little time she would remain in Constantinople.

I was alone with her. I took advantage of it to reveal my plans for her. But although I had thought them over carefully and was certain that she would react favorably, I found it surprisingly difficult to spell out my proposition. As I gazed at Théophé, I felt far more moved to express my passionate feelings for her than to propose bluntly the relationship I had in mind. However, this troubled state of mind not being sufficient reason to abandon a resolution I was determined to bring to a successful conclusion, I told her rather timidly that my concern for her happiness having convinced me that her departure would be a very dangerous enterprise with little chance of success, I had resolved to offer her a much more pleasant situation that would also enable me to guarantee her both the tranquility she appeared to desire and complete protection against any plots by Condoidi. "At a short distance from the city," I continued, "I have a house that has very attractive surroundings and an extraordinarily beautiful garden. I invite you to come live there. You will be free and respected. Forget harem life, that is, constant solitude and constraint. I will join you there as often as my work permits it. I will invite only a few selected French friends, with whom you can become accustomed to our social practices. If my affection, my attentiveness, and my kindness help to make your life more enjoyable, you will never see me slacken in my efforts. In short, you will see how different it is for a woman's happiness to share an old man's affections in a harem or to live with a man of my age, who will do everything in his power to please you and make you happy."[23]

I had kept my eyes lowered in speaking to her, as if I had assumed too much as regards my power over her and feared abusing it. More preoccupied with my feelings for her than with the arrangement I had planned with such pleasure, I was much more impatient to hear her admit her attraction to me than discuss the prospect of tranquility and safety that I was offering her in my home. The slowness of her response began to worry me. Finally, seeming to surmount with some difficulty her reservations, she told me that, although she had not changed her mind about the necessity of leaving Turkey, she had to agree that she would be better off in the country than in the city while she waited for me to find the opportunity I had promised to seek for her; and coming back to her gratitude, she added that my kindness knowing no bounds, she no longer even wondered what I expected from her in return, since by helping a poor wretch who could offer me nothing, I must be acting out of pure generosity. It would have been natural with the desire that was consuming me to unburden myself by speaking more plainly, but all too happy to see her agree to come to my country home, I made no attempt to learn if she had understood my intentions, or if her response was an acceptance or a refusal, and I urged her to leave with me immediately.

She made no objection. I ordered my valet to have a carriage brought around quickly. It was scarcely nine in the evening. I intended to dine with her in the country, and what pleasures could I not anticipate afterward from this happy night? But just as I began to express my joy, the tutor came in, clearly troubled, and taking me aside informed me that the selictar, accompanied by only two slaves, was asking to see Théophé. His clear distress as he told me this news prevented me at first from understanding that this eminent official was himself at the door. "Ah! Didn't you inform him," I said, "that Théophé cannot see him now?" He admitted, with the same embarrassment, that unable to guess that it was the selictar, and taking him for one of his servants, he had thought he could get rid of him by telling him that I was with Théophé. But this gentleman became all the more insistent on coming in and had even ordered him to inform me of his visit. I could see no way of avoiding this unfortunate contretemps, and if I marveled at what love could drive a man of this rank to do, it didn't occur to me that it was no less true of me; I was just upset to see him get in the way of my plans for Théophé. It was clear to me that this was another betrayal by the tutor, but not lowering myself to castigate this scoundrel, I hastened to urge Théophé not to compromise herself in any way with a man whose intentions she knew all too well. My anxiety should have finally made her understand my own intentions. She assured me that only her submission to my wishes could bring her to agree to see him.

I went to greet him. He embraced me affectionately, and joking about such a strange meeting, he told me that the beautiful Greek girl would be very ungrateful to complain about the affection and love that surrounded her. Then, repeating everything he had told me previously about his attraction to her, he added that given the trust he still had in my word, he was very pleased that I was there to witness the proposals he was going to make to her. I confess that this statement and the ensuing scene I anticipated with Théophé were equally troubling for me. How different I felt now compared to my state of mind when I had assured him that I was only interested in Théophé's welfare out of generosity. And being now acutely aware of the nature of my own feelings, how could I be expected to stand by calmly while my rival laid out his proposals or sweet-talked her? Nonetheless, I was forced to control myself, hiding my feelings all the more painfully since I had myself strictly imposed this stance. Théophé was extremely distressed upon seeing him appear with me. Her discomfort increased even more when, approaching her, he spoke openly of his passion and inflicted on her all the apparently rehearsed sentimental rhetoric that Turks are wont to employ in these situations. I attempted several times to interrupt this comical performance that was surely more unbearable for me than for Théophé, and I went so far as to answer in her place that since she intended to use her new liberty to leave Constantinople, she could only regret not being able to respond to the tender sentiments he expressed so graciously. But what I thought would dampen his ardor, or at least bring him to moderate his language, had the opposite effect: he hastened to reveal the offers he had prepared. He reproached her a plan whose only purpose, he said, could be to make him miserable. Still persuaded, however, that he could touch her heart by explaining what he wanted to do for her, he told her of a magnificent house he possessed on the Bosphorus that he wished to put at her disposal for the rest of her days, along with an allowance that matched the splendor of her abode. Not only would she live there free and independent, but she would also have complete authority over everything that belonged to him. He would give her thirty slaves, including both sexes; all of his diamonds, whose quantity and beauty would stun her; and the unquestioned right to ask for anything that she fancied. He enjoyed the favor of the Sublime Porte and had no need to fear anyone's envy. Nothing was more secure than the situation he was offering. And to leave her no doubt as to his sincerity, he made me a witness to all his promises.

I found these offers, presented with the bombast that comes naturally to the Turks, so splendorous that I feared they would make too great an impression on Théophé. It seemed so surprising to me that they were so similar to my own, and in fact far surpassed them, that I found myself trembling for my own carefully constructed plan and began to despair of ever obtaining for myself what had been refused the selictar. But how greatly were my fears compounded when Théophé, pressed for an answer, appeared far more receptive to his proposal than even the selictar had expected? An expression of satisfaction that spread over her features made her even more attractive than she had been since I had met her. I had always seen her sad or worried. Struck by a sudden pang of jealousy, I was sure I saw love burning in her eyes. My jealousy turned into fury when I heard her add that she would need only twenty-four hours to make up her mind. She brought this scene to a close by beseeching him, and him alone, to take his leave. Then, realizing that the selictar could be shocked that she did not include me in this dismissal, or that she did not wish him to remain in a place where he had found me upon his arrival, she very cleverly added that she was less formal with a benefactor to whom she owed her liberty than with a stranger whom she had barely seen three times.

Perhaps these final words would have sufficed to diminish or completely relieve the distress that was consuming me, if my superior position had left my mind free enough to realize the extent to which they were flattering and comforting for me. But struck by the length of time she had asked to give her response, in despair over the selictar's joy, and very nearly suffocating from the violent effort it took to hide my inner turmoil, my only thought was to get out into the street in the hope of finding some relief in a few sighs. However, lacking the resolution to let the selictar leave alone, I was subjected to a new torment in finding myself, as we left together, forced to listen to him rejoice at his good prospects for over an hour. I could not convince myself that Théophé's receptive attitude toward him was just an isolated incident, and knowing his sincerity, I asked him to explain this rather surprising visit. He willingly revealed to me that having sent various gifts that same day, gifts that Théophé had accepted, he said, without replying to his letter, he had approached the tutor with his plan to come secretly to his home, and that the hope of a reward had prompted this mercenary soul to admit him. He had warned him, in all truth, that I regularly spent my evenings there, "but feeling as you know I do toward her," the selictar continued, "and being aware of the nature of your own feelings, I was not troubled by your presence, and I am in fact delighted that you were there to witness the sincerity of my promises." He repeated that he was determined to make good on all of them, and that he wanted to taste a form of happiness that was unfamiliar to Moslems.

I could not help but praise the nobleness of his conduct. When I considered the despair I had just experienced, the thought of my good relationship with the selictar, and a thousand scruples dictated by honor that I just couldn't ignore, I resolved to resist feelings for Théophé that I had allowed to become too obsessive, and I took leave of the selictar in this frame of mind. But he had scarcely moved a few steps away when I heard someone call my valet, who was the only servant I had with me. I recognized Jazir, the slave I had assigned to Théophé. The thoughts I had been entertaining upon taking leave of the selictar were still so firm that I opened my mouth to give him some orders that would have appeared harsh to his mistress. But before I could get the words out, he delivered his own message. Théophé had sent him to ask me to come back to her room and had advised him to wait at some distance until I had left the selictar. I felt my heart torn between the spite that had been magnified by the conversation I had just finished and the strong desire that still made me regret the loss of the hopes I had entertained. But I thought I could avoid the embarrassment of a discussion with Théophé by using as a pretext for returning to her room a motive that had nothing to do with my troubled feelings. I had forgotten my watch that I liked particularly for its fine craftsmanship. So not even asking myself if it might not be more appropriate to send my valet for it, I went back with the slave, only too happy to have this pretext to close my eyes to my weakness. What will the unfaithful girl say to me? What excuse will this ingrate use to justify her fickleness? I voiced these complaints as I walked, and far from considering that the injurious terms I was using assumed that I had rights over her that she had never granted me, my imagination grew more and more heated as I approached her room. I would have inevitably launched into the harshest reproaches if she had appeared the slightest bit fearful or embarrassed. But my own embarrassment became extreme when I found her instead calm, laughing, and apparently ready to rejoice at the happiness she had just been promised. She didn't leave me in doubt for long. "You will have to agree," she said, "that that was the only way I could get away from the selictar's pestering. But if your carriage is ready, we must leave the city before daybreak. And I would be upset to learn," she added, "that you have informed your tutor of our plans, because I'm beginning to see clearly that he has not been honest with us." As I was even more overwhelmed by my joy than I had been by my pain, she had time to tell me that when she had confided her departure plans in him, she had been pleased to find him very willing to help her, but that it was easy to see that his eagerness was motivated only by his own interest. He had asked permission to keep the selictar's gifts for himself, suggesting that it shouldn't matter in the slightest to her what people thought when she was gone. What he had said to her in private at the port was an entreaty not to reveal this arrangement to me. And although he seemed not to be so bereft of integrity that he would sink so low as to steal, given that he had gone to the trouble of obtaining her permission, she had no doubt that he was somehow involved in the selictar's visit and propositions.

Finally, she felt inclined, for a multitude of reasons, to accept my offer to take her to my country home, and if I were kind enough to yield to her impatience, I wouldn't wait until the next day to undertake the trip.

I was so enchanted at what she said, and so determined not to put off for a moment what I wished for much more than she, that without even taking the time to give her an answer, I repeated my orders to get my carriage back as quickly as possible. It had come while I was conversing with the selictar, and I had ordered my valet to send it back home. While it was not difficult to hide Théophé's departure from the tutor, my immense joy couldn't prevent me from thinking of the selictar, and I was rather worried about how he would take this turn of events. To the extent that I could easily defend my integrity, I felt that I needn't fear his reproaches. The description I had given him of my feelings was sincere at the time. I hadn't said that they couldn't change, and not even having stood in the way of his proposals to Théophé, he had no right to complain about me if she preferred my own. Nevertheless, she had given him some reason to hope, and the deadline she had set to make her decision was a kind of commitment that at the very least required her to see him again and explain her intentions clearly. I was afraid to cause her some embarrassment by reminding her of this. But she had thought of everything. Returning to her room after giving my orders, I found her pen in hand. "I'm writing to the selictar," she said, "to prevent him once and for all from drawing the wrong conclusions about the answer I gave him. I will leave my letter with the tutor, who will no doubt be very happy to be of service to him again." She continued writing, and I only responded briefly to praise her decision. I continued to control myself to conceal all my joy in my heart, as if the fear of meeting some new obstacle might force me to stifle my ecstasy. The tutor, whom I was ignoring and who was perhaps prompted by his remorse to seek a way to make amends, asked permission to come in. "By all means," Théophé replied for me and, seeing him appear, told him that, having resolved to leave Constantinople, and the reasons she had given me forcing me to approve her decision myself, she was happy to convey to the selictar her gratitude for all of his kindness. She gave him her letter, which she had just finished. "You will carry out this commission all the more faithfully," she added mischievously, "as you have already been rewarded, and neither the selictar nor I will bring up the subject of the gifts." I couldn't prevent myself from taking advantage of these remarks to level some sharp criticism at my cowardly confident. He swore to me, to justify himself, that he hadn't thought he was being disloyal to me. Reminding me of his frankness in admitting his role in Théophé's departure when he had seen how deeply distressed I was, he begged me to judge the character of his sentiments by this strong proof of their sincerity. But it was not difficult to discern the role that his fear of my punishment had played and, dismissing him from my service, I entrusted him only with telling the selictar that I hoped to see him again very soon.

Indeed, I was already contemplating several infallible ways to keep this nobleman's friendship despite our conflict of interests. But hearing my carriage arrive at that moment, I put everything else aside and took Théophé's hand to escort her to it. I squeezed it with a passion I could no longer disguise; and although it had occurred to me to send her off with my valet, to make it more difficult for the tutor to figure out where she was going, I couldn't resist the pleasure of finding myself alone with her in the carriage, master of her destiny and of her person since she had freely consented to leave with me; master of her heart, for why would I hide the happiness I eagerly anticipated? And what other explanation could I give to her decision to throw herself into my arms with such confidence?

No sooner was I beside her than, kissing her passionately on the lips, I had the pleasure of finding her receptive to this tender gesture. A sigh, which she could not stifle, gave me an even more favorable impression of what she was feeling. During the whole trip I held her hand tightly in mine, and it seemed to me that she took as much pleasure in it as I did. I said nothing that did not include some expression of my amorous feelings, and my very words, despite being as measured as my actions owing to my natural decency, constantly betrayed the passion that burned ever stronger in my heart.

If Théophé sometimes objected to my passionate expressions, it was clearly not out of scorn or severity. She simply asked me not to use so inappropriately this sweet and loving language with a woman who had known only the tyrannical customs of a harem; and when this type of resistance only encouraged me to increase my attentions, she added that it was not surprising that women were so happy in my country, if all the men there treated them with such excessive kindness.

It was around midnight when we arrived at my country estate, which was located near the village of Oru. Although I hadn't given orders for any unusual preparations, the house was always stocked with whatever was needed to entertain properly my friends, whom I sometimes brought home with me at the most unexpected times. Upon arriving, I suggested we have a late dinner. Théophé responded that she needed rest more than food, but I insisted that we at least restore ourselves with a light, tasty snack. We spent little time at the table, and I used it less to eat than to begin to gratify my desires by my playful bantering and passionate looks into her eyes. I had designated the apartment where I intended to spend the night, and one of the reasons I had urged Théophé to have some refreshments was to give my servants time to decorate it with the utmost elegance. Finally, telling me again that she needed rest, I interpreted this as a discreet way of expressing her impatience to be alone with me. I even congratulated myself to discover in her a charming mistress who was both spirited enough to be impatient to share my bed and possessed enough modesty to disguise her desires.

My servants, who had witnessed a number of my trysts at the Oru house, and who in any case had my orders to prepare only one bed, had laid out in the same apartment everything that Théophé and I could possibly need for the night. I led her there, my joy and amorous attentions increasing at each step. Her slave and my valet, who were awaiting us, approached us to perform their normal duties, and I jokingly urged Bema (her slave's name) not to risk incurring my wrath by being too slow. It had seemed to me up to that point that Théophé was completely in agreement with my plans, and I was so sure that she had the same intentions as I did that I hadn't made the slightest effort to hide my designs. I certainly didn't feel obliged to be overly demure, as is sometimes necessary to soothe the modesty of an inexperienced young lady, with a woman who had so frankly shared with me her experiences in Patras and in the harem. Nor should have I expected, if I may be permitted another thought, any excessive shyness and virtue from a woman over whom I had acquired so many rights and who had given herself to me so freely. Consequently, from my point of view all the passionate desire I had felt for her up to that time was simply due to an enlightened libertinage that led me to prefer her to any other woman, because with such stunning looks she seemed to offer me so much more pleasure.[24]

However, scarcely had she noticed that my valet had begun to undress me than she pushed away her slave, who was trying to do the same for her, and remained for a moment in thought, as if she were uncertain about what to do, all the while refusing to look at me. At first I just attributed this change in attitude to the darkness of the night, which, as I looked at her across the room, could have just given me the impression that her expression had changed. But as she continued to stand there, with Bema standing idly by, I became concerned and made some playful comments about my fear of becoming bored if I had to wait too long for her. This manner of speaking, whose meaning was apparently all too clear from the situation, threw her into a state of utter dejection. She moved away from the mirror where she was still standing, and dropping listlessly down on a couch, she remained there, her head in her hands, as if she were trying to hide her face from me. At first I feared that she had suddenly become ill. We had made the trip during the night. Our snack had consisted only of some fruit and sherbet. I rushed to her side anxiously and asked her if she was not feeling well. She remained silent. Growing more and more concerned, I grabbed one of her hands, the very one her head was resting on, and tried to draw it toward me. She put up some resistance. Finally, using the same hand to wipe away some tears that I could still see on her face, she asked me if I would be so kind as to send away the two servants so that we could speak for a moment in private.

As soon as I was alone with her, she lowered her eyes and voice and told me with an air of dismay that she could not deny me whatever I demanded of her, but that she would never have expected this from me. She fell silent after these few words, as if distress and fear had prevented her from continuing, and I understood from the difficulty she had breathing that she was overcome with emotion. My surprise, which was extreme, and perhaps a feeling of shame that I couldn't completely suppress, reduced me to the same state, with the result that we were a most bizarre spectacle, both of us as prostrate as if we had been suddenly struck down by some illness.

However, I forced myself to overcome my lethargy, and seeking Théophé's hand again, I finally managed to overcome her resistance. "Just for a moment," I said to her during this tender struggle, "please just let me hold it for a moment while we speak." She appeared to yield to the fear of offending me, rather than to any desire to please me. "Alas! Do I have the right to deny you anything?" she repeated with the same listlessness. "Is there anything in my power that does not belong to you more than to myself? Even so, I never, never would have expected this from you." A flood of tears prevented her from continuing. Despite the embarrassment that I felt at this scene, I had some doubts as to her sincerity. I could recall hearing on many occasions that the majority of Turkish girls make it a point of pride to resist at length granting sexual favors, and with this in mind I was ready to ignore her resistance and her tears. Nonetheless, the ingenuousness I detected in her grief, and the shame I would have felt not to live up to the good opinion she had of me if she were sincere, prompted me at the same time to control my desires. "Do not be afraid to look at me," I said to her, upon seeing her eyes still cast downward, "and rest assured that I am the person who is the least inclined of anyone in the world to make you unhappy or thwart your wishes. My desires are a natural response to your attractiveness, and I had thought that you would not refuse me what you gave so willingly to the son of the governor of Patras and to the pasha Cheriber. But we are not free to love as we wish . . ." She interrupted me with an exclamation that seemed to be laced with bitterness; and just when I thought I had found the right words to soothe her feelings, she made it clear that I was only making her distress more acute. Completely confused by this strange turn of events, and not daring to add a single word for fear of further misunderstanding her intentions, I begged her to explain to me what I should do, what I should say to undo the unhappiness I had caused her, and not to think badly of me for something she really couldn't consider offensive. It seemed to me that the tone I used in this entreaty caused her to fear that she had shocked me by her laments. Clearly anxious, she clasped my hand tightly and said, "Oh! The best of all men," using an expression very common among the Turks, "do not judge badly the sentiments of your miserable slave, and do not think for a moment that there can ever be anything offensive between you and me. But you have saddened me beyond words. All I ask of you," she added, "since you have given me the freedom to express my wishes, is to leave me alone with my sad thoughts tonight, and to allow me to share them with you tomorrow. If you find your slave's request too bold, wait at least to learn my feelings before you condemn them." She tried to throw herself at my feet, but I stopped her, and getting up from the couch where I had sat down to listen to her, I adopted a pose as casual and detached as if it had never occurred to me to make any advances toward her. "Please do not use terms that no longer apply to your situation," I said. "Far from being my slave, I would have been all too happy to become yours. But I would not want to owe your love to my power over you, even if I had the right to use force. You will spend this night, and the rest of your life if you so desire, as tranquilly as you seem to wish." I immediately called her slave and ordered her to perform her duties; and withdrawing with the same appearance of coolness, I asked my valet to take me to another apartment where I went quickly to bed. I was still somewhat agitated, despite all my efforts to calm down, but I was sure that a night's rest would soon bring back my peace of mind and soothe my aching heart.

However, as soon as the darkness and silence of the night had begun to allow me to compose myself, all the events that had just taken place before me were just as vividly seized upon by my imagination. Since I hadn't forgotten a single word that Théophé had said, my first reactions, as I thought about them, were of course spite and embarrassment. It was not hard for me to understand that the ease with which I had made the decision to let her be, and all the indifference I had affected upon leaving her, had the same cause. I became all the more convinced of this as I berated myself for my lack of resolve. Shouldn't I be ashamed of so foolishly allowing myself to become enamored of a girl of this sort, and should my attraction to her have become important enough to cause me such concern and distress? Wasn't Turkey full of slaves who could give me the same pleasure? That's all I needed, I added, mocking my own folly, to fall in love with a sixteen-year-old girl whom I had helped get out of a harem in Constantinople, and who had perhaps joined Cheriber's only after trying out all the others. Reflecting then on her refusal to grace me with her favors after she had bestowed them on so many Turks, I congratulated myself on my refinement, which had led me to value so highly old Cheriber's leftovers. But I was still more amazed that Théophé had learned so quickly the value of her charms, and that the first man she had approached, and whom she was forcing to pay so dearly for them, was a Frenchman who knew his way around women so well. "She has imagined," I said, "because of my kind appearance and manners, that I was going to become her first dupe; and this young coquette, whom I thought to be so naïve and innocent, thinks perhaps that she can just lead me around by the nose."

But after having tempered my resentment with these insulting thoughts, I began little by little to contemplate the situation more objectively. I recalled Théophé's behavior with me from the moment I had seen her in Cheriber's seraglio. Had she done a single thing or said a single word that would justify my suspicions about her intentions? Hadn't I been surprised instead at seeing her, over and over again, seize the opportunities I had given her to develop her thoughts and turn them to the most serious moral questions? And hadn't I even admired the astuteness and soundness of judgment that were so evident in all of her reflections? It is true that she had sometimes gone on far too long, and it was perhaps this sort of exaggeration that had prevented me from taking her seriously. At most, I had taken the constant reasoning for her way of exercising her mind, or for the effect of a multitude of new impressions that the continual explanation of our principles and social customs had had on her lively and anxious imagination. But why should I do her this injustice rather than believing, in fact, that with her good character and keen intelligence she had been deeply impressed by so many principles that resonated deep in her heart? Hadn't she flatly rejected the selictar's proposals? Hadn't she even tried to leave me to go to Europe in search of a life in harmony with her new principles? And if she had then agreed to put herself in my hands, wasn't it natural for her to have confidence in a man to whom she owed the notions of virtue that she was beginning to savor? In this supposition, was she not now a respectable woman? And for whom more than for myself, who had come to her aid disinterestedly, and who, far from troubling her aspiration to decency by insane libertine propositions, should instead be proud of a conversion that was undisputedly my doing?

The more I thought about it, the more I found that this view of my liaison with Théophé was flattering for me; and since I had always prided myself on the loftiness of my principles, it cost me very little to sacrifice the pleasures I had envisioned in the hope of turning Théophé into a woman as distinguished by her virtue as by her physical charms. "It was never really my intention," I said to myself, "to encourage her to become virtuous; and the inclination that I am discovering in her can only be the happy effect of her own natural goodness, stimulated by a few random comments of mine. What might happen if I were to make a serious effort to cultivate the rich personal qualities with which she has been endowed?" Entranced, I contemplated the status I could help her to achieve. But struck by this vision, I added, "How would she then be any different from the finest lady in the world? Is this possible? Théophé could become as attractive by her qualities of heart and mind as by her beautiful looks? Ah, what man of honor and taste would not be happy to be united for life . . ." I left this thought incomplete, as if I were frightened at the eagerness with which my heart seemed to embrace it. It came back again and again until my passion was lulled; and far from experiencing the incessant turmoil I had feared, I spent the rest of the night in deep, satisfying sleep.[25]

The first thoughts I recalled the next morning were the same ones that I had so blissfully entertained as I fell asleep. They had spread throughout my mind with such force that they had supplanted my earlier plans, leaving no trace of the desires that had so preoccupied me for the past several days. I was burning with impatience to see Théophé, but it was in the hope of finding her as I had taken so much pleasure in imagining her, or at least with the frame of mind I had assumed she possessed. I was so excited that I was suddenly afraid that I had presumed too much. As soon as I learned that the curtains had been opened in her room, I requested permission to come in. Her slave asked me to be so good as to wait until she had gotten up from her bed. However, I hastened to get there before she had arisen, if only to show her, by my moderation, the change that the previous night had wrought in me. She seemed a little upset at seeing me arrive so quickly, and in her embarrassment she apologized for the slowness of her slave. I reassured her with some soothing comments meant to allay any fears that she might have had regarding my intentions. How beautiful she was nonetheless in this state, and how easily such charms might have made me forget my good resolutions!

"You promised," I said to her gravely, "to give me explanations that I am eager to hear; but please allow me to give you mine first. Despite the desires that I expressed yesterday, you must have understood by my submission to yours that I do not desire from a woman what she is not willing to give me of her own free will.[26] To this proof of my sentiments, I am adding today a declaration that will confirm them. Whatever may have been your intentions in agreeing to come here with me, you will always be free to follow them, just as you are now free to explain them." I fell silent after these remarks and resolved not to interrupt her until she had finished hers. But, to my surprise, after looking at me for a moment her tears began to flow again; and when my concern prompted me, despite my resolution, to ask her the cause, I was even more astonished by her answer. She told me that no one was more deserving of pity than she, and that what I had just said to her was precisely the misfortune that she had expected. I urged her to speak more clearly. "Alas!" she continued, "in declaring your sentiments, how little justice you do mine! After what happened here yesterday, you can only take this tone with me in the same spirit; and I am devastated that all my efforts to help you see into my heart have failed so miserably to bring you to understand my feelings."

This lamentation only threw me further into the dark, and I confessed with complete frankness, matched only by the expression on my face, that everything about her, from the first moment I had laid eyes on her, had been a perpetual enigma for me, an enigma that her present statement made it even more difficult to understand. "Please speak plainly," I added. "Why do you hesitate? In whom can you confide more freely?"

"It is your very questions," she answered finally. "It is your insistence that I speak clearly that is the source of my distress. Good grief! Do you really need an explanation to understand that I am the most miserable woman in the world? You who opened my eyes to my shame, you are surprised that I cannot bear to look at myself, and that my only thought is to hide from the eyes of others? Ah! What is my lot now? Is it to satisfy your desires or the selictar's, when I see them condemned by the very maxims you have taught me? Is it to go live in the countries whose customs and principles you have so praised only to find there, in the practice of all the virtues of which I was kept ignorant, a perpetual reproach of my scandalous past? I nonetheless tried to leave this corrupt nation. I attempted to flee both those who stole from me my innocent youth and you who taught me what I had lost. But where was I being led by my shame and remorse? I understand only too well that without protection and a guide I wouldn't have been able to take a single step without plunging into a new abyss. I was stopped by your entreaties. Although you were the most dangerous of all men for me, because you knew better than anyone the extent of my misfortune, although each time you looked at me it felt like a death sentence, I returned to Constantinople with you. I tried to reassure myself: does a sick person have to be ashamed of his most embarrassing wounds? Moreover, after I had understood that an ill-prepared voyage was extremely risky, I was encouraged by your promises to think that you would find a safer way for me to leave. However, it is you who are now forcing me back toward the precipice you saved me from. I considered you my teacher in the ways of virtue, and you want to lure me back into debauchery; and this is all the more dangerous that if it could hold any attraction for me, it would be because you are the source. Alas! Have I failed to express myself clearly, or are you pretending not to understand me? The limits of my intelligence, as well as the disorder of my ideas and my words, could have misled you as to my feelings; but if you are beginning to understand them through my efforts to explain them, do not be offended by the effect that your own lessons have had on my heart. Even if your own principles have changed, it is clear to me that I must remain faithful to those you taught me first, and I beg you to allow me to continue to adhere to them."²⁷

I've related only the parts of this speech that have remained the clearest in my memory, but it was long enough to give me time to understand its full force and to prepare my response. Still filled, as I was, with the thoughts that had occupied me during the whole night, I had been much less offended by Théophé's reproaches and much less aggrieved by her sentiments and her resolutions than I was, on the contrary, enchanted to find them consonant with the conclusions I had already drawn. Thus, the impression I had begun to have of her, and the virtuous satisfaction that I had felt because of it, had continually grown while I listened to her; and if she had paid attention to my reactions, she would have noticed that I was receiving each word she spoke with some sign of joy and approbation. I was careful, nonetheless, to be measured in my response in order to avoid appearing either flippant or too emotional after such serious remarks. "Dear Théophé!" I said, in a senti-mental flourish, "you humiliated me with your complaints, and I will not hide from you the fact that yesterday I was completely taken aback by them; but I have a better understanding of your feelings now, and I've come to admit my guilt. If you were to ask me how I came to misjudge you so badly, I can only say that it would have been too difficult to persuade myself of the truth of what I've just heard with such admiration, and which would still seem unbelievable to me if I hadn't received such convincing proof. I blame myself for having had for you, until now, more admiration than esteem. Ah! When you know how rare it is to discover a true penchant for virtue in the countries most favored by heaven, when you feel yourself how difficult it is to practice it, can you easily believe that in the heart of Turkey, coming out of a harem, a person of your age has not only instantly grasped the idea but even conceived a strong inclination for the most virtuous behavior? What did I say? What did I do to inspire this in you? Could a few casual thoughts on our customs have planted this happy penchant in your heart? No, no, you owe it to yourself alone; and your education, which has repressed it until now by the force of habit, is just a misfortune for which you are not responsible.²⁸

"The first conclusion I would like to draw," I continued just as calmly, "is that you would be equally unjust to be offended by the plans I had for you, since there was no way that I could immediately perceive yours, and to believe that anyone could use your past to deny you the respect you will deserve by a conduct worthy of your feelings. Forget your travel plans; young and inexperienced as you are, you can expect nothing good to come of them. Although they may have very sound ideas of virtue in Europe, they scarcely practice it any better than in Turkey. You will encounter passions and vices in all the countries where men live. But if you will have confidence in my promises, you may rely on my new sentiments, whose sole aspiration will be to perfect yours. My house will be a sanctuary; my example will inspire all of my servants to respect you. You will find a constant source of support in my friendship; and if you have appreciated my principles, perhaps you will also be able to profit from my advice."

She was looking at me in such an uncertain manner that it was impossible for me to tell if she was satisfied with my answer. I even feared from her silence that she still had doubts about my sincerity, and that after my behavior the night before she didn't dare trust my declarations. But in fact she was worrying about herself. "Can I ever imagine," she said after remaining silent for a long while more, "that with your idea of virtue you could look without contempt upon a woman whose sins you know only too well? I have confessed everything to you, and I don't regret it. I owed you this honesty, given the keen interest you showed in learning about my misfortunes. But isn't this the best reason for me to leave you, and can I ever be far enough away from those who can reproach me my shameful life?" Her words put me beside myself, and losing all control, I interrupted her. My entreaties must have been very touching and my arguments quite persuasive, since I managed to get Théophé to admit that the better I knew the value of virtue, the more I was forced to admire her own sentiments in this regard. I convinced her that for reasonable people only misdeeds that are committed intentionally are worthy of contempt, and that what she called her sins did not deserve that name, since such a judgment would suggest that she already knew what she only learned in our discussions in the seraglio. In the end I promised to respect her without fail and to do everything in my power to complete the education that I was so fortunate to have undertaken with her, and I gave her my most solemn oath that I would leave her free not only to leave me but to detest and scorn me if she ever saw me violate the conditions she set out. And to remove any ambiguity from my promises, I immediately outlined a plan whose every detail I submitted for her approval. "This house," I said, "will be your residence, and you may organize it however you choose. I will see you only as often as you like. You will see only the people you wish to receive in your home. I will see to it that you have everything you need for your chosen activities and entertainment. And in view of your interest in everything that can help improve your mind and fortify your heart, I intend to teach you my country's language, which will be extremely useful in opening up to you a whole new world of excellent books. You may remove anything you like from this proposal, or you may add anything that appeals to you, and you will never fail to see your desires fulfilled."

I didn't stop to ask myself the source of the eagerness behind all of these offers, and nor did Théophé. My candor itself seemed to convince her to yield to my pleading. She said that since she owed everything to my generosity, she feared that she would appear unworthy of it if she were too obstinate, and she was happy to accept these all-too-wonderful offers if I indeed kept my word. I do not know how I found the strength to refrain from throwing myself to my knees before her bed, as I so wanted to do, and thanking her for her consent as if it were a great favor. "We will begin immediately," I said, unable to contain my joy, "and you will realize one day that I am worthy of your confidence."

I was sincere. I left her without even permitting myself to kiss her hand, although it was the prettiest one in the world, and her movements during our conversation had moved me to do so a hundred times. My plan was to return immediately to Constantinople, not only to obtain for her all the things I thought she would need to entertain herself in her solitude, but also to give her the time to establish her authority and organize my household as she wished. I informed the small number of servants I left with her of my intentions in this regard. Bema, whom I had summoned to be witness to my orders, asked for the liberty to speak with me in private and gave me quite a surprise with what she had to say. She told me that the very liberty and authority that I was granting her mistress made it clear to her that I was not familiar enough with the character of the women of her country; that her experience in several harems had put her in a position to give useful advice to a foreigner; that the loyalty she owed her employer did not permit her to hide from me all that I had to fear from a mistress as young and beautiful as Théophé; that, in a word, I had little confidence in her wisdom if, instead of giving Théophé absolute authority in my house, I didn't subject her to the guidance of a faithful slave; that this was the custom of every lord in Turkey; and that if I judged her worthy of this function, she promised to serve me with such vigilance and devotion that I would never regret my confidence in her.

Although I hadn't found this slave clever enough to suppose that she could be of exceptional use to me, and given my good opinion of Théophé I had no need of an Argus at her side, I took a middle path between her advice and what I thought prudence dictated. "My conduct is not governed," I said to Bema, "by the principles of your country, and I want it to be clear, in any case, that I have no rights over Théophé that allow me to lay down any laws for her. But if you can be discreet, I would be happy to have you keep an eye on her behavior. The reward will depend on the quality of your service, and especially on your discretion," I added, "because it is essential that Théophé never be aware of the role I am giving you." Bema seemed extremely pleased with my answer. I would have perhaps found her joy a little suspicious if she hadn't come to me so highly recommended for her good sense and reliability. But I could see nothing in such a simple task that required more than a modicum of those two qualities.

What preoccupied me the most upon returning to the city was the difficulty I was going to have in mollifying the selictar, who would soon discover that Théophé had left the tutor's house, and that I had given her shelter in my home as well. Ever since I was assured of having control over her, I had suddenly ceased to worry about her, and without asking myself what I hoped to gain personally from this situation, it seemed to me that whatever feelings I might conceive for her, the future clearly offered some promising possibilities. But I couldn't avoid a discussion with the selictar about Théophé, and the arguments that I had prepared the day before, which I had thought would suffice to calm him down, seemed weaker and weaker to me as the moment to try to get him to accept them drew nearer. The one that I thought the most convincing was the fear of her father, who would have claimed even more fiercely his right not only to exclude her from his family but to seek to have her punished if she had willingly compromised herself with a Turk. My protection, in her present situation, was more reassuring than anything the selictar could offer her. However, in addition to his opinion of his standing with Théophé, I couldn't very well reveal to him that she was at my estate without once again finding it necessary to receive his visits there as often as he wished. That was an obvious source of aggravation for both Théophé and myself. In my uncertainty I chose a completely different course, and perhaps the only one that had any chance of succeeding with such a generous person as the selictar. I went directly to his home. I didn't wait for him to make my undertaking more difficult with his complaints, and before he could even ask me any questions I informed him that the reason that the young Greek girl had rejected his offers was a dedication to virtues that are not typical of women in Turkey. I didn't even hide from him that I too had been quite surprised, and that I hadn't begun to believe in her sincerity until I had put her principles to the test. Since I could only admire such feelings in a person so young, however, I was determined to do everything in my power to help her perfect such noble aspirations, and knowing him, I had no doubt that he would be inclined to support my efforts. I had chosen my words very carefully, but I immediately regretted my final statement. The selictar replied by protesting that he respected Théophé's feelings such as I had depicted them, and that he had never intended to exclude them from the relation he had envisioned with her; but he took advantage of my good opinion of him to assure me that his affection was only enhanced by his growing respect for her, and he was all the more eager to let her know how important she was to him. My only resistance to his request to accompany me occasionally to Oru was to offer him the same liberty I granted all my friends to visit me, with the stipulation that Théophé was free to see him or not, since I had given her my word that she could choose freely whom she wanted to admit into her solitude.

Although I was understandably unhappy with myself for having given the selictar an opening he was clearly determined to exploit, I was so pleased to have managed to skirt so deftly the ethical dilemma that had troubled me that I gave little importance to the discomfort of seeing him at Oru. He could easily have taken offense if I had hesitated to accede to his desires, and the suspicions that had been dispelled up until then by both his own honesty and his opinion of mine would perhaps have been aroused and eventually ruined our friendship. My only thought on leaving was to fulfill the promises I had made to Théophé. Knowing her interest in painting, which had been limited to depicting flowers because of the law that forbids Turks to paint any living beings, I sought out a painter who could teach her drawing and portraiture. While selecting other tutors for the arts and various activities practiced in Europe, I had an idea that I resisted at length, but that Providence, whose aims are ever unfathomable, finally imposed in spite of all my objections. Since I was convinced that the youngest Condoidi son was her brother, it seemed to me all the more natural to have them educated together, as most of the tutors that I was going to give them were the same. This plan assumed that Condoidi would live at Oru also; and far from finding anything objectionable in this perspective, I was instead delighted at the idea of giving Théophé a regular companion who could relieve the boredom of living alone. To tell the truth, the principal difficulty that I had to combat was not very clear in my mind, and it was perhaps the obligation I felt to block it out that prevented me from contemplating other issues that should have given me more concern. Without daring to admit it to myself, I felt vaguely that the constant presence of this young man would prevent me from being alone with Théophé; but having decided once and for all to keep my promises to Théophé scrupulously, I rejected this idea in the end.

Synèse (the name of the Condoidi boy) was overjoyed to learn the decision that my esteem and affection for his sister had led me to make. He was no less happy at my plan to have him live with her and give them the same education. I had him leave the same day for Oru, with everything I had acquired for Théophé's entertainment. Their father, who was now aware that I had taken his son under my protection, and who had already come to thank me, came back again when Synèse informed him of my arrival. He was astonished to see who I was, and I was convinced by his embarrassment that Synèse had followed faithfully my orders not to let him know what was really going on. I had wanted both to enjoy his surprise and to take advantage of his initial reactions to again plead for Théophé. But the latter hope was shattered when this stubborn old man declared flatly that his religion and honor forbade him recognize a daughter who had been raised in a harem. Even my offer to resolve all of the practical problems by assuming any paternal duties could not make him budge. He remained so inflexible that I couldn't control my resentment and told him that he needn't bother coming back, and that he wasn't welcome in my house.

I didn't return to Oru until the next day. I couldn't hide from myself my impatience to see Théophé, and despite the fact that I had absolutely given up all my claims on her, I had no intention of denying myself the simple pleasure of an affection that violated neither her virtuous principles nor my promises. This sort of sentimental indulgence saved me from having to admit the terrible difficulty I would have experienced had I attempted to stifle my feelings entirely.[29] I found Synèse with her, both of them delighted with their studies and equally grateful for my decision to have them live together. I admired Théophé's outer tranquility, which seemed to increase her natural freshness, and which was the fruit of her newfound contentment. I wanted to know from Bema what use Théophé had made of the authority I had granted her in my home. This slave, offended to have so little power herself, didn't dare tell me that her mistress had abused hers, but she repeated all the reasons she had already stated to convince me of the danger I was courting. The cause of her insistence was so obvious that, smiling, I encouraged her to be less apprehensive. Based on some comments by the people who had bought her for me, she had expected me to give her a certain authority over Théophé, and this sign of confidence that she had received in some seraglio was the highest mark of distinction for a slave. I declared to her that a Frenchman was not guided by Turkish customs, and that we had our own, advising her moreover to take advantage of them to improve her own lot in life. While she was not so bold as to complain, it was perhaps from this moment on that she began to develop an antipathy for both Théophé and me, and she would easily find an opportunity to make us feel it.

The demands of my office being less pressing than they had been for a long while, I took advantage of the beautiful weather to spend several weeks in the country. I had feared at first that Théophé might exercise too severely the freedom I had given her to refuse to see me. But it seemed to me, on the contrary, that she took pleasure in our conversations, and I found myself spending entire days in her company. Being so close to her constantly, I became more and more familiar with all the fine qualities with which nature had endowed her character. It was from me that she received her first lessons in our language. She made remarkably quick progress. I had praised highly the advantages of being able to read French, and she was impatient to have in her hand a French book that she could understand. I was no less impatient than she, and I tried to make the wait easier for her by giving her a rough idea of what she could expect to discover more fully developed in the works of our great authors. I kept my feelings for her to myself. I was virtually intoxicated by the innocent pleasures of seeing and hearing her. I would have been afraid of diminishing by any sign of weakness her new confidence in me; and what I found the most surprising was that I did not at all suffer from the natural cravings that tend to make the deprival of certain pleasures rather difficult for men of my age; I renounced them effortlessly and didn't even think about them, even though up until then I hadn't denied myself much as regards women, especially in a country where the demands of nature seem to increase with the freedom to satisfy them. In reflecting later on the cause of this change, it seemed to me that the natural faculties that are the source of our desires perhaps follow a different course in a man who is in love than in those whose only stimulus is the lust innate to our sex. The impression that beauty makes on all our senses divides the action of our physical nature. So what I prefer to call "natural faculties," in order to avoid ideas that might appear lewd, rise through the same channels that brought them into the normal regions of the body, spread throughout our blood, provoke that sort of fermentation or fire that can be considered the sign of love, and do not follow the path reserved for the act of physical love until they are called upon to do so.[30]

The selictar occasionally troubled this delightful existence with his presence. I had prepared my pupil for his visits, and since I wanted to accustom her to viewing the company of men differently from Turkish women, who can not imagine any relation with them outside of love, I had recommended to her that she receive courteously a man who honored her with his admiration, and whose affection should no longer be a source of concern for her. He had lived up to my opinion of him by behaving so moderately that I couldn't help but wonder about his feelings. I found it rather difficult to understand their nature, because the only course that could have given him any hope to gratify them was now closed by his own resolutions, as well as by Théophé's refusal. Consequently, the future held nothing for him, and all the present could offer him was the simple pleasure of serious conversation, which wasn't even as long as he would have liked. Théophé, who was kind enough to admit him into her presence each time he came to Oru, was not always willing to put up with it when he overstayed his welcome. She would leave us to continue her studies with her brother, and when she was gone I would have to listen to the selictar pour out his love for her. Since he no longer had a clear plan, and he allowed himself only vague evocations of his admiration and love, I eventually became convinced that since he had often heard me speak of the refined kind of love based on sentimental inclination, so rare in his country, he felt so drawn to the idea that he wished to experience it himself. But how could one imagine that he would be satisfied with simple sentimental pleasures without manifesting more disappointment and impatience at getting nothing in return?

These doubts did not make his presence disagreeable to me, since the comparison of his situation and my own still seemed more promising for my hopes, carefully dissimulated, than for the selictar's. But I was less sanguine after another discovery, for which I can take no credit and which triggered the revelation of several intrigues that would cause a great deal of bitterness in my life. I had been residing for about six weeks at Oru, and being privy to everything that happened in my house, I was delighted at the peace and contentment I witnessed there. Synèse was constantly with Théophé, but no more than I was myself. I had noticed nothing in their relationship that cast doubt on my understanding that they were of the same blood, or rather, since I hadn't the slightest doubt that they had the same father, I had no reason to be concerned about their living together on such familiar terms. Synèse, whom I treated with the affection one has for a son, and who proved himself worthy of it by his gentle character, came to see me alone one day in my apartment. After some small talk, he casually brought up the problem of his father's unwillingness to recognize Théophé as his daughter and, voicing thoughts that I had never heard from him before, told me that despite the pleasure he felt at the idea of having such a charming sister, he hadn't been able to convince himself sincerely that he was her brother. Taken aback by such an unexpected declaration, I waited for him to continue. "The confession of the wretched individual who had been executed by the judge's order was enough," he said, "to justify his father's refusal. What interest would a man who was facing death have had to hide the identity of Théophé's father? And wasn't it clear that after declaring that Condoidi's daughter had died with her mother, he had only changed his tune in a vile attempt to curry favor with the judge, or to have his punishment postponed?" It was hardly any more likely, Synèse added, that such a sublime person as Théophé was the daughter of this scoundrel, any more than she could be Paniota Condoidi's, and numerous circumstances he remembered being discussed in his family had never allowed him to take this idea seriously.

Although there was no reason to doubt Synèse's sincerity, the fact that these ideas came from him, and were so contrary to the affection he had always demonstrated for Théophé, made me extraordinarily suspicious. I knew that he was clever enough to be capable of dissimulation, and I hadn't forgotten the selictar's proverb about the sincerity of Greeks.[31] I immediately surmised that Synèse's feelings had changed, and whether it be hate or love, he didn't have the same attitude toward Théophé as before. After this admission, it didn't seem to me that I needed to fear being duped by such a young man. Resolved on the contrary to lead him to reveal his intentions without his realizing it, I pretended to share his concerns, more readily than he had perhaps anticipated, about the problems he had just evoked. "I am no more certain than you," I said, "about Théophé's birth, and I think, when all is said and done, that the most important opinion on this matter is your family's. So if you all agree not to recognize her, it would be inappropriate for her to pursue her claims any further." It was easy for me to see that he was very pleased with this response. But when he was apparently getting ready to confirm what he had said with some additional proof, I added, "If you are as convinced as you appear to be that she is not your sister, not only do I not wish you to continue to give her that name, but I would not pardon myself if you were forced to live with her any longer. You will return to Constantinople this very evening." This declaration threw him into a state of bewilderment that was even easier to see than his earlier rejoicing. I didn't give him time to recover. "Since you must have understood," I added, "that it is out of consideration for her that I invited you to live in my home, you certainly should have foreseen that I wouldn't allow you to stay when I no longer had that reason. Therefore, I am going to give orders for you to be taken back to your father's home tonight."

I had said everything that I thought might help me discover Synèse's intentions. I stopped a moment, feigning to ignore his anguished state, but to push him over the edge I advised him to say his good-byes to Théophé, since it was highly unlikely that he would ever see her again. After changing colors twenty times and becoming pitifully flustered, he protested timidly that his doubts about his sister's birth would diminish neither the esteem nor the affection that he felt for her; that he considered her, on the contrary, to be the most wonderful woman alive, and that he couldn't have been happier to have had the liberty to live with her; that his feelings would never change in this regard; that he wanted to devote his life to proving them to her, and if he could combine the satisfaction of pleasing her with the honor of my protection, he wouldn't exchange his fate for any in the world. I interrupted him. Not only did I think I could see into his heart, but this fervor that told me everything I needed to know about his sentiments also produced another suspicion that troubled me greatly. "Brother or not," I said to myself, "if this young man is in love with Théophé, if he was able to deceive me up to now, who can assure me that Théophé doesn't share his passion, and that she hasn't been just as clever in hiding it? Who even knows if they are not conniving together to free themselves of an inconvenient family tie that is preventing them from satisfying their desires?" This idea, which all the circumstances seemed to support, threw me into a state of despair that I would have been no more able to dissimulate than Synèse. "Leave me," I said. "I need to be alone, and I'll see you in a short while." He left the room. Still worried, however, I watched carefully to see if he would go directly to Théophé's apartment, as if I could draw some conclusions from the eagerness I assumed he had to share our conversation with her. I saw him walk sadly into the garden, where I had no doubt he was going to indulge his grief at having failed so miserably in his undertaking; but his distress must have been extreme if it was greater than mine.

My first act was to summon Bema, whose observations would doubtlessly shed some light on this matter. She appeared not to understand my questions at all, and I eventually came to the conclusion that, since she had always thought that Synèse was Théophé's brother, she had paid no attention to their relations and never had any reason to be suspicious. I was determined to discuss this with Théophé and to go about it as shrewdly as I had with Synèse. Since I was certain that he hadn't had the opportunity to see her since he had left my presence, I sounded her out first on my plan to send him back to his family. She was quite surprised, but when I added that the only source of my displeasure with him was his reluctance to recognize her as his sister any longer, she couldn't hide her chagrin. "What little faith," she said, "can one have in men's appearance! These past few days he has shown me more esteem and affection than ever before." "I have every reason to believe," I said, "that he has fallen in love with you. He feels constrained by his status of brother, which is clearly in conflict with his feelings."[32] Théophé interrupted me with such sharp protests that I had no need of any other proof to confirm my confidence in her. "What are you telling me?" she exclaimed. "Good heavens! You think that he has other feelings for me than brotherly affection? What have you exposed me to?" Then, telling me with surprising naïveté everything that had happened between the two of them, she provided details of their relations that left me trembling. As her brother, Synèse had led her to give him caresses and favors that must have delighted him as her lover. He had managed to convince her that it was an established custom between brothers and sisters to give each other constant demonstrations of innocent affection, and following this principle, he had accustomed her not only to live with him in the greatest familiarity, but also to allow him to gratify his passion continually with her charms. Her hands, her mouth, even her breasts had become the infatuated Synèse's private domain.[33] I extracted all of these admissions from Théophé, and I was reassured as regards further fears only by the very sincerity of her regrets at the thought of what she had already allowed him to do with her. My own resolution to control my desires could not protect me from the bitterest feelings I have ever experienced. "Ah! Théophé," I said, "you have no idea how much you are hurting me. I am doing extreme violence to my own feelings in order to leave you free to bestow your affections upon whomever you choose, but if you give them to another, your heartlessness will certainly cause my death."

I had never before spoken to her so frankly. She was so stunned that her cheeks began to burn. Lowering her eyes, she said, "You can not consider me guilty of a crime that can be attributed only to my ignorance; and if you have the opinion of me that I have strived to deserve, you will never suspect me of giving to someone else what I haven't given to you." I gave no reply. The pain that still weighed on my heart left me perplexed and taciturn. I could find nothing in Théophé's response that flattered my desires enough to give me cause to applaud myself for finally declaring them openly. What could I hope to obtain if she clung to her devotion to virtue, and what could I possibly expect for myself if she had relented in favor of Synèse? This reflection, or rather the indifference I thought I had perceived in her reply, renewed all my anxiety, and I left her, looking more dejected than affectionate, to go tend to the business of ridding myself of Synèse.

He had returned from the garden; and when I gave orders to summon him, I learned that he was in my quarters. But I received at the same time news from Constantinople that gave me serious cause for alarm regarding the safety of several of my best friends. I was informed by telegram that the aga of the janissaries had been arrested the night before, on suspicions that concerned no less than the life of the Sultan himself, and that it was feared that the same fate awaited the selictar and the bostangi bachi, who were considered to be his best friends.[34] My secretary, who had sent me this news, added his own speculations. Given the power and authority the bostangi bachi exercised in the Sultan's seraglio, he doubted, he wrote me, that they would dare to harm him; but he was all the more convinced that they would not spare his friends, among whom the most highly placed were the selictar, Cheriber, Dely Azet, Mahmouth Prelga, Montel Olizun, and several other lords with whom, like him, I had relations. He inquired if I would not try to intervene in their favor, or if, at the very least, I wasn't disposed to offer them some form of help in their perilous situation. The only thing I could do for them was to appeal to the grand vizir; but if it was an affair of state, I foresaw that my entreaties would fall on deaf ears.[35] However, the notion of my "help" had a broader sense. In addition to the means to flee that I could easily provide, it was no less easy for me to help some of them out in the same way that my predecessor had done willingly for Mahomet Ostun, that is, to shelter them secretly in my residence until the storm was over; and in a country where anger cools quickly after the initial outburst, there is no great danger for people who manage to keep out of the way long enough.[36] However, since the duties of my function didn't always leave me free to indulge imprudently my devotion to my friends, I decided to return quickly to Constantinople to take the measure of the situation with my own eyes.

But while reading my letters I had noticed Synèse, who was indeed waiting for me, and his timid manner seemed to promise a new scene. I was preparing to treat him to some scathing comments, but scarcely had he seen me finish reading the letters when he threw himself at my feet in a display of humiliation that comes easy to Greeks and begged me to forget everything he had said about Théophé's birth and to allow him to continue to live at Oru, since he was more disposed than ever to recognize her as his sister. He couldn't understand, he added, by what whim he could have doubted for a second a truth that he embraced with his whole heart, and despite his father's injustice he was determined to declare publicly that Théophé was his sister. I had no trouble seeing through the young Greek's shrewdness. His earlier stratagem having failed, he wanted to at least hold onto the pleasures he had been enjoying. He obviously felt no remorse for them, since he had indulged himself tranquilly for so long a time, and it was apparently just to obtain yet greater favors from her that he had attempted to escape the inconvenience of being her brother. But my answer dashed all of his hopes. Without reproaching him his love, I told him that since the truth was independent of his acceptance or repudiation, it was neither what he had said to me nor the ease with which he changed his tune that would determine my opinion on his sister's birth; but that his behavior made the state of his feelings abundantly clear; his words were useless against the pleadings of his heart; and, to sum up in a few words what I thought of him, I considered him to be a coward who had recognized that he was Théophé's brother, who had then denied that title, and who was now trying to take it back for reasons that were far more despicable than his father's. I have to admit that these rather insulting remarks were prompted by my extreme resentment. Then, forbidding him to reply, I called one of my servants and ordered him to accompany the young man back to Constantinople. I took my leave, ignoring his misery, and remembering that I had given him my permission to say good-bye to his sister, I withdrew it and forbade him to speak to her, under any pretext, before leaving.

Trusting my servants to carry out my orders, I immediately got into my carriage, which I had had prepared after reading my letters, and went back to my residence in Constantinople to learn the latest news before taking any action to help my friends. The crime of the head of the janissaries was to have visited Ahmet, one of the Sultan Mustapha's brothers, in his prison. The bostangi bachi was suspected of arranging this visit, and they wanted to get the truth out of the aga. Since he had been on bad terms with the grand vizir for some time, no one doubted that this minister, eager for his rival's downfall, would show him no mercy; and what distressed me the most was to learn that Cheriber had just been arrested with Dely Azet, for the sole reason that they had both spent part of the day preceding his crime at the aga's home. I would have rushed immediately to the grand vizir's house, if it were only a question of my friendship for Cheriber. But since I could not hope to gain much from a vague appeal, I thought I could be of more use to my friend if I saw the selictar first and determined with him the best way to proceed. I went to his home. He was out, and the gloom that pervaded his house convinced me that they were extremely concerned over his absence. A slave in whom I knew he had confidence came and told me in secret that his master had left in great haste at the first news of Cheriber's arrest, and that he had no doubt that the misfortune of his friend had prompted him to seek safety in flight. I replied that he should take this precaution without delay, if he hadn't yet taken it, and I went on to instruct the slave to offer him the shelter of my house at Oru, provided that he come at night and with no retinue. In addition to the example of my predecessor, I had that of Pasha Rejanto, who had earned an eternal reputation for taking in Prince Demetrius Cantemir. Moreover, it wasn't a matter of helping a criminal avoid punishment, but rather of protecting a gentleman against unjust suspicions.[37]

However, since I was no further along in my plans to help my friends, I decided to go see several Turkish lords who might at least be able to provide more information. A rumor was spreading that the aga of the janissaries, after confessing under torture, had already been strangled to death by the Mutes.[38] It was a good sign for the selictar that he had not been arrested yet, and there was no suggestion that he was suspected of any other crime than his friendly relations with the aga. But the public outcry against Cheriber and

Dely Azet, two of my best friends, was so worrisome that I felt compelled to act. I went to the grand vizir's residence. I made no attempt to use elaborate arguments to gain the vizir's ear in this affair of state. I simply insisted on my deep friendship for the two men, and assuming that my friends had not been accused of some misdeed that I could not imagine them committing, I begged the vizir to give some consideration to my entreaties. He listened to me solemnly. "You surely understand," he said, "that the Sultan's justice is not blind, and that it can distinguish between guilt and innocence. Have no fear for your friends, if they have nothing to hide." He added, nevertheless, that my appeals would never be taken lightly at the Porte, and he promised me that the two pashas would benefit from them. But suddenly breaking into laughter, he told me that the selictar must think my influence very powerful, since his fear had prompted him to seek asylum in my house. I did not grasp the meaning of this banter. He continued in the same vein, even pretending to praise my discomfort and silence, which he attributed to my discretion. But when I protested in the clearest possible terms that I did not know where the selictar had hidden, he informed me that he had sent spies out after him, and that he knew that he had gone the night before to my house in Oru, with such a small suite that there seemed little doubt that he had gone into hiding there. "I do not believe he is guilty of anything," he added, "and I do not see anything criminal in his former relations with the aga of the janissaries. But I thought it wise to keep him under surveillance, and I am not at all sorry that he was frightened enough to become a little more careful in the choice of his friends." He gave me his word, after these remarks, that he would not make any trouble for him while he was at my house, but he made me promise not to reveal to him what he had just told me, in order to let him stew a little longer.

It was still difficult for me to understand that the selictar was at Oru. I had left there in the middle of the day. How could it be possible that he was there without my involvement, and that he had convinced my servants to hide his arrival from me? His passion for Théophé was the first idea that struck me. Wouldn't he think less about his safety than about satisfying his love? And if it is true, I said to myself, that he has been hidden in my house since last night, could he possibly be there without Théophé's complicity? Draw whatever conclusions you like about my feelings for her. If I do not deserve to be called her suitor, let me be regarded as her guardian or as her moral mentor; but the least of these titles sufficed to throw me into a state of panic. I couldn't get back to Oru quickly enough. Upon arriving I asked the first servant I saw where the selictar was, and how he happened to be in my house without my knowledge. It was the man that I had instructed to take Synèse back home. Although I was surprised to see him back so soon, I concluded that he could have managed it if he went as fast as possible; and it was only after he had assured me that the selictar wasn't there that I asked him how he had carried out my orders. It is improbable that there was no trace of discomfort in his replay, but having no reason to be suspicious, I paid no attention to his manner when he answered that he had taken Synèse to his father's home. Nonetheless, I was equally deceived on both accounts, with the difference that he was sincere in the first case, and that in the second he had lied to cover up a betrayal in which he was complicit. In short, when I was convinced that the selictar hadn't come to my house, and that Synèse had left it, they were both there, and I was unaware of it for several days.

Synèse had received my order to leave as if it were a death sentence. Having only his ingenuity to avoid obeying me, it had occurred to him that my staff was not aware of my motives, and that he might be able to persuade them to let him at least stay at Oru until my return. Then, out of fear that I might return very unexpectedly, as I sometimes did, he had lowered himself to bribing, albeit handsomely, the lackey I had trusted to take charge of him. I have no idea what pretext he used to make his proposition attractive, but after winning him over, he had pretended to leave with him, and both of them had come back a few moments later. Synèse had locked himself in his room, and the lackey had reappeared in the house after a few hours, as if he had just returned from the city after discharging his duty.

The selictar's escapade was more complicated. It will be remembered that Bema was very much dissatisfied with her position, and whether she was offended at how little confidence I appeared to have in her, or if it was her vanity alone that led her to feel that she did not enjoy the status she deserved in my household, she considered me to be a foreigner who didn't appreciate her talents sufficiently and whom she could take no pleasure in serving. The selictar had been a frequent visitor, and she was too perspicacious not to have discovered what drew him there. Well versed in scheming by her lengthy experience in harems, she took pleasure in plotting how to avenge the slights she had suffered. She had found the opportunity to speak to the selictar, and offering to serve his amorous interests, she had succeeded in convincing him that his happiness depended on her. The hopes she had given him were far greater than those she entertained herself; being well aware of the terms I was on with Théophé, she could hardly think that it would be easy to obtain favors for the selictar that she knew had been denied to me. But she used this very knowledge to encourage a lover's illusions. After reinforcing his long-held impression that I had no amorous relationship with my pupil, she claimed to know well enough the inclinations and temperament of a girl of that age to assure him that she would not forever resist the attraction of pleasure, and the first promise she had made was based on the hope she would meet no resistance.

It is true that since she was always in Théophé's company and was so adept at governing young women, she was more to be feared in this matter than the natural yearnings on which the selictar had founded all his hopes. However, no matter how cleverly she had acted, her plan could not have gotten very far when the downfall of the aga of the janissaries had thrown the selictar into a state of panic. All of his fears couldn't dampen his passion, however, and he had exhorted Bema all the more since, uncertain of what to do, he had wondered if he shouldn't seek asylum among the Christians with whatever he could save of his fortune, all of which he would have willingly sacrificed if Théophé would have agreed to accompany him in his flight. But the scheming Bema, who hadn't dared promise him such a quick success, had ventured to offer him a hiding place near Théophé. My house was organized according to our customs; that is, since I didn't even submit to Turkish practices as regards women's lodgings, they simply occupied the rooms that my majordomo had assigned them. Bema's room was adjacent to Théophé's apartment. It was in this tiny space that she offered to hide the selictar. She made him feel all the more secure in that I was not aware of how he was being accommodated in my house, so he need not fear that I might sacrifice our friendship to political concerns. Moreover, I was certain to be very pleased, after the danger had passed, to learn that I had been of service to my friend. It is far less strange that such a plan would have occurred to a woman experienced in all sorts of intrigues than it is that a man of the selictar's eminence could have approved it. I thus found this event so extraordinary, after learning all of the circumstances, that I would offer it as an example of the greatest follies of love, if there hadn't been an additional motive, that is, the selictar's fear for his life.

But I can add that the haughtiness of the Turks is the first thing that disappears when they encounter adversity. Since all of their prestige is borrowed from their master's, whose slaves they profess to be, not a trace is left at the slightest fall from grace; and for most of them, their reasons to be proud are extremely weak when they are reduced to their own merit.[39] However, I knew that the selictar possessed enough fine qualities to make him a formidable rival for Théophé's affections, especially since she was raised in the same country and would not be offended by what we would find disgusting in a Turk. I said nothing to Théophé about the concerns that had brought me back from Constantinople. On the contrary, finding myself all the freer with her since I felt that a weight had been lifted from my heart, I couldn't hide during our conversation a feeling of satisfaction that was so apparent to her that she asked me why I was so cheerful. It was an opportunity to repeat more enthusiastically what I had declared to her that morning when I was feeling so sad and listless. But as certain as it was that she reigned over my heart, I was still just as uncertain what course I should allow my feelings to take; and finding my mind unburdened now that I had been relieved of my fears, I had the strength to restrain my impulse to speak to her of my love. Today as I reflect on the past, I perhaps have a clearer understanding of my feelings then, and it seems to me that what I secretly desired was for Théophé to feel for me some of the penchant I had for her, or at least that she let me see some evidence of it; for I was still inclined to flatter myself that she had more affection for me than for anyone else, but held back by my principles of honor as well as by my promises, I would not have wanted to owe the conquest of her heart to my talents at seduction; and I would have been happy if only she had seemed to desire from me what I wanted from her.[40]

End of Book One

It was the most beautiful season of the year. Since my garden contained the most pleasant things imaginable in a country estate, I invited Théophé to join me there for a breath of fresh air after dinner. We strolled down some of the prettiest lanes. Despite the relative darkness, I thought I spotted the figure of a man in several nooks. I imagined that it was either my shadow or one of my servants. In another place I heard the rustling of leaves, but having no reason to be suspicious I assumed that it was just the wind. It had suddenly become chillier. I took the movement I had heard for an indication that a storm was coming, and I hurried Théophé toward a small pavilion in the garden where we could find shelter. Bema was following us with another female slave. We sat down for a few minutes, and I thought I heard someone walking slowly a short distance from the pavilion. I called Bema and asked her some question or other to check how far away she was. She was not on the side where I had heard the sound of footsteps. I began to suspect that someone was listening to us, and not wishing to frighten Théophé, I found a pretext to get up and go see who could be capable of this indiscretion. It didn't yet occur to me that it could be anyone other than one of my servants. But seeing no one, I calmly rejoined Théophé. Night was falling quickly. We returned to her apartment without meeting anyone else.[1]

However, as I could not get it out of my mind that I had heard someone moving around near us, and it seemed important to punish this boldness on the part of my servants, I decided, upon leaving Théophé, to linger for a while at the garden gate, which was not far from my apartment. My idea was to surprise the indiscreet fellow who had followed us when he decided to leave. It was an iron gate through which one had to pass to get out. It wasn't long before I caught sight of a man coming toward me in the darkness, but he saw me too, although it was impossible for him to recognize me, and he turned around and went quickly back into the woods. In my impatience I went after him. I even called out loudly to let him know who I was, ordering him to stop. He paid no attention to my command. My resentment was so keen that, taking another tact to shed some light on this matter, I went back into my house and gave orders to summon all my servants at Oru. There were not very many of them. I had seven, who all appeared at the same time. I became so flustered that I didn't even reveal the reason why I had asked them to come, and then recalling the selictar, with all the suspicions that the thought of him couldn't fail to provoke, I grew indignant at this indisputable act of treachery. It seemed clear to me that he had taken lodgings in some nearby house with the hope of sneaking into mine during the night. But was it with Théophé's consent? This question immediately came to mind and plunged me into an unspeakable state of bitterness. I would have given orders to my whole staff to search the garden if I had not been halted by another thought that prompted me to make a completely different decision. It seemed to me that it was much more important to discover the selictar's intentions than to arrest him. I resolved to see to this matter myself. I dismissed all my servants, including my valet, and returning to the garden gate I hid myself more carefully than I had the first time, in the hope that the selictar would return before the night was out. But I was disappointed once again, for I had just wasted my time.

He had come back into the house while I was getting my servants together. Bema, who had led him into the garden herself, had guessed my suspicions and, finding some pretext to leave her mistress, had called him back quickly enough to prevent me from finding him. I spent the whole following day in a state of dejection that I could not conceal. I didn't even visit Théophé, and the concern for my health that she expressed that evening struck me as a form of treachery I vowed to avenge. To add to my woes, I received the news at the end of the day that the pasha Cheriber's life was in the greatest danger, and his friends, who were already aware of my efforts on his behalf, were begging me to see the grand vizir again to renew my appeals for clemency. What an inconvenience, at the beginning of a night that I had resolved to spend again at the gate to my garden with the enjoyable perspective of covering the selictar with shame! However, I could not hesitate between my love interests and my duty to a friend. The only course that would take both of them into account was to make the trip to Constantinople quickly enough to be back at Oru before the night was too far along. But considering everything I had to do, even acting with the greatest haste I couldn't be back home before midnight; and how could I be sure that no one would take advantage of my absence?

I gradually began to regret having rejected Bema's advice; and in this extremely urgent situation I could see no other alternative than to follow it, at least in this instance. I sent for her. "Bema," I said, "I have to go to Constantinople to tend to matters of critical importance. I cannot leave Théophé on her own, so I feel it necessary to give her a governess like you whom I can count on. While I cannot give you the official title, you will have the same authority until I return. I entrust you with her health and her behavior." Never has anyone exposed himself so foolishly to treachery. However, this wretched woman confessed to me, when circumstances later forced her to be sincere, that if instead of limiting her promotion to the time of my absence, I had instead given her the hope that she would retain her authority in my house for the rest of her life, she would have renounced her commitments to the selictar and served me with complete loyalty.

I departed extremely relieved, but my trip was of no use to my two friends. I learned upon arriving home that the grand vizir had twice sent one of his principal officers, who had expressed great regret at not finding me at home, and some muffled rumors that had begun to spread made me very fearful for the fate of the two pashas. This news, in addition to what I had been told about the grand vizir, prevented me from taking a moment's rest. I went to the minister's residence even though it was around ten in the evening, and on the pretext that I was impatient to learn what he desired of me, I urgently requested to see him for a moment, even if it meant leaving his harem, where I was given to understand he was. He did not make me wait long, but he shortened my visit and my pleas by anticipating what I was going to say. "I did not want you to be able to accuse me," he said, "of having lacked consideration for your testimony; and if my officer had found you at home, he was charged with informing you that the Sultan had no choice but to pass sentence on the two pashas. They were guilty."

However much I may have wanted to try to vindicate them, I could say nothing in the face of such a categorical statement. But while agreeing that

crimes of state deserve no indulgence, I asked the grand vizir if the one committed by Cheriber and Azet was to remain a mystery to me. He replied that
their crime and punishment would be made public the very next day, and that
he could grant me the small favor of informing me of them a few hours earlier. Aurisan Muley, the aga of the janissaries, had been irritated for a long
time with the court, which had taken steps to diminish his authority; he had
concocted a plan to put on the throne Prince Ahmet, the Sultan's second
brother, whom he had raised when he was a small child, and who had been
consigned to a cramped prison cell for a few months for some mocking
remarks about his brother he had let slip. It had been necessary to ascertain
this prince's feelings on the matter and establish some means of communication with him in his prison. The aga had succeeded in doing so quite
shrewdly by means that hadn't yet been elucidated, and this was the only
element that continued to trouble the minister. In yielding to the terrible
torture that had compelled him to confess his crime, he had steadfastly
refused to betray his friends, and the vizir himself admitted to me that he
could not help but admire him; but his close relations with Cheriber and
Dely Azet, who had succeeded each other as the last two pashas of Egypt,
had prompted the divan to have them arrested.[2] They both possessed immense fortunes, and their influence was still so powerful in Egypt that no
one doubted that they were the principal backers of the aga's plot. Indeed,
fearing the cruelties of torture, the thought of which was intolerable at their
age, they were forced to confess that they had been party to the conspiracy;
and the plan of the conspirators was to flee to Egypt with Ahmet if they
weren't immediately successful in placing him on the throne. Despite this
confession, they were subjected to various tortures in the hope of extracting
from them the names of all their accomplices, and especially to find out if
the bostangi bachi and the selictar were guilty. But whether they really didn't
know or they were as steadfast in their loyalty as the aga, they had gone to
their deaths without implicating them in any act of treason. "Four hours
ago," the grand vizir told me, "you would have found them stretched out on
the floor of my antichamber, for it was I who conducted their final interro-
gation, and the Sultan gave orders to have them executed as soon as I had
finished with them."[3]

Despite the shock I felt at such a recent catastrophe, whatever friendship
I still felt for the selictar prompted me to ask the minister if he had been
sufficiently vindicated to appear in public without fear. "Listen," he said. "I like

him and have no intention of harassing him for no good reason; but his flight has provoked some serious resentment at the council, and I would prefer that he not resurface without having leaked to the public some credible explication of his mysterious absence. And since he made the decision to seek asylum in your house, keep him there," he added, "until you hear from me." I took the vizir's show of confidence in me for another favor, and I thanked him for it; but since I was still unaware that the selictar was in my home, I thought it in my interest to disabuse him of this idea, and I protested so sincerely that I had just come from Oru, where I had spent the night before and the whole following day, and was certain no one had seen the selictar there, that he preferred to believe that his spies had misinformed him rather than put my honesty into question.

My trip being considerably shortened by this unfortunate outcome, I was delighted at the idea of getting back to Oru before night's end, and I felt sure I could be there early enough to surprise the selictar in my garden. I was already calculating how I could keep him from getting away. But when I returned to my house in Constantinople, I found my valet waiting for me with the utmost impatience; he asked to speak with me immediately and in private. "I bring you news," he said, "that will be both shocking and distressing for you. Synèse is dying from a wound he received from the selictar. Théophé has been scared to death and is scarcely better off than Synèse. Bema is a miserable wretch who I believe is at the bottom of all this commotion, and I've taken the precaution of having her locked up until your return. I believe that your presence is sorely needed at Oru," he continued, "if only to thwart the selictar's plans; he cannot be far from your estate, and he is capable of returning with enough men to take it over. His show of remorse for his violent acts seems very suspect to me. As he was alone, I would have had him arrested myself if I had not feared incurring your displeasure. However," my valet added, "since I've put the rest of the servants on their guard, you should not have to worry about anything he may attempt."

Since such an unexpected event could hardly leave me free of worry, I left immediately, taking the precaution of bringing along with me four well-armed servants. The state of anxiety in which I found my servants at Oru was clear proof that nothing had been exaggerated. They were standing guard at my gate, with a dozen rifles I used for hunting. I asked them for news of Théophé and Synèse, as I was still in the dark about what had happened to them. They were as unaware as I that he hadn't left my house, and since no one knew how the selictar had gotten in, this scene was becoming downright comical because of all the precautions they were taking to prevent him from getting into the house, whereas he had never left it. Nonetheless, having asked them to explain more fully the circumstances, I learned everything that they had managed to discover. Synèse's cries had drawn them to Théophé's apartment, where they had found the young man struggling with the selictar and already suffering from a dagger wound that could well have been fatal. Bema seemed to be siding against him also and was urging the selictar to punish him. They had separated them. The selictar very adroitly slipped away, and Synèse was left bathed in his own blood, while Théophé, trembling and nearly in a faint, pleaded with my servants not to lose a moment in informing me of the events.[4]

The fact that she had thought of me touched me so deeply that I went immediately to her apartment. I was even more reassured by her obvious delight at seeing me. I approached her bed. She seized my hand and held it tightly in hers. "Good heavens!" she said, pouring out her apparently heartfelt relief. "What horrors I've seen during your absence! You would have found me dead of fright if you had not returned so quickly." The tone in which she spoke these few words seemed so natural and tender that I felt not only all my suspicions evaporate, but also the attention I should have been paying to the events that had occurred, and I was tempted to respond to the first real sign of affection she had demonstrated for me. However, I kept all my joy hidden in my heart, and contenting myself with kissing her hands, I said to Théophé, with ill-concealed emotion, "Tell me what I am to think of the horrors you complain of. Tell me how you can complain of them when they took place in your room. What was the selictar doing here? And what about Synèse? None of my servants knows. Will you tell me the truth about all this?"

"This is precisely what I had feared," she said. "I knew that you would find everything that has happened here incomprehensible, and that you would not be able to avoid some suspicions about me; but I swear to heaven that I understand no better than you what has just happened. You had scarcely left," she continued, "and I was preparing to go to bed when Bema came and treated me to a long harangue to which I barely paid any attention. She made fun of my penchant for reading and for the other activities I enjoy. She spoke to me of sentimental involvements and of the enjoyment women of my age find in the pleasures of love. She told me a hundred love stories that seemed to be intended as reproaches for not following such attractive examples. She sounded out my feelings with various questions; and as this excessive attention, which she had never paid me before, was becoming annoying, I suffered all the more from having to listen to her since she had given me to understand that you had granted her a certain authority over me, and that she was determined to use it to make me happy. She finally left after putting me to bed, and hardly a moment had passed when I heard someone open my door quietly. I recognized Synèse in the candlelight. I was more surprised than frightened at seeing him; however, recalling everything you had told me, I would have expressed some concern if it hadn't occurred to me that you might have forgiven him upon arriving in Constantinople, and that you might have sent him back to Oru with some orders for me. Since that would have explained his visit, I allowed him to approach. He launched into a series of complaints about his fate, which I interrupted when it became clear to me that he hadn't been sent by you. Amid a new stream of laments about his suffering, he threw himself to his knees before my bed in a state of extreme agitation. It was at this very moment that Bema entered the room with the selictar; please do not ask me to recount what my increasing confusion prevented me from seeing clearly. I heard Bema's cries berating Synèse for his audacity and urging the selictar to punish him for it. They were both armed. Threatened, Synèse prepared to defend himself. But when he was wounded by the selictar, he grabbed onto him, and I could see the two daggers flashing in the air as they each attempted to strike the other and parry his blows. The noise of their struggle rather than my cries, which my terror rendered too feeble to be heard, brought your servants running; and all that I have been able to gather since that moment is that someone had left at my urging to beg you to return immediately."

Her innocence was so clear in this account that, regretting having suspected her, I endeavored on the contrary to relieve her of the fear I could see still lingering in her eyes. And perhaps, in the midst of my ardent expressions of devotion, which appeared to touch her, I might have gradually gained what I had given up asking from her, if my own resolutions had not fortified me against my desires. But my plan was set; and I believe that, in view of my renewed feelings for her, I would have been disappointed to find in her a licentiousness that would have lowered her somewhat in my esteem.

However, while I didn't allow myself to give any indication of the pleasure I was feeling, I derived enough satisfaction from this encounter to consider the mysteries I had yet to solve to be events of less importance to me, which I was going to examine with my mind at ease. "Remember," I said to Théophé, to share with her some of my hopes, "you have given me today a glimpse of what I expect to discover some day more fully." She appeared uncertain of the meaning of my words. "I think I've been clear enough," I continued, and I was convinced in fact, when I left her, that she had pretended not to understand me. I sent for Bema immediately. This duplicitous slave thought for a few minutes that she could deceive me with lies. She attempted to persuade me that it was by pure chance that the selictar had arrived at my estate at nightfall, and having noticed at the very moment that she had met him that Synèse was in Théophé's apartment, she had been prompted by her devotion to the honor of my house to beg this lord to punish the insult I was suffering from this reckless young man. Having seen the selictar disappear before she was put under arrest, she was sure that if he hadn't simply left my house, he would have secretly returned to his hiding place, and in either case she would have time to inform him of the story she had concocted to defend him. But I had lived too long in Turkey not to know the power that a master has over his slaves, and seeing no reason for the selictar to slip away if he had come to my house with honest intentions, I resolved to resort to the harshest measures to get to the truth. The reasons why my valet had arrested Bema had to carry at least as much weight for me as for him. In short, I spoke of torture to my slave, and since the tone I used led her to take my threats seriously, she began trembling and proceeded to confess her whole scheme.

When I had satisfied myself that the selictar hadn't seen Théophé other than during the events of that evening, I was inclined to see in his adventure more reason to tease him about his bad luck than to be offended by his stay in my house. Bema succeeded in dispelling any lingering traces of my resentment by informing me of the principal reasons that had led him to hide his presence from me. But since whatever served to mitigate my friend's guilt could in no way justify her actions, I informed her that I would determine in good time the punishment she deserved for betraying my trust; and it was then that she swore by the Prophet that I would have had nothing to reproach her if I had only granted her my full confidence. My anger was greatly mollified by this frankness. It remained to learn from her what could have become of the selictar. She answered promptly that she thought he had returned to her room; and to find out for sure, all I had to do was check to see if the door was closed. Since this was indeed the case, there was little doubt that he was there, and the only revenge I planned for him was to leave him there until hunger forced him to come out, and to post my valet at the door to take charge of him when he was forced to make his appearance. Bema, whom I had left under arrest, was in no position to interfere with the satisfaction I anticipated from this scene.

She had not been able to shed any light on Synèse's presence, since no one had been more surprised than she when she had seen him in Théophé's apartment. But he caused me so little concern that when I learned that his wound was indeed very serious, I simply ordered that he be given the care he needed and put off seeing him until he had begun to recover. Whether he had never left my house, or whether he had returned after leaving, I was simply dealing with the disloyalty of one of my servants, and this was hardly important enough for me to rush to punish him. And as soon as I was assured of Théophé's honorable behavior, I was so little concerned with this young Greek's love for her that, on the contrary, I foresaw that she might be able to use it to her advantage with her father. This thought had not occurred to me at first, but my reflections since my last conversation with him had led me to conclude that if his passion continued to burn so fiercely, it would provide me an opportunity to put his father to another test by pretending to want to marry him and Théophé. If Lord Condoidi hadn't completely lost his sense of honor and religion along with the paternal sentiments normally dictated by nature, I found it impossible to believe that he would not oppose this incestuous union; and in a country where fathers' rights were extremely limited, I could force him to resort to this objection to prevent it from occurring.

Thus these incidents that had caused me such acute alarm had no other unfortunate consequences than Synèse's wound and the chastisement of some servants. I got rid of Bema a few days later, with the added humiliation for her that I sold her for only half of what she had cost me. It is a kind of punishment that is reserved for the wealthy, who are at the same time kind enough not to treat a guilty slave too rigorously; but to the extent that these wretched creatures have feelings at all, they are all the more chastened in that they have lost some value in their own eyes and feel reduced, if that is possible to conceive, even lower than their sad station in life. Nonetheless, I learned that Bema had appealed to the selictar, who, out of gratitude, had bought her for his seraglio.

As for him, I was denied the pleasure I had hoped for in seeing him yield to thirst or hunger. That very night, deducing from the long absence of his confidante that she had been detained and that he was going to find himself in an extreme dilemma without her help, he resolved not to wait for daybreak to leave his hiding place, and being familiar with my house, he was confident he could easily escape under cover of darkness. He was grabbed by my valet, who was already at his post. I was perhaps exposing this loyal fellow to die from a stroke of the selictar's dagger; but being aware of the danger himself, he was careful to reassure the selictar quickly so that he understood at once that he was in no danger, and that I intended only to treat him graciously and offer him my good services. He allowed himself to be led to me, remaining on his guard. I was in bed. I hastened to arise, and feigning extreme surprise, I cried out, "What in heaven? It's the selictar! How on earth . . . ?" He interrupted me somewhat sheepishly. "Spare me," he said, "the mockery I deserve. Your reproaches are completely justified if you limit them to the visit I tried to pay Théophé last night; I only used my dagger with the intention of serving you, although it became clear, from the urgency with which your men tore from my grasp the young man I wounded, that my ardor was misguided; and as for the liberty I took in hiding in your home without consulting you, you should only see in my behavior the concern of a friend who, in choosing your house as a refuge, did not want to expose you to the displeasure of the court." I interrupted him in turn to assure him that I required no justifications from him, and as regarded Théophé herself, the only thing I found reprehensible in his conduct was what surely had to be offensive to him as well; that is, a course of action that did not seem to reflect the refinement that he had exhibited in his sentiments up until then. He made no objection to this rebuke. "The opportunity," he said, "overwhelmed my virtue." The remainder of this conversation was just playful banter. I assured him that the most serious consequence of his adventure would be to have more comfortable lodgings and to receive better treatment than in Bema's room, without being any more exposed to the dangers that had prompted him to go into hiding. I then told him what I had learned from the grand vizir, which relieved him greatly on his own account while provoking deep sympathy for the aga of the janissaries and the two pashas. However, he protested that he had less sympathy for them if they were guilty and added that far from joining their plot, he would have been capable of breaking off relations with them completely if he had had any reasons to suspect them. He appeared ready to leave immediately and spoke of alerting two slaves whom he had told to wait for his orders in the neighboring village. But I explained to him the precautions the grand vizir had advised him to take before returning to Constantinople. Among several courses of action he could adopt, he decided to follow my advice and go to his country estate, as if he had just returned from visiting the Black Sea arsenals. I even agreed to accompany him, and to show him that I harbored no ill will for what had happened, and that I still had the same good opinion of him that had led me to seek his friendship, I suggested that we bring Théophé along on our outing.

He could scarcely convince himself that this offer was sincere; but I was so serious that after spending the rest of the night with him I accompanied him to Théophé's apartment myself to seek her approval of our plan. The impression left by my last conversation with her made me feel invulnerable to any sort of jealousy, and I was so certain that the selictar would never be able to touch her heart that I virtually exulted over the useless attempts he was going to make to gain her affections. In any case, whatever success my own feelings might meet, I didn't want him ever to be able to reproach me for creating the slightest obstacle to his. I owed him this indulgence after having perhaps contributed to the rise of his own sentiments by approving them so nonchalantly at the outset; and if Théophé ever developed the feelings I desired from her, I would be very much relieved that my friend had lost all hope before learning that I was more fortunate than he.

If Théophé at first expressed some surprise at our plans, she made no objection when she understood clearly that I was to be at her side at all times, and that it was just a matter of accompanying me. I gave her a retinue that would allow her to appear with some distinction at the selictar's home. He had referred to his house as the center of his power and pleasures; that is, along with all the embellishments prized by the Turks, there was a harem and an enormous number of slaves. I had heard it praised, moreover, as the most beautiful place in the country surrounding Constantinople. It was eight miles from my house. We didn't arrive there until evening, so I was denied that day the pleasure of the view, which is perhaps unparalleled in any other place in the world. But the selictar immediately lavished upon us all the riches and elegant accessories that he had amassed within the buildings, and I was forced to admit from the very first moment that I had never seen anything in either France or Italy that surpassed this beautiful sight.

I promise you no description.[5] These details are always tiresome in a book; but I feared for a moment that I would have reason to regret bringing Théophé along on this trip when the selictar, after gaining her admiration for so much magnificence, offered to put it at her entire disposal, while repeating all of his earlier declarations. I had some difficulty hiding the flush of emotion that spread over my face, despite myself. I glanced at Théophé and awaited her response with an anxiety that she later confessed had not escaped her. While assuring the selictar that she was sensitive to his sumptuous offers, and that she felt all the gratitude that he had a right to expect, she described her feelings to him as the most bizarre mixture in the world and the least likely to lead her to appreciate the benefits that usually appeal to a woman's vanity. Although the tone of her response seemed quite light-hearted, she made remarks about wisdom and happiness that were so judicious and so sensible that I couldn't help admiring such an unexpected disquisition, and I wondered in my amazement where she had gotten her ideas. The conclusion she drew was that the rest of her life would be devoted to the practice of the principles that she admitted she owed to my teaching, and for which she believed she owed me much more gratitude than for her liberty. The discomfort I had suffered earlier was now beginning to appear on the selictar's face instead. He complained bitterly of his fate; and addressing me now, he beseeched me to lend him some of the power that Théophé attributed to my words. I replied, bantering, that the desire he expressed was contrary to his own interests, since if his desires were fulfilled he would only succeed in reinforcing Théophé's principles. In fact, my heart was bursting with joy, and no longer doubting my good fortune, I thought it was more clearly assured by this declaration than by all the reasons I already had to feel confident. I stole a moment to congratulate Théophé on her noble sentiments, and I took her response for yet another confirmation of my hopes.

The selictar, who was as distressed as I believed I was happy, continued nevertheless to offer us with the same attentiveness everything that did honor to his graciousness and to the beauty of his home. He permitted us that very evening to enter his harem, and his intention was perhaps to tempt Théophé by the sight of a charming domain where she could reign supreme. But if she was struck by something, it was neither the riches nor the pleasures that abounded on all sides. The memory of the condition that she had escaped came back to her so poignantly that I saw her fall into a deep melancholy that afflicted her for several days. The very next day she took advantage of

Le Seliktar-Agassi, ou porte épée du Grand Seigneur.

Fig. 5 The selictar, or the sword bearer of the Sultan. From Ferriol, *Recueil de cent estampes*, 1714. Art and Architecture Collection, Miriam and Ira D. Wallach Division of Art, Prints and Photographs, The New York Public Library, Astor, Lenox and Tilden Foundations.

the liberty that the selictar had given us to return to the harem on our own as often as we liked to spend part of the day there, where she passed her time conversing with the women whose appearance had touched her the most. The selictar was enchanted by the pleasure she seemed to take in such a long visit, whereas I couldn't help feeling a little alarmed. But since I could not follow her without being indiscreet, I waited until she came out to rejoin her. She seemed so sad that I couldn't bring myself to reprove her. I asked her, on the contrary, what had happened that had changed her mood so drastically. She invited me to take a walk in the garden with her, without answering my question. Her continued silence began to puzzle me when she finally indicated by a long sigh that she was going to speak. "What variety there is in the vicissitudes of life!" she said, with that philosophical turn she spontaneously gave to all her observations. "What strange sequence of things that are so dissimilar and so incongruous! I have just made a discovery that has affected me deeply and given me some ideas that I wish to share with you. But I first need to soften your heart with a story.

"The keen interest," she continued, "that I couldn't help taking in the fate of so many unfortunate women, an interest I am sure you will deem excusable after my own misfortunes, led me to question a few of the selictar's slaves about the circumstances that had brought them to the seraglio. Most of them are girls from Circassia or from neighboring countries who were raised for this life, and who do not feel humiliated by it.[6] But the one whom I just left is a foreigner whose sweetness and modesty made an even greater impression on me than her striking looks. I took her aside. I praised her beauty and youth. She reacted sadly to my flattery and astonished me with her response: 'Alas!' she said. 'If you are capable of feeling any pity, far from prizing these miserable advantages, consider them rather a tragic gift from heaven that makes me detest life every moment of the day.' I promised her much more than pity, and giving her to understand that I could help console her, I urged her to explain to me the cause of such strange despair. She told me, after shedding some tears, that she was born in Sicily of a father whose superstitions had cost her both her liberty and her honor. He was the son of a mother who had ruined her reputation by debauchery, and the same unlucky star had led him to marry a woman who, after deceiving him for a long while by her virtuous pretenses, had in the end brought dishonor upon herself by her blatant dissipation. When his daughter, now the selictar's slave, was born, he had sworn to heaven that he would keep her virtuous by such an austere upbringing that she would be able to restore the family's honor. When she was still very young, he had shut her up in a castle that he had in the country, under the supervision of two elderly and virtuous ladies, whom he had admonished, upon giving them their charge, not to let his daughter know that she was blessed with any exceptional physical qualities, and never to speak to her of a woman's beauty as if it were an advantage deserving of any attention. In addition to these precautions, they brought her up in the constant practice of all the virtues and succeeded in making her life so innocent until the age of seventeen that she had never entertained anything in her heart or mind that would have been contrary to her father's goals. She had noticed, on the rare occasions that she appeared in public with her two governesses, that she drew stares from a number of people who seemed to be moved by some peculiar emotion upon seeing her. However, since she had never used a mirror, and the two old women were constantly vigilant to keep out of her presence anything that could lead her to think about how she looked, she had never had the slightest suspicion that she was attractive. She was living in this state of innocence when her governesses allowed into the castle one of those peddlers who roam the countryside with their pack of jewelry; solely by chance she picked up a little box that contained a mirror. She was so naïve that she imagined that the reflection of her face was a portrait attached to the box, and her gaze lingered so long on this agreeable sight that the two old women finally noticed it. Their shrieks and the rebukes they hastened to shower upon her would have alone sufficed to disabuse her if the peddler, who had understood the cause of their admonishments, had not taken a moment to approach the young Sicilian and slip her one of his mirrors, suggesting to her that it was a great wrong to deprive her of this object. It was her shyness alone that prompted her to accept it, since she still had no idea of its use, but as soon as she was alone it took her only a moment to understand. Even if she had not been capable of perceiving by herself the gifts nature had bestowed upon her, a comparison with the two old women whom she constantly had before her eyes would have been enough for her to notice that the difference was distinctly to her advantage. She soon found so much pleasure in gazing at herself constantly, arranging her hair, and dressing more attractively that, while not knowing what use she could put these charms to, she began to understand that what gave her so much pleasure would inevitably have the same effect on others.[7]

"During this time the peddler, who had been extremely amused by his adventure, delighted in relating it everywhere he went. His description of the young Sicilian's charms piqued the curiosity and the desires of a Knight of Malta who had just taken his final vows to his order with little intention of respecting them.[8] He found his way to the castle and managed to smuggle in to this young lady a mirror that, in a larger box than the peddler's, contained opposite the mirror the portrait of a very handsome young man, along with a tender letter designed to inform her of everything that had been so carefully hidden from her. The portrait, which was that of the knight, produced the intended effect, and the information in the letter became so useful that it served to overcome many obstacles. The young lady, whose governesses had never referred to men other than as instruments that heaven had chosen to help women propagate the human race, and who had prepared her to respect the sanctity of marriage, was careful not to listen to the knight's declarations of love without asking him if he intended to become her husband. He spared no promises when he realized how he could benefit from them, and alleging personal reasons for keeping his commitments secret, it took him only a few days to subvert her father's plans and circumvent the vigilance of the two governesses. This affair went on untroubled for some time. But since the Sicilian girl was beginning to feel some remorse, as well as some fear for the future, she became more insistent over the promises she had exacted. It became impossible for the knight to disguise any longer that he was a member of an order that forbade him to marry. Tears and reproaches prevailed for a few days. However, they were sincerely in love. The worst misfortune of all would have been to be separated. Any other miseries were trivial in the face of this fear, and to escape the dire consequences they could not avoid, they resolved to leave Sicily and take refuge in some country ruled by the Turks. The two lovers had no reason to feel guilty; since they both were born into a great fortune, each was making the same sacrifice for love.

"Their intention to take refuge voluntarily in a Turkish country would have protected them from slavery had they been able to prove it. But having embarked on a Venetian ship with the intention of getting off in Dalmatia, confident they could push on farther from there, they had the misfortune to be taken captive at the entrance to the gulf by several Turkish vessels that were trying to provoke the State of Venice. The explanation of their plan was taken for an attempt at deception. They were sold separately in a Morean port, from which the unfortunate Sicilian girl was brought to Constantinople. If it was the height of misfortune to see her lover torn away from her, what words could begin to describe the situation in which she soon found herself! Since her incessant weeping had altered her features somewhat, the merchants in Constantinople did not realize immediately the profits they could reap from her beauty. An old woman who had a sharper eye used part of her fortune to buy her, certain that she could resell her for twice as much. But this was the most disastrous thing that could have befallen the Sicilian girl. Given the principles of modesty and virtue in which she had been raised, the attempts that this odious mistress made to enhance her charms and to make her more appealing to Turkish men were such a torture that she would have found death less cruel. In the end she had been sold for a large sum to the selictar, who had shown her great affection at the beginning but, inevitably put off by her deep sadness and perpetual tears, subsequently neglected her after satisfying his desires."

The account of the adventures of this sad foreigner did little more than surprise Théophé. What really filled her with compassion was seeing how acutely she suffered from the ignominy of her fate and discerning in her such shame and grief that she had not been able to determine what afflicted her the most, the loss of her honor or of her lover. I was so accustomed to these kinds of situations by the tales I heard every day that I hadn't listened to hers with the level of sympathy she had expected. "You do not seem to be moved," she said, "by what I thought would touch you as much as it did me. Do you not feel that this girl deserves the interest I have taken in her predicament?" "I feel sorry for her," I replied, "but much less so than if she had not been responsible for her plight by a deliberate moral failing. And that is the difference," I added, "between your misfortunes and hers. You may well be the only example of a comparable hapless woman who has retained her innocence and the only member of your sex who, after being dragged over the precipice without realizing it, was instantly transformed into an honorable woman at the first mention of the name and concept of virtue. And this is what makes you so admirable in my eyes," I continued in my enthusiasm, "that I put you above all the other woman in the world." Théophé shook her head, smiling very gently; and without responding to his remarks about her, she returned to the Sicilian girl's feelings, which she deemed worthy of any efforts we could make to obtain her freedom. "Your wish is my command," I replied, "and I don't want you to owe even this favor to the selictar." He was coming to join us when I promised to speak to him about it that very day. I decided to make my request immediately. And taking him aside as if I wanted to hide my remarks from Théophé, I asked him casually if he were so attached to the Sicilian girl that it would be difficult for him to let me have her. "She is yours as of now," he said; and when I spoke of the price, he rejected the very idea as if it were an insult. I judged by his joy, moreover, that in addition to the satisfaction it gave him to do me a favor, he was convinced that this would be yet another reason for me to support his overtures to Théophé, not to mention that my example might lead her to think more about the pleasures of love. But in granting me the liberty to open his harem's door for his slave, he informed me of a detail that she had hidden from Théophé. "At first I assumed she was stricken only by the loss of her liberty, and I did my utmost to reconcile her to her fate; but I discovered by chance that she is passionately in love with a young slave from her country who was clever enough to get a letter to her in my harem, and whom I refrained from punishing out of consideration for his master, who is one of my friends. I have no idea how this affair began, and I simply put my servants on alert to protect my house from this kind of disorder. But it served to dampen my affection for my Sicilian slave, whose many charms I had truly admired." This information, which the selictar thought he owed our friendship, would have been a very wise precaution if I had been subject to the desires he assumed I had. But since my only interest was to please Théophé, I imagined on the contrary, to my delight, that the young slave the selictar was complaining about could only be the Sicilian knight, and I foresaw that I would soon be forced to free him from his chains as well. I nonetheless waited to be alone with Théophé to let her know that the Sicilian girl was ours. She was so ecstatic to hear me add that I thought the knight was nearby, and that I was planning to reunite him with his mistress, that she thanked me on their behalf with extraordinary emotion. Since I interpreted everything in relation to my own desires, I had no doubt that this sentimental interest she took in the happiness of two lovers was a sign that her heart had softened, and I reached the conclusion that my own chances were much more promising than the selictar's.

The Sicilian's name was Maria Rezati, and the name she had taken or been given as a slave was Molene. I did not consider it appropriate to inform her of what I had done for her until the day of our departure. I simply advised Théophé to tell her that she could anticipate an unexpected happy event. The news that the selictar received from Constantinople having reassured him, I was called back to the city by my own affairs and suggested to Théophé that she return to Oru. But in addition to the disappointment I felt at not being able to discourage the selictar from accompanying us on our trip, I was forced to witness a very awkward scene upon leaving his house with him. The Sicilian knight, who was indeed a slave at a nearby estate, had enough freedom of movement to steal from his duties a few hours each day that he used to observe the walls of the selictar's house. The peril to which he had been exposed by the betrayal of another slave had done so little to cool his passion that he had attempted numerous times to find a way into the compound despite the constant danger. We were leaving around the middle of the day in a large barouche that I had acquired for use in the country. He was stationed twenty feet from the gate, and he saw several of my people come out on horseback, gathering together to wait for me. Struck by their French attire, he asked them in our language, which he spoke rather fluently, who their master was. I have no idea what plan he could have formulated based on their response, but scarcely had he heard it when, seeing my coach come out carrying the selictar, the two ladies, and myself, he easily recognized his mistress. His excitement was beyond his control. He leapt to my door and clung to it despite the lively pace of six powerful horses, begging me to give him a moment to explain. He was so frenzied that he was out of breath, and his frantic efforts to hold on and to gain my ear made him look like a madman out to do some evil deed. We hadn't noticed that Maria Rezati, or Molene, had fainted on the seat beside us. But when the selictar's servants, who were following with his baggage, spotted a slave who seemed to be acting disrespectfully toward their master and me, they rushed up and tore him violently from my door. Suspecting what was really going on, I cried out to the coachman to stop. He finally managed to rein in his horses. I called off the selictar's men, who were still roughing up the young slave, and ordered them to bring him over to me. The selictar was utterly perplexed by this scene and by my interest in it. But the knight's explanations soon elucidated for him what I had already understood. This unfortunate young man managed to calm down enough to get his breath back, and assuming naturally the demeanor that befitted his high birth, he spoke to me in a manner so touching that I could never reproduce it here. After briefly relating his story and his mistress's, he noticed when he went to introduce her that she was lying unconscious beside me. "Ah! Look at her," he suddenly cried out, beside himself with worry. "She is dying. Do something for her. Alas! She is dying," he continued, "and you are doing nothing to help her!"

It was not difficult to revive her. Joy serves only to restore one's strength when it doesn't suffocate you immediately.[9] She turned toward Théophé: "It's he," she cried. "Ah! It's the knight; it's he." I didn't need her confirmation to understand what was going on. After reassuring the young slave with my reply, I asked the selictar if his relations with the slave's master were good enough for him to guarantee that his absence would not have serious consequences. He assured me that he was one of his best friends; and with a courtesy that I admired in Turkey, when I had informed him of my desire to take the knight to Oru, he sent one of his men back to ask his friend, who was an army officer, permission to use his slave for a few days. "I foresee," he said after giving his orders, "that you are going to have further recourse to my services, but in anticipating your request by offering my help, I must inform you that whatever Nady Emir refuses to do for me he will do for no one else." We had extra horses. I gave one to the knight, who was overcome with joy. However, he managed to get himself under control, and aware of the behavior that his garb and position still required, he refrained both from approaching his mistress and from speaking in a manner that did not befit his miserable state.

During the remainder of our trip I couldn't avoid admitting to the selictar that it was my desire to help out these unfortunate lovers that had prompted me to ask him to free Molene, and I accepted his offer to serve as intermediary in the efforts to obtain the young knight's release from Nady Emir. Théophé's keen interest in the matter further fueled his desire to be of service. We arrived at Oru. The knight moved away discreetly while we were getting out of our carriage, but he asked me a moment later to let him see me in private, and the favor he asked me on his knees, calling me his father and savior, was to permit him to dispense with his slave's garb immediately. Although the slightest disguise is a crime for a slave, I didn't think it would be dangerous for him under the circumstances. He appeared a few moments later dressed in a way that changed his manners as much as his figure; and knowing already that his mistress was free, or that I was now her only master, he asked me permission to embrace her. This scene touched us even more. I once again pleaded with the selictar to intervene in his favor, and even though I had no particular relationship with Nady Emir, I was confident that the esteem in which I was held among the Turks would suffice to obtain what I sought from him myself.

The selictar's stubborn insistence on accompanying us forced me to rein in feelings that, I now confess, could scarcely have been stronger. With the certainty that my charming Théophé would be forever virtuous, I was no less certain that I had gained her affections and resolved to speak to her so clearly that she would be able to overcome her shyness, which I now believed was the only thing that restrained her. But I wanted to be free for such an important undertaking. The selictar had assumed that we would return together to Constantinople. To get him to agree to hasten our departure, I exaggerated the importance of the affairs that required my presence there. The knight made the trip with us. In addition to the reasons regarding his liberty, I had another motive not to leave him at Oru in my absence; or at the very least I had to make a decision about a difficulty that troubled me somewhat. Since it was very unlikely that he intended to return to Sicily with his mistress, and since it was even less likely that he could be alone with her without resuming their amorous relations, I wondered if it were proper for me to allow such licentious behavior in my house. My principles were no stricter than those governing typical love affairs, and I did not consider it a crime for these two lovers to make each other as happy as I would have liked to be with Théophé, but if the passion of youth causes people to forget sometimes the laws dictated by religion, moral respectability serves to set limits, and I was myself constrained by the proprieties of my office, which imposed on me a multitude of obligations. These scruples would have led me to make some decisions that would not have been to the knight's liking if he hadn't spared me this trouble upon our arrival in Constantinople. He declared that after the favor I was going to do for him, he planned to go back to Sicily, not only in order to procure the means to reimburse me the expenses I was going to incur in obtaining his liberty, but also to find out if there was any hope for him to be able to repudiate his vows. His misfortune had given him a more mature outlook. He realized that Maria Rezati was an only child whose virtue and prospects of inheritance he had ruined. She possessed countless qualities that he continued to love; even the thought of her service in the harem was indifferent to him; and she had enough wealth to satisfy his ambitions. All of these reflections, which he shared with me very calmly and wisely, had brought him to the decision to spare no effort to obtain the freedom to marry her.

I praised his intentions, although I foresaw difficulties that did not appear to daunt him. The selictar wasted no time seeing Nady Emir, who had returned to the city. He obtained ownership of the knight as easily as he had expected. But despite his generosity, which still led him to prefer to give him to me as a gift, I used the fact that I would myself be reimbursed as a way to convince him to accept from me the thousand sequins he had given Nady. After learning of the young Sicilian's feelings, I did not hesitate to send him back to his mistress. He intended only to say his good-byes to her, and in his burning desire to undertake a trip on which his happiness depended entirely, it was only with some difficulty that I persuaded him to rest a few days at Oru. However, when I saw him there two days later I was quite surprised from the moment of my arrival to learn that he had changed his mind. I wasn't able to perceive immediately what was behind this mysterious change of heart, so I simply asked him what plans were going to replace the ones he had abandoned. He told me that after a great deal of additional reflection on the difficulty of bringing off his initial project successfully and on the risks of getting into trouble with his order or with the Rezatis, he had returned to his former idea of taking up residence in Turkey; that several promising prospects had opened up for him in Morea, and that he would still marry his mistress because since he was giving up his status as a Knight of Malta he didn't feel obliged to fulfill the duties of a vocation whose advantages he had completely forsworn; and finally that since he hadn't yet touched a rather large sum of money that was being held for him in letters of change for Ragusa that he had left in cash with a banker in Messina, he felt sure that he would be rich enough to pay me back the amount I had given the selictar and then lead a simple life in the country where he wanted to make his home.[10] He added that his mistress was the daughter of a very wealthy father who would not live forever, and since she could not be denied the rights that nature gave her to this inheritance, sooner or later she would receive more than either of them desired to make their life quite comfortable and to leave something to their children, if it pleased heaven to grant them any.

A plan conceived so quickly seemed to me too well devised not to suspect that it came from some extraordinary event. Nonetheless, I would never have suspected that it came from Synèse. The knight hadn't been able to spend two days at Oru without learning that this young Greek was also there, with a dangerous wound. He had gone to see him out of courtesy, and finding him quite amiable, he quickly became such good friends with him that he told him his adventures. The distress that his marriage plans were causing him had led Synèse to concoct this admirable plan by which he was persuaded he could serve his own interests also. He had offered the knight a refuge in his father's lands, and revealing in his turn the torments of his heart, they had come to believe, confiding more and more in each other, that Théophé, by love or by interest, would let herself be convinced to join them. They had in no way obtained her consent, and Synèse had warned his friend about the delicate nature of this negotiation; they felt certain that with the help of Maria Rezati, who had embraced wholeheartedly this plan, they would get her to understand that whether she was Paniota Condoidi's daughter or whether she fell in love with Synèse, she could not hope for a happier outcome for a girl from the same country.

Although the knight had raised my suspicions, they were so little focused on Synèse and my own interests that not wanting to pry further into his affairs, I did not make the slightest objection to his project. "The cost of your freedom," I said, "should not be a subject of concern to you, and I would have gladly given a greater sum if it would have contributed to your happiness." However, I imagined that Théophé must be at least aware of the new plot. I couldn't wait, of course, to see her. My impatience was so acute that the three days I had been forced to spend in the city had seemed intolerably long, and when I occasionally reflected seriously on the state of my heart, I was somewhat embarrassed to have allowed it to assume such power over me. But having made up my mind to devote myself to a passion that my complete happiness now depended on, I dismissed anything that could have diminished the force of such a delightful feeling.

I entered Théophé's apartment resolved not to come out without having reached a clear agreement with her. I found her with Maria Rezati. What a dreadful constraint! They had become extremely fond of each other, and the Sicilian, unable to imagine that we were anything but lovers, had already made some allusions to the happiness of an affair so serene as she assumed ours to be. These remarks had displeased Théophé. Scarcely had she received my first compliments when she turned to her companion: "Given your misunderstanding," she said to her, "you will be surprised to learn from Monsieur that I owe nothing to his love, and that I can only attribute the favors he has showered upon me to his generosity." They both seemed to be waiting for my response. I couldn't see clearly what they had been discussing; and speaking from the heart I answered that I had in fact never fallen in love just for a woman's beauty and had been motivated only by my admiration when I first came to her aid. "But your character becomes so quickly obvious," I continued, turning my impassioned gaze on her, "and when one has discovered all your qualities, it is simply impossible not to devote all one's love . . ." Théophé, seeing where this language was leading, interrupted me shrewdly. "I have to recognize," she said, "that your own favors may indeed have induced you to feel some friendship for me, and this is a treasure that I consider so precious that I will forever prefer it to wealth or pleasure." She immediately changed the subject. I was so uncertain about what to think that it put me in a very strange state of mind. But not being able to bear this anguishing situation for long, I resolved to do something that would appear childish to anyone but a person in love.

I entered Théophé's sitting room alone, and only too aware of how severely my hopes had been set back, I took up my pen in order not to put off any longer what I foresaw that I would not have the strength to say to Théophé's face, given the fear and bitterness the preceding scene had caused me. I put briefly into words the most intense and touching things a heart brimming with respect and love could say to appeal to her affections; and although there was nothing obscure in my language, I reiterated at the end, to be perfectly clear, that I was not speaking of friendship, which was far too cold a sentiment to describe the passion reigning in my heart, and that I was devoting my whole life to love.[11] I added nonetheless that while I had managed to keep my love in check up to then with a measure of restraint that she had to acknowledge, I still wanted it to depend on the desires of the person I loved. My only hope being that she shared my feelings, I left it to her to choose her manner of expressing it.

I returned much calmer after having unburdened myself with this declaration, and I asked Théophé coolly to step into the other room by herself. She soon reappeared with a solemn expression and beseeched me to go back into the room she had just left. Below my message, I found another written by her. It was so short and so extraordinary in nature that I've never forgotten it. "A miserable creature," she wrote, "who had learned from me the name of honor and virtue, and who still hadn't succeeded in learning that of her father, the slave of the governor of Patras and of Cheriber, did not feel capable of inspiring anything but pity." Therefore, she could not recognize herself as the object of my other feelings. A sharp cry escaped me upon reading this strange response. Fearing that I had had an accident, she appeared quickly in the doorway. I held out my arms to her to invite her to come hear me out, but despite the fact that she clearly saw this passionate gesture, she left to rejoin her companion as soon as she was reassured that I had not become ill. I stood there absolutely shattered. However, I couldn't simply renounce all my hopes, so I took up the pen again to erase the horrible portrait that she had painted of herself and composed another that depicted her on the contrary with all the perfections with which nature had adorned her. "Here is what I love," I added, "and the traits are so deeply engraved in my heart that it is impossible for me to be mistaken." I got up, walked to her side in the adjoining room, and suggested again that she go back into her sitting room. She smiled and begged me to give her more time to examine what I had left there.

This response consoled me. I nonetheless took my leave to try to dispel completely the distress I was still feeling. It seemed so astonishing to me that I needed to take such precautions to express my feelings to a girl I had plucked from a Turk's arms, and who in the first days of her freedom would perhaps have been only too happy to come right into my own, that despite the intoxication of my love, I reproached myself for a timorousness that was so at odds with my age and my experience. But in addition to some secret remorse that I could not avoid feeling when I recalled the chaste principles I had explained a thousand times to Théophé, and the fear of provoking her scorn by a passion whose object could, after all, only be the corruption of the virtuous feelings that I had helped her acquire, I would have to be able to give an adequate idea of her person to make it possible to understand that feminine charms that could only set a heart on fire became for this very reason eminently capable of imposing fear or respect when, instead of meeting the acquiescence that such attractiveness made one desire and that so many graces seemed to promise, one was not only halted by the fear of displeasing her, which is typical of anyone in love, but virtually kept at bay by the decency and respectability, by the appearance and language of all the virtues that one hardly expected to find behind such a seductive guise. Over and over again, following my natural principles of rectitude and honor, I resolved to stifle my passion and give free rein to Théophé's virtuous inclinations; but swept away by a passion that my very silence and moderation had constantly intensified, I could only manage each time to promise heaven to respect the limits I had set for myself, and I felt I was being extremely moderate by sticking to my resolution to ask of Théophé only what she was willing to give me of her own accord. I spent the rest of the day rather calmly, awaiting the new response for which she had requested more time to reflect, and I did not seek out any opportunities to speak to her alone. She appeared to avoid them also. I even noticed in her eyes a troubled look that I had never seen before.[12]

When I arose the following day, one of the slaves who served her brought me a letter carefully sealed. How eager I was to read it! But in what deep despondency I fell immediately upon finding in it a categorical condemnation that seemed to destroy the slightest hope I may have harbored. This devastating letter that Théophé had spent all night composing would have deserved to be related here in its entirety if certain reasons, which will be revealed later, and which I cannot recall without pain and shame, had not caused me to tear it to pieces in a terrible fit of spite. But the first reactions it provoked were only sadness and consternation. Théophé reiterated therein all the circumstances surrounding her story, that is, her misfortunes, her sins of the flesh, and my favors. And reasoning on the foregoing with more force and good sense than I've ever seen in our best books, she concluded that it behooved neither her, who had as many moral failings as tribulations to repair, to respond to a passion that could only renew them, nor me, who had been her moral mentor, to abuse both the rightful power that I held over her and the very inclination that she felt to love me for the purpose of destroying principles that she owed as much to my advice as to her own efforts. If, nonetheless, she ever became capable of forgetting moral obligations whose extent she was beginning to understand, she protested that I was the only man who could bring her to give in to that weakness. But in the name of this confession itself, which reflected the state of her affections, she begged me not to renew these declarations and attentions whose danger was clear to her; or if her presence was as harmful to my well-being as it appeared to her, she asked me for the liberty to adopt her former plan, which had been to retire to some peaceful spot in a Christian country so she couldn't be accused of undermining the happiness of a master and father to whom she owed, at the very least, the sacrifice of her own satisfaction.

I am giving short shrift to the ideas themselves that I remember from this letter, because I despair of rendering them with all the grace and force they had in their original expression. At the age I've reached upon writing these memoirs, I have to admit with some embarrassment that I didn't at first take so many sensible reflections as an homage to virtue. On the contrary, only seeing in them the frustration of all my desires, I abandoned myself to the regret of having given such strong weapons against myself to a girl of seventeen. "What possessed me," I said to myself bitterly, "to play the preacher and the catechist? How ridiculous for a man of my position and age! I needed to be sure that I could find in my precepts the remedy I need for myself. I needed to be convinced of all the things I was preaching to make them my own guide. Isn't it just pitiful that a man so attached to carnal pleasures as I am took it upon himself to try to make a girl chaste and virtuous? Ah! Such folly deserved to be punished." And pushing my ravings further, I recalled my conduct from the beginning in order to justify to myself in a certain sense the madness I was admitting. "But is it my fault?" I added. "What did I teach her that could have engendered in her this inflexible devotion to virtue? I drew to her attention the ignominy of love as it is practiced in Turkey, this overly facile acquiescence to men's desires, this vulgarity in the use of pleasures, this ignorance of everything that is called taste and feeling; but did I ever intend to make her averse to respectable love, to a proper affair, which is the most charming of all pleasures and the greatest advantage that a woman can derive from her beauty? She is the one who is mistaken, and who has misunderstood me. I want to make her aware of this; my honor obliges me to. It would be just too ridiculous for a man of the world to have led a young woman with such qualities to espouse principles that are suitable only for a convent."

Far from easily overcoming this first reaction, it occurred to me that my cardinal error was to have put into Théophé's hands a few works on morality whose principles, as it happens in most books of this kind, tended to be overly stern and could have been understood too literally by a girl encountering them for the first time. From the time that she had begun to master our language well enough to read our authors, I had put Nicole's *Essais* at her disposition, for the sole reason that I saw she was naturally inclined toward reflection, and I wanted to introduce her to a writer who constantly developed ideas. She had become a devoted reader. *La logique de Port Royal* was another book that I thought could serve to mold her judgment.[13] She had read it with the same diligence and appreciation. I surmised that works of this nature may have caused more harm than good to a lively imagination, and that in short all they had accomplished was to give her false ideas. This thought helped to put my own mind somewhat at ease, since it would be easy for me to obtain other books for her that I hoped would soon produce quite a different effect. My library contained works of all sorts. I did not intend to give her lascivious books, but I thought that our good novels, poetry, plays, and even a few books on morality whose authors were well versed in human desires and the ways of the world might bring Théophé around to less unsociable principles; and I derived such consolation from my plan that I had the strength to control my expression and my feelings when I found myself in her presence again.[14] I seized an opportunity to speak to her in private. I could not avoid expressing some disappointment about her letter, but I did so very moderately, and emphasizing my admiration for her virtue rather than my regret at her rejection of me, I referred to her resistance to my attentions only as a reason for me to try to keep my passion under control.

I immediately changed the subject to the progress of her education, and speaking glowingly of some new books that I had received from France, I promised to send them to her that afternoon. Her reaction couldn't have been further removed from the restraint I was affecting. She expressed her joy in a passionate outburst. She took my hand and pressed it to her lips. "I have my father back!" she said. "I have recovered my good fortune, my happiness, and everything I hoped for when I appealed to his generous friendship. Ah! Who could have a happier fate than I?" This emotional outburst touched me to the bottom of my heart. It overwhelmed me, and leaving her without adding a single word, I took refuge in my study where I abandoned myself at length to the agitation that dominated all my thoughts.

"How sincere she is! How innocent she is! Good heavens, how charming she is!" A thousand other exclamations escaped me before I was able to gather my thoughts. However, it was virtue incarnate that had appeared to speak through her mouth. My scruples were the first reactions to fill my heart. "And I would sacrifice such virtue to a lecherous passion!" I had my books before my eyes. I glanced at the ones I had intended to give to Théophé. It was *Cléopâtre*, *La princesse de Clèves*, etc. But am I going to fill her imagination with a thousand pipe dreams that will be of no use to her judgment? Supposing that she were to become more sensitive to love, would I really be satisfied to owe it to romantic fictions that are capable of awakening normal emotions in a heart that is naturally disposed to feel affection, but that would not bring happiness to my own if I owed it solely to my trickery? I know her. She will go back to her Nicole, to her *Art de penser*, and I will be left with the grief of seeing the illusion burst far more quickly than I would ever have been able to bring it to life; or if she were faithful, my happiness could only be imperfect, for I would constantly attribute it to motives in which I played no part.[15]

It was with reflections of this nature that I gradually managed to calm the emotions that had troubled me. "Let's just see," I continued more calmly, "where my reason is capable of leading me. I have two difficulties to overcome, and I have to choose which one to confront. I have to overcome either my passion or Théophé's resistance. Where shall I apply my efforts? Isn't it more appropriate that I turn them against myself, and that I try to achieve a peace of mind that Théophé can share as well? She is inclined to love me, she says; but she has repressed this inclination. What can I hope for from her love? And if I am trying to serve her interest as well as my own, wouldn't we both be better off if we confined ourselves to a simple friendship?"

In fact, this was the most reasonable conclusion I could reach, but I was sadly mistaken if I thought I could control my heart as easily as my behavior. If I immediately gave up my plan to employ other means than my own attentions to reach Théophé's heart, and if I imposed on myself even severer restrictions than ever given the close contact I couldn't avoid in living with her, I remained no less smitten with my love for her. Therefore, the most interesting part of my existence, that is, my personal life, was going to become a constant struggle for me. I realized it from the outset, and I abandoned myself blindly to this variety of torture. How little did I foresee, however, the torments that lay in wait for me!

Synèse, whom I had not yet seen since he received his wound, and who was beginning to get back on his feet, sent for the first time one of my servants, who interrupted my gloomy meditations to offer his apologies. I had neglected him since the incident, and not feeling much offended by a lover's initiative, I had merely given orders to take good care of him and to send him back to his father's home when he had recovered. But the deference he had shown me made such a good impression that I inquired in greater detail about his health and asked to be shown to his room, which he couldn't yet leave. He would have gladly sunk into the bowels of the earth if it had only opened up to hide him from my gaze. I quickly reassured him and asked him only to explain his intentions, which, I added, I already knew for the most part. This request was somewhat ambiguous, although I wasn't thinking of anything beyond his visit to Théophé's room. I saw him tremble with fear, and his agitated state making me more suspicious than I had previously been, I intensified it by insisting on an answer. He tried to get up, and when

I forced him to remain where he was, he begged me to take pity on an unfortunate young man who had never intended to offend me. I listened, maintaining a severe expression. He told me that he was still prepared to recognize Théophé as his sister, and he would defend this position more zealously than his brothers when his father agreed to discuss the question; but that in all truth since he couldn't confirm her birth sufficiently to execute this plan successfully, he had fallen back on other sentiments that could become just as advantageous to Théophé as the revelation of her birth and the piddling sum she might inherit from Condoidi; in short that he offered to marry her, and despite the law governing his family that passed on all of his father's property to the eldest son, he would inherit something from his mother; that with these intentions he did not feel he was lacking respect for me by putting off his return to Constantinople in order to seek an opportunity to communicate his feelings to Théophé; that he dared to hope on the contrary that I would deign to approve them; that with respect to the offers he had made to the knight, he had always assumed that they would not be put into effect without my consent. In explaining to me their plans to take up residence in Morea, he was trying to take credit for telling me sincerely everything he feared I had learned from other sources.

In examining his comments and intentions calmly, I found him less guilty than frivolous and imprudent for not seeing that, given his own opinion of Théophé's birth, his marriage proposal required imperatively that such an important difficulty be cleared up beyond any doubt. I couldn't in any case see anything criminal in his attempt to steal from me a heart he had no idea I had designs on. Therefore, far from frightening him by reprimands, I simply attempted to make him realize how childish his plan was. Although he couldn't have hoped for it after my comments, I promised to speak to his father once again in an effort to clear up the question of Théophé's birth, and I wished him a speedy recovery so that he would be able to go fetch Lord Condoidi, with whom I would agree to speak only in his son's presence. This promise and the kindly manner in which I was careful to articulate it did more to help him recover from his wound than any of his medicines.

I was not committing to anything that I did not intend to carry out; but Synèse was not the one I was trying to help, and all of my plans were meant to be to Théophé's advantage. There would never be a better opportunity to get to Condoidi than through his fear of his son's marriage. I had already adopted this course of action, and I still do not dare to confess what my heart hoped to gain from it. After several days, far too long for Synèse's impatience, he came to inform me that he felt strong enough to return to the city. "Bring your father to me then," I said, "but be careful not to let him suspect the reasons for which I wish to see him." They arrived at Oru that very evening. I greeted Lord Condoidi respectfully, and then turning immediately to my reasons for sending his son back to him, I said, "What scandal have you exposed us to, and if pure chance hadn't revealed to me Synèse's intentions, what would you have made us guilty of? He has made up his mind to marry Théophé. Let's see if you can make up yours to allow this marriage to take place." At first the old man seemed disconcerted. But recovering quickly, he thanked me for having put a halt to his son's reckless inclinations. "I have found him a match," he added, "who will be more fitting for him than a girl whose sole advantage is the protection with which you choose to honor her." I tried again, suggesting to him that he might not always be in a position to thwart the burning passion of a young man. He answered frostily that he had all the means to do so that he needed, and changing the subject, the wily Greek evaded for over an hour all of my efforts to bring him back to the question at hand. Finally, taking leave with the utmost politeness, he ordered his son to follow him, and they both set out on the road to Constantinople.

Several days later, very much surprised not to have any news about Synèse, out of curiosity I sent one of my men to Constantinople with instructions to learn how his wound was healing. His father, who knew that I was behind the inquiry, thanked me for my concern and added somewhat maliciously to this courteous response that henceforth I need have no worries about his son's marriage, because he had sent him under good guard to Morea and was certain he would not easily escape from the place where he had ordered him to be locked up. I was kindhearted enough to be troubled by this severity. Théophé expressed the same sympathy. And since I did nothing to keep this news quiet, the knight, who was more deeply affected by his friend's misfortune than I would have thought, made a decision that he carefully hid from us. On the pretext of going to Ragusa to cash his bills of exchange, he set out to free Synèse from his prison, and the risks he took out of friendship will soon testify to the nobility of his character.

I did not hide from Théophé the new attempts I had made to soften her father's heart. She was distressed by my lack of success, but not excessively so, and I was enchanted to hear her say that with all the kindness I showed her, no one would ever suspect that she had no father. Imagine how I would have responded to this tender mark of gratitude if I had given my heart free rein! But remaining steadfast in my resolutions, I contented myself with expressions of paternal affection and assured her that she would always be like a daughter to me.[16] An event that perturbed both Constantinople and the neighboring countries finally made it clear how much my dear Théophé cared for me. A contagious fever spread throughout the region and long frustrated attempts to discover a remedy. I fell victim to it. My first order was to have myself transferred to a lodge in my garden where I forbade entry to anyone other than my doctor and my personal valet. This precaution, which was an act of charity, was also a measure of prudence, because I would not have been able to rid my house of this deplorable illness once it had infected my servants. But an order that was meant for Théophé in particular was no more effective than fear itself in preventing her from following me. She entered the lodge over my servants' objections, and it was impossible to stop her from taking care of me. She fell sick herself. My entreaties, my pleadings, my lamentations could not convince her to remove herself from my presence. They set up a bed for her in my antechamber, where she remained constantly preoccupied with my illness despite her own serious condition.

What feelings filled my heart after we had both recovered! The selictar, who had been informed of my illness, paid me a friendly visit as soon as he thought he could without being indiscreet. His feelings were in a state of turmoil. He had spent his time away from Oru struggling against a passion that he was beginning to feel would never be gratified. But he could not listen to me speak about the loving care she had given me without betraying by his discomfort and blushing a jealousy that he hadn't felt up until then. He fidgeted impatiently during the rest of our conversation. And when the time came to leave, he ignored the fact that my weak condition obliged me to stay in my apartment; he asked me to accompany him to the garden. I accepted immediately. After having remained silent for a few steps, he said angrily, "My eyes are now open, and I am embarrassed to have kept them closed so long. It is easy for a Frenchman," he added sarcastically, "to dupe a Turk."

I admit that I had not expected in the least this sudden vehemence, and having intended only to emphasize the natural kindness of Théophé's character in my enthusiastic praise of her actions, I sought for a while how to defend myself. However, whether my natural restraint kept me from being blinded by my resentment, or whether the exhaustion brought on by my illness made me less aggressive, I offered the haughty selictar a response that was less offensive than firm and modest. "The French (because I put the interest of my country before my own)," I said to him, "do not tend to indulge in subterfuge and seek better ways to achieve their aims. As for me, who never intended to shut your eyes, I have no regret that they are now open, and I can tell you only that they are deceiving you if they lead you to doubt my friendship and sincerity." These remarks tempered the selictar's ire but did not placate him completely. "What?" he said. "Didn't you tell me that your relations with Théophé were only a matter of friendship, and that you took an interest in her only out of generosity?" I interrupted him calmly: "I did not deceive you when I told you that; it was an accurate description of my initial motives," I said, "and I would be unhappy with myself if my heart had begun with any others. But since you insist on knowing the state of my feelings, I confess that I love Théophé and have been no better able to resist her charms than you. However, I would add to this confession two circumstances that should put your mind at ease: I did not feel this way when I helped her to leave Cheriber's harem, and it has done me no more good than you to have changed my feelings since. That," I continued with less haughtiness than courtesy, "should satisfy a man whom I love and esteem."

He had sunk during this time into the darkest thoughts, and recalling everything he had noticed in our relations since I had received Théophé from his hands, he would not have hesitated to pounce with all the venom in his heart upon the slightest observations that might have appeared suspicious to him. But since he could only reproach me with the innocent evidence I had received of this sweet girl's devotion, he finally concluded that I would not have boasted about it so recklessly if I had thought it was a proof of her love. This thought was not enough to give him back his peace of mind and his happiness; but soothing at least his darkest misgivings, it helped him to take leave of me with neither hatred nor anger. "You will not have forgotten," he said upon leaving, "that I offered to sacrifice my passion for you when I believed that it was my duty as a friend. We will see if I have understood your principles well and what the difference is between your customs and ours that you have bragged about." He gave me no opportunity to answer.

This incident forced me to examine once again if I deserved any blame as regards my behavior in relation to love and friendship. I would have agreed that I deserved the selictar's reproaches only in the event that my love had been reciprocated, leading him to fear that my competition had diminished the affection he would have received. But since the moment I had fallen in love with Théophé, it hadn't even occurred to me to promote myself at the expense of my rival. She had made it clear to me that she felt no attraction to him, and the obstacle that he accused me of not respecting was precisely the only one I did not have to confront. Moreover, I had so many complaints to make about my own unhappy lot that I was perhaps less sensitive to those of anyone else, and I decided to make fun of his disappointment in order to relieve my own. I went back to Théophé in this frame of mind and asked her playfully what she thought of the selictar, who accused me of being loved by her, and who had taken me severely to task for a happiness that was so far out of my reach. Maria Rezati, whose friendship for Théophé grew each day stronger, had become too perceptive through her experiences not to recognize quickly the nature of my feelings. Constantly in her company, she was astute enough to draw her into discussions that soon gave her considerable influence over her manner of thinking. She suggested to her that she did not realize what she was spurning and that a woman of her worth could derive extreme advantages from a passion as keen as mine. Finally, in an attempt to raise her hopes, she pointed out that I was not married; that nothing was so common in Christian countries than to see a woman make her fortune with an advantageous marriage; that I looked so favorably upon her that I discounted her past life as the misfortunes of an unkind fate and would in all likelihood judge her solely on her conduct since the time she had gained her freedom, and that being so far from my homeland, I would listen only to the dictates of my heart. She repeated over and over the same advice, growing somewhat impatient to see Théophé react so coolly; and unable to obtain from her anything but modest responses that bespoke a soul cured of ambition, she declared that she was going to approach me on her own and purely for the sake of friendship to try to bring me around eventually to the idea of making her friend's fortune and happiness. Despite Théophé's strenuous objections and arguments, her resistance was simply dismissed as fear and weakness.

Her embarrassment was beyond description. Apart from her manner of thinking, which absolutely precluded any dreams of wealth and social position, she trembled at the thought of the opinion I was going to form of her vanity and boldness. After renewing to no avail her attempts to dissuade her friend, she resolved to warn me about a proposal that would at the very least, she thought, result in the loss of both my esteem and my affections.

But after struggling at length to overcome her timidity, she finally gave up, and the only resource left her was to appeal to the services of a *caloyer*, the head of a Greek church two miles from Oru, whom she had come to know.[17] This fellow agreed readily to act on her behalf. He explained her problem in a joking manner; and with still greater admiration than he already had for such an extraordinary young lady, he asked me if I saw much difference between these virtuous qualms and those that would move a simple caloyer to go into hiding to escape a promotion to a high post in the church. I laughed at his comparison. With a little more experience than he in the vanity and the shrewdness of women, I would have been suspicious of anyone but Théophé, and I would perhaps have viewed this exhibition of modesty as a clever ruse to make me aware of her aspirations. But I would have done a grave injustice to my charming pupil. "She had no need of this precaution," I told the caloyer, "to make me think well of the disposition of her heart, and I would like you to emphasize to her that if I were free to follow the dictates of my own, I would hasten to show her what a fine opinion I have of her." This was the only answer that seemed appropriate to my situation. Dare I confess that it was much more restrained than my true desires?

I communicated exactly the same response to Théophé and was virtually forced to pursue her to find an opportunity to speak with her in private. I had renounced the visits that I formerly made to her alone in her apartment. I no longer invited her to walks in the garden. She had become so intimidating to me that I couldn't approach her any longer without trembling. The happiest moments of my life were nonetheless those I spent in her company. I couldn't get her out of my mind, and I was sometimes ashamed to discover, while performing my most serious functions, that I couldn't escape the memories that constantly assailed me. My acquaintanceship with the caloyer that Théophé had arranged led me to participate in several outings that were perhaps ill suited to the dignity of my position; but it was enough for me just to accompany Théophé to forget everything but the pleasure of being beside her. However, I could not forget the circumstances of the first visit we paid the caloyer. In fact, he was, properly speaking, merely a priest who deserved respect for his advanced age and because of the esteem he had earned among all the Greeks. His income had grown owing to his frugal ways, and the gifts that he constantly received from the faithful members of his congregation were sufficient for him to lead an enjoyable and comfortable existence. The ignorance in which he had lived to the age of seventy did not prevent him from possessing a library that he considered to be the principal attraction of his house. It was in this room that he received me because of the great esteem in which the Greeks hold the erudition of the French. But when I expected to see him display his literary riches, I was surprised to hear him draw our attention first to an old chair sitting in a corner. "How many years," he asked, "would you guess that this piece of furniture has spent in the same place? Thirty-five years. For I have had my present position for thirty-five years, and I have been amused to note that no one has ever sat in it." It seemed that even the layer of dust with which it was covered had been respected. But glancing at the same time at the books that were next to it, I noticed that they were no less dusty. This observation gave me an amusing idea, which was to measure the thickness of the dust on the books and the chair; and finding it about the same, I offered the caloyer to wager that the books had gotten no more use than the chair during the past thirty-five years. He could not figure out how I had made my calculation, even though he had followed my procedure quite closely; and he came to the conclusion, admiring my erudition, that I had an extraordinary talent for discovering the truth.

He had been married three times, despite the fact that the laws of the Greek church forbade its clergy from marrying more than once.[18] The reason he had alleged to obtain this dispensation was that his first two marriages had produced no offspring, and that one of the goals of marriage being to contribute to the propagation of society, it was incumbent upon him to take a new wife for each one he lost in order to fulfill more perfectly the legitimate purpose of a union between a man and a woman. The Greek Council had allowed itself to be persuaded by this strange logic, and the caloyer, who had had no more success rendering his third wife pregnant than he had the first two, was very much distressed to discover that he was unfit for marriage or that he hadn't been able to fulfill its functions any better. Such is the vulgarity of the leaders of a church of considerable size, although it is not nearly as large as they would like to believe. I observed so much variety in their principles that they appeared to be united solely by the fact that they shared the Christian faith and by their mutual tolerance for one another's errors.

However, Maria Rezati had not forgotten the promise she had made to Théophé; and the fact that I had been forewarned allowed me to take great pleasure in observing all the clever devices used by a woman to achieve her ends. But I eventually tired of a stratagem that I had no trouble seeing through, and taking advantage of her actions to convey to Théophé what I no longer felt bold enough to tell her myself, I encouraged the Sicilian girl to share her friend's certitude that the object of my affections would never change. This is a promise that I have never betrayed. My common sense persuaded me that I had to leave it at that. But I didn't yet realize what I had to fear from my weakness.

It had been six weeks since the Sicilian knight's departure when Maria Rezati received a letter from him in which he related how his friendship for Synèse Condoidi had led him to overcome myriad difficulties and informed her that the young Greek, who had nothing to fear any longer from his father's wrath since he had become free enough to feel he could defend himself, was still disposed to offer them refuge in a part of the property he had inherited from his mother. He added that he counted on her to persuade Théophé to join them, and that if she hadn't yet succeeded in bringing her around, Synèse was determined to return to Constantinople to appeal to her in person to accept his offers. They didn't seem to be concerned about my consent to this plan, and I had the satisfaction of noting that they had a very favorable opinion of my relationship with Théophé, since they thought me capable of being so indifferent to her departure. But they had been careful not to reveal their full intentions in their letter. In the event that they were to meet any resistance from Théophé or from me, they were determined to employ any courage and tactics necessary to wrest her away from me.

The test to which they had just put themselves clearly encouraged them to attempt additional exploits. They owed their freedom to live in peace in Acade to the indulgence of the governor, who had turned a blind eye to a reckless act for which he could have punished them. Synèse, locked up by his father's orders in an old tower that constituted the major part of their castle, had no idea how long he was to be kept there and saw no possibility of escaping by himself. His guards consisted solely of a small number of servants who would have been easy to bribe if the knight had had more money; but having left with a modest sum that I had lent him for his trip, he had no recourse other than shrewdness or force to free his friend from his prison. His poor grasp of either Greek or Turkish constituted yet another obstacle, and I've never understood how he surmounted it. He might have been less bold had he realized how difficult his endeavor was going to be; indeed, a good half of foolhardy individuals succeed only because they are oblivious to the danger involved. He arrived alone in Acade. He took lodgings near

Condoidi's castle, which is only a short distance from the village. He spent the next few days informing himself as to the location of Synèse's prison and studying the layout. There was no question of forcing his way in, as it was extremely difficult just to approach the entrance. But using an iron rod that he heated in a stove, he managed, in one night, to burn through the end of a thick joist that ran the length of the tower; and either because he had received knowledge in advance or because it was just blind luck, it turned out that the spot he had chosen to work on was precisely where Synèse's room was located. Once he had begun the opening, nothing was easier than removing the neighboring stones and making a hole all the way through the wall. His only hope at that point was to be able to communicate with his friend, because he couldn't make a hole large enough for him to get through in one night, and daylight would have given him away if there had been too much debris. But having succeeded in identifying himself to Synèse, he informed him of his intentions and of what he had done up until then in the interest of his freedom. After deliberating together, they agreed to meet each night, and that Synèse, repeating to his servants everything he had learned in their conversations, would earn the reputation of having a personal genie who kept him abreast of everything that was happening in the empire. Indeed, this absurd story soon spread not only throughout Acade but in all the neighboring cities, and the two young men took great delight for a while in the public's gullibility.

They had imagined rightfully that such an extraordinary novelty would rouse a great deal of curiosity about Synèse's situation, and that the sympathy of the Turks, who are extremely superstitious, would help to free him. But although the governor of Acade himself had expressed admiration at what had been reported to him, he did not appear to be any more prepared to breech paternal authority by setting a son free against his father's wishes. Therefore, not having achieved anything with his trickery, the knight resorted to violence. He managed to smuggle a sword in to Synèse, and having befriended several of the castle's servants during his stay in the area, he took advantage of one of their visits to Synèse's prison to help him fight his way out with such vigor that Condoidi's entire household, brought running by the racket, was unable to prevent their escape. They were brazen enough to speak about their exploit in public, without reflecting that they were risking punishment both for having cast Synèse's revelations in a religious light and for having used weapons in his escape, two reckless acts that the Turks rarely pardon. But the governor of Acade, informed of the reasons behind the young Greek's incarceration, deemed his father's severity to be excessive and easily resolved himself to overlook an enterprise that he considered a tribute to friendship.

It was just after their triumph that the knight had written to Maria Rezati. He had added that they were leaving together for Ragusa, where Synèse had insisted upon accompanying his friend, and that they would make further plans according to Théophé's response, which they hoped to find upon their return. The tone of this letter was so moderate that Maria did not hesitate to share it with us. This openness convinced me at the very least that I had no reason to suspect her of any bad intentions. She hadn't waited so long to confide in Théophé; or rather she had sounded her out as soon as the plan had been conceived, and discovering that she was drawn only to Christian countries, she had virtually given up all hope after learning of Synèse's imprisonment. But upon seeing the abandoned plan resurrected, and judging by my attitude, which she witnessed every day, that I had left Théophé free to determine her own fate, she had no reason to think she would incur my displeasure or to suspect that she could cause me any grief by showing me the knight's letter.

However, my natural self-restraint suddenly gave way to a burst of emotion that led me to greet this news with greater resentment than I should have shown to a woman.[19] I dismissed their plan to go live in Morea as a libertine adventure that may have been logical for Maria Rezati, given the grave error she had committed in fleeing her father's house, but that was shameful to propose to a girl as respectable as Théophé. I went so far as to denounce as betrayal and ingratitude the plan that they had concocted in my house. "I forgave Synèse," I said, "whose ideas seemed as lunatic as those for which his father rightfully punished him, and I didn't wish to add, by my reproaches, to the misfortune he had experienced in my house. But I cannot easily excuse this action by a woman from whom I would have expected some gratitude and loyalty."

If these complaints were too harsh, the consequences were too dire as well. They led Maria to harbor for me a hatred that was indefensible in the light of all I had done for her. I realize that it may be offensive to reproach someone for not appreciating a favor you've done. But there was nothing overly humiliating in my remarks, and I might add that you wouldn't expect to find such oversensitivity in a woman who had just left a harem after fleeing her homeland with a Knight of Malta, and whose presence, to do myself justice, I should not have suffered so long either in my house in Constantinople or in my country estate. Théophé gave her unhesitatingly the best response she could have chosen to soothe my aggravation. The success of this plan, she told her, was so improbable that she was surprised that it had been taken seriously. Beside the fact that the frivolity of two young men did not bode well for the seriousness of their undertakings, there was no doubt that Lord Condoidi would soon take steps to halt a project formed without his consent. As for her, whom they were so kind as to wish to include in their plans, she did not understand by what right they did so, and she felt as uninterested in Synèse's current project as she was indifferent to the one that his father persisted in opposing. Her words put my mind more at ease. However, fearing at the same time that Maria Rezati's counsel might make more of an impression on her in my absence, I decided to help the Sicilian girl find a way to go join her lover. I learned that there was a ship leaving in a few days for Lepanto.[20] I appealed to the captain to take aboard a lady called to Morea on business, and I gave her one of my servants as an escort. Our leave-taking was so strained that it was clear to me that I could no longer count on Maria Rezati's friendship. Théophé herself, whose affection for her had cooled considerably since she had observed several indications of her indiscretion, observed her departure with little regret. But neither she nor I were prepared for the demonstration of hate she reserved for us.

I enjoyed more peace of mind after her departure than I had known for a long time; and without changing the behavior I had resolved to maintain for the rest of my life with Théophé, it was such a pleasure to find myself less constrained with her that I scarcely missed all the joys of love that I no longer dared to hope for. The selictar seemed to have given up any claim on Théophé. In the end it had cost me his friendship, for he had not come to Oru since my illness, and if I happened to cross his path in my frequent trips to Constantinople, there was no longer any trace of the warmth with which he had always rushed to greet me and shower me with all sorts of kind gestures. Nonetheless, I changed nothing in my behavior toward him. But after treating me so coldly for several weeks, he appeared offended at my equanimity, and I learned that he had complained bitterly about my attitude. I felt obliged to ask him to explain his grievances against me. Our exchange began so acrimoniously that I feared it would end badly. I had been offended by some of his remarks that, I had learned, were quite critical of me, and I knew very well that there were limits to restraint and silence when one's honor was at stake. He denied nonetheless the story I had been told. He even promised me to force the individual who had done him this disservice to retract his words publicly. But he was still no less intractable on the subject of Théophé, and he criticized me just as sharply as he had at Oru for sacrificing his love to mine. My own grievances had been satisfied. Therefore, reviving all the affection I had for him, I did my best to revive in him the opinion he had formerly held of my sincerity. After again admitting my feelings for Théophé, I protested in terms that make the greatest impression on a Turk that not only was my love just as unrequited as his, but that I had no intention of trying to improve my situation. His response could not have been more prompt if he had prepared it in advance. "But you still want her to be happy, right?" he said, looking me straight in the eye. "Yes," I replied immediately. "Very well," he continued, "if she is in the same state as you received her from me when she left Cheriber's seraglio, I have made up my mind to marry her. I know her father," he continued. "I've gotten him to agree to recognize her as his daughter on this condition; he was won over by some financial offers that I intend to honor fully. But at the very moment that I thought I was ready to carry out a plan that had cost me infinite pains, I found myself afflicted by cruel thoughts that I've been unable to overcome. Your example has made me too scrupulous. Your conversations and principles have turned me into a Frenchman. I could not bring myself to coerce a woman who I thought had given her heart to another man. How I suffered! However, if you give me your word of honor that what I have just heard is true, all of my intentions are revived. You know our customs. I will make Théophé my wife, with all the rights and honors that this position will bestow on her."

There were few surprises that could have appeared so horrible to me. My honor that I had just pledged, my unfortunate passion that had not abated, a thousand thoughts that were immediately transformed into cruel barbs that tormented my mind and tore my heart filled me instantly with more bitterness than I had ever tasted in my whole life. My distress did not escape the selictar. "Ah!" he cried. "If I judge by how you are acting, my worst fears will be realized." I understood that he was calling my integrity into question. "No," I said, "you have no reason to insult me with your suspicions. But if I am familiar with your laws and customs, do I not have the duty to remind you or inform you that Théophé is a Christian? How could her father have forgotten this? I recognize that she was raised according to your practices, and since she has been in my house I've scarcely even wondered what she thought as regards religion; but she has become close to a caloyer who visits her often, and although I haven't seen her put into practice either your religious principles or ours, I believe that she is drawn toward Christianity by her birth, or at least by the fact that she has always been aware of her homeland." The selictar, struck by this thought, replied that Condoidi himself assumed she was Moslem. He added other reasons that led him to hope that whatever her religion might be, she would not prove to be any less docile than most other women, who readily adopt the religion of their masters or their husbands in Turkey.[21] I had had time to recover my composure while he spoke, and understanding that I was not the one to be formulating objections, I told him finally that it was useless for him to worry about a point that he could easily clear up in his next visit to Théophé. This response had two goals: to prevent him from asking me to approach Théophé with his proposal and to put a prompt end to this new torment that doubt and delay would have only exacerbated for me.

It is quite certain that it had never clearly occurred to me that Théophé could ever have anything but amorous relations with me; and in the event that she allowed herself to be dazzled by the honor of becoming one of the most exalted women in the Ottoman Empire, I felt myself capable of sacrificing all of my love to her good fortune. I would have felt jealous of the selictar's happiness, but I would not have troubled it, even if it had cost me unspeakably violent despair; and perhaps I might even have contributed by my own efforts to the elevation of a woman whom I loved above all others. However, after leaving the selictar, who promised to come to see me at Oru that evening, I hurried back there as quickly as I could. I got right to the point with Théophé, wanting to learn her reaction quickly rather than working up to the subject gradually. My heart cried out for immediate relief. "You are going to learn," I said, "the nature of my feelings. The selictar intends to marry you, and far from being opposed to his plan, I approve everything that may ensure your fortune and your happiness." She was so little moved by these remarks that I understood instantly what her answer would be. "Far from contributing to my happiness," she said, "you are preparing additional miseries for me with a proposal that I can foresee I will not be able to refuse without deeply offending the selictar. Was it from you," she added, "that I had to hear such an odious proposition? Either you do not have all the affection for me that I had come to believe, or I have simply failed to make you understand how I feel."

I was so ecstatic at this flattering rebuke, so aware of how well it appeared to bode for my own amorous interests, that I reiterated the selictar's intention for the sole pleasure of hearing her repeat what had filled my heart with joy and admiration. "But have you considered," I said, "that the selictar is one of the most eminent lords of the empire, that his wealth is enormous, that the proposal you are receiving so coldly would be embraced eagerly by all the women in the world, and that it is to men of his stature that the sisters and daughters of the Sultan are married every day? Have you considered, finally, that this is a man who has loved you for a long time, who has not only love but a great deal of esteem for you, and who intends to behave toward you much differently than Turks normally do with their wives?" She interrupted me. "I consider none of this," she said, "because the only thing that interests me is to live peacefully under your protection, and I seek no other happiness." After so many promises to myself to maintain my silence, I could no longer express my joy overtly; but what was transpiring secretly deep in my heart was far more powerful than anything I've reported about my feelings up to now.

True to his word, the selictar came to Oru that evening. He asked me anxiously if I had spoken to Théophé about his plans. I couldn't hide from him the fact that I had ventured some overtures that did not meet as favorable a reception as he might have wished. "But perhaps you will have better luck yourself," I added, "and I would encourage you to make your proposal in person." This suggestion was not devoid of a certain malicious pleasure. I was very impatient not only to see his irksome solicitations put to an end by a refusal that would obliterate all hope, but even more to savor fully my triumph in seeing my rival humiliated before my eyes. This was the only pleasure that I had derived from my passion up until then, and I had never before allowed myself to indulge in it with such enjoyment. I accompanied the selictar to Théophé's apartment. He revealed to her the reason for his visit. Having had time to prepare her response, she was careful to avoid saying anything that might have been humiliating for him; but her refusal seemed so definitive to me, and the reasons she gave were presented with such force that I had no doubt that he had immediately reached the same conclusion as I. Therefore, he did not ask her to repeat them. He stood up without saying a single word, and appearing less distressed than irritated as we left together, he said several times, "Can you believe that? Who in the world would have expected that?" And when he was ready to take his leave, having declined my invitation to spend the night, he added as he embraced me, "Let us remain friends. What I was planning to do was sheer folly; but I'm sure you will agree that the folly you have just witnessed is far greater than my own." He continued to give vent to his resentment until he had taken his seat in his carriage; I saw him raise his hands as he left and clasp them together in a gesture that bespoke, or so I imagined, his shame as much as his pain and astonishment. Despite the feelings I have admitted, my friendship for him was strong enough that I couldn't help feeling sorry for him, or wishing at least that such a painful experience would help to cure him.

But it was perhaps not he who should have been the object of my compassion, if I could have foreseen what new trials lay in store for me and the great disappointment and humiliation that his very disgrace was going to cause me. Scarcely had he left when upon returning to Théophé's apartment I found her so pleased at his departure, which she had just learned of, and her naturally lighthearted and lively disposition led her to make so many amusing comments on the good fortune she had refused that, completely mystified by the principles of a woman who was capable of treating with such scorn everything that most people value, I begged her, after listening to her for a few moments, to explain to me what she hoped to achieve with a behavior and sentiments that never ceased to fill me with astonishment. "One sets goals for oneself," I said, looking at her with a pensive air owing to my troubled feelings, "and the more extraordinary the paths one chooses to take, the nobler and loftier must be the goal to which one aspires. I have the greatest admiration for yours, but I fail to grasp exactly what it is. I know you have confidence in me," I added. "Why have you consistently hidden your intentions, and why will you not share with me out of friendship what I no longer dare ask you for other reasons?" I had spoken in a purposely serious manner to convince her that I wasn't asking this question out of mere curiosity, but despite my efforts to remain within the bounds I had set for myself, she was too perceptive not to be continually aware that my heart was very heavy. However, without changing the cheerful tone she had adopted in commenting on the selictar's departure, she insisted that her only goal was the one that she had repeated to me over and over, and she was surprised that I could have forgotten it. "Your friendship and your generous protection," she said, "repaired instantly all of my misfortunes; but the regrets, the determination, the efforts I will need to make for the rest of my life will never repair the immorality of my past. I am indifferent to anything that will not help to make me more virtuous, because virtue is henceforth the only treasure I desire, and every day I discover more and more that it is the only one I lack."

Answers of this nature would have again given rise to fears that her reading and meditation had warped her judgment if I hadn't observed on the contrary an admirable equanimity in her character, a consistent moderation in all her desires, and the same charm in her words and manners. At this point I would begin to blush at my weakness if I hadn't prepared my readers to excuse it in the light of so fine a cause. It was impossible for me to reflect on so many marvelous events without feeling myself penetrated more deeply than ever by all the emotions that I had repressed for several months owing to my promises. The offers of a man of the selictar's rank, and the refusal that I had witnessed, had transformed Théophé to such an extent in my eyes that I imagined her adorned with all of the titles that she had rejected. She was no longer a slave whom I had bought, a stranger that her own father refused to recognize, an unfortunate girl exposed to the debauchery of a harem; along with all of the qualities that I had adored for so long, I could now only see in her a person ennobled by the very grandeur that she had scorned and worthy of a position far more exalted than fortune could ever offer her. With this image of her growing ever stronger as I thought about her over the next few days, I soon found myself disposed, without feeling the slightest repugnance, to marry her myself; and what was surprising to me after spending nearly two years without daring to entertain this thought even for a moment, I immediately found my plan so natural that my only concern was how to bring it to fruition.[22]

There were no obstacles for me to overcome from my imagination, since my every thought tended to favor my love; nor were there any from my family, who not only had no power to oppose it, but given how far I was from my homeland, would not even learn of my decision until long after the event. However, in yielding to my heart's desire I did not forget what I owed to the demands of decorum; and if only to avoid the expense and the commotion, I decided to confine my marriage celebration within my own walls. But in the midst of the pleasure I found in gratifying my deepest desires, I would still have liked Théophé to give some indication that she was yielding to my affection for other reasons than those I was going to propose to her, and I felt some regret at having to use this course to obtain a little love from her. Although I had flattered myself on more than one occasion that I had made an impression on her heart, it was sad for my own that I had never been able to extract from her the slightest admission of it. Without really hoping to lead her openly to such a declaration, I felt assured at least that by intimating to her somewhat vaguely what I was resolved to do for her, it would be impossible for her to avoid, in the resurgence of the deep gratitude she had expressed so often, some remarks that I felt would bring comfort to my heart, and that would afford me an opportunity to declare to her on the spot what my love for her had moved me to do for her happiness and mine. In all these reflections it had never even occurred to me that her refusal of the selictar's proposal was a reason for me to fear the same fate; and I took yet greater pleasure in persuading myself that even if it were not precisely to save herself for me that she had rejected one of the greatest fortunes of the empire, it was at least indicative of such a clear preference for our nation that she would be all the more pleased to receive the same proposition from me.

Finally, after several days devoted to this kind of mental preparation, I had chosen as the moment that would determine my happiness an afternoon in which nothing could trouble the conversation I wished to have with her. I was on the point of entering her apartment when my blood suddenly turned cold at a thought that all my reasoning had neglected, and that prompted me to beat a retreat as anxious and frightened as I had been serene and resolved when I arrived. I remembered that the selictar had at least gone to the trouble of reaching an agreement with Condoidi concerning Théophé's birth, and I trembled at the force of a passion that had blinded me to the point of ignoring proprieties that even a Turk had considered indispensable. But this cause for alarm was not the only one that threw me into a state of complete consternation. I reflected that as necessary as it was for me to speak to Condoidi and to bring him to do for me what he had offered to do for the selictar, it was going to be just as difficult and humiliating for me to see my course of action depend on the whims of a man whom I had treated with so little consideration. What could I do if he were to take pleasure in seeking revenge for both the way I had badgered him about his daughter and the trouble he suspected I had caused him with his son? Nonetheless, I didn't see that I had any choice, and I was only surprised that such an essential precaution had escaped my attention. But would you believe that after chastising myself for this oversight and thinking long and hard about how I could go about remedying my negligence, I decided in the end to go back to Théophé and make the proposal I had thought I needed to postpone for such good reasons. I will not attempt to justify the rationale that brought me to this decision. I would not be able to convince anyone that love had not taken precedence over prudence here. However, it seemed to me that obstacles I had no doubt I could overcome shouldn't be a reason to defer a declaration that would finally reveal to Théophé the full force of my passion, and that would undoubtedly dispose her favorably toward my plans, at least as regards her desires. When I informed her of my decision to marry her, I had no intention of hiding from her that the same day I was going to become her husband I meant to give her back a father. Should I admit it? However successful I might be with Condoidi and with Théophé herself, I felt sure that she would be so touched by the decision I had taken in her favor that she would show her appreciation through her feelings and grant me sooner or later, even without marriage, the love that she would see I was determined to deserve at any cost.[23] My head was spinning with a multitude of thoughts that were perhaps not all that clear when I returned to her apartment. I did not give her time to express any concern over my anxious state. I hastened to forestall any questions from her so that I could explain my plans, and having begged her to listen to me without interrupting, I spoke at length, revealing all my feelings in the greatest detail.

The ardor that had led me to so many strange actions had not only continued unabated but seemed to increase during my speech; and the presence of such a cherished object affecting me far more than all of my thoughts, I found myself in a state in which nothing could be compared to the intensity of my love and my desires. But a glance at Théophé plunged me into a fright that was infinitely more violent than the one that had stopped me in my tracks before her door an hour before. Instead of the expressions of gratitude and joy that I had expected to see spread over her features, I saw only signs of the most profound sadness and extreme dejection. She seemed deeply moved by everything she had just heard; but I could see only too well that what continued to silence her was the shock of surprise and apprehension rather than feelings of admiration and love. Finally, despite my own dismay, I was on the point of expressing concern for her state when she threw herself to her knees before me, and no longer able to hold back her tears, she wept with such violence that she was unable to speak for a moment. I was myself in such emotional turmoil that I didn't even have the strength to raise her back up to her feet. She remained in this position despite my wishes, and I was forced to listen to a declaration that pierced my heart through and through. I will not repeat the abusive and contemptuous remarks that the thought of her faults, which she could not forget, led her to make about herself; but after describing herself in the most odious terms, she beseeched me to open my eyes to the picture she had painted and not to permit myself to be blinded any longer by an unworthy passion. She reminded me what I owed to my birth, to my rank, to honor and reason even, which I had myself brought to her awareness, and whose principles I had taught her so well. She accused fate of crowning her misfortunes by using her not only to destroy her father's and her benefactor's peace of mind but to corrupt the principles of a heart whose virtues, she claimed, had been her sole and unique model. And abandoning finally her expressions of pain and her complaints for a darkly menacing tone, she vowed that if I did not suppress these desires that offended both my duty and hers, if I did not confine myself to the titles of protector and friend, to those cherished and precious names that she still asked heaven to lead me to accept in my heart, she was determined to leave my house without so much as a good-bye and to use her liberty, her life, in short all of the things that she confessed she owed to me, to flee my presence forever.

After this cruel protest, she got up from the position in which she had remained, and begging me in a calmer tone to pardon her for some disrespectful terms that the acuteness of her anguish had torn from her, she asked my permission to go hide her distress and recover from her shame in an adjoining study, adding that she was resolved only to come out either to take her leave from me definitively or to rejoice at the pleasure of finding me again in the disposition we both should desire for my happiness and hers.

She indeed went into the next room, and I didn't dare make the slightest effort to stop her. My ability to speak, to move, to think, all of my natural faculties were virtually paralyzed by my astonishment and confusion. I would have plunged into an abyss if one had opened up before me, and the very thought of the situation in which I found myself seemed unbearable torment. Nonetheless, I remained in this state for a long time without being able to muster the strength to shake myself out of it. I must have appeared absolutely devastated, since the first servant that I met was alarmed by the strange look on my face, and sounding the alarm in my house, he assembled around me all of my servants, who hastened to do everything they could to help me recover. Théophé herself, alerted by all the commotion, forgot her resolution not to come out of her study. I saw her rush over to me, clearly distraught. But the sight of her only intensified my despair, and I pretended not to notice her presence. I assured my servants that their concerns were unfounded, and I quickly left to shut myself up in my apartment.[24]

I remained there more than two hours, which seemed no more than an instant. What bitter thoughts and violent emotions! But in the end they brought me to the conclusion that I had to accept the situation that I had tried to change. I was finally convinced that Théophé's heart was impervious to the efforts of any man, and whether it was owing to her natural character or to the virtue acquired by her studies and reflections, I considered her to be an extraordinary woman whose behavior and principles should serve as an example for her sex and ours. What dismay I still felt from her refusal became easy to dispel as soon as I had reached a definitive conclusion about her. I even wanted to receive some sign of appreciation from her for rallying so quickly to her position. I went into the room where she had withdrawn, and declaring that I was bowing to the force of her example, I promised to confine myself as long as she wished to the role of her most ardent and affectionate friend. But this promise was nonetheless intensely disputed by the yearnings of my heart, and her presence was only too capable of making me retract what I had recognized as just and inescapable in a moment of solitude!

If the image I am going to give of her in the remainder of these memoirs does not correspond to the one that the reader has conceived up to now based on the ordeals that her virtue has overcome so gloriously, do I not have to fear that people will distrust my version of the events and suspect me of harboring some jealous resentment that may have altered my own state of mind rather than imagine that a girl so devoted to virtue could have lost some of the moral rectitude that I have taken such pleasure in offering for everyone's admiration until now?[25] Whatever opinion one might form about this, I only ask this question in order to be able to answer that people will find me as sincere in my doubts and suspicions as I've been in my praise, and that after relating honestly some events that have plunged me into the deepest uncertainty, I wish to leave the final judgment to the reader.

But the new pact that I had made with Théophé was followed by a rather long period of calm, during which I was pleased to see her continue to practice all of her virtues. I had learned from the guide that I had given to Maria Rezati that this troubled Sicilian had not lived up to our expectations, not to speak of those of her lover. The captain of the ship on which I had booked her passage to Morea was strongly attracted to her and had coaxed her into revealing her past adventures and her plans. He had used this knowledge to paint her such a vivid picture of the wrong she was going to do to herself for the rest of her life by rejoining the knight that he eventually succeeded in getting her to agree to be taken back to Sicily, where he was convinced that she would have no trouble reconciling with her family. He had anticipated, of course, that he would be the principal benefactor of this by a marriage that, it was easy to foresee, would meet little opposition; and if I was to believe the word of a servant, he had not waited to disembark at Messina to establish his rights. Having finally introduced himself to his young lady's father, who was only too happy to get his daughter and heir back, he had, upon presenting himself as an Italian of high birth, obtained permission to marry Maria Rezati before the news of her return had spread; and this was indeed the only way for her to return to her country with her honor intact. She had insisted that the guide whom I had given her accompany her to her father's home in an effort to increase her chances of winning over this kind old man by giving him this proof of the interest I had taken in her welfare. He hadn't left Messina until after the wedding ceremony, and he brought me a letter from Signor Rezati containing the warmest expressions of his gratitude.

Théophé had received one also from Maria, and we had both believed that we were finally free of her. It had been around six weeks since my valet had returned when, being in Constantinople, I learned from another of my servants who had just come back from Oru that the knight had arrived there the day before, and that the news Théophé had given him had plunged him into a state of despair that did not bode well. Nonetheless, he sent me his excuses for the liberty he had taken in coming to my estate, and he begged my permission to stay there a few days. I sent a message immediately assuring him that I would be glad to see him there, and no sooner was I free than my impatience to inform myself of his feelings and plans prompted me to leave the city. I found him in the state of distress that had been described to me. He even chided me for causing his misfortune by giving his mistress the liberty of leaving my house without informing him; I excused his reproaches, attributing them to a lover's sorrow. But in a few days my consolation and my advice brought him around to a more reasonable position. I got him to recognize that the decision his mistress had made was the very best one she could have made for both him and her, and I persuaded him to take advantage of the help I offered to make peace with his family and his order.

Having calmed down, he told us all about his adventures with Synèse, since we had only learned about the principal events in his letter. They had traveled together to Ragusa, and not having any trouble cashing the bills of exchange, they had taken steps to carry out deliberately and successfully their plan to establish residence. But what he could not bring himself to confess at first was that Synèse had come with him to Constantinople. Maria Rezati's response, which they had found upon their return from Ragusa, having led them to understand that Théophé would not agree to join them, they had come in the hope of being able to convince her in person; and the knight, grateful for the gracious reception he had received in my house, did not hide from me that Synèse was determined to resort to violence, since the other avenues he had employed had proved to be fruitless. "I am betraying my friend," he said, "but I am sure that you will not use my revelation to do him harm; on the other hand, in hiding his plan from you I would be betraying you all the more grievously, since it would be impossible for you to defend yourself against the attack that threatens your home." He added that if he had agreed to help Synèse, it was only because, expecting to find his mistress at my house and return with her to Morea, he could think of no more amiable a companion for her than Théophé, who, sharing the pleasures of their company, would also, he was sure, discover in Acade a happier life than she had expected. Being aware moreover of the attempts I had myself made to persuade Condoidi to recognize her, he had convinced himself that I would not be offended if they led her, even against her will, to become a member of a family with which I wished to see her reunited. But since the plan to establish their residency in Acade was now ruined, he was warning me of Synèse's intentions, which he could no longer consider safe or advantageous for Théophé.

She was not privy to this revelation, and I asked the knight not to let her know anything about it. It was enough for me to be forewarned to be able to frustrate easily Synèse's plot, and I concluded moreover that without the knight's help he would have neither the means nor the boldness to bring it off. I nonetheless wished to learn how he had intended to proceed. They were to choose a day when I would be in the city. I left few servants at Oru. As they both were familiar with my house, they felt certain they could get in easily, and that they would meet little resistance since Maria Rezati was leaving with them willingly, and they could thus convince my servants that even if Théophé seemed to accompany her against her wishes, it was nonetheless with my approval. I have no idea if this brash plan would have succeeded. But I relieved myself of all kind of fears by having Synèse informed that I was aware of his plan, and if he persisted in the slightest way I promised him that he would be punished even more severely than he had been by his father. The knight, whose friendship for him had not abated, also helped persuade him to give up the plans they had concocted together. However, he could not extinguish a passion that drove his friend to a number of additional wild schemes.

What confidence can one have in people of this age despite their fine character? This same knight, whom I thought had finally come to his senses, and who continued in fact, until his departure, to deserve by his good conduct the consideration I never failed to show him, returned to Sicily only to fall back into libertinage that was still more inexcusable than that which he had renounced. I used my strongest recommendations to the Grand Master of Malta and to the Viceroy of Naples to obtain for him far more leniency than he dared hope for. He appeared openly in public in his homeland, and his flight was looked upon as an error of youth. But he could not avoid seeing his mistress, or rather he most likely had the weakness to seek out the opportunity to do so. Their passion was rekindled. Scarcely had four months passed since his departure when Théophé showed me a letter written from Constantinople in which he informed her very timidly, after beating around the bush at length, that he had returned to Turkey with his mistress and, not being able to live without each other, had finally decided to renounce their homeland forever. He recognized the extent of his folly; but although he offered as an excuse the violence of a passion that he was unable to vanquish, he felt, he said, that propriety prevented him from appearing before me without having sounded out my good will, and he entreated Théophé to revive it in his favor.

My response was immediate. This case was so different from the first, and I was so little inclined to receive in my home a man who was committing a multitude of moral infractions by this new elopement that, dictating personally Théophé's letter, I declared to the knight and his companion in flight that they couldn't count on me for favors or protection. But they had taken enough precautions to be able to dispense with my help, and their purpose in coming straight to Constantinople was much less to see me again than to rejoin Synèse, with whom they wanted to resurrect their former project. However, as they still intended to include Théophé, and the close relationship they had had with her led them to believe she would be overjoyed to see them, they had no trouble deducing that her response had been dictated by me; and far from being discouraged by a refusal that they attributed to me alone, as soon as they were certain that I was in the city they both hurried to Oru. Théophé, disconcerted by their visit, told them frankly that after being informed of my intentions she didn't even have the right to consider whether or not she was happy to see them, and she begged them not to expose her to the danger of displeasing me. They urged her so insistently to listen to them, and the interview they requested of her was so brief that, not being able to use force to get rid of them, she had no choice but to show them the indulgence they were demanding.

Their plan was prepared, and the letter with which the knight had attempted to find a way back into my house was only an expression of his remorse on the eve of a new scheme that gave him qualms of conscience. Although I had never explained to him what I thought of his previous plan to settle in Morea, and although I had been even less candid about my reaction upon discovering that they wanted to include Théophé, he perceived clearly enough that she would not have been treated in my house with such solicitude and consideration if I had not taken pleasure in her presence there, and that he could not win her over or spirit her away secretly without offending me. He would have liked therefore to obtain my approval of his plan, as much to please his mistress as to help out his friend, and despite the fact that I had refused to see him, he hadn't lost hope yet that he could gain my approval after obtaining Théophé's consent. Accordingly, he spared no effort in trying to get her to see how advantageous and enjoyable it would be for her to join their little group. But she had no need of anyone's help in resisting such frivolous propositions.

I was busy at the time with the preparations for a celebration that was talked of throughout Europe. The difficulties that I had met on several occasions in carrying out the duties of my office had not prevented me from remaining on very good terms with Grand Vizir Calaïli, and I dare say that the energy with which I had upheld the privileges of my position and the honor of my country had served only to increase the respect I enjoyed among the Turks. The king's birthday approaching, I intended to celebrate it more brilliantly than it had ever been before. The fireworks were to be spectacular, and my house in Constantinople, which was in the Galata suburb, was already filled with all of the artillery that I had found on our nation's ships.[26] As these dazzling festivities are forbidden without a special permit, I had requested one from the grand vizir, who had granted it to me most courteously. But on the very eve of the day I had chosen, and when, being satisfied with my arrangements, I had returned to Oru to rest that night before returning the next day to the city with Théophé, whom I wanted to have at my party, I learned two pieces of news that put a damper on my joy. The first that greeted me upon arriving was the news of the knight's visit and his efforts to persuade Théophé to follow him. Learning at the same time that he was more strongly allied than ever with Synèse, my suspicions went far beyond her, and I had little doubt that after her refusal and mine they would be capable of renewing all the schemes that the knight had confessed to me. However, I was not particularly alarmed, since I was to take her to Constantinople the next day, and I had all the time I needed to take measures in the future to guarantee her safety at Oru.

But when I was chatting with her that evening about all the things she had told me, I was informed by my secretary that Grand Vizir Calaïli had just been deposed, and that he had been replaced by Choruli, a highly arrogant individual with whom I had never had any relations.[27] I understood immediately the seriousness of my predicament. This new minister could block my gala, if only out of the capriciousness that usually prompts officials like him to modify the existing state of things and to revoke all of the permits granted by their predecessors. My first thought was to pretend not to be aware of this change and to maintain the arrangements that I had made by virtue of the *ferman* given me by Calaïli.[28] However, given the conflicts I had experienced and that I had surmounted with my honor intact, and considering it perhaps wise to proceed more tactfully, I decided in the end to request another permit from the new vizir, and I sent a man to get it. He was so busy with the initial problems he had to handle in his new position that it was impossible for my secretary to gain a moment's audience. I learned only the next day that he hadn't been able to speak with him. Growing ever more impatient, I resolved to see him in person. He was at the *galibe divan*, after which there would be the solemn procession that is customary when there is a change of office.[29] I lost any hope of seeing him. All of my preparations were done. I returned to my original thought that Calaïli's permit was sufficient, and I began my fireworks as night fell.

Le Grand Visir,
en Habit et en Turban de ceremonie.

Fig. 6 The grand vizir. From Ferriol, *Recueil de cent estampes*, 1714. Art and Architecture Collection, Miriam and Ira D. Wallach Division of Art, Prints and Photographs, The New York Public Library, Astor, Lenox and Tilden Foundations.

The vizir was of course informed of it. Highly resentful, he immediately sent one of his officers to inquire as to my intentions and to ask me by what right I had organized such an event without his approval. I answered politely that since I had obtained Calaïli's approval two days before, I didn't think I needed a new *ferman*, and that I had moreover not only sent officials several times but had myself tried to see him to renew it. The officer, who apparently had his orders, informed me that the vizir wished me to stop my festivities immediately, or he would use force to make me obey. This threat made my blood boil. My response was no less sharp, and when the officer, becoming irritated in his turn, added that if I made any show of resistance, orders had already been given to bring up a detachment of janissaries to put me in my place, I didn't mince my words: "Tell your master," I said, "that his action is utterly contemptible, and I know no fear when the honor of my king is at stake. If he goes to the extremes with which you are threatening me, I have no intention of trying to defend myself against an enemy that will crush me by its superior numbers; but I am going to have brought to this room all the gunpowder I have amassed here, and I will put a match to it myself to blow up my house along with myself and all of my guests. After that, I will leave it to my master to avenge me."[30]

The officer withdrew, but the news of this conflict immediately produced considerable anxiety among all the French nationals that I had invited to my party. As for me, I was in a rage that would have made me capable of carrying out my threat. And determined above all not to allow the slightest suggestion of fear to be seen in my behavior, I issued orders for a salvo to be fired immediately by my whole artillery, which was composed of more than fifty canons. My servants trembled as they carried out my orders. My secretary, more alarmed than all the others, thought he was acting in my interest by extinguishing part of the torches and lanterns, that is, by taking care to put out several of them here and there, to be able to claim that we were obeying the vizir's orders. I did not immediately notice what was happening; but the hasty exodus of part of my guests, who doubtlessly feared that I might carry out the drastic measures with which I had threatened the minister's envoy, increased my aggravation. I called cowards and traitors the people that I couldn't stop from leaving; and soon becoming aware that the brilliance of my light show was diminishing, I flew into a new fury when I learned of the timid precautions of my secretary. I was in this state of mind when I heard the cries of a woman who was calling for help. I had no doubt that it was the detachment of janissaries that was beginning to insult my servants, and not wanting to start anything before I was sure, I ran toward the place where the cries were coming from, accompanied by a few loyal friends. But what did I see? Synèse and the knight, with the help of two Greeks, were trying to kidnap Théophé, whom they had managed to draw aside, and were attempting to stuff a handkerchief into her mouth to stifle her cries. There was no need for all the outrage that I already felt to drive my wrath to its fullest. "Get those scoundrels!" I said to my companions. They followed my orders only too well. They pounced on the four kidnappers, who tried to put up a fight. The two Greeks, less adept or less resolved, fell beneath the first blows. The knight was wounded, and Synèse, finding himself in a hopeless situation, surrendered his sword. I would perhaps have had him arrested, and in the heat of the moment he would have been treated harshly if someone had not been sent to inform me that the vizir, placated by the appearance of submission that he owed to my secretary, had called back his troops and declared that he was satisfied. Feelings of pity soon took over when my anger had dissipated. We even had to take some precautions to hide the death of the two Greeks. I dismissed Synèse, emphasizing the leniency I was showing him, and gave orders for the knight's wounds to be dressed with care. Fortunately, I had only Christians in my house, and all of them felt it was in their interest to cover up this incident.

However, my own incident with the vizir was followed by several other events that have no relevance to this account other than they led to my return to my homeland.[31] No sooner had I received the king's orders than I reflected on how I was going to behave with Théophé. I loved her too much to hesitate to invite her to follow me, but I could not at all be sure that she would accept. Thus, my uneasiness being linked only to her inclinations, I sounded them out very discreetly. She spared me part of my trouble by expressing doubts about whether I would permit her to accompany me. I got up passionately, and giving her my word that the sentiments she knew I had for her would never change, I left her the choice of the conditions it pleased her to impose upon me. She explained them to me simply: my friendship, to which all the other favors, she said graciously, seemed to be attached, and the freedom to continue to live as she had lived in my house until then. I swore to observe them faithfully. But I got her to agree to allow me, before our departure, to make additional efforts to win over the coldhearted Condoidi. She foresaw that they would be useless. Indeed, although I had been optimistic, despite her opinion, that he would become more receptive at the thought of her leaving Turkey for good, I wasn't able to get anywhere with this callous old man, who imagined instead that the pretext of my departure was just an attempt on my part to deceive him. Synèse, whom I hadn't seen any more than the knight since their foolhardy action, had no sooner learned that she was going to accompany me to France than, overcoming all his fears, he came to beg me to allow him at least to make his final farewells to his sister. The quality of "sister" that the wily Greek feigned to give her, and the tender manner in which he enveloped his entreaties, persuaded me not only to permit him to see her immediately but to grant him the same favor several times before our departure. The measures I had taken in the country and in town gave me complete peace of mind regarding the safety of my house, and I knew Théophé too well to be suspicious of her. This easy access nonetheless gave new hope to Synèse. He had scarcely seen her four times when, requesting the liberty to speak to me, he threw himself at my feet and beseeched me to take him back into my heart; and taking heaven for his witness that he would consider Théophé to be his sister for the rest of his life, he asked me to take him with me and to be a father to him as he was to her. The nature of his plea, his tears, and the good opinion that I had always had of his character would inevitably have led me to yield to his request if I had been able to convince myself that it wasn't just love hiding behind deceptive appearances. I did not give him a positive response. I wanted to consult Théophé, suspecting that she was in league with him and had been won over by their sibling bond or by his tears. But she replied without the slightest hesitation that although she would have urged me to grant this favor if she ever became certain that she was his sister, she begged me not to expose her to the constant quandary of not knowing how to act with a young man who harbored such passionate feelings for her if he wasn't her brother. Thus the sorrowful Synèse had to satisfy himself with the consolation he no doubt found in the knight's friendship, and I have no idea what became of them after our separation.

The few weeks that elapsed between the king's order and my departure were employed by Théophé in activities that would fill a whole book if it were my intention to pad these memoirs. Her reflections, as well as her own experience, had led her to feel that the most dreadful of all misfortunes for a person of her sex was slavery; and from the beginning of her stay at Oru she hadn't missed a single opportunity to learn which were the largest harems and who were the lords who most valued this kind of wealth. With the help of some slave dealers, who were as well known in Constantinople as our most famous horse traders are here, she had discovered several unfortunate girls, Greeks or foreigners, who found themselves in this sad situation against their will, and her hope had always been to discover some way to obtain their freedom. She had understood that I couldn't ask this kind of favor of all the Turkish lords one after the other, and her discretion had prevented her in addition from soliciting money from me too often for this purpose. But finding herself on the point of leaving, she became less timid. She began by selling all the jewels she had received from Cheriber as well as several presents of considerable value that I had insisted she accept. After confessing that she had converted them into money, she informed me of the use she intended to make of this sum and appealed to my charitable instincts to persuade me to add some of my own money to it. I sacrificed ten thousand francs that I had intended to use to purchase various Levantine curios. I never felt moved to find out how much of her own money Théophé had spent, but I soon saw in my house several extremely attractive girls whose bondage could only have been broken for considerable sums, and if you add the expenses she incurred in sending them back to their homelands, there is little doubt that her generosity went far beyond my own. I was greatly entertained for several days by the stories of this charming troop, and I was careful to write them down almost immediately to guard against the inconstancy of my memory.

We finally left the port of Constantinople on a ship from Marseilles. The captain had warned me that it would be necessary to drop anchor at Livorno for a few weeks, and I was not sorry to have the opportunity to visit this famous port.[32] Théophé appeared overjoyed to set foot on Italian soil. Having left my whole entourage on board, since I was obliged to travel incognito for a multitude of reasons, I took lodgings in an inn where I did not disdain to dine in the company of some good people who were there also. Théophé passed for my daughter and I for an ordinary man returning from Constantinople with his family. From the first meal we took with the other travelers, I noticed that a young Frenchman around twenty-five years old was struck by Théophé's charms and was making every effort to draw her attention by his flattery and courtesies. His gracious looks and manners, as well as his elegant conversation, led me to believe that he was a nobleman who was also traveling incognito, although the name that he gave, the comte de M. Q., did not evoke for me any well-known family. He showered me with compliments

because he took me for Théophé's father. At first I only saw in his overatten-
tiveness the gallantry that was typical of the French, and during the walks
that I took in the city the following days, it didn't even occur to me that
there was any danger in leaving Théophé alone, with a woman from her
country to wait on her.

However, in less than a week I noticed that her mood had changed. Since
the fatigue from the trip itself could have affected her adversely, I felt little
need for concern; I asked her nonetheless if she had any reason to be sad or
had any complaint. She replied that she was not aware of any problem, but
she answered in such a constrained manner that I would have been alerted
to something immediately if I had had any reason to be suspicious. Moreover, I was unaware that the comte de M. Q. had been keeping her company
during the whole time I was visiting the city's points of interest. We had been
in Livorno for two weeks before the slightest incident could have prompted
me to watch more closely what was going on. If I came back before mealtime,
I found Théophé alone, since the count was careful to take his leave before my
return. I noted that she still appeared somber and preoccupied, but seeing no
other indication of the decline in her health that I had feared, I thought it
enough to combat these appearances of melancholy by promising her that
she would find life in France much more enjoyable than in an Italian inn.

There is no doubt that she seemed to be on more familiar terms with the
count at the table than would have been warranted were he just a passing
acquaintance. Their glances and winks seemed to imply a certain complicity
between them. Their eyes often met, and the count's polite gestures were
received quite differently than they had been at the beginning. However,
since it would have taken a miracle to render me suspicious after so many
proofs of Théophé's virtue and even her coldness, I found innumerable reasons to excuse her. She had enough natural taste to recognize in the count's
noble demeanor the difference between our manners and those of the Turks.
She was studying the count as a model. These excuses, which I made for her
quite naturally, were all the more plausible since I had noticed a thousand
times that she had studied me as well, and without finding in me as much
elegance and finesse as in the count, she had benefited considerably as
regards her imitation of our manners. More than a week more went by
before I was led to entertain the slightest suspicion, and I've never known
how this secret liaison might have ended if I hadn't by pure chance returned
one day at a moment when I was so completely unexpected that, entering

suddenly into Théophé's room, I surprised the count on his knees. The sight of a snake that was going to sink its poisonous fangs in me could not have shocked or dismayed me more. I was able to withdraw discreetly enough to be sure that I hadn't been seen. But kept at the door in spite of myself by my fears, my suspicions, and my grim reflections, I attempted to increase the despair that was gnawing at my heart by recalling everything that could make Théophé appear even more guilty. To be honest, I did not discover anything indecent in her conduct. However, I remained where I was until dinner, burning with impatience as if I wished to see or hear what I most terribly dreaded.

What reason did I have to be jealous? What commitment had Théophé made to me? What had she led me to hope? What had she promised me? On the contrary, hadn't I renounced any kind of claim on her heart, and wasn't the freedom to follow her own penchants one of the two articles of our pact? I could not deny it; but it seemed so cruel that after all my failed attempts at gaining her affection, another had succeeded so easily. Supposing that she were capable of falling for someone, I would have preferred that it not be the result of a chance encounter with the first fellow who came along. Or to reveal my feelings completely, I was indignant that all those appearances of virtue that I had respected had been so quickly undone. I even blushed at having been the dupe of those fine principles that she had repeated to me so often and with such airs, and I blamed myself less for my kindness than for my gullibility and weakness.

Along with a great deal of embarrassment and spite, there was so much malice in my thoughts that far from giving a favorable interpretation to the reserve the count had exhibited in her presence, I felt inclined to conclude that it was the calm of a sated lover whose tranquil state was perhaps only an indication that he had already obtained everything that could stimulate his desire. What additional violent emotions this thought provoked in me! But I had enough self-control not to undertake any rash action. Following my plan to surprise the cruel Théophé in the midst of her pleasures, I arranged to speak with her maid, less to take her into my confidence, which I did not want to risk, than to extract from her any information that she might let slip naïvely; she was a Greek with whom I had replaced Bema, and who had entered my service of her own accord. But either she was more loyal to the mistress I had given her than to myself, or she had been cleverly deceived, like me, by the count and Théophé, I learned nothing from her but their frequent conversations, which she didn't even appear to try to hide from me.[33]

I was careful not to stray far from our rooms, and pretending that a slight indisposition forced me to stay there, I did not leave Théophé's side the rest of the day. The count requested permission to join us that afternoon. Far from objecting, I was delighted that he was going to subject himself to my surveillance, and for more than four hours I gave my full attention to his words and gestures. He did not give himself away by the slightest misstep, but I noticed how cleverly he slipped into our conversation remarks intended to increase the affection I imagined Théophé felt for him. He related a few of his amorous affairs in which he had consistently distinguished himself by his love and fidelity. Whether it was truth or fiction, his only true love had been a Roman lady who had at first made him pay dearly for the conquest of her heart; as soon as she had become acquainted with his fine character, however, she gave herself to him unreservedly and showered him with unbounded love. It was this liaison that had kept him in Italy for two years, and that would have led him to forget his country for good if the most horrible of all misfortunes hadn't severed such a beautiful bond. After he had enjoyed his love tranquilly for a long period, his mistress's husband had become aware of their affair. He had poisoned them both during a meal. The young lady had died; as for him, his robust constitution had saved him, but he recovered only to learn of the death of the woman he loved, and his grief had suddenly plunged him once again into a far more dangerous state than the one from which he had just emerged. In despair that his grief nonetheless had no greater effect than the poison, he had sought death by means that were less criminal than if he had taken his life with his own hand, but that he thought would be nearly as certain. He had confronted the husband whose hate he had earned, and chiding him a thousand times for his barbarity, he had offered up to him, baring his stomach, the victim who had escaped him. He took heaven as his witness that he had thought his death ineluctable, and that he would have willingly accepted it. But this cruel husband, mocking his emotional display, had replied coldly that far from still wishing to put him to death, he was overjoyed to see that he could obtain no sweeter revenge than by letting him live, and he was deeply gratified that he had survived a poison that would have put an end to his suffering too quickly. Since that time he had led a miserable life wandering throughout the Italian cities in an effort to erase memories that made his life perpetual torture and attempting to repair his stricken heart by seeking the company of the most attractive women he could find. But he had arrived in Livorno without having achieved the slightest change in a heart where his sadness continued to preclude any feelings of love.[34]

It was quite clearly implied that this miracle was reserved for Théophé. Nonetheless, I hadn't noticed any trace of this profound melancholy, which should still have been evident when we arrived unless he had been cured since that time. But the keen attention with which Théophé listened to all of his tales left no doubt in my mind that they had made upon her exactly the impression he intended. Evening fell. I was waiting for her impatiently in order to clear up far more horrible suspicions. Théophé's room was next to mine. I got back up as soon as my valet had put me to bed and sought out a vantage point from which I could see anyone approaching our apartment.

However, I couldn't help feeling deep remorse at the outrage I was inflicting on the adorable Théophé; and in the throes of myriad feelings that were pleading in her favor, I wondered if my dark suspicions were sufficiently grounded to justify such insulting surveillance. I spent the whole night without observing anything untoward. I even moved close to the door several times. I listened intently. The slightest noise made me suspicious, and I was tempted, believing I had heard some movement, to knock sharply on the door to be let in. Finally, at sunup, I was going to leave when Théophé's door swung open. A deadly shudder suddenly made my blood run cold; it was she going out accompanied by her servant. Such an early rising troubled me at first; but I then remembered that she had told me several times that to combat the excessive heat of the season she went for walks in the garden, which overlooked the sea. I watched her as she left and was not reassured until I had seen her head in that direction.

One would think that I should have been pleased with the use I had made of the night, and that after an ordeal of this nature the best thing for me to do was to get some sleep, which I badly needed. However, my heart was not yet unburdened. I was still concerned about the movement I had heard in the room. The key was still in the door. I went in, hoping to find some trace of what had alarmed me. It was perhaps a chair or a curtain that Théophé herself had pushed. But in examining carefully every inch of the room, I detected a little door that opened onto a hidden set of stairs and whose existence had escaped me until then. All of my anxiety was revived at this sight. "That is how the count gets in," I cried in my distress. "There is the source of my shame and of your crime, wretched Théophé!" I can hardly describe the fervor with which I examined all the passageways to discover where the stairway could lead. It led to an isolated courtyard, and the door at the bottom of the stairs appeared to be carefully closed. But couldn't it have been opened during the night? It occurred to me that the best place I could hope to find any evidence was in Théophé's own bed, which was still unmade. I pounced eagerly on this idea. I approached her bed with even greater apprehension, as if I were on the point of discovering some indisputable proof. I observed every single detail, the appearance of the bed, the state of the sheets and blankets. I went so far as to measure how much room Théophé needed and to try to determine if the bed had been rumpled beyond the limits of her size. There was no way I could be mistaken; and even though it occurred to me, as hot as it was, that she might have thrashed about in her bed as she slept, it seemed to me that nothing could prevent me from recognizing where she had lain. This examination, which went on for a long while, produced an effect that I had not at all foreseen. Since my observations served only, little by little, to relieve my fears, the sight of the place where my dear Théophé had just rested, the outline of her body that I could still see in the sheets, a trace of warmth that still lingered there, the dampness left by her gentle perspiration, moved me so profoundly that I pressed my lips a thousand times to the places she had touched. Tired as I was from staying awake all night, I lost myself so entirely in this pleasant activity that my senses succumbed to sleep, and I remained in a deep slumber in the very place that she had occupied.[35]

During this time she was in the garden, where it wasn't surprising that she had met the count, since it was virtually an established practice at this inn to go out to enjoy the sea air before the heat rose during the day. Various people in the neighborhood also appeared there, turning the place into a kind of public promenade. By chance, that very day the captain of a French ship that had arrived in the port the day before was there with several passengers he was bringing back from Naples. The sight of Théophé, always a cause for admiration, drew the foreigners to her, and the count, who recognized the captain as a Frenchman, managed to gain his confidence by a few ingratiating remarks. He not only learned from him about his own business but also a bit about my own; that is, the captain, who had seen our ship upon arriving in the port, had inquired of several sailors on the decks where they came from and whom they had on board; and these vulgar individuals, whose silence I had neglected to procure when I left the ship, had revealed the position I had previously occupied. When the count heard me referred to by this title, he was extremely surprised not to have known that I was in Livorno, since the captain's comments clearly suggested that I had been there for several days already. After some reflection, he concluded that I must be the person in question, and that for some reason I had preferred to remain incognito. But unable to control his initial reaction as his thoughts turned to Théophé, he expressed some embarrassment at not having shown her the deference he thought he owed my daughter. But what has always convinced me, without knowing him any better, that he was not of common birth was that on the basis of the knowledge he had just received, he came up with a plan that hadn't yet occurred to him, which was to offer his hand in marriage to Théophé, under the assumption that I was her father. Having sought a way to bring her to approve this plan before they left the garden, their walk lasted much longer, with the result that it was late in the morning when he gave her his hand for the walk back and returned her to her apartment.

She had listened to his proposition with all the embarrassment one can imagine, and understanding immediately that she owed it only to the mistaken opinion he had of her birth, she had resisted with vague excuses that he had no way of understanding. However, remaining no less firm in his intentions, he told her as they entered her apartment that he would not let the day pass without informing me of his sentiments; and if anything could reassure me about their relations, it was both the promptness with which he broke them off after the incident I'm going to relate and the desire he had shown to unite his fate with hers solemnly through the bond of marriage. I was still in the position in which I had fallen asleep, that is, wearing my dressing gown, of course, but lying in Théophé's bed; and as I was jolted awake by the noise they had made when they opened the door, I had heard the count's last words. I would have preferred to dissimulate my presence, and despite the discomfort I felt at being caught in this position, I would have taken advantage of my situation to hear the rest of their conversation. But the bed curtains were open, and the count was the first to catch sight of me. He had no trouble seeing that I was a man. "What is this?" he blurted out in utter astonishment. Théophé, who spotted me almost at the same moment, let out a scream as much from fright as from embarrassment. It would have been useless to try to slip away. The only recourse I could think of was to try to put on a smile and, making the best of a bad situation, turn the incident into a joke. "I found your door open," I said to Théophé, "and not getting a shred of rest all night, I thought that I might sleep better in your bed than in my own." She had cried out at first in shame and embarrassment, but finding nothing in her ensuing thoughts that might explain a behavior so incompatible with the terms of our relationship, she expressed her uncertainty and dismay by her silence. The count, for his part, thought he understood instantly what he had not even suspected and offered me his apologies for an indiscretion that he considered criminal; and assuring me that he respected me far too much to interfere with my pleasures, he took his leave in such a manner that it was easy to see that he was no longer unaware of my identity.

I remained alone with Théophé. Despite the effort I had made to give a humorous turn to the events, it was difficult for me to avoid feeling an embarrassment that was greatly increased by hers. I saw no other way to get out of this predicament than by frankly sharing with her my suspicions about her behavior; especially since the promises I had heard the count make were a new cause for concern about which I was extremely impatient to hear her explanation. As deeply as she had flushed when she had caught sight of me in her bed, the color now drained from her face upon hearing my first admonishments. She nonetheless interrupted me, trembling, to protest that my suspicions were an outrage, and that nothing had happened between her and the count that was contrary to the principles I knew she possessed. Such an absolute denial turned my resentment into indignation. "What! You deceitful creature," I said, as if I had any right to censure her betrayal. "Didn't I see the count at your feet? Haven't you treated him, during our stay in Livorno, with more kindness than you ever had for me? Didn't he, just this moment, promise to spare no effort today to guarantee his happiness by making you his own? What did he mean by that promise? Speak to me. I want to hear it from you. I will not spend my life being the plaything of an ingrate for whom my love and favors have never inspired anything but cruelty and hatred."[36]

My wrath must have been at its peak for me to use such harsh terms. She had never heard from me anything but expressions of esteem and love or complaints so tender that she must have felt my respect for her even in any reproaches prompted by my unhappiness. Therefore, she was so shocked at my words that, with tears streaming down her face, she begged me to listen to what she had to say in her defense. I forced her to sit down; but as the bitterness that filled my heart still dominated the pity that her distress inspired in me, I did not soften the severity of my voice or of the expression on my face.

After repeating to me, with additional protests, that she had granted nothing to the count for which she deserved any blame, she admitted to me not only that he was in love with her, but that in a change of heart that she herself found difficult to comprehend, she had felt an extremely strong attraction to him. "It is true," she continued, "that I didn't resist this inclination as much as I should have in the light of my own principles; and if I dare tell you the reason, it is because I didn't believe that he had any knowledge of my wretched past, so I flattered myself that I could enjoy with him the ordinary rights of a woman who has pledged herself to honor and virtue. He told me that he normally lived in the country. That is another reason that convinced me that he would never learn about my misfortunes; and as long as he took you for a merchant, I didn't feel that I was deceiving him to his disadvantage by allowing him to think that I was your daughter. However, I must confess," she added, "that ever since he learned of your position—and this knowledge prompted his decision to ask for my hand this very day—I have had scruples that I would not have waited long to share with you. Those are my honest feelings," she added, "and although you saw him at my feet, I neither tolerated him in that position nor authorized him to take it by any reprehensible encouragement."

She appeared to be reassured after this declaration, and expecting me to approve her intentions, she looked at me more calmly. But her opinion of her innocence was precisely the cause of my despair. I was profoundly offended that she was so unconcerned with my feelings, or that she was so indifferent to them that she didn't even appear to have any fear of hurting me, and that she felt completely free to abandon herself to a new penchant. However, my feeling of shame led me to repress this bitter spite deep within me, and trying to react to the situation in a reasonable way, I said, "I am inclined to believe your explanations, and it would not be easy for me to be convinced that you have deceived me by false displays of virtue; but if the count knows me, what hope can you harbor that he thinks you are my daughter when he knows or will find out shortly that I have never been married? If he knows it already, you are too intelligent not to perceive that his intentions cannot be sincere, and that you are only a source of amusement for him. If he is not yet aware of it and intends to marry you under the mistaken impression that you are my daughter, won't this plan fall to pieces when he learns that I am not your father? But you know that only too well," I continued, unable to contain the jealousy that was tearing at my heart. "You aren't so naïve that you think a nobleman would marry you just like that. You are attracted to him. You simply followed the dictates of your heart, and perhaps you went much further than you dare to admit. Why do you imagine I am in your room?" I added in another surge of bitterness. "It is because I've discovered your affair in spite of you. I read your passion in your eyes, in your speech, in every aspect of your behavior. I wanted to catch you in the act and cover you with shame. I would have done it last night if my former affection had not compelled me to spare you. But you may be sure that I saw everything, heard everything, and that a person has to be as weak as I still am to treat you with so little scorn and resentment."

It is easy to perceive my purpose in making this speech. I wanted at all cost to free myself from the doubts that were still tormenting me, and I pretended to be well informed about all the things I feared to discover. Théophé's denials were so emphatic and the signs of her distress so natural that if any credence may be lent to the justifications of a woman who is just as clever as she is in love, I would not have had the slightest reason to doubt her sincerity. But it is not yet time to submit this case to the judgment of my readers. The trial of this ungrateful woman is far from over.

The two of us spent the remaining time before dinner in other discussions that shed no light on the situation. Finally we were informed that dinner was being served. I was impatient to see how the two lovers were going to act in my presence, and I was especially curious about how the count was going to greet me. I imagine that my impatience was matched only by Théophé's embarrassment. But I didn't see the count at the table; it was only in conversing with the other guests that I learned that he had left in a post chaise after saying good-bye to everyone in the inn. However surprised I was by this piece of news, I pretended not to give a second thought to his departure, and sneaking a glance at Théophé I noted that she was making a supreme effort not to allow any sign of distress to appear on her features. She withdrew to her room after dinner. I would have followed her immediately if I hadn't been detained by the French captain I mentioned earlier, who, having had the discretion until then not to reveal that he knew me, came up to me finally to pay me the respects that he thought were due me. I still did not know by what quirk of fate he had managed to learn my name. In chatting with him,

I learned not only what had happened in the garden but also the reasons behind the count's rapid departure. The captain offered his apologies, as if he had feared a rebuke from me. "Not having been apprised," he said, "of the impression you had created here regarding the status of the young lady who is with you, I answered the count's questions frankly. He spoke of your daughter. I carelessly answered him that you did not have one, and without knowing you personally, I knew like everyone else in France that you weren't married. He asked me to repeat this answer several times, and I understood from what I could gather that my indiscretion may have disturbed your plans."

I assured the captain that he had given me no reason to complain, and that if I had changed my name or disguised myself in any other way at Livorno, it was solely to avoid the bother of any ceremonies. I gave him no other reason to respect my desire to remain out of the public view. But it was obvious to me that when the count had learned that Théophé was not my daughter, he had surmised that she was my mistress. The position in which he had surprised me in her room must have led him to that conclusion; and in his embarrassment at having proposed to her, he could think of nothing else to do but simply leave without seeing her. I hastened to return to Théophé's room. I could only guess at her despair, for scarcely had she caught sight of me when, doing her best to look calm, she asked me with a smile if I weren't surprised at the count's sudden decision. "You see," she added, "that his feelings were not all that serious, since he was capable of shedding them so quickly that he left without even telling me good-bye." I pretended not to see beyond this feigned serenity. "He did not love you very deeply," I said to her solemnly, "and if his tokens of affection were no more ardent than his actions, this passion certainly did not cause him to forget his Roman lady." Our conversation, which lasted all afternoon, was thus a continuous charade in which Théophé pretended steadfastly to be indifferent to her loss, while for my part, with a malicious satisfaction that came doubtlessly from the hope that I felt rising anew in my heart, I continued to denigrate the count's passion and to speak of his departure as if it were a matter of extreme rudeness and an outrage. She somehow found the strength to make it through this scene. Since the captain of the ship on which I had arrived appeared willing that very evening to set sail as soon as I agreed to it, I requested only the following day to make my preparations. It was less any pressing business that led me to ask for a day than the precautions I thought were necessary for Théophé's well-being. I had observed all too clearly the efforts she had to make constantly to dissimulate her grief, and I wanted to be sure that her health would not suffer in any way.

She held up until we embarked; but as soon as she had lost any hope of seeing the count again, she took to her bed, succumbing to her broken heart, and did not leave it until our arrival in Marseilles. I tended her with all the care that my paternal duty would have prompted me to give a daughter, or that my love would have led me to give a cherished mistress. However, it was impossible for me to see her languishing for another man without discovering that the most ardent love is eventually chilled by hard-heartedness and ingratitude. Little by little I noticed that my heart was becoming less heavy, and without losing my desire to be useful to Théophé, I was no longer prone to the distress that had plagued me for the past several years. I had ample time to recognize this change during a calm that lasted more than a week and left us stranded near the entrance to the Gulf of Genoa. No one had ever seen such absolute stillness of both air and water. We weren't even six leagues from the shore, and the surface of the water being so calm that we seemed fastened to the same place, I was tempted several times to get into a lifeboat with Théophé and several of my servants to row ourselves ashore. I would have spared myself a serious fright caused by a few scoundrels who, letting their imagination run wild in their forced idleness, planned to take over the ship by killing the captain and the other officers. This conspiracy had perhaps been cooked up before our departure, but the opportunity to carry it out couldn't have been better. We had on board five Italians and three men from Provence who, like myself, were traveling as simple passengers; people whom, given their gear and manners, the captain and I had not been at all tempted to get to know better. They had limited their frequentations to several sailors from their own country, with whom they spent their time imbibing constantly; and it was during these cheerful drinking bouts that they had plotted to knife the captain and his lieutenant, convinced that they would meet little resistance from the rest of the crew, who were very few in number. Their plan with respect to me and my servants was to put us ashore on some isolated place on the coast of the island of Corsica and to seize everything I had brought with me. Through an extraordinary act of Providence, my valet fell asleep on the deck during the night. He was awakened by the talk of these abject assassins, who, having met to discuss how to carry out their plans, were already assigning the main roles, deciding who

would be in command, and dividing up the booty. Since the captain was in
the habit of appearing on the upper deck at the end of the day, it was decided
that they would do away with him at that moment, while two accomplices
would knock on the lieutenant's door and cut his throat as soon as he opened
it. The others were to spread out on the ship and keep everyone else under
control through threats and a show of weapons. While agreeing to treat me
with a semblance of respect and to leave me on the island of Corsica with my
servants, one of them offered to take Théophé as the most valuable part of
my possessions. But after a short discussion, they came to the conclusion
that such a beautiful woman would only serve to create dissension among
them, so they decided instead to put her ashore with me.

Although he was trembling from his horrible discovery, my valet had
enough presence of mind to understand that our only hope for salvation lay
in speed and secrecy. It was around midnight. By the grace of heaven he
managed to sneak along the upper deck and reach the captain's room, which,
as luck would have it, adjoined my own. He awakened us with the same care
and, after urging us to keep silent, gave us a terrifying account of the calam-
ity we were facing. The darkness had prevented him not only from recognizing the conspirators but also from being able to calculate their number.
However, having recognized the ringleaders from their voices, he named several of them and surmised that there could be a dozen of them in all. I cannot
be suspected of excessive vanity if I boast of my courage, for there are abun-
dant well-known examples. With the eight servants in my retinue, the captain, his lieutenant, and myself, there were eleven of us who were capable of
defending ourselves. There were also several sailors whom we knew we could
count on and a few other passengers who were no less interested than we in
protecting themselves from abuse by a band of thugs. The only difficulty we
faced was getting everyone together. I took this task upon myself, and after
having several torches lit, I sallied forth armed to the teeth, followed by all
of my servants, whom I had armed as well. I encountered no difficulties in
reaching all those we thought could help us, and having led them to my
room, we set up our defenses so that we had nothing to fear until daybreak.
However, our enemies, becoming aware of our movements, began to fear
even more for themselves than we had for ourselves. They were not as well
armed as we were, nor were their numbers as great, to say nothing of the terror that always accompanies a crime. Understanding that it would be difficult for them to resist our efforts in the daylight, they hastened to take the

only course that could save them from punishment. With the help of the sailors who had joined their plot, they lowered the lifeboat and rowed to the nearest shore. They could not conceal their actions from us; but even though it would have been easy for us to cut them to pieces while they were preparing their escape or to shoot them down in the lifeboat with our muskets and pistols, I decided that we should allow them to get away.

It was impossible to hide this event from Théophé. The clinking of weapons and the commotion that she noted around her put a scare into her that she had trouble surmounting, or perhaps this was just what she called the surge of grief that was secretly devouring her since our departure from Livorno. Her lethargy turned into an out-and-out fever, which was accompanied by several extremely dangerous lapses. Her health had not improved when we arrived in Marseilles. Whatever reasons I had to hasten my return to Paris, her condition was so serious that I could risk neither exposing her to the jolting of a coach nor leaving her in the care of my servants in a city so far from the capital. I watched over her with the same kindness and devotion I had shown her throughout our voyage. With every passing moment it became clearer to me that it was no longer love that made her so dear to me. It was the pleasure I took in seeing and hearing her. It was the esteem I felt for her character. It was my own largess that seemed to draw me to her as if she were my creation. No expressions of passion crossed my lips, nor a single complaint about the torment I saw her suffering for my rival.

She gradually recovered after having been so ill that the doctors had despaired more than once of her surviving. But her attractiveness was affected by such extreme suffering; and if she could not lose the evenness or the delicateness of her features, I found the beauty of her complexion and the brightness of her eyes greatly diminished. She remained nonetheless a very pretty woman. Several people of distinction with whom I had become acquainted during her illness often came to my residence to see her in particular. M. de S . . . , a young man who was to come into a great fortune, made no effort to hide the love he had conceived for her. After bantering about it for a long time, he became so serious that he sought an opportunity to broach the subject with her. He found her just as cold as she had been to me, as if she had been able to respond only to the lucky count who had discovered the key to her heart. She even asked me to spare her the irksome attentions of this new suitor. I promised to render her this service without taking advantage of the situation to remind her of my own desires. And to be perfectly frank, they had died out to the point that they could not be distinguished from simple feelings of friendship.

The results of the discussion I had with M. de S . . . were far from what she had expected; he felt, on the contrary, all the more entitled to besiege her with constant expressions of his love. He had hesitated at first out of fear of finding himself in competition with me. But when he learned that I was only a friend of Théophé's, and the only reason I was opposed to his attraction to her was the wish she had expressed to me, he announced that with the keen passion he felt for her, he could not let himself be discouraged by an attractive woman's indifference, and he still had the hope, commonly entertained by a suitor, to win by his perseverance what he hadn't been able to gain by his qualities or by the lady's inclinations. I informed him that after Théophé's declaration all of his efforts would be in vain. His ardor was no less dampened, especially when I protested on my honor that I had never received any favors from her that could lead him to doubt her virtue. As soon as she had recovered enough to enjoy entertainment, he set out to dispel her melancholy with parties and concerts. She went along with it, less out of any inclination than just to be kind, especially when she saw that far from being opposed, I was happy to share these distractions with her. M. de S . . . was just a merchant's son; and if it was an appreciation of her good qualities that attracted him to such a lovely girl, I saw nothing shocking in his apparent desire to marry her. Condoidi's stubborn refusal to recognize her as his daughter would not have prevented me from testifying that she was, and the evidence I had seen was convincing enough to make me feel quite certain about this. However, M. de S . . . , who occasionally spoke to me of his passion, never mentioned marriage. I tried in vain to suggest the idea to him by various reflections that should have at least led him to understand that I only approved of his feelings on this condition. Since I didn't find him as enthusiastic about this idea as I would have liked, and to justify at the very least the indulgence I had shown toward his amorous behavior, I resolved to speak to him frankly. Thus, in a very strange turnabout, I found myself securing Théophé's conquests and preparing to separate myself from her forever by making her the wife of another man. Above and beyond her interests, which were my primary motive, I couldn't ignore the fact that it would be difficult for me in Paris to avoid the suspicions that would arise concerning my relationship with her; and even though I was not so old that love had become unseemly for me, I had plans that hardly accommodated liaisons of this nature.

If I spoke frankly with M. de S . . . , he responded in the same manner, replying that he loved Théophé enough to wish to make her his wife, but having myriad precautions to take with his family, he did not dare commit himself recklessly to an undertaking that might lead to his father's disgrace; nonetheless, no longer being a minor he was quite willing to marry her in secret, and he left it up to me to work out all the details. I reflected at length on this offer. Although it assured me of obtaining everything I had wanted, it did not seem worthy of me to contribute to a clandestine marriage that promised little hope of happiness for Théophé, given that she would be forced to hide her status for a long period, and that could be detrimental to M. de S . . . 's fortunes by getting him into trouble, sooner or later, with his family. I replied curtly that a clandestine arrangement was not suitable for Théophé, and I left him distressed at the thought that I was even offended by his proposal.[37]

However, since I didn't yet know Théophé's own inclinations, and since having already been mistaken about her feelings once before, I could be wrong again in assuming that she would not stray from her first declaration. I wanted to sound her out and inform her of the good fortune that love was prompting someone to propose to her. I was hardly surprised to hear her reject the love and the hand of M. de S . . . ; but when I insisted in her own words on how advantageous it would be for her to receive all the rights due virtue and honor by a marriage that could erase all of her memories of the past that continued to haunt her, and the only response I received was that she was not inclined to get married, a rush of spite prompted me to rebuke her for misleading me when she had claimed with such a show of sincerity that this was the only reason that she had suffered the count's attentions. She was disconcerted by this objection, but attempting to overcome her discomfiture by adopting an air of kindness and candor that had always worked with me, she beseeched me not to misinterpret her feelings or, if I preferred, not to judge her weaknesses too severely. And reminding me of my promises, she took heaven as her witness that whatever inconsistencies I may have noticed in her conduct, she had never ceased to consider the hope I had given her to live with me as the greatest good she could ever desire.

I thanked her for her kind words and assured her that I would keep all of
my commitments to her. Her health improving as each day passed, we soon
began planning our departure. M. de S . . . strove in vain to stop us, often
with tearful appeals. He heard from Théophé's own mouth the decision that
condemned him to repress his passion, which did not prevent him, under
some pretext he invented pertaining to his father's business, from accompanying us as far as Lyon in a post chaise just behind my berlin. And when he
was obliged to take his leave, he whispered in my ear that he planned to
travel to Paris immediately, where he was sure that he would be able to
choose a bride more freely out of his father's view. I've always been convinced
that he had tried secretly to obtain his family's consent, and that it was upon
his father's refusal that he had proposed a clandestine marriage.

Constantly occupied for a long period by my personal affairs, I was no
longer able to keep close track of Théophé's behavior. I took her into my
home, treated her with all the respect I had always shown her, and granted
her the same rights she had enjoyed at Oru. My friends formed varying
opinions upon seeing me arrive in Paris with this beautiful Greek girl. They
were not satisfied with the frank account I gave them of some of the events
of her past; and since I was ever careful to hide those that had besmirched
her early years, they saw in my praise for her principles and conduct the
exaggerations of a man in love. Others, when they had come to know her
better, recognized in fact all of the qualities I ascribed to her and were all
the more convinced that I was in love with this young lady whom they
couldn't imagine I had brought from Turkey for any other reason. Thus,
they all agreed, as I had foreseen, that I had more intimate relations with her
than I did, and even the demands of my business concerns, which sometimes
prevented me from seeing her for three days at a time, could not change their
opinion. But the general public held even more varied and bizarre views on
the subject. At first they said she was a slave that I had bought in Turkey and
had become so enamored of that I had gone to great lengths to see that she
was educated. This was not so far from the truth. But then they added, and I
met various people in the Tuileries who told me this without knowing who I
was, that the Sultan, having fallen in love with my slave after being told of
her charms, had asked me for her, and this was the sole cause of all the conflicts I had had in Constantinople. And since Théophé's looks, despite how
attractive she still was, were no longer striking enough to have conceivably
provoked such admiration, they claimed that in order to escape the torments

of jealousy, I had destroyed part of her beauty with an acid that I had had prepared. Others claimed that I had abducted her from a harem, and that it was this audacity that had cost me my post.[38]

I kept myself above all these tales by listening to them calmly, and I was always the first to joke about them. Théophé had made a very good impression on all the people in my social circle, and she soon had a large number of admirers at her feet. It seemed unlikely to me that she could fend off forever the devoted attention she was receiving from so many dashing young men, but I thought it my duty to give her some advice about the precautions women have to take. The episode with the comte de M. Q. had shown me that she was vulnerable to suave looks and fine manners. That represented a constant danger in Paris, and if I was no longer motivated by love, I was at least obliged by honor to protect my house from anything that might lead her into unacceptable behavior. She listened to my counsel with her normal docility. Her taste for reading had not lessened, and I even noted in her an increased enthusiasm for learning. Perhaps vanity was now beginning to accomplish what I had always been led to attribute to a passion to enrich her heart and mind. However, whether I was no longer observing her closely enough to keep track of her conduct, or whether she was cleverer than I had given her credit for in disguising it, I noticed nothing offensive in her behavior until the arrival of M. de S . . . , who provoked suspicions that I never would have entertained otherwise.

He did not have the good fortune to become an object of them himself. But after spending several weeks in Paris and appearing quite often in my house, where I received him with the utmost courtesy, he spoke to me in private one day to air some very bitter complaints. The purpose of his trip, he said, was the same as he had told me in Lyon; but his fortune had changed considerably. Instead of only having to overcome the coldness of his mistress, he found himself in competition with several active suitors, and he had a multitude of reasons to believe that she was not equally indifferent to all of them. He was particularly disheartened by the attention she was showing M. de R . . . and the young comte de . . . , who seemed to be courting her the most zealously.[39] She was not seeing them in my house; but this very exception was the source of the extreme unhappiness of the young man from Marseilles, who was convinced that the special treatment she accorded them, as compared to the many other suitors whose visits she received with apparent indifference, clearly indicated a strong penchant for them. But was it conceivable that she loved them both at the same time? He still had not solved this mystery. But having trailed her to church, on her walks, and to the theater, he had constantly spotted these two troublesome rivals hanging around her, and the look of satisfaction that appeared on her face when she caught sight of them was enough to betray her feelings. He did not add anything that might have fueled my suspicions, and the request that accompanied his complaint tended on the contrary to allay them. He beseeched me to help him gauge his chances more clearly and at least not to permit feelings as honorable as his to be rebuffed with undisguised scorn.

I promised not only to look after his interests most enthusiastically but to get to the bottom of an intrigue I was entirely unaware of. To keep Théophé company, I had found an elderly widow whose advanced age would normally protect her from the follies of youth; and even if I had been less sure of the behavior of the young Greek girl, I would have been confident in the example and guidance of such an experienced governess. They never left each other's side, and I was pleased to see that they were drawn together as much by friendship as by my intentions. I only revealed to the governess a part of the accusations against her charge, because M. de S . . . had admitted to me that he had never seen Théophé alone, so if one of them deserved any recriminations, the other did as well. The elderly widow listened to mine with such equanimity that I was immediately inclined to attribute M. de S . . .'s anguish to his jealousy. She even named him as the source of my worries. "He is unhappy," she said, "that Théophé is so unresponsive to his love. He plagues her constantly with his chatter and his letters. We began to make fun of such an annoying passion, and he probably went to complain to you out of resentment. As for what he calls our crimes, you know very well what they are," she added, "since I was only following your orders by providing some entertainment for Théophé." She described their pleasures to me forthrightly. They were the ordinary distractions of respectable Parisians; and if the two rivals who were causing M. de S . . . such alarm were sometimes included in their walks or in other equally innocent activities, they received no special treatment of which they could take advantage.

This response put my mind at rest, and I could only console M. de S . . . by urging him to do what he could to make himself worthy of Théophé's heart, which I assured him was pure and innocent. His suppositions were nonetheless not completely baseless. While she was incapable of participating in or approving inappropriate behavior, my elderly widow still had enough self-esteem and vanity to be the dupe of two young men, one of whom had tried to help his friend by pretending to be in love with a woman who was at least sixty years old. Her gaze, focused solely on the attention she was receiving, saw nothing of what was going on with her companion, and her blindness even led her to believe that Théophé was quite happy to share the flirting she thought was directed to her alone. Neither the testimony given by M. de S . . . , who finally discovered this farce, nor any evidence other than what I had seen with my own eyes would ever have been able to convince me of it.

One day, particularly well chosen because I was enjoying a respite in both my official duties and my infirmities, M. de S . . . beseeched me to join him in his carriage to go witness a scene that would finally bring me to lend more credence to his complaints. He had discovered, through his constant vigilance, that Théophé and the elderly widow had agreed to an outing that was to conclude with a lunch in the Saint-Cloud gardens. He had learned both the place and the arrangements of the party; and what had gotten him so worked up that he included threats in his account was that he knew that M. de R . . . and the young count were going to be alone with the two ladies. However the widow might try to present this outing, I found it so imprudent that I condemned it out of hand. I allowed myself to be driven to Saint-Cloud, determined not only to observe what was happening in such a licentious setting, but also to cover the two ladies with admonishments that even the innocence of their intentions could not spare them. They were already there with their two gallants. We saw them stroll around a while in a place so open that it seemed useless to follow them. M. de S . . . took care to choose an observation post where we could miss nothing that happened during their collation. He wanted to be able not only to see them but to hear them as well. Having learned that the spot where the preparations were being made was a circle of lawn in the upper part of the garden, we made our way there in a very roundabout way and were fortunate to find a place behind an arbor just ten feet away.

They arrived shortly after us. There was nothing unseemly in their demeanor. But scarcely were they seated on the grass when their party began with a long session of playful banter. It began with the widow, and I understood suddenly that the flattery and compliments of the two young men were just a lot of mockery that they had prepared in advance. After a hundred vapid compliments on her charms, after comparing her to nymphs, they adorned her with grass and flowers, their admiration seeming to grow at the sight of her in this comical toilette. She was touched by the slightest flattery, and her modesty leading her to resort to various circumlocutions to express her pleasure, she praised the wit and charm she found in each word. How ridiculous a woman is, I reflected, when she forgets her age and looks! I found the old governess so justly punished that if I had not had more important concerns, I would have found this spectacle highly amusing. But I could see the count taking advantage of some lulls to turn to Théophé and, adopting a more serious tone, address remarks to her occasionally that we could not hear. The fervor that was consuming M. de S . . . was blazing in his eyes. He was fidgeting so much that I was afraid that the noise of his movements was going to betray our presence; and if I had not restrained him several times, he would have leapt up to put a stop to a spectacle that was cutting him to the heart. What difficulty I had keeping him under control when he saw the count lower his head near the grass to secretly kiss one of Théophé's hands that she seemed in no hurry to withdraw!

The snack was exquisite and quite lengthy. The animated atmosphere was sustained by a large number of tales and witty comments. While the drinking was not excessive, they tasted several kinds of wines and did not shy away from the liqueurs. Finally, although nothing clearly reprehensible had transpired, all that I had seen left me with a feeling of displeasure that I was resolved to convey in the very near future. However, I would have endured it until our return to Paris, and believing the ladies ready to go back to their carriage, I was contemplating how to avoid being seen when we returned to ours when M. de R . . . , offering his arm to the governess, steered her into a covered path that led to nothing less than the park's gate. The count accompanied likewise Théophé, and imagining that he was going to follow his friend, I intended only to watch them leave. But I saw them take a different route. The danger seemed urgent. I did not want to wait for further evidence, and I had no need of M. de S . . . 's exhortations to head off the problem quickly. Having at least obtained his promise to remain calm, I soon caught up to the four lovers with M. de S . . . at my side, and I pretended that having come to Saint Cloud for the pleasure of taking a walk, I had just been informed of their party and told where I could join them. They were so disconcerted that despite the joviality and lightheartedness I tried to assume, they were slow in regaining their composure; and it was only after a rather long silence that they politely offered to share with us what remained of their meal.

I was hardly tempted to accept, being solely concerned with immediately breaking off a dangerous affair, and declared to the two ladies that I had several matters to address with them that obliged me to ask for a seat in their carriage. "These gentlemen did not come without their own vehicle," I added in turning toward them, "and if not, mine would be available to them." M. de R . . . had ordered his carriage to follow them. We took the paths that led directly to the gate, and the two suitors suffered the humiliation of seeing M. de S . . . take one of the places they had occupied.

It would have been too harsh to criticize the ladies for their wayward behavior in front of a stranger. I put off the moralizing until our return to Paris; but upon getting a close look at the governess, who was sitting across from me, I couldn't resist laughing at my memory of her adornment or paying her a few compliments on her charms in the same vein as the ones she had received earlier. It seemed to me that she was so daffy that she thought they were sincere. Théophé was smiling maliciously, but I was preparing a compliment for her that I was sure would sober her up. She nonetheless had time to give one to M. de S . . . too that took away any hope he may have been harboring. Whether she had some suspicion of the reasons that had brought us to Saint Cloud and was convinced that it was his idea, or she was in fact just fed up with his attentions, which, as I had noticed myself, sometimes bordered on harassment, she took advantage of the moment when he gave her his hand to help her down from the coach. Asking him to trouble her no longer with visits and attentions that she had never cared for and that she would no longer tolerate, she declared that she considered this their final good-bye. He was so thunderstruck that when she turned her back on him and walked away, he didn't have the nerve to follow her. He addressed his complaints to me. I was quite sympathetic since I found something in Théophé's behavior that was extremely contrary to the natural gentleness of her character, and I could not imagine that she had been pushed to such extremes without being propelled by a violent passion. I urged M. de S . . . to try to get over it, like all suitors who meet the same fate, and although it was not much consolation, I promised him my continued friendship. I valued his sincerity much more than his fortune and looks. "Come visit me," I said, "as often as you like. I will not violate Théophé's wishes, but I will remind her of what she is losing in rejecting your suit, and I will certainly make her ashamed of her feelings if she is guilty of indulging in some wanton passion."

My physical ailments forced me to take my meals in my rooms, depriving me of the pleasure of living with my family.[40] But the same concern that had led me to Saint Cloud demanded that I open my heart to Théophé before nightfall. I inquired as to the time she would retire for the night, and having gone to her room with an informality born of a long established habit, I confessed upon arriving that some extremely serious reasons had brought me there. I do not know if she suspected the reason for my visit, but I saw her face fall. She nonetheless listened to me raptly. It was one of her good qualities to strive to understand what was being said to her before attempting to respond.

I got quickly to the point. "You have made no secret of your eagerness to live with me," I said, "and you know the reason you evoked over and over again: your desire for a quiet, virtuous life. Haven't you found that in my house? Why then do you go off to Saint Cloud in search of distractions that are so foreign to your principles, and what are you doing fooling around with M. de R . . . and the comte de . . . , you who have insisted on your devotion to virtuous conduct that is so contrary to their practices? You are not yet familiar with our customs," I added. "That is the excuse my affection finds for you, and the guide I have given you is a foolish old woman who has lost sight of them. But this party at Saint Cloud, this intimate familiarity with two young men who in no way share your manner of thinking, what am I to think of that? This flouting of the most basic proprieties causes me grave concerns that I can hide no longer."

I lowered my eyes when I had finished, and I wanted to give her all the time she needed to prepare her reply. She didn't make me wait long. "I fully understand," she said, "all of your suspicions, and the weakness I exhibited in Livorno is certainly enough to justify them. However, you do me a grievous wrong if you think that either in Saint Cloud or in any other place that you have observed me I have been untrue for even an instant to the principles I carry in my heart. You have repeated a thousand times yourself," she continued, "and I learn every day in the books that you put in my hands, that one must accommodate the weaknesses of other people, learn to live in society, show indulgence toward the faults and passions of one's friends; I am putting into practice your ideas and the principles that I derive constantly from my books. I know you," she added, looking me straight in the eye. "I know that I can confide in you; but you have given me a companion who has foibles I have to humor. She is your friend, she is my guide; what choice do I have but to obey her and do what pleases her?"

It was more than enough to put a halt to my rebukes and even to lead me to regret having expressed them so freely. I suddenly thought I understood what was going on. The count was in love with Théophé. M. de R . . . was pretending to love the elderly widow to help out his friend. And Théophé was tolerating the count's overtures out of consideration for her governess, whom she thought she was helping by facilitating her love affair. What a heap of illusions! But what a surge of renewed esteem I felt for Théophé, in whom I saw again all the wonderful attributes that I formerly knew her to possess. My infirmities were making me gullible.[41] I embraced my lovely Théophé. "Yes," I said, "I am the one you should complain about. I gave you as a guide a mad woman whose ridiculous fantasies must be, I imagine, a constant source of aggravation for you. I am speaking of what I saw with my own eyes. I witnessed it. All I needed to do you the justice you deserve was to understand your intentions better. But let us leave it at that. Tomorrow I will free you from this troublesome bondage, and I already have my eye on a companion who will suit you much better."

It was night. I was in my dressing gown. For me, Théophé had lost none of the overpowering charms that had touched my heart so deeply. The evidence of virtue that could be seen so clearly in her sincere kindness rekindled in me feelings that I thought had been completely stamped out. Even my weakened state was no obstacle, and I am still trying to understand how impressions of honesty and virtue had the same effect on me as the image of vice.[42] I kept my desires no less under control; but this visit renewed a passion that I thought I had finally gotten over, given both my constant ailments and the voice of reason in an older man. A feeling of shame at my weakness did not hit me until I was on my way back to my room, that is, after completely abandoning myself to it. In fact, I put up no more resistance to my feelings than I had back in Constantinople, and if the state of my health hardly permitted me to develop serious desires, I felt all the more justified in indulging in feelings that I had to keep hidden away in my heart. But beginning that very night, they produced an effect that I had not foreseen. They rekindled the intense jealousy that had gripped me for such a long time, and that was perhaps the least suitable to my condition of all the weaknesses of love. I had hardly gone to bed when, unable to understand how I could have grown indifferent to such a charming object, I was infused by regrets at not having taken better advantage of the opportunities I had had to gain her favor, and at the idea that I had brought her to France only to see some adventurer harvest the fruits that I would have obtained sooner or later with a little more zeal and perseverance. Finally, if my passion was prevented by my poor health from regaining its former violence, it became proportional to my current condition, that is, capable of dominating my whole being.

In this state, it didn't take much effort on Théophé's part to satisfy my desires. The only indulgence I intended to ask of her was to keep me company often in my room, where my suffering sometimes kept me bedridden for entire weeks. The new companion that I planned to give her was quite wise and kind enough to submit to this habit without finding anything repugnant in the company of a sick man. The idea of this new plan was so alluring that it helped me to sleep peacefully. But Théophé having requested early the next morning to see me in my room, all of my plans were upended by the proposal she had come to make. Whatever the source of her unhappiness, she had been so affected by my rebukes, or so offended by the incident in Saint Cloud, that bemoaning all of her distractions and the type of life she was leading, she had come to ask me permission to retire to a convent. "The pleasure of seeing you," she said obligingly, "which was the only reason why I wished to live with you, is a favor I am constantly denied by your illness. What am I doing in the tumult of a city like Paris? The flattery of all the men is just a bother for me. I find the excessive distractions far more boring than amusing. I would like," she added, "to organize my life as it was in Oru, and of all the places I have come to know here, I see none that suits my inclinations better than a convent."[43]

Who wouldn't have thought that the unveiling of my own plan was the best response that I could give to this request? Therefore, I hastened to tell Théophé that far from being opposed to her desires, I wanted to help her find in my home all of the advantages she hoped for in a convent; and explaining to her the advantages that I would myself find in having her constantly in my company, reading, painting, and conversing or playing with a new companion, in short, enjoying all the activities that she loved, I expected in all simplicity that she was going to eagerly embrace a proposal that contained everything she had appeared to desire. But reiterating her decision to retire to a convent, she begged me anew to grant her wish. Nothing surprised me more than to notice that she hadn't made the slightest reference to the constant pleasure of seeing me that, she had told me, she was so distressed to

be denied by my infirmities, and that was consequently the first consideration that should have occurred to her. I couldn't keep myself from dwelling
on this. But returning to her idea, after assuming that I would be satisfied
with a few polite comments, she continued to speak of the convent as if it
were the only place that had any appeal for her now. I felt so humiliated by
her indifference that out of pure resentment I declared to her rather testily
that I could not approve of her plans, and that as long as she still had any
consideration for me, I preferred that she put this idea out of her mind for
good. I gave orders at the same time to send for the person whom I had chosen to be her companion and whom I had alerted the day before in a brief
letter. She was a lawyer's widow to whom her husband had left very little
income, and who had been overjoyed at a proposal that could be very advantageous for her. She lived in my neighborhood; as a result she arrived almost
immediately, and I explained to her more thoroughly the service she could
render me by becoming good friends with Théophé. They enjoyed each other's company as much as I had hoped, and Théophé submitted to my wishes
without so much as a murmur.

Such sweet company acted as a charm against all of my torments. I refused
to take anything except from my dear Greek girl's hand. I spoke only to her.
I was interested only in her replies. In the most cruel throes of an illness to
which I am condemned for the rest of my life, I was comforted by her slightest attentions, and the pain I lived with did not prevent me from feeling
sometimes the most delightful sensations of pleasure. She seemed to be sensitive to my situation, and I never got the impression that the additional time
she spent by my side was a burden to her. In any case, a day did not go by
when I did not encourage her to take a few hours to enjoy a walk or some
form of entertainment with her companion. Sometimes I had to insist. Her
absences were short, and she never appeared to find her return home a disagreeable duty. Nonetheless, in the middle of such a charming situation, her
first governess, who was extremely vexed by her dismissal, came once again
to disturb my rest by suspicions that I have never been able to elucidate. It is
here that I completely abandon the judgment of my woes to the reader, and
where I leave him free to form whatever opinion he will on everything that
may have struck him as obscure and uncertain in the character and conduct
of Théophé.[44]

The accusations of this woman were severe. After pitying me for being in
an unfortunate situation that prevented me from becoming aware of what

was going on in my house, she informed me bluntly that the comte de . . .
was seeing Théophé regularly, and that he had succeeded in gaining her
heart, something that he had never accomplished when she was under her
tutelage. And not waiting for me to recover from my initial surprise, she
added that the two lovers saw each other at night in the very apartment
occupied by Théophé, who left me in the evening only to go throw herself
into her lover's arms.

She chose a time when Théophé was absent to do me such an awful favor.
I would not have been able to hide the devastating impression her words
made on me, and in a matter of this nature, it was important not to make a
public spectacle of suspicious behavior that had first to be studied with the
greatest discretion and caution. My initial thoughts were nonetheless in
Théophé's favor. I remembered her entire conduct since she had resolved to
constantly keep me company in my solitude. Other than the time I insisted
she take for her walks, she was never away from my apartment for more than
a quarter hour. Was it these short moments that she was devoting to her
passion, and is love capable of such constant moderation? It was always late
at night when she left me. In the morning she was always just as fresh and
lively as usual. Would this be the case if she had spent the night with a passionate lover? And what's more, didn't she appear proper and modest as she
always had? And wasn't what I treasured most in her this continual combination of prudence and gaiety, which seemed to indicate as much moderation in her desires as order in her thought? Finally I knew the frivolity and
imprudence of her accuser; and although I did not think her capable of slan-
der, I had no doubt that she had been piqued enough by my censuring of her
behavior to seek revenge on me or Théophé or on the person with whom I
had replaced her.

However, since she was still living in my house, and I would not have
wanted the secret she had shared betrayed by either her or me, I replied that
such serious charges required two kinds of precautions that I was certain
she would respect: the first that they be kept secret, as much for the honor of
my house as for that of the young Greek girl; the second that they not be
considered to be absolutely true before being confirmed by convincing testimony. "Discretion," I said, "is a necessity that I urge you to take so seriously
that any failing in this matter would make me your mortal enemy; and as for
the certainty I require, you must understand that it is all the more necessary
that you have exposed yourself to strange suspicions if you are unable to

prove your accusations." We took our leave very much dissatisfied with each other; for if she would have liked me to show more confidence in her story, I had noticed in her zeal more bitterness and vehemence than I should have expected if her only wish was to be of service to me.

Two days went by, days that seemed like centuries of apprehension and torment because of my strained relations with Théophé. As much as I wanted not to find her guilty, I would have been just as upset, if she were, not to learn the full extent of her licentious behavior. Finally the evening of the third day, no more than a half hour after she had left me, her enemy came to my apartment in an agitated state and whispered in my ear that I could catch Théophé with her lover. I made her repeat several times this cruel and humiliating news. She reiterated it with a host of details that removed any possible doubt.

I was in bed, suffering from my normal pains, and I needed to put forth a considerable effort to prepare myself to follow her. How many precautions did I need moreover to hide it from my servants? It is true that these preparations took quite some time. My repugnance and my fears slowed me down as well. Nonetheless, I eventually found myself ready to go to Théophé's rooms. We only had a candle to light our way, and Madame de . . . was carrying it herself. It went out a couple of steps from the door. It took us several moments more to light it again. "I greatly fear," my guide said as she rejoined me, "that her beau has taken advantage of this delay to make his escape! However," she added, "the door could not have been opened and closed without making some noise." We knocked. I was trembling, and my mind was in such a jumble that I could not notice anything. After making us wait a few moments, Théophé's servant opened the door and was clearly astounded to find me at her mistress's door so late at night.

"Is she alone? Is she in bed?" I asked her several questions of this nature, driven by my extreme anxiety. The accuser wanted to burst into the room. I held her back. "It is impossible," I told her, "for anyone to escape now without being seen. This is the only door. And I could never forgive myself for the offense we would be committing to Théophé if she were not guilty." The maid assured me in the meanwhile that her mistress was in bed, and that she was sleeping peacefully. But the noise we were making was in itself enough to awaken her; we heard some movements that seemed to render her enemy even more impatient. I had to follow her and traverse the antechamber. Théophé, after calling in vain for her chambermaid, who slept in a small adjoining room, had apparently reacted to her fear at the noise she heard at her door. She had gotten up, and I was, to be truthful, extremely surprised to see her arrive in person to open the door for us.

It had not taken her very long to dress. She was covered only by a very light robe; and nor was I surprised to find a light in her room, because I was quite aware that this was her habit. But she was up, whereas I had just been assured that she was sleeping. She looked afraid and ill at ease, and I couldn't attribute this merely to her surprise at seeing me. In short, my imagination overwrought by all of the charges brought by her accuser, the slightest disorder that I thought I saw in her room appeared to me to be signs of her lover's presence and proof of the indecent behavior she was being accused of. She asked me, trembling, what brought me to her room so late. "Nothing," I said, in a far brusquer tone than I was accustomed to using with her; and looking all around me, I continued to note everything that could help to resolve my suspicions. The room was so open that nothing could escape my scrutiny. I opened a closet where it would have been no easier to hide. I bent down to look under the bed. Finally, having left no corner unexamined, I withdrew without having spoken a single word, and without even bothering to respond to various questions that Théophé asked in her astonishment at this scene. If shame and indignation were the source of my agitation upon arriving, my feelings were no different when I left, fearing that I had been guilty of a grave injustice. The accuser had remained in the antechamber, as if she were on guard. "Come," I said in a strangled voice. "I am very much afraid that you have led me to take an action that is absolutely scandalous." She seemed as perturbed as I was, and it was only after we had left the room that she protested that the count must have gotten away, since she could assure me that she had with her own eyes seen him come up the stairs and enter the apartment.

I had so few objections to make regarding both the testimony of a woman whom I did not dare suspect of lying and the results of my own investigation that had discovered nothing in Théophé's room that, seeing nothing but horror and embarrassment in this incident, I resolved to return quickly to my bed to try to recover from the cruel torment I felt. However, the memory of the agitated state in which I had just left Théophé and innumerable feelings that pleaded in her favor in my heart prompted me to send one of my servants to reassure her that all was well. I reproached myself for the stubborn silence I had maintained. She could have drawn terrifying conclusions, and what impression must they have made on her mind and heart if she were not guilty? I was informed that she had been found sobbing, and that she had only responded to my message with sighs and complaints about her fate. I was so moved that if I had obeyed my feelings of compassion I would have gone back to her room to console her. But the doubts that still clouded my mind, or rather the nearly insurmountable reasons that seemed to prevent any hope of finding her innocent, kept me in spite of myself in a state of despair that lasted the entire night.

I had decided to forestall her reaction the following day by paying her a visit, as much to calm her spirits as to obtain from her a confession of the misconduct of which she was accused. Having lived with her for such a long time and learned to divine her moods, I hoped that it would not take me long to discover the truth; and if I was forced to lose my esteem for her, I intended at least to save her from her enemy's mockery by hiding from the former governess whatever my personal efforts might turn up. This was part of the reason for keeping my silence during my search the night before. I did not want to be criticized for closing my eyes to the truth, and I would not have spared Théophé had I had the misfortune of catching her with the count; but a glimmer of hope continued to moderate my fears, and I was determined to seize on the slightest pretexts to force the governess to abandon her suspicions. Nothing had perturbed me more than hearing her insist on what she had seen with her own eyes just as I was going to accuse her of jumping to conclusions too hastily.

I was thus getting ready to go up to Théophé's room when I was informed that she was entering my apartment. I was grateful to her for taking the first steps. The care she had taken to compose herself did not prevent me from noticing the marks her tears had left. Her eyes were swollen, and for a while she did not dare look up at me. "Well! What about this, Théophé?" I said before she could utter a word. "So you have been capable of forgetting all your fine principles? You are no longer this sensible, modest young woman whose virtue has always been dearer to me than her beauty? My God! Lovers during the night! I was spared the agony of catching you with the comte de . . . , but he was seen entering your room, and this horrible adventure is not the first." I was watching her with the greatest attention to catch her slightest reactions. She wept for a long time, she sobbed, unable to speak; and not seeing anything yet that could help me form an opinion, I was as gripped by my impatience as she seemed to be by her distress. Finally, regaining the use of her voice: "He was seen entering my room?" she cried. "Who saw him? Who dares make such a cruel accusation against me? It is Madame de . . . , of course," she added, naming her former governess, "but if you give any credence to her hate, it is useless for me to try to defend myself."

I found this statement rather surprising. I focused my entire attention on it. It led me to conclude not only that Théophé was already aware of the subject of my complaints, but that she knew this woman was determined to do her harm. "Listen," I replied, interrupting her. "I will not hide from you that is was indeed Madame de . . . who saw the count. Did I have any reason to be suspicious of her testimony? But if you know anything that might discredit it, I am prepared to listen to you." This encouragement appeared to give her heart. She told me that ever since the day that this lady had ceased to accompany her, M. de R . . . , who no longer took the trouble to see her, had replied rather harshly to some letter in which she had given him to understand that he could continue to pay her visits despite some changes that did not concern her in any way. He had declared to her that the game was over, and that the reasons that had prompted him to participate had disappeared with the changes of which she had informed him. This declaration having opened her eyes to the humiliating role she had played, she had become convinced that Théophé must be on better terms with her lover than she thought she was with hers, and the desire to take revenge had led her to seek all sorts of means to obtain proof of it. "I was completely aware of her tricks," Théophé said. "She had me followed each time I went out, and imagining finally that I was entertaining the count during the night, her malice was so extreme that she had even had my bed carefully inspected. What offers did she not make to my chambermaid? Only two days ago she seized at the door a letter the count had written me. She brought it to me immediately, already opened; and irked to find nothing but respectful expressions in it, she gave it the worst interpretation her spite could invent and threatened to inform you of it."[45]

"I had no doubt," Théophé added, "in seeing you in my room with her yesterday, that her accusations had brought you there. But your presence, or rather the despair that I felt at seeing you listening to my enemy, plunged me into a state of complete dismay, as you may have noticed. Today I have come to entreat you to deliver me from this vicious persecution." Then, tears streaming down her face and adopting Greek gestures of submission she should have long abandoned in France, she threw herself to her knees before my bed and begged me to grant her what I had refused her previously. "A convent," she said, in a voice choked with tears, "a convent is the only choice left to me and also the only one I desire."

I do not know how I would have replied; for as moved as I was by her tears, and convinced by her defense, I felt just as disinclined to consider her accuser to be the meanest and vilest of all women. I remained for a time unsure what to do, and none of my thoughts shed any light on the matter. My door opens. It is Madame de . . . , Théophé's enemy, perhaps mine also, and the source of all our grief. What was I to expect from her visit, some clarity or just more obscurity? I had no time to form an opinion. She couldn't have been unaware that Théophé was in my apartment, and it was apparently the fear that she might gain my confidence that brought her to attack her or defend herself. Thus she immediately began badgering her mercilessly. She reproached her so harshly that, innocent or guilty, poor Théophé could not bear this torrent of insults. She collapsed into a deep faint, and it took my servants a long while to bring her back to her senses. The governess having renewed her accusations even more heatedly, I could see nothing in this horrible dispute other than the stubborn claim of the one that she had seen the comte de . . . enter the room where we had looked for him, and Théophé's steadfast insistence that it was a horrible lie.

I suffered more than she from such a violent scene. Finally, prey to a thousand conflicting emotions that were too painful to try to sort out, unable either to abandon my faith in Madame de . . . 's honor or to bring myself to feel hate and contempt for Théophé, I made the decision, with many a sigh, to order them both to be silent and to recommend to them that they erase the very memory of an incident that we should all hold in horror. "You will not leave me," I said to Théophé, "and you will maintain a conduct that is beyond reproach." "You," I said to Madame de . . . , "will continue to live in my house, and if you ever dare to renew accusations that are not better founded, you will immediately go seek another abode." I had every right to make this threat, since my generosity was her sole means of subsistence.

Since this strange episode I have continued to enjoy Théophé's company, seeking no other satisfaction than the pleasure of seeing and hearing her. The seriousness of my illness, and perhaps the lingering effects of such an unfortunate scene, have gradually cured me of any of the woes caused by love. If she has been guilty of any other indiscretions, the public will have to wait to learn of them from her lovers. No such news has reached me in the quarters where I have been confined by my illness. I did not even learn of her death until several months after the tragic event, owing to the care that my family and all the friends who came to see me in my solitude took to conceal it from me. It was immediately after receiving this news that I began to plan to record in writing the whole story of my relations with this lovely foreigner, and to put the public in a position to judge if my esteem and love were misplaced.

End of the Second and Last Part

Appendix 1

Excerpts from Demetrius Cantemir, *The History of the Growth
and Decay of the Othman Empire*, translated by
Nicolas Tindal (2:423–25n33)

Ferriol and the sword incident

When *Châteauneuf* was recalled, he was appointed to succeed him, on account of his being supposed to have acquired, by long use, a perfect knowledge of the manners and customs of the Othman court. But he behaved in
this post quite otherwise than his friends had expected; for, either through
his haughtiness and natural obstinacy, or by the treacherous advice of some
whom he took for his friends, he not only opposed the *Port* in many respects,
but also demanded several things that never used before to be granted to any
ambassador, and were contrary to the usages of the Othman court. In the
very beginning of his embassy, when he was, according to custom, to have
his first audience of the Sultan, he came into the inner room with his sword
by his side. *Maurocordato*, who assisted at that ceremony as chief interpreter
of the court, friendly told him to take off his sword; for it was an old custom
in the Othman court, not to suffer any one person armed to come to the
Sultan: but he boldly answered, he had received his sword from his King,
and would not take it off for any man. The Sultan having notice of it, sends
Ferriol orders to take off his sword, and if he refused, commands he should
be thrust out of doors. The *Capuji basbi* executes this order, and rudely
pushes back *Ferriol* as he is endeavouring to enter. The ambassador, thus

repulsed, in a very great passion makes his interpreters pull off the Caftans, which, according to custom, they had put on in the outer court, and, trampling upon them, goes out of the palace. When the Sultan heard of it, he ordered all the presents the ambassador had brought (and which also he demanded, affirming they had not been sent by the King, his master, but were of his own purchasing) to be restored to him; and would never after give him admittance, especially as he constantly refused to come without a sword.

The celebration of the birth of the Duke of Brittany, the king's grandson

The last disturbance he raised at Constantinople was in the Vizirship of *Calaily Ahmed Pasha*. He had obtained leave from his predecessor, *Silabdar Hasan Pasha*, to make rejoicings for the birth of the King his master's grandson, by firing guns and making bonfires: and had accordingly got a sumptuous entertainment ready, and made all other preparations for that solemnity. But the very day the rejoicings were to begin, *Silabdar Hasan Pasha* was deposed, and *Calaily Ahmed Pasha* put in his room. *Ferriol*, hearing of this change, sends immediately his chief interpreter to the Vizir's house, to procure a confirmation of the former *Ferman*; and had now a *Ferman* given him to quiet the troubles with his regiment, without further orders, and if the ambassador refused to obey, to extinguish the candles by force, and destroy all his preparations. To this *Ferriol* replies, "If you will violently infringe the rights of the King, my master, and the privileges of ambassadors, I, who am bound to sacrifice my own life for my master's honor, will blow up this house with gun-powder, and in it my self and those that come to offer any violence; and will leave the King, my master, to demand satisfaction for the injury done me." During this disturbance, *Ferriol's* chief interpreter, one *La Fontaine*, a man well versed in the affairs of the *Othman* court, privately puts out the candles that were lighted abroad; not in the order in which they stood, but some here, and others there, so that they might seem to have been blown out by the wind: and the guests perceiving the danger they were in, withdrew by degrees; so that *Ferriol* was forced to do, for want of company, what he would not do for the Sultan's order, that is, put an end to his rejoicings.

Ferriol's descent into madness, excerpted from
Antoine de La Motraye, *Voyages du Sr. A. de La Motraye en Europe,
Asie, et Afrique* (410–11)

A few days later, Monsieur de Ferriol was subject to the indisposition that
has been identified as madness and that occurred in the following manner.

He had invited to the village of Belgrade several ladies and various other
people from his nation, along with a few guests from Holland. The weather
was extremely hot when he and most of the other men mounted their
horses, around nine or ten in the morning. The ladies went by boat to a village named Buyukdery on the shore, not far from Belgrade, which they
then reached by coach. His Excellency entertained the whole party gathered there with his normal lavishness. They had a fine meal, danced, and
sang; in short, everyone had a most enjoyable time. But as they were returning home by the same path, M. de Ferriol saw or thought he saw a snake
cross the road just in front of M. de Marigny's horse, which was on his left.
He said to him, *Be careful that your horse doesn't step on that snake crossing
the road.* When M. de Marigny replied that there was no snake, the ambassador was offended at being contradicted and gave him a rather hard blow
on the back with his riding crop. M. de Marigny responded sharply, *My
Lord, that is not how a nobleman is treated here. Yes it is,* replied M. de Ferriol, *when he speaks like you just did.* This exchange, which was followed by
harsh words and threats from His Excellence, was not interpreted in his
favor, and the rest of the company thought that the heat and the fatigue
from riding, which he had hardly done since his audiences, had affected his
senses; they gestured to the nobleman not to contradict him anymore. In
any case, His Excellence, who appeared more and more overwrought upon
his return to the palace of France and who was unable to sleep the following night, spoke and acted like a man who had become violently delirious;
he was so difficult to deal with that his entourage was finally forced to tie
him up. This treatment seemed to make his illness even worse, and M. de
Marigny having been involved to the point of putting his hands on him
when he was restrained was subjected to threats and violent reproaches of
ingratitude. But what upset M. de Ferriol even more was that they took
away from him an Armenian girl whom he called his *figlia d'anima*, or his
"soul daughter," and whom the malicious gossips called his "body daughter."

This girl even accompanied him out in the streets, holding his hand, when he went to various churches or convents in Galata or when he visited shop-keepers.

The agitated state of the ambassador was such a poorly kept secret that all the other nations represented there knew of it in less than six days. His insomnia, which exacerbated his condition more and more and awakened in his heart all his passions, led him to threaten loudly those who he felt had offended him. Since he had always attempted to thwart the czar's negotiations with the Porte, whereas Knight Sutton had orders from his court to support them, which he had done with such success that it had provoked Ferriol's jealousy, the ambassador challenged him to a duel, of which M. de Marigny informed him in a joking manner. . . . It was at this time that M. Brue, having told the vizir that the ambassador had gone mad, received the response that I related in my note about the audience. It was also he who, shortly thereafter, carried to France an attestation of his madness, signed by the principal merchants of his nation and by the Jewish doctor Fonseca. . . . He returned with M. de Ferriol's order to return to France and the news of the appointment of M. Des Alleurs to succeed him as ambassador.

Excerpts from *Nouveaux mémoires du comte de Bonneval* (112–23)

The comte de Bonneval and the French girl at the slave market

I couldn't resist the desire to speak to her. I had her brought over to ask her how she happened to be in this place. . . . She had a good figure, but nothing out of the ordinary; she wasn't particularly pretty, although her face was not unpleasing; perhaps her grief had diminished the features that would have made her attractive. Here is her adventure as she told it to me. [She had boarded the ship in Marseilles, with her mother and her brother, to go join her father "in one of the islands of the Archipeligo the closest to Chio." The boat having been attacked by Turkish pirates, she was taken prisoner by the captain, who brought her to Constantinople, where he put her in his harem.]

"He had me put in his women's apartment and gave me an old French slave to serve me. They left me in peace for a few days. This woman, following the pirate's orders, spoke to me of his love for me and offered a thousand reasons to convince me to accept it. I resisted all her arguments and constantly repeated that I would rather die. They threatened to use violence or to give me to people who would have no respect for me. They took away the nice clothes they had given me and turned me into a simple servant. I remained intractable. After five or six months of persecution, the pirate's mother persuaded him to sell me. He sent me here under the guard of his most loyal eunuch. I've been in this house for six weeks. These lineups that they make us go through from time to time are more unbearable than the cruelest death. No matter how sad my life here may be, there is nothing I fear more than leaving it.

"You are a Frenchman, Monsieur; you look like a Turkish Lord. . . . Might I be so fortunate as to have the honor of speaking to the comte de Bonneval?" I introduced myself. "Ah!" she cried. "You are a man of honor, you used to be a Christian, and perhaps you still are in your heart. You know the horror a well-bred Christian girl must feel at the idea of the kind of prostitution they want to force on me. In the name of God, take me away from here. . . . If everything people say about you is true, you are generous enough to pay for the pleasure of doing such a fine deed."

Her prayers and tears softened my heart; I granted her request immediately. Since the trader was afraid that she might die from grief, he let me have her for five hundred crowns. I had her brought to my castle. Her joy at being free quickly restored her to good health, and she became her old self, that is, perfectly lovely. I had such a thorough investigation conducted that we finally discovered where her mother and brother were. . . . As regards Mme Letori, a rich old Moslem had bought her. After having tried in vain to get her to submit to him, he had sent her off to one of his country homes to work as a servant. She cost me a thousand crowns.

The comte de Bonneval and the beautiful Persian slave

At one of these traders I found several Persians on the list. One of them appealed to me very strongly. She was tall and had a perfect figure. The fairness of her complexion was dazzling, which further enhanced both her eyes and black hair. What struck me even more was a certain air of dignity on her face, which led me to think she was of noble birth. I sent for her and spoke to her; I was just as pleased with her intelligence as I had been with her physical attributes. "I would be inconsolable," she told me, "to find myself in a foreign country, if I did not know that my sex condemns me to spend my life locked up in a harem, subject to the will of whomever my destiny has given me to. . . . The pasha's expression," she continued, "allows me to hope for a happier fate than a slave can usually expect. Mighty Mohammed," she cried, "make him think kindly of me." I didn't need any further inspiration; her beauty and wit had already made as great an impression on me as she could desire. I told her that her hope would not be in vain and that her apparent desire to belong to me was a reason to cherish her even more. "But," I added, "is this inclination sincere, and is it not just your desire to escape from this place that makes you speak in this way?" "No," she replied, with a hint of spite and anger in her voice, "I am not in the habit of faking my feelings, and although I am a slave, nothing in the world could lead me to lower myself to use deception to plead for a man's affections, whoever he may be."

1697   Antoine-François Prévost is born in Hesdin, France (April 1).

1711–15   He attends elementary and secondary schools in Hesdin, joins the army, spends a year studying philosophy in Paris, and begins his novitiate with the Jesuits.

1717–18   He continues his novitiate with the Jesuits in La Flèche, returns to the army, leaves the army, and flees to Holland.

1721   He takes vows with the Benedictines in Jumièges (Nov. 9).

1721–26   He continues studying theology, publishes the satirical novel *Les avantures de Pomponius, chevalier romain; ou, l'Histoire de notre tems* (The adventures of Pomponius, Roman knight; or, The history of our times, 1724), begins his translation of Jacques-Auguste de Thou's *Historia sui temporis* (*Histoire de M. de Thou*) in Sées, and is ordained a priest in Rouen.

1726–28   He teaches humanities in Saint-Germer, preaches in Evreux, resides at the monastery of the Blancs-Manteaux in Paris, and works on the *Gallia christiana* (Christian France) at the convent of Saint-Germain-des-Prés in Paris.

1728   The first two volumes of *Mémoires d'un homme de qualité* (*Memoirs of a Man of Quality*) are approved for publication (March 13 and

April 5). Prévost leaves Saint-Germain without permission (Oct. 18), and the Benedictines obtain an order for his arrest (Nov. 6). Volumes 3 and 4 of the *Homme de qualité* are approved for publication (Nov. 19). Prévost flees to Holland again, then crosses the channel into England.

1729–30   He serves as tutor for Sir John Eyles's son, seduces Sir John's daughter, writes the first two volumes of the *Histoire de M. Cleveland*, then leaves London for Amsterdam.

1731   The last three volumes of the *Homme de qualité* (April), including his most famous novel, *Manon Lescaut* (vol. 7), are published. Volumes 1 and 2 of *Cleveland* are submitted for approval (April 2), and volumes 3 and 4 appear in October. Prévost engages in a financially ruinous love affair with Lenki Eckhart.

1732   He translates the first volume of the *Histoire de M. de Thou*; his financial situation is more and more precarious.

1733   *Histoire de M. de Thou* is published (Jan.). Prévost finds himself bankrupt the same month and flees to England with Lenki, while his furniture is sold at a public auction. The first issue of his journal *Le Pour et Contre* (The pros and cons) is published (April). In December Prévost is jailed, then released (narrowly escaping the hangman) for forging a check to himself from his former pupil, the son of Sir John Eyles.

1734–35   He returns to France, and Pope Clément XII grants him a pardon for his transgressions. In August 1735 he begins a second novitiate at La Croix-Saint-Leufroy. The first volume of *Le doyen de Killerine* (The Dean of Coleraine) appears the same month.

1735   He translates John Dryden's tragedy *All for Love* (*Tout pour l'amour*).

1736   Prévost is named chaplain (unpaid) in the home of the Prince de Conti.

1738   Volume 6 of *Cleveland* is published (April), but his financial situation becomes critical again.

1739   Volume 7 of *Cleveland* (March), then volumes 2 (April) and 3 (June) of *Le doyen de Killerine* are published. He *abandons Le Pour et Contre* for eight months; *Histoire de Marguerite d'Anjou* is published (July).

1740   Prévost is in desperate straits. Threatened with arrest, on January 15 he offers to write a defense of Voltaire and his works for fifty louis, but the philosopher declines. Publication commences the same month of volume 4 of *Le doyen de Killerine*. He resumes writing *Le Pour et Contre* (Feb.).

     Histoire d'une Grecque moderne (*The Greek Girl's Story*) is published (Sept.).

1741   On January 26 Prévost flees to Brussels, then to Frankfort. He publishes *Mémoires pour server à l'histoire de Malte; ou, Histoire de la jeunesse du commandeur de . . .* (Memoirs serving the history of Malta; or, Story of the youth of the commander of . . . , Jan.), then *Campagnes philosophique; ou, Mémoires de M. de Montcal* (Philosophical campaigns; or, The memoirs of M. de Montcal, March). He returns to France in November.

1742   *Histoire de Guillaume le Conquérant* (Story of William the Conqueror) is published (May). Prévost returns to Paris (Sept.).

1743   He translates Thomas Middleton's *Life of Cicero* (*Histoire de Cicéron*, Dec.).

1744   *Lettres de Cicéron* (June) and the *Voyages du capitaine Robert Lade* (Nov.) are published.

1745   *Mémoires d'un honnête homme* (Memoirs of a decent man) is published (Nov.).

1746–48   Prévost publishes *Histoire générale des voyages*: volumes 1 (May) and 2 (Nov.), two volumes a year in 1747 and 1748, then one volume a year until 1759 (vol. 15). He takes up residence in Chaillot with his "governess," Claude Catherine (Robin) de Genty.

1750   *Manuel lexique* (Lexical handbook) is published.

1751–58   He translates Samuel Richardson's novels *Clarissa; or, The History of a Young Lady* (*Histoire de Miss Clarisse Harlowe*, 1751) and *The History of Sir Charles Grandison* (*Histoire du chevalier Grandisson*, 1755–58).

1753   New, corrected edition of *Manon Lescaut* is published.

1754   Prévost is awarded the priory of Gennes, with a modest prebend.

1755   *Journal étranger* (Foreign journal) is published (Jan. 15–Sept. 1).

1760   Prévost publishes *Le monde moral* (The inner world), volumes 1 and 2 (April), and translates David Hume's *History of the House of Stuart* (*Histoire de la maison de Stuart*, April).

1762   He translates Frances Sheridan's *Memoirs of Miss Sidney Bidulph* (*Mémoires pour servir à l'histoire de la Vertu, Extraits du Journal d'une Dame*, April).

1763   Prévost translates John Hawkesworth's *Almoran and Hamet: An Oriental Tale* (*Almoran et Hamet: Anecdote orientale*, June). He dies from a ruptured aneurysm (Nov. 25).

1764   Prévost's translation of *Letters to a Young Nobleman* (*Lettres de Mentor à un jeune seigneur*, April) and volumes 3 and 4 of *Le monde moral* (May) are published.

Notes

Except where indicated, all translations from the French are my own.

Introduction

1. The most complete and accurate biography of Prévost is Sgard's *Vie de Prévost*.

2. "Key novels" were very popular in this period, especially in the case of satirical oriental novels, and in some cases a key to the names (linking each fictional name with its real-life equivalent) was even provided at the beginning of the book (Dufrenoy, *Orient romanesque en France*, 1:323).

3. In the *Explication des cent estampes*, Ferriol, or rather his spokesman, relates at length the "sword incident," which occurred at the beginning of his ambassadorship, when he arrived at the Sultan's palace to present his credentials. He provoked a tremendous scandal by refusing to take off his sword, despite the prohibition of weapons in the presence of the Sultan. He was denied entrance into the reception room and reacted in an extremely boorish fashion. In issues 292 and 293 of his journal *Le Pour et Contre*, Prévost gives the French translation of several notes from Tindal's English translation of Cantemir's work, including a very interesting excerpt concerning this incident (see app. 1).

4. The narrator of Prévost's novel *Le monde moral* (*The Moral World*, 1760, 1764) tells the same anecdote but replaces "his *fille de corps*" with "his own daughter," which is a little kinder to the ambassador.

5. Sgard also emphasizes the importance of Bonneval as a model for the narrator-hero of *The Greek Girl's Story*: "In the disconcerting Ferriol character he imagined a new Bonneval, enjoying the same favorable status with the Sultan, indulging in the same quarrels, showing the same indifference to dogmas, and, like his model, seeking happiness in love" ("Aventure et politique," 418).

6. For a convincing argument in favor of Théophé's sincerity, see Hill, "Virtue on Trial."

7. See, respectively, Engel, *Véritable abbé Prévost*, 199; Sgard, *Prévost romancier*, 429; Pruner, "Psychologie," 146; and Monty, "Romans de l'abbé Prévost," 172.

8. Herman takes this perspective on the novel to its ultimate conclusion, asserting that Théophé is a veritable metaphor for "narrative polysemy" (*Récit génétique*, 110).

9. The analysis of amorous jealousy offered by the psychoanalyst Daniel Lagache is a striking commentary on the narrator's reference to the "enigma" of Théophé: "The jealous person's

project to dominate the psyche of the partner is defeated, and this failure is transcended by attributing to the partner an enigmatic, indecipherable character" (*Jalousie amoureuse*, 2:54).

10. As Rousset observes, "Everything depends here on the identification of the narrator with the impassioned hero . . . , and it is the consequences of this identification that constitute the real subject of this novel: the impossibility of seeing things other than through his own eyes and of arriving at any objective truth through the subjective vision to which the narrator is condemned" (*Narcisse romancier*, 128). Bokobza-Kahan pushes beyond the notion of "subjectivity" and develops a persuasive psychoanalytical argument with respect to the unreliability of the narrator in Prévost's novel, suggesting that not only is the hero a paranoid psychotic afflicted by pathological jealousy but that the paranoia contaminates the narration itself so that the ambassador's discourse is no less aberrant than his behavior in the story he relates (*Libertinage et folie*, 253).

11. For a more in-depth development of this perspective, see Singerman, "Quand le récit devient procès."

12. Cf. Douthwaite's position on this question: "A male author lends such authority to his male narrator's negative preconceptions about the 'oriental character' that he effectively undermines the reader's trust in the heroine's words" (*Exotic Women*, 35). But does the narrator in fact completely succeed in undermining the reader's trust? And is that the *author's* clear intention (that the reader lose faith in Théophé's honesty)? Mall notes that the real reader is not duped by the narrator's attempts to discredit the heroine and rejects any identification with the "powerless and superfluous" intradiegetical reader to whom the narrator appeals ("Modalité et déplacement," 345).

13. Cf. Francis: "It is clear that the reader must assume that any of Prévost's narrators is likely to be unreliable. What is less clear is how far it is suggested that they deliberately try to deceive" (*First-Person Narrators*, 73).

14. We borrow the concept of "psychological decomposition" from Rogers, *Psychoanalytical Study*.

15. For a broader analysis of the narrator-hero's possible doubles in the novel, see our commentary in Singerman, *Abbé Prévost*, 236–74. Sempère remarks, similarly, that a whole series of minor figures—Bema, the diplomat's language tutor, M. de S . . .—serve as a mise en abyme of the narrator's equivocal attitude toward Théophé ("Double prix," 235). Walsh, another reader who finds that Prévost's novel lends itself to psychoanalytical considerations, states, "The characters who act as doubles in the story also illustrate the "topography" of the hero's mind, of which one part, the repressed part of the *ego*, envies the unimpeded libidinal force of his rivals in love, and tries to control the whims of the *id*. . . . The other part, representing a differentiation within the *ego*, the *super-ego* or *ego-ideal*, tries to reconcile his actions with the social and moral norms which, as a prominent public figure and nobleman, the hero is compelled to respect" (*Abbé Prévost's "Histoire d'une Grecque moderne*,*"* 73–74).

16. Or alternatively, as Miller suggests, "*Theo* ('godliness') and *phé* ('brightness') are signs of both her Greek ethnicity and her transformation in leaving the harem" ("*Histoire d'une Grecque moderne*," 5). Douthwaite, for her part, offers a somewhat different interpretation: "The neologism Théophé combines the Greek symbol of divinity, *theo*, with *phé*, derived from the Greek *phema* (voice, rumor, reputation), from *phanai*, to speak. Hence Théophé means 'God's voice' or 'divine reputation,' the ultimate signifier for this eighteenth-century woman who so fervently desires a good reputation" (*Exotic Women*, 53).

17. Francis notes the existence of parallel episodes in a number of Prévost's novels that render it possible "to make comparisons and judgments leading beyond the narrator's words, and to find means whereby Prévost may signal criticisms of his narrators which the discerning

reader can interpret for himself" (*First-Person Narrators*, 320). For a more thorough treatment of the layer of irony in *The Greek Girl's Story*, see Singerman, "Relecture ironique."

18. As regards the problem of equivocal language and the *malentendu* (misunderstanding) in *The Greek Girl's Story*, see also Calder, "Résistance langagière," 115–16; and Leborgne, "Orient vu par Prévost," 453–54.

19. Dufrenoy has shown that the number of works of oriental fiction published in France increases from nine in 1730 to seventeen in 1740 and reaches its zenith with twenty-five works in 1746 (*Orient romanesque en France*, 2:15–18). Martino explains this phenomenon, for the most part, by the diplomatic relations between France and the Sublime Porte during this period: "The diplomatic intervention of France in the war between Turkey and Austria and the role of mediator that it played at the Belgrade Congress [1739] suddenly doubled the number of novels or comedies with a Turkish subject" (*Orient dans la littérature*, 180).

20. The French ambassador's scornful attitude is also an attempt on Prévost's part to give an accurate portrait of his historical model. Ferriol was well known for his contemptuous attitude toward the Ottoman ministers from the beginning of his appointment in Constantinople. His arrogance was the subject of repeated complaints by the Ottoman authorities, culminating in their request, in 1708, that he be recalled. This request was granted the following year, although it took more than a year and a half to remove Ferriol from his post, and this was accomplished only by the use of force by the French authorities to get him on a ship back to France (Moronvalle, "Connaître et représenter," 65).

21. See Gôçek, *East Encounters West*, 5–10; and Bilici, "Relations franco-ottomanes," 60–61.

22. See, for instance, Douthwaite, *Exotic Women*, 53, 60.

23. La Motraye, whose book Prévost knew very well, refers several times to the integrity of the Turks and compares them favorably to Westerners. He states, for example, "Sincere and faithful in their promises, they consider it a point of honor to be absolutely true to their word. ... What more can I say? In a word, I find the Christian superstitious and libertine and the Turk devout and wise; the first vain and disloyal and the second modest and bound to integrity. This comparison could, I assure you, be extended quite far in favor of the *Mahomedan*" (*Voyages*, 1:259–60).

24. Cf. Hartmann: "In keeping with the spirit of the Enlightenment, Prévost's Orientalism, just like Montesquieu's, serves less to promote Western values than to throw them into suspicion" ("Femme étrangère/femme étrange," 58).

25. Bokobza-Kahan explores in considerable depth the libertine character of the ambassador, remarking that, throughout the novel, he "remains attached to an essentially phallocratic ideology, openly displayed in the Orient, much more insidiously in the Western World" (*Libertinage et folie*, 241). Sgard himself is led to suggest that "the misfortune of the little immigrant girl becomes, in the final analysis, an image of the fate of women"—"*une image de la condition féminine*" ("Titre comme programme," 239).

26. Viewing the East-West opposition in *The Greek Girl's Story* through another contemporary critical lens, Ohayon proposes a Lacanian reading: "Metaphorically, the Orient may well represent the imaginary realm and the West the symbolic. In the novel, the diplomat strives to control and master the Imaginary and circumscribe it within the Symbolic. The quest to decipher and capture Théophé translates as a relentless metonymic pursuit of signifiers" ("Prévost's *Histoire*," 33). Since Lacan defines the functioning of desire precisely as a metonymic pursuit of signifiers, well, yes. For a particularly lucid analysis of the East-West opposition in Prévost's novel, see Tremewan, "Orient et Occident."

Book One

1. As regards this portrait of the diplomat, Prévost does not hesitate to mix fact and fiction. While it is true that the comte de Ferriol spoke Turkish when he assumed his functions as ambassador, having lived six years in Constantinople (1692–98) as a special envoy of the king, and that he was reputed to have become "Turkified" during his long stay there, he hardly enjoyed the harmonious relations with his hosts that the narrator describes. Proud and quick-tempered, obsessed with questions of honor, Ferriol provoked frequent quarrels over his prerogatives of rank and brought all kinds of woes down upon himself throughout his ambassadorship. The most famous example is the "sword incident" at the very beginning of his appointment (see introd., note 3, and app. 1).

If Prévost's model here was not Ferriol, he may have been thinking of the comte de Bonneval (see introd., 9–10) or even of Ferriol's predecessor, the marquis de Châteauneuf, who also managed to maintain exemplary relations with his hosts. Often dressed in the Turkish style, Châteauneuf "had close relations with the high Moslem officials who, although it was virtually unheard of, admitted him to their table" (Roman d'Amat, "Châteauneuf"), which was not at all Ferriol's case.

2. One may suspect here an ironic reference to Usbek's illusions about the "felicity" of Roxane (and her harem companions) in Montesquieu's *Persian Letters* (1721): "How fortunate you are! You live in my seraglio as in the home of innocence, safe from the evil intent of all humans" (letter 24).

3. The selictar is the Sultan's sword bearer and the captain of his guard. As Sgard remarks in his 1989 edition of Prévost's novel, the selictar was also charged with recruiting concubines for the Sultan's harem, so he was, in fact, the best person for the French diplomat to ask for help in this matter (Prévost, *Histoire d'une Grecque moderne*, 27n1).

4. The heroine's name change is of considerable interest as regards her character. Names beginning with "Z" were a virtual sign of orientalism or exoticism—and eroticism in the case of women characters—in eighteenth-century France and were very much in fashion. Dufrenoy notes 112 names of main characters beginning with "Z" in novels published in France from 1700 to 1750 (*Orient romanesque en France*, 23). When the heroine of *The Greek Girl's Story* changes her name from "Zara" to "Théophé," she symbolically sheds her former (concubine) identity in favor of a new identity that evokes God's will or God's love in Greek (see introd., 16–17, and note 16).

5. Théophé's behavior here is an expression of her education not only as a concubine but as a woman in Turkey at this time, if we are to believe La Motraye, who tells us that when a pasha sends for one of his concubines, "she . . . caresses him as her duty dictates, calls him her emperor and gives him all of the ordinary and extraordinary compliments she can think of. Education . . . teaches women in Turkey to caress men, and that is the practice there just as it is the opposite in our country, at least among respectable women" (*Voyages*, 1:337).

6. Morea is the former name of the Peloponnesus, whose most important city is Patras.

7. It was apparently common, again according to La Motraye, for children to be sold to the Turks by their parents. Since it was forbidden for the Turks to take their servants and concubines from among the Sultan's subjects, "they have to buy them from among women who have been captured in wars or sold by their own parents or by their princes, as is done in . . . Georgia, Circassia, and in other countries whose princes sell their subjects, and fathers and mothers their children, like we sell horses in France" (*Voyages*, 1:186). When Prévost writes that not even four of the twenty-two concubines in Cheriber's harem are Turkish, it is one of several minor cultural errors that indicate the haste with which he was composing this novel.

8. Knowing her "father's" plans for her, we can easily guess the nature of the education he gives to her, which must have resembled that which the slave merchants reserved for future concubines: "The merchants normally keep them in private houses where they instruct them in the art of pleasing men and stimulating their sexual desire, like how to dance in a lewd manner, to sing erotic songs, and to play various instruments" (La Motraye, *Voyages*, 1:260).

9. According to Tournefort, *cadis* are common judges: "The judges in the big cities are called *moula-cadis* ["high judges"]; those in the little cities, towns, and villages are known as *cadis*. The whole system of justice is in the hands of these people in Turkey" (*Relation*, 2:385-86).

10. Thévenot tells us that the Sultan was, indeed, in the habit of confiscating "all the possessions of criminals" (*Voyages*, 1:204).

11. The "desire for a good" of which one is ignorant may be an allusion, on the one hand, to the Pascalian theme of an "unknown good" (*un bien inconnu*) whose faint memory comes from our original innocent nature, before the Fall, and which is thus attached to the notion of grace, the attraction to spiritual life. On the other hand, this desire may also be interpreted, as does the diplomat, as the desire to know love, sentimental happiness. We recall the opposite error of the doyen de Killerine, who takes for a penchant toward virtue, that is, for a latent religious vocation, this "devouring need, this absence of an unknown good" that prevents his stepbrother, Patrice, from finding happiness and that turns out to be, on the contrary, the need for sentimental fulfillment (Prévost, *Doyen de Killerine*, 3:19, 20).

12. As Deprun has shown convincingly, the theme of "uneasiness" (*inquiétude*) belongs to the Malebranchian thematic repertory from which Prévost frequently borrows. Théophé's constant state of *inquiétude*, combined with the idea of a *bien inconnu* (as in the long philosophical meditation of Cleveland in Saumur) recalls the dynamic psychology of the Oratorian theologian according to which man lives normally in a state of agitation, which is nothing but an unrecognized desire to find God ("Thèmes malebranchistes," 158-59).

13. See the introduction (16-17) for our commentary on this apparent moral coup de foudre, which seems to be a corollary to the amorous coup de foudre that strikes so many heroes in Prévost's novels.

14. This lengthy autobiographical narrative by Théophé resembles, as Pruner observes, a "confession." In this optic, the diplomat thus becomes for the Greek girl a confessor, the guardian of her "sins," and the agent of her moral rehabilitation—which may explain much about her subsequent behavior ("Psychologie," 141, 145). Mall develops this perspective further, observing that the ambassador is responsible for the sudden birth of moral conscience in the Greek concubine, her new consciousness of the distinction between Good and Evil, and the concomitant experience of shame, much like Adam and Eve. The harem thus becomes, Mall muses, a "perverse" version of the Garden of Eden, where the heroine was living in a state of innocence, that is, in complete ignorance of the concept of sin ("Modalité et déplacement," 343).

15. The diplomat's reference to "ancient times" is most likely an allusion to the famous words in the *Aeneid*: "Quidquid id est, timeo Danaos et dona ferentis" (Whatever the case, I fear the Greeks, even in their offerings to the gods) (bk. 2, line 49). The reputation of the Greeks in Prévost's times is scarcely any better, judging by the travel literature of the period. Thévenot declares, for example, that "the Greeks are greedy, untrustworthy, and treacherous, pederasts, extremely vindictive, and moreover very superstitious and hypocritical" (*Voyages*, 1:262).

16. Cheriber's anger is hardly exaggerated here, given that it was expressly forbidden under the Ottoman Empire to force a free girl to become a concubine: "The Sultan would not be permitted to keep a free girl in his harem unless he married her; such a commerce would be considered incestuous; the law is the same for everyone; you must marry a free person" (Ferriol, *Explication des cent estampes*, 4). As observed in Book One, note 7, it was also forbidden to lock

up in the harems of Constantinople any Turkish, Greek, or Armenian women, all of whom were subjects of the Sultan; only women captured in enemy countries could be forcibly placed in harems (Grosrichard, *Structure du sérail*, 176n2).

17. One may wonder if Prévost, in emphasizing Théophé's penchant for reflection, is not alluding to the "taste for intellectualism which was typical of Hellenism" noted by Mirambel (*"Histoire d'une Grecque moderne,"* 42) and which suggests a Greek atavism that is quite different from the reputation for dishonesty (*mauvaise foi*) that the narrator draws to our attention earlier.

18. The narrator's observations on the deficiencies of the Turkish system of justice are, again, confirmed by the contemporary travel literature. Tournefort writes, for example, "How many blatant injustices are committed? . . . The cadis are most often corrupted by money and guided by their passions" (*Relation*, 2:300) and adds later, "It is often useless to appeal the cadis' sentences, because they never reinvestigate cases; thus the sentence would always be confirmed, because the cadi himself led the investigation; this results in horrible abuses" (2:386).

19. Prévost is playing fast and loose with history here: the Venetians having reoccupied most of the Peloponnesus between 1687 and 1714, it is highly unlikely that there were any provinces still under Turkish administration in the first years of the eighteenth century, where the action of the novel is placed. In any case, Prévost was never overly concerned with historical chronology in his novels; we remember the correspondence between Cleveland and Descartes . . . twenty years after the celebrated philosopher's death! As Sgard so aptly remarks, Prévost "knows history, but he reinvents it in his novels" (*Prévost romancier*, 463).

20. We meet once again the theme of the "voice of nature" (*la voix du sang*) that Prévost develops in *Cleveland* when Fanny reunites with her long-lost daughter, Cécile: "This extraordinary penchant that I felt for her, was it not the voice of nature? A hundred times, my dear Cécile, I felt my blood cry out while holding you in my arms" (Prévost, *Histoire de M. Cleveland*, 2:451).

21. The name "Condoidi" seems to come from a note by Cantemir in which he speaks of the Greek scholars of his time, including one Anastasius Condoidi who had been the tutor of his own children. This note is placed precisely at the point in his text where Cantemir is telling about the siege of Constantinople by Mohammed II (1453) and the efforts by the Greek emperor to repulse the attacks by the Turks (*History* 1:100n10). This allusion to the siege of Constantinople may have contributed to the origin of the episode, apparently apocryphal, concerning the illustrious ancestor of Paniota Condoidi.

22. The suffragan bishops are prelates attached to the patriarch (the head of the Greek Orthodox Church).

23. Sermain points out the "duplicity" of the diplomat's language, observing that "the perversity of male discourse in Europe comes from the fact that he perpetuates his dominance by adopting a façade of liberalism, by declaring his respect for the rights and dignity of women" (*Rhétorique et roman*, 87–88). Cf. Vissière, who comments that Prévost "deserves credit for denouncing the hypocrisy of a European society that behaves like Turks in its treatment of women but refuses to recognize it and hides reality behind fancy language" ("Paradoxes du voile," 152).

24. We recall that the diplomat, given the difficulty of meeting women in Turkey, had resolved to repress the penchant he had for the ladies. This minor inconsistency in the narrative, caught by Holland (Prévost, *Histoire d'une Grecque moderne*, 8:295), is perhaps just an oversight owing to Prévost's intense literary activity at that time (see introd., 3). Leborgne, however, suggests that the ambassador's statement may in fact be an example of Freud's *Verneinung* ("denial"), which is a form of unconscious bad faith reflecting here a "fundamen-

tal lack" in the diplomat. Leborgne refers to the hero as "cet ambassadeur eunuque" and conjectures (perhaps a bit overventuresomely) that his talk of libertinism in his memoirs is just a façade to hide his sexual inadequacy, his fear of women ("Orient vu par Prévost," 451, 456–57, 459–61).

25. It seems clear that Prévost is alluding to the Pygmalion legend here. Like the Cypriot sculptor who marries his beautiful statue after transforming it into a flesh-and-blood woman, the ambassador dreams of the happiness of being "united for life" to this former concubine that he could transform into "the finest lady in the world." See James Jones's commentary on the influence of two myths, Pygmalion and Don Juan, in Prévost's novel ("Textual Ambiguity," 247–51).

26. We can almost hear in this declaration the voice of the master libertine Valmont as he plots the seduction of Mme de Tourvel in Choderlos de Laclos's *Les liaisons dangereuses* (1782): "It is not enough for me to possess her; I want her to give herself to me" (letter 110). Prévost demonstrates here a canny intuition of Sartre's existential psychology as regards desire and liberty: the lover does not want his mistress to give herself to him like a slave. "On the other hand, the man who wants to be loved does not desire the enslavement of the beloved. He is not bent on becoming the object of passion which flows forth mechanically. He does not want to possess an automaton. . . . Thus the lover does not desire to possess the beloved as one possesses a thing; he demands a special type of appropriation. He wants to possess a freedom as freedom" (*Being and Nothingness*, 343). Or as Mall remarks, regarding the diplomat's project, "What he is intent on conquering and dominating is [Théophé's] free will, not in place of her body but along with it" ("Modalité et déplacement," 339).

27. One cannot help being struck here ("each time you looked at me it felt like a death sentence") by the allusion to the gaze of the other (*le regard d'autrui*) and its corollary Sartrian theme, "Hell is others," that will become so famous in the postwar years. The diplomat is, of course, no less prisoner of Théophé's gaze, which traps him in the intolerable role of moral mentor (see introd., 18–19).

28. Prévost introduces here the nature-nurture opposition that will become so important when Maria Rezati's story (in Book Two) is contrasted with that of Théophé's.

29. The retrospective lucidity of the narrator (the "narrating I"), undeniable here, alternates with moments of blindness that he shares with the hero (the "narrated I"), so that the character becomes complex and difficult to decipher. As Rousset points out, Prévost's narrators do not possess the same analytical detachment as those of his contemporary Marivaux (*Narcisse romancier*, 136–37).

30. This passage is a most curious description (based on Cartesian psychophysiology) of the sexual phenomenon that will later be identified by Freud as "sublimation." We note, however, the distinction that Prévost establishes here between love and lust, a distinction that may be germane to the conflict that will arise subsequently between the selictar and Théophé's brother Synèse (see Book Two, note 4).

31. Another example of Prévost's haste in writing this novel: the proverb about the sincerity of Greeks that the diplomat cites after Théophé tells the story of her life does not come from the selictar but from the narrator himself.

32. Given the hero's own situation vis-à-vis Théophé, his status as "father," the dramatic irony of this statement is painfully obvious.

33. The suggestion of incest is an unambiguous allusion to the diplomat's historical model, the comte de Ferriol (see introd., 5). However, the theme of incest held a clear fascination for Prévost long before *The Greek Girl's Story*. Des Grieux plays the role of Manon's younger brother to dupe M. de G . . . M . . . , and we recall the highly suspicious sentiments that Cleveland harbors for his long-lost daughter, Cécile, even after he barely avoids seducing her (see Lebois, "Amitié").

34. The aga, or commander, of the janissaries was in charge of the Sultan's personal guards, who were referred to as the "janissaries of the Porte," and of the entire Turkish infantry corps, somewhat abusively called janissaries also (Tournefort, *Relation*, 2:285). The bostangi bachi, according to Cantemir, was the captain of the imperial palaces who was responsible for the safety of the Sultan's family (*Histoire de l'empire ottoman*, 1:xxxvii); he was "one of the most powerful officers of the Porte" (Tournefort, *Relation*, 2:285). Based on later allusions in the novel to the Sultan Mustapha and to his brother Ahmet, we know that Prévost is referring to the events that surrounded the revolution of July 3, 1703, in which Mustapha II was indeed deposed in favor of his younger brother Ahmet III, following a revolt by the janissaries. Prévost makes only a vague reference to these vicissitudes of Ottoman history, a summary of which he could have read in Cantemir (*History*, 2:433–40) or in La Motraye (*Voyages*, 1:323–36), as well as in Ferriol's *Explication des cent estampes* (2–3).

35. The grand vizir was the Sultan's powerful prime minister: "The Sultan puts at the head of his ministers the Grand Vizir . . . to whom he delegates all of the empire's affairs. The Grand Vizir is not only in charge of the finances, foreign affairs, and civil and criminal justice; he also has the War Office and is Commander-in-Chief of the Armies" (Tournefort, *Relation*, 2:292). As Tavernier tells us in *Nouvelle relation de l'intérieur du sérail* (1712), his power is "so absolute that in all the Empires and Kingdoms in the world there is no Prime Minister who exercises such authority as the Grand Vizir" (quoted by Grosrichard, *Structure du sérail*, 92).

36. This is a reference to Pierre-Antoine de Castagnères, marquis de Châteauneuf, who was ambassador to the Porte from 1689 to 1699. We were unable to find in Châteauneuf's political correspondence any allusion to this incident, which appears to have been invented by Prévost.

37. Demetrius Cantemir (1674–1723), a Moldavian (Romanian) prince and writer, was the author of the celebrated work *The History of the Growth and Decay of the Othman Empire* (published in Latin in 1716). Prévost, who knew Cantemir's life well, and at least this work (the 1734–35 English translation by Tindal), gives his biography in his journal *Le Pour et Contre* in 1740 (vol. 19, no. 274, pp. 145–57). For the purpose of his novel Prévost changes the facts as regards the person who sheltered the banished prince; it was not just some obscure pasha but, as Cantemir tells us in his *History*, the comte de Ferriol himself who hid him in his residence (2:424n33). The narrator could hardly use himself as a precedent here!

38. The Mutes were servants of the Sultan whose name came from the fact that they communicated between themselves by signs in order not to disturb the Sultan when he was resting (Tournefort, *Relation*, 2:287). The *capigis* (palace porters), who also served as executioners, were sometimes accompanied by Mutes, who used a silk rope to strangle the political officials condemned by the Sultan before cutting off their heads (Thévenot, *Voyages*, 1:200–201).

39. These remarks could apply equally well to the whole class of courtesans that derived their prestige, under the Old Regime, from whatever favor they could curry at the Versailles court; one may well suspect that Prévost is indulging in irony here.

40. The first part of the novel thus concludes with a summing up of the hero's basic psychological dilemma, the conflict between his intense desire to possess Théophé and his sense of honor (or *amour-propre*) that prevents him from pressuring her, against her will, to submit to his desires. How this conflict plays out will be a principal focus of the second part of *The Greek Girl's Story*.

Book Two

1. In the nineteenth century the "shadow" will become a virtual synonym of the *Doppelgänger* (psychological double), as seen, for example, in Hans Christian Andersen's "The Shadow"

or Chamisso's *Peter Schlemihl*. Whether the shadow here is Synèse or the selictar, it is tempting to consider the possible symbolism as regards the diplomat's inner world, as does Walsh in his Freudian take on the novel: "The characters who act as doubles in the story also illustrate the 'topography' of the hero's mind, of which one part, the repressed part of the *ego*, envies the unimpeded libidinal force of his rivals in love, and tries to control the whims of the *id*. . . . The other part, representing a differentiation within the *ego*, the *super-ego* or *ego-ideal*, tries to reconcile his actions with the social and moral norms which, as a prominent public figure and nobleman, the hero is compelled to respect" (*Abbé Prévost's "Histoire,"* 73–74).

2. The divan was the daily (except Friday) council of ministers at which the grand vizir dealt with all the affairs of state.

3. In *Nouveaux mémoires* the author states that the rebellious janissaries "asked for the heads of several pachas, and they had to be satisfied" (53), which may be the source of Prévost's account, as Holland remarks (Prévost, *Histoire d'une Grecque moderne*, 8:305). Whatever the case, there is considerable fictionalizing here, as Prévost embroiders freely on the circumstances that surrounded the successful revolution of 1703, which he mixes with those of a second revolt by the janissaries in 1704, which was indeed suppressed (La Motraye, *Voyages*, 1:375). If the allusion to historical events adds some local color and contributes to the "authenticity" of the novel, this incident seems to function also as a presage of the perhaps metaphorical violent struggle that will break out in the diplomat's home immediately afterward. As Murphy remarks, "With the news of the political intrigue, and the hiding of the Selictar and Synèse in the villa, the stage is set for the exterior confusion and agitation which parallel the inner turmoil of the diplomat's emotions throughout Book Two" ("Narrative Techniques," 32).

4. If it was indeed Prévost's intention to give an allegorical dimension to Synèse and the selictar, this violent conflict between the two characters may suggest both the intensity and the character of the psychological struggle gripping the hero. In this context it is interesting to note that *synèse* is derived from the Greek word for "union," suggesting a distinction that classical Christian moral theology makes between *amour de bienveillance* (benevolent love) and *amour d'union* (lust), that is, between generous, self-sacrificing love that seeks its object's happiness and purely carnal desire that seeks only its own satisfaction in physical union (see Malebranche, *Traité de morale*, 42).

5. Prévost refuses systematically, here as in his other novels, to indulge in detailed descriptions of physical settings. It is the psychological world (*le monde moral*) that interests him, the "inner springs of actions . . . the knowledge of motives and feelings" (Prévost, *Monde moral*, 6:287).

6. Cf. La Motraye: "Turkish women, or women raised for the Turkish harems, are not sensitive to this broad freedom that European women enjoy . . . but they are only unhappy, in this respect, in your imagination. Their education has taught them to take great pleasure in the distractions that they share with each other, like their songs, dances, and the music they play on their instruments" (*Voyages*, 1:337–38).

7. Maria Rezati's story—her education and subsequent behavior—is diametrically opposed to that of Théophé, creating a contrast that provides a potentially illuminating perspective on the character of the heroine (see introd., 15–16).

8. The Knight of Malta, as characterized by Prévost here, corresponds to an eighteenth-century stereotype, as Engel demonstrates in her study, "Chevalier de Malte."

9. The danger of excessive joy—fainting or even dying—has been a commonplace in French literature since the preceding century. Descartes describes this phenomenon in the article "About Fainting" in his 1649 treatise, *The Passions of the Soul*, and Chimène, the heroine of Corneille's play *Le Cid* (1636), speaks of it as well (4.5). Prévost echoes this theme in his novel *Cleveland* (1731–39), when Fanny faints upon recovering her daughter, Cécile: "The

overwhelming effects of such a sudden joy had constricted her heart. Her eyes were covered with a thick cloud. . . . The sickness of my wife was only a fainting caused by joy" (449–50).

10. Ragusa was a small republic on the Dalmatian coast, under Turkish authority since the sixteenth century. It took its current name, Dubrovnik, when it was absorbed into Yugoslavia in 1919.

11. It is difficult not to reflect on the implications of this *mise en abyme* of the act of writing within Prévost's narrative. The goal of the diplomat-hero's letter, like the narrator's text, is to convince, to "seduce" the receiver (in one case Théophé, in the other the novel's reader). Gossman remarks that Prévost may be suggesting here an analogy between writing and desire—if not out-and-out orgasm ("Male and Female," 31n3).

12. We have not forgotten—and in all probability nor has Théophé—the declaration by the diplomat that "only misdeeds that are committed intentionally are worthy of contempt" and his later comment that he would have had more sympathy for Maria Rezati "if she had not been responsible for her plight by a deliberate moral failing."

13. The *Essais de morale* by the Jansenist theologian Pierre Nicole, written between 1671 and 1678, belong to the most morally strict Augustinian tradition. *La logique de Port Royal*, whose real title is *L'art de penser* (*The Art of Thinking*, 1662), is a work co-authored with Antoine Arnauld, the celebrated head of the Jansenist movement. Both works were immensely popular in their time and widely used for educational purposes. Taken together they refer to both the intellectual and moral edification of the young Greek girl.

14. The Jesuit priest in Prévost's *Cleveland* prescribes the same kind of "therapy" for the hero, suggesting that he read a light moral booklet, *La dévotion aisée* ("Easy Piety"), to cure him of his despair (312). Prévost is poking fun at a fashion of the times, "worldly Christianity," as demonstrated, for example, in the *Traité du vrai mérite* (Treatise on true worth) by Maître de Claville (1734), which offers "an easy and seductive compromise between the world and Christian morality" (Mauzi, *Idée du bonheur*, 94n2).

15. *Cléopâtre* (1647–58) was a popular heroic-romantic novel by La Calprenède. The reference to Mme de Lafayette's 1678 masterpiece *La princesse de Clèves* (generally considered to be the first modern psychological novel in France), which portrays the torments of jealousy and the tragic consequences of amorous intrigues, is perhaps not completely innocent in the context of *The Greek Girl's Story*.

16. The allusion to the quasi-incestuous relationship between the ambassador Ferriol and his goddaughter Mlle Aïssé seems particularly transparent here.

17. Prévost is confusing here Greek monks (caloyers) and priests.

18. This is confirmed by Thévenot (*Voyages*, 1:260): "It is permitted for their priests to have married once in their life to a virgin, and they keep their wife when they become a priest; but if she dies, they may not take a new one." He adds, however, "The Greek calogers are not permitted to marry at all," which emphasizes Prévost's error noted above. The relative opulence, as well as the ignorance, of Greek priests are characteristics that Prévost could have found both in La Motraye (*Voyages*, 1:188–89) and in Ferriol's *Explication des cent estampes*: "The Greek priests are ignorant, crude, and greedy; they take advantage of their penitents and make money from taking confession" (18).

19. The narrator's reference to his "natural self-restraint" is a measure, among other elements, of the extent to which Prévost has fictionalized his historical model Ferriol, who was notoriously short-tempered. Asse remarks that Ferriol's intemperate character "led him into perpetual difficulties with his Ottoman hosts, who nicknamed him *Deli-Iltchi*, the mad minister" ("Baron de Ferriol," 45).

20. Lepanto is the name that the Venetians gave to Naupactus, a Greek port at the entrance to the Gulf of Corinth that they occupied from 1417 to 1699.

21. Here again Prévost is writing quickly and not checking all his facts. La Motraye, one of his principal sources of information on Turkish culture, makes it clear that a woman's religion was not a problem in marriage: "A husband and a wife are never concerned about having different religions," to which he later adds, "They [new wives] are not required to change religion if they already have one" (*Voyages*, 1:227, 337).

22. On the literal level of the story (whatever allegorical role the selictar may play as a double), the rivalry between the selictar and the diplomat as regards the state of the latter's feelings here may be seen as a strikingly prescient illustration of René Girard's concept of "mimetic (or triangular) desire," since the selictar's declarations always precede those of the diplomat and can be perceived as a suitor's rivalry that shapes the evolution of the diplomat's own feelings toward Théophé rather than just mirroring them. "Rivalry," Girard says, "does not arise because of the fortuitous convergence of two desires on a single object; rather, *the subject desires the object because the rival desires it*. In desiring an object the rival alerts the subject to the desirability of the object. . . . We must understand that desire itself is essentially mimetic, directed toward an object desired by the model" (*Violence and the Sacred*, 145–46).

23. The unfortunate confusion of gratitude and love is also an important motif in Prévost's novel *Le doyen de Killerine*, which he finished writing in 1740, the same year as *The Greek Girl's Story* (see Book Two, note 36). The role that the hero expects Théophé's "gratitude" to play here in furthering his amorous designs casts considerable suspicion on the sincerity of his marriage proposal.

24. The "strange look" on the diplomat's face, produced by the unbearable emotional shock he has just suffered, suggests a severely altered mental state. The theme of madness, introduced here, will be developed in a much more spectacular manner in the episode of the king's party.

25. We note in passing this "model labyrinthine sentence," cited by Sgard as a prime example of Prévost's prose style, characterized by "cascades of subordinate phrases," embedded relative phrases, symmetries, parallels, and oppositions: "A sentence like this could only have been written by Prévost" (*Abbé Prévost*, 211–15).

26. Prévost is misinformed here by Cantemir, who states that Ferriol lived in Galata (*History*, 2:424n33). From 1646 on, the French ambassador always lived in Pera, a village adjoining Galata (Mantran, *Empire ottoman*, 167).

27. Here again Prévost is a little cavalier with historical fact. In his journal *Le Pour et Contre*, in which he presents Cantemir's *History*, one of the translated footnotes relates very precisely the order of succession of the grand vizirs during the period in question (20:242–60). According to Cantemir, Grand Vizir Calaïli Ahmet, who took office in 1703, was followed not by Chorluli Ali but by Baltagi Mehemed. Moreover, Chorluli, who became grand vizir in 1705, is lauded by Cantemir as a man "of great genius and most peaceful character" (20:256), certainly not "highly arrogant," as the narrator of Prévost's novel describes him. As regards Ferriol's party, in any case, the grand vizir in question (according to La Motraye, *Voyages*, 1:369) is Calaïcos Achmet, appointed in 1704, who was rather corrupt and extremely hostile to Christians. The sudden change of grand vizirs in the novel is in keeping with the generally precarious position of the Ottoman prime ministers. As Thévenot remarks, "When a Grand Vizir lasts six months, he is a clever man indeed" (*Voyages*, 1:200).

28. A *ferman*, La Motraye explains, is an "order from the Porte" or, as the case may be, a "privilege" (*Voyages*, 1:292).

29. The *galibe divan* is the Sultan's council, which met every Sunday and Tuesday, as opposed to the daily divan of the grand vizir (Cantemir, *Histoire*, 1:xxxix).

30. The preceding paragraph, like the first part of the one that follows, leaves little doubt as to Prévost's principal historical source for this episode. It is the version of the events given by Cantemir in his *History of the Growth and Decay of the Othman Empire* and concerns a party

given in 1704 to celebrate the birth of the king's grandson, the Duke of Brittany (2:424–25n33; see app. 1). La Motraye also relates the episode, but his version differs considerably in the details (*Voyages*, 1:369–71).

31. These "other events" refer clearly to the one that led to Ferriol's recall in 1710 and that is recounted by La Motraye (see *Voyages*, app. 1). This incident is at the origin of the "madness" motif in *The Greek Girl's Story* that Prévost presents, as Sgard remarks, as a consequence of love and jealousy (*Prévost romancier*, 432). Nonetheless, the novelist telescopes rather severely the chronology of the historical events: the aborted celebration of the Duke of Brittany's birth (1704) is separated from Ferriol's mental breakdown by five years (1709).

32. Livorno (Leghorn) was a regular port of call for maritime traffic between Marseilles and the Orient. La Motraye makes a stop there (and writes a brief commentary) upon returning to Constantinople (*Voyages*, 1:445), as do Montesquieu's famous oriental travelers en route to France in *Persian Letters* (1721): "We have reached Livorno after forty days at sea. Livorno is a new city that bears witness to the genius of the dukes of Toscany, who transformed a swampy village into the most flourishing city of Italy" (letter 21).

33. Or there was no misconduct to report, but, significantly, the narrator does not even consider this possibility, as jealousy and paranoia begin to dominate his behavior in this phase of the novel.

34. This grim drama, dominated by spite and the desire for vengeance, reflects the classical analysis of jealousy found in the novels of Mme de Lafayette (see Delhez-Sarlet, "Jaloux et la jalousie," 282). One might well wonder if there is not an analogy to be drawn between the story of the comte de M. Q., which serves as a catalyst for the hero's jealousy, and the subsequent behavior of the diplomat toward Théophé, as well as its effects on her hopes for happiness.

35. It does not take a psychiatrist to recognize a severely neurotic behavior: the hero is reduced to indulging his erotic fantasies; he beds the phantom of his desires. The trace of Théophé's body on her bedsheets is "the perfect symbol of the operation of a jealous mind that creates its object with nothingness, that makes a body out of a shadow, because all of its pleasures and pains are the fruits of an imagination that is no longer based on reality" (Rousset, *Narcisse romancier*, 151).

36. While the word "ingrate," in classical sentimental language, is commonly used to describe a woman who does not share her suitor's love, it also suggests moral condemnation, as we see in *Le doyen de Killerine* when Patrice is forced to marry Sara Fincer to settle a debt of gratitude. As the dean, his older half brother, tells him, "You cannot deny love and gratitude to Sara without bringing eternal shame to yourself" (Prévost, *Doyen de Killerine*, 3:93). We also recall, as regards the diplomat's accusations, the bitter complaints voiced by Cécile in *Cleveland* about the tendency of men "to think that their love is a right to demand to be loved" (Prévost, *Histoire de M. Cleveland*, 2:602).

37. When we recall the hero's own spurious plans for a clandestine marriage, also kept secret from his own family in France, his comments here are strongly tinged with romantic irony. M. de S . . . 's subsequent jealous, spiteful, and inquisitorial behavior will further emphasize the similarity of the two characters.

38. Knowing that the diminished beauty of Théophé was largely a result of her suffering from the hero's jealous comportment, one might be inclined to interpret metaphorically the "acid" he was thought to have prepared and which might call to mind the "vitriolic" spite whose excesses brought about her disfigurement. We can well imagine the swarm of rumors that swirled around Ferriol, Fontana, and Aïssé after the ambassador's return to Paris (see introd., 5, 8). Prévost is coyly emphasizing here the "key" to his novel in the obvious hope of furthering the *succès de scandale* he wishes to achieve.

39. We recall that "the young comte de . . ." was, in Prévost's original manuscript, "le chevalier D.," which brought strong protests from the chevalier "Daydie" (d'Aydie), Mlle Aïssé's former lover, and some of her close friends (see introd., 8–9).

40. The diplomat, who was "in [his] prime" when he met Théophé, has aged abruptly here, implying a significant temporal ellipsis since his return to France—or, more likely, an effort on Prévost's part to match his narrator-hero more closely to Ferriol, who was around sixty (and still very virile) when he was repatriated in 1711, but who had become seriously ill and debilitated in his final years before passing away in 1722 (Courteault, "Aïssé," col. 1044).

41. One cannot fail to note here Prévost's clever use of the resources of the double register of narration to maintain the ambiguity he cultivates in his novel: the hero has no sooner expressed his renewed faith in Théophé's character when the narrator steps in to undermine his positive appraisal of the Greek girl by asserting his "gullibility."

42. The Don Juan theme is brought to the fore here: Théophé's dedication to virtue has been one of the principal obstacles to the satisfaction of the hero's desire for possession, and the obstacle, whatever it may be, always serves as the primary stimulus for the libertine in his drive to seduce the object of his affections. Valmont's seduction of the virtuous Mme de Tourvel, in Laclos's *Les liaisons dangereuses*, is certainly the most striking example of this motif in French fiction.

43. It was common knowledge in Prévost's time that Aïssé had received propositions from the regent, the duc d'Orléans, and that several of his former mistresses, including Mme de Ferriol, had put so much pressure on her to submit that she eventually "threatened to retire to a convent" if they did not stop (Andrieux, *Mademoiselle Aïssé*, 94). This may well be the origin of this idea in *The Greek Girl's Story*.

44. The diplomat's illness, his rather unmotivated physical debilitation, may be, as Gossman suggests, a metaphorical allusion to his ultimate impotence to discover the truth about his protégée ("Male and Female," 31). On the other hand, as we saw in Book One, note 24, Leborgne takes the suggestion of impotence literally, portraying the hero-narrator as a eunuch figure.

45. The contemporary reader could not avoid being influenced here by the novels "key," that is, the quasi-public affair between Mlle Aïssé and the chevalier d'Aydie. However, we cannot ignore the striking similarities between the inquisitorial conduct of the governess and that of the diplomat in the comte de M. Q. episode in Livorno. The behavior of the old governess seems to reflect the pathological jealousy and spite of the hero himself, which leads Sermain to comment, "At the end of the book, the jealousy of the ambassador speaks through the voice of the governess, who is a veritable symbol of madness wrought by passion" (*Rhétorique et roman*, 135).

Works Consulted

Andrieux, Maurice. *Mademoiselle Aïssé*. Paris: Plon, 1952.

Asse, Eugène. "Le baron de Ferriol et mademoiselle Aïssé." *Revue Retrospective: Recueil de Pièces Intéressantes et de Citations Curieuses*, n.s., 19 (July–December 1893): 1–48, 97–144, 169–210.

———, ed. *Lettres de Mlle Aïssé à Mme Calandrini*. In *Lettres portugaises avec les réponses: Lettres de Mlle Aïssé, suivies de celles de Montesquieu, et de Mme du Deffand au chevalier d'Aydie, etc.* Paris: Charpentier et Cie, 1873.

Balteau, Jules, Marius Barroux, Michel Prevost, Jean-Charles Roman d'Amat, Roger Limouzin-Lamothe, Henri Thibout de Morembert, Jean-Pierre Lobies, and Yves Chiron, eds. *Dictionnaire de biographie française*. 20 vols. Paris: Letouzey et Ané, 1933–2011.

Beaumont, Ernest. "Abbé Prévost and the Art of Ambiguity." *Dublin Review* 229 (1955): 165–74.

Bilici, Faruk. "Les relations franco-ottomanes au dix-septième siècle: Réalisme politique et idéologie de croisade." In *Turcs et turqueries (seizième–dix-huitième siècles)*, edited by Gilles Veinstein, 37–61. Paris: Presses de l'Université Paris-Sorbonne, 2009.

Billy, André. *Un singulier bénédictin, l'abbé Prévost, auteur de "Manon Lescaut."* Paris: Flammarion, 1969.

Bokobza-Kahan, Michèle. *Libertinage et folie dans le roman du dix-huitième siècle*. Louvain: Peeters, 2000.

Bouvier, Emile. "La genèse de l'*Histoire d'une Grecque moderne*." *Revue d'Histoire Littéraire de la France* 48 (April–June 1948): 113–30.

Bray, Bernard. "Structures en série dans *Manon Lescaut* et *Histoire d'une Grecque moderne* de l'abbé Prévost." *Studies on Voltaire and the Eighteenth Century* 192 (1980): 1333–40.

Breuil, Yves. "Une lettre inédite relative à l'*Histoire d'une Grecque moderne*." *Revue des Sciences Humaines* 33 (July–September 1968): 391–400.

Calder, Martin. "La résistance langagière de la 'Grecque moderne.'" In Francis and Mainil, *Abbé Prévost*, 111–17.

Cantemir, Demetrius. *Histoire de l'empire ottoman*. Translated by A. de la Joncquière. 4 vols. Paris: Le Clerc, 1743.

———. *The History of the Growth and Decay of the Othman Empire*. Translated by Nicolas Tindal. 2 vols. London: Knapton, 1734–35.

Conroy, Peter V., Jr. "Image claire, image trouble dans l'*Histoire d'une Grecque moderne* de Prévost." *Studies on Voltaire and the Eighteenth Century* 217 (1983): 187–97.

Corneille. *Le Cid*. 1636. In *Théâtre complet*. 2 vols. Paris: Gallimard, 1950.

Coulet, Henri. "Sur les trois romans écrits par l'abbé Prévost en 1740." *Cahiers Prévost d'Exiles* 2 (1985): 7–19.

[Coulet, Henri], ed. *L'abbé Prévost: Actes du colloque d'Aix-en-Provence, 20 et 21 décembre 1963.* Aix-en-Provence: Ophrys, 1965.

Courteault, Henri. "Aïssé (Charlotte-Elisabeth)." In Balteau et al., *Dictionnaire de biographie française*, vol. 1, cols. 1043–49.

———. *Mademoiselle Aïssé, le chevalier d'Aydie et leur fille.* Paris: Société des Bibliophiles Français, 1908.

Delhez-Sarlet, Claudette. "Les jaloux et la jalousie dans l'oeuvre romanesque de Madame de Lafayette." *Revue des Sciences Humaines* 115 (July–September 1964): 279–309.

Deprun, Jean. "Thèmes malebranchistes dans l'oeuvre de Prévost." In Coulet, *Abbé Prévost*, 155–72.

Descartes, René. "About Fainting." In *The Passions of the Soul.* 1649. Translated by Stephen Voss. Indianapolis: Hackett, 1989.

Douthwaite, Julia V. *Exotic Women: Literary Heroines and Cultural Strategies in Ancien Régime France.* Philadelphia: University of Pennsylvania Press, 1992.

Dufrenoy, Marie-Louise. *L'Orient romanesque en France, 1704–1789.* 2 vols. Montreal: Editions Beauchemin, 1946–47.

Engel, Claire-Eliane. "Le chevalier de Malte, type littéraire du dix-huitième siècle." *Revue des Sciences Humaines* 71 (July 1953): 215–29.

———. *Le véritable abbé Prévost.* Monaco: Editions du Rocher, 1957.

Ferriol, Charles de, Marquis. *Recueil de cent estampes.* Paris: Le Hay, 1714. Republished with additional material under the title *Explication des cent estampes.* Paris: Collombat, 1715.

Francis, Richard A. *The Abbé Prévost's First-Person Narrators.* Oxford: Voltaire Foundation, 1993.

Francis, Richard A., and Jean Mainil, eds. *L'abbé Prévost au tournant du siècle.* Oxford: Voltaire Foundation, 2000.

Gilroy, James P. "Prévost's Théophé: A Liberated Heroine in Search of Herself." *French Review* 60, no. 3 (1987): 311–18.

Girard, René. *Violence and the Sacred.* Translated by Patrick Gregory. Baltimore: Johns Hopkins University Press, 1977.

Gôçek, Fatma Müge. *East Encounters West: France and the Ottoman Empire in the Eighteenth Century.* New York: Oxford University Press, 1987.

Gossman, Lionel. "Male and Female in Two Short Novels by Prévost." *Modern Language Review* 77, no. 1 (1982): 29–37.

Grosrichard, Alain. *Structure du sérail: La fiction du despotisme asiatique dans l'Occident classique.* Paris: Seuil, 1979.

Harrisse, Henry. *L'abbé Prévost: Histoire de sa vie et de ses oeuvres d'après des documents nouveaux.* Paris: Calmann-Lévy, 1989.

Hartmann, Pierre. "Femme étrangère/femme étrange: Le personnage de Théophé dans l'*Histoire d'une Grecque moderne* d'Antoine Prévost d'Exiles." *Revue Francophone de Louisiane* 8, no. 2 (1994): 51–61.

Herman, Jan. *Le récit génétique au dix-huitième siècle.* SVEC 11. Oxford: Voltaire Foundation, 2009.

Hill, Emita B. "Virtue on Trial: A Defense of Prévost's Théophé." *Studies on Voltaire and the Eighteenth Century* 67 (1969): 191–209.

Holland, Allan. "The Miracle of Prévost's *Grecque moderne.*" *Australian Journal of French Studies* 16, no. 2 (1979): 278–80.

Jones, James F., Jr. "Textual Ambiguity in Prévost's *Histoire d'une Grecque moderne.*" *Studi Francesi* 27, no. 2 (1983): 241–56.

Jones, Shirley. "Virtue, Freedom, and Happiness in the *Histoire d'une Grecque moderne.*" *Nottingham French Studies* 29, no. 2 (1990): 22–30.

Laclos, Choderlos de. *Les liaisons dangereuses.* 1782. Paris: Garnier, 1961.

Lagache, Daniel. *La jalousie amoureuse: Psychologie descriptive et psychanalyse.* 2 vols. Paris: Presses Universitaires de France, 1947.

La Motraye, Antoine de. *Voyages du Sr. A. de La Motraye en Europe, Asie, et Afrique.* 2 vols. The Hague: Johnson and Van Duren, 1727.

Lebois, André. "Amitié, amour et inceste dans *Cleveland.*" In Coulet, *Abbé Prévost*, 125–37.

Leborgne, Erik. "L'Orient vu par Prévost dans l'*Histoire d'une Grecque moderne:* L'ambassadeur et l'eunuque." *Dix-Huitième Siècle* 29 (1997): 449–64.

Malebranche, Nicolas. *Traité de morale.* 1684. Vol. II of *Oeuvres complètes.* 20 vols. Paris: Vrin, 1958–78.

Mall, Laurence. "Modalité et déplacement de la violence dans l'*Histoire d'une Grecque moderne.*" In *Violence et fiction jusqu'à la révolution*, edited by Martine Debaisieux and Gabrielle Verdier, 337–46. Tübingen: Narr, 1998.

Mantran, Robert. *L'empire ottoman du seizième au dix-huitième siècle.* London: Variorum Reprints, 1984.

Martino, Pierre. *L'Orient dans la littérature française aux dix-septième et dix-huitième siècles.* Paris: Hachette, 1906.

Mauzi, Robert. *L'idée du bonheur dans la littérature et la pensée françaises au dix-huitième siècle.* Paris: Colin, 1960.

Mercier, Roger. "Le thème oriental dans les romans de Prévost." In Coulet, *Abbé Prévost*, 85–92.

Miller, Nancy K. "L'*Histoire d'une Grecque moderne:* No-Win Hermeneutics." *Forum* 16, no. 2 (1978): 2–10.

Mirambel, André. "L'*Histoire d'une Grecque moderne* de l'abbé Prévost." *Bulletin de l'Association Guillaume Budé* 3, no. 3 (1951): 34–50.

Montesquieu, Charles-Louis de Secondat, baron de. *Persian Letters.* 1721. Translated by Margaret Mauldon. Oxford: Oxford University Press, 2008.

Monty, Jeanne. "Les romans de l'abbé Prévost: Procédés littéraires et pensée morale." *Studies on Voltaire and the Eighteenth Century* 78 (1970): 167–89.

Moronvalle, Jeff. "Connaître et représenter l'Orient au siècle des Lumières, le *Recueil de cent estampes* [1714] de Charles de Ferriol." In *L'orientalisme les orientalistes, et l'empire ottoman de la fin du dix-huitième siècle à la fin du vingtième siècle*, edited by Sophie Basch, 61–79. Paris: Actes du Colloque International, 2011.

Murphy, Patricia. "A Study of the Narrative Techniques of the Abbé Prévost as Illustrated in *Manon Lescaut* and l'*Histoire d'une Grecque moderne.*" PhD diss., University of Wisconsin, 1968.

Nouveaux mémoires du comte de Bonneval. The Hague: Van Duren, 1737.

Ohayon, Ruth. "Prévost's *Histoire d'une Grecque moderne* or the Emerging Self." *Atlantis* 14, no. 2 (1989): 31–35.

Orsini, Dominique. "Les enjeux de la narration dans l'*Histoire d'une Grecque moderne.*" In Francis and Mainil, *Abbé Prévost*, 209–18.

Pizzorusso, Arnaldo. "Prévost: Ipotesi e velleità." *Belfagor* 33, no. 3 (1978): 279–96.

Prévost, Abbé. *Le doyen de Killerine.* 1735–40. In Sgard, *Oeuvres de Prévost*, 3:3–415, 8:187–269.

———. *Histoire du chevalier des Grieux et de Manon Lescaut.* 1731. Edited by Frédéric Deloffre and Raymond Picard. Paris: Garnier, 1965.

———. *Histoire d'une Grecque moderne.* Amsterdam: Desbordes, 1740.

———. *Histoire d'une Grecque moderne.* Amsterdam: Desbordes, 1741.

———. *Histoire d'une Grecque moderne*. Corrected edition. Amsterdam: Catuffe, 1741.

———. *Histoire d'une Grecque moderne*. Edited by Alan J. Singerman. Paris: Flammarion, 1990.

———. *Histoire d'une Grecque moderne*. Edited by Allan Holland. In Sgard, *Oeuvres de Prévost*, 4:5–121, 8:271–321.

———. *Histoire d'une Grecque moderne*. Edited by Jean Sgard. Grenoble: Presses Universitaires de Grenoble, 1989.

———. *Histoire d'une Grecque moderne*. Edited by Robert Mauzi. Paris: Union Générale d'Editions, 1965.

———. *The History of a Fair Greek, Who Was Taken Out of a Seraglio at Constantinople, and Brought to Paris by a Late Embassador at the Ottoman Port*. London: Roberts, 1741.

———. *Le monde moral*. 1760 (vols. 1–2), 1764 (vols. 3–4). In Sgard, *Oeuvres de Prévost*, 6:283–479, 8:475–511.

———. *Le philosophe anglais ou Histoire de M. Cleveland*. 1731–39. In Sgard, *Oeuvres de Prévost*, 2:3–663, 8:81–186.

———. *Le Pour et Contre*. 20 vols. Paris: Didot, 1733–40.

———. *The Story of a Fair Greek of Yesteryear*. Translated by James F. Jones Jr. Potomac, Md.: Scripta Humanistica, 1984.

———. "The Story of a Modern Greek Woman." Unpublished translation by Peter Tremewan. Christchurch, New Zealand: University of Canterbury, Department of French and Russian, 1999.

———. "The Story of a Modern Greek Woman." Translated by Lydia Davis. In *The Libertine Reader: Eroticism and Enlightenment in Eighteenth-Century France*, edited by Michel Feher, 543–717. New York: Zone Books, 1997.

Pruner, Francis. "La psychologie de la *Grecque moderne*." In Coulet, *Abbé Prévost*, 139–46.

Roddier, Henri. *L'abbé Prévost: L'homme et l'oeuvre*. Paris: Hachette-Boivin, 1955.

Rogers, Robert. *A Psychoanalytical Study of the Double in Literature*. Detroit: Wayne State University Press, 1970.

Roman d'Amat, Jean-Charles. "Châteauneuf (Pierre-Antoine de Castagnéry, marquis de)." In Balteau et al., *Dictionnaire de biographie française*, vol. 8, col. 773.

Rougemont, Denis de. *L'amour et l'Occident*. Paris: Plon, 1956.

Rousset, Jean. *Narcisse romancier: Essai sur la première personne dans le roman*. Paris: Corti, 1973.

Said, Edward W. *Orientalism*. New York: Vintage Books, 1979.

Sainte-Beuve, Charles Augustin. *Portraits littéraires*. 3 vols. Paris: Garnier, 1862–64.

Sartre, Jean-Paul. *Being and Nothingness*. Translated by Hazel E. Barnes. New York: Citadel Press, 1966.

Sempère, Emmanuelle. "Le 'double prix' de l'*Histoire d'une Grecque moderne*: Eléments pour une analyse de l'étrangeté du récit." In *Les expériences romanesques de Prévost après 1740*, edited by Erik Leborgne and Jean-Paul Sermain, 227–36. Louvain: Peeters, 2003.

Sermain, Jean-Paul. "L'*Histoire d'une Grecque moderne* de Prévost: Une rhétorique de l'exemple." *Dix-Huitième Siècle* 16 (1984): 357–67.

———. *Rhétorique et roman au dix-huitième siècle: L'exemple de Prévost et de Marivaux (1728–1742)*. Studies on Voltaire and the Eighteenth Century 83. Oxford: Voltaire Foundation, 1985.

Sgard, Jean. *L'abbé Prévost: Labyrinthes de la mémoire*. Paris: Presses Universitaires de France, 1986.

———. "Aventure et politique: Le mythe de Bonneval." In *Romans et lumières au dix-huitième siècle*, edited by Werner Krauss, 411–20. Paris: Editions Sociales, 1970.

———, ed. *Oeuvres de Prévost*. 8 vols. Grenoble: Presses Universitaires de Grenoble, 1978–86.

———. *Prévost romancier*. Paris: Corti, 1968.

———. "Le titre comme programme: L'*Histoire d'une Grecque moderne.*" *Revista di Letterature Moderne e Comparate* 47, no. 3 (1994): 233–39.

———. *Vie de Prévost.* Sainte-Foy: Les Presses de l'Université de Laval, 2006.

Singerman, Alan J. *L'abbé Prévost: L'amour et la morale.* Geneva: Droz, 1987.

———. "The Abbé Prévost's *Grecque moderne*: A Witness for the Defense." *French Review* 46, no. 5 (1973): 938–45.

———. "Narration and Communication in Prévost's *Grecque moderne*: A 'Semiolinguistic' Approach to the Question of Ambiguity." *Nottingham French Studies* 29, no. 2 (1990): 31–44.

———. "Quand le récit devient procès: Le cas de la *Grecque moderne.*" *Eighteenth-Century Fiction* 9, no. 4 (1997): 415–27.

———. "Relecture ironique de l'*Histoire d'une Grecque moderne.*" *Cahiers de l'Association Internationale des Etudes Françaises* 46 (May 1994): 355–70.

Thévenot, Jean de. *Voyages de Mr. de Thévenot en Europe, Asie et Afrique.* 5 vols. Amsterdam: Le Cène, 1727.

Tournefort, Joseph Pitton de. *Relation d'un voyage du Levant.* 2 vols. Lyon: Anisson et Posuel, 1717.

Tremewan, Peter. "Orient et Occident dans l'*Histoire d'une Grecque moderne.*" In Francis and Mainil, *Abbé Prévost*, 119–26.

Virgil. *The Aeneid.* Translated by Sarah Ruden. New Haven: Yale University Press, 2008.

Vissière, Isabelle. "Les paradoxes du voile et de l'enfermement dans *Histoire d'une Grecque moderne.*" In *Le forum et le harem: Femmes, hommes, pratiques et représentations*, edited by Geneviève Dermenjian and Monique Haicault, 145–52. Aix-en-Provence: Publications de l'Université de Provence, 1997.

Walsh, Jonathan. *Abbé Prévost's "Histoire d'une Grecque moderne": Figures of Authority on Trial.* Birmingham, Ala.: Summa, 2001.

Weil, Françoise. "L'abbé Prévost et le gazetin de 1740." *Studi Francesi* 16–18 (1962): 474–77.